Shadow Over the Heartland

A Novel

By

Thomas Annino

Copyright © 2023 by – Thomas Annino– All Rights Reserved.

ISBN: 978-1-916787-92-6

This is a work of fiction. Unless otherwise indicated, all the names, characters, businesses, places, events and incidents in this book are either the product of the author's imagination or used in a fictitious manner. Any resemblance to actual persons, living or dead, or actual events is purely coincidental.

To Lisa, Hayley, Nick & Eric

&

My Bishop Creek Brothers

Acknowledgements

I am very blessed to have had so many people in my corner supporting me in finishing my debut novel. It was a long time coming and on my mind for over a decade. But, given a hectic full-time job, I was only focused on moving it forward as best as possible in the last eight years.

My beautiful wife Lisa was a great encourager and understood when I disappeared to the library or our retreat place in Lewes, Delaware. My daughter Hayley and sons Nick and Eric excelled in English in college and helped me immensely. I appreciate them not laughing out loud at me struggling with punctuation! I can't thank you all enough for being by my side with patience and loving support.

After many years in business, I retired at the end of 2022. The retirement intentionally allowed me to scratch my itch to write and finalize the novel in my heart. Work was challenging and allowed me to travel to many countries, which made my perspective on the world a lot wider. Some of that international experience found its way into the storyline. I also greatly appreciated the interest and support from my DLL Group colleagues.

Sadly, my parents, Joan and Jerry, didn't have an opportunity to read the novel as they passed away in 2019. I wish they had the chance to read the final product. Similar to my mother-in-law Jeanne, who passed away in 2022. She was a wonderfully positive person and a great supporter of my writing. I am glad that she read what was effectively the final version of the novel. I can still visualize her sitting alone in a quiet room for hours, flipping the pages.

I was assisted by many people, and I would like to thank them all here. Given the long road, I'm pretty sure I've missed some names, and for that, I'm sorry. The professionals who supported and educated me encouragingly: were Laura Maylene Walter, Laura Pritchett, Megan McKeever, and Karen Boston.

Also, I greatly appreciate friends who provided valuable input and encouragement, including Jeanne Rioux, Mickey Graham, Nicoleta Onuta, and Dave Swavely.

Lastly, thank you to the Amazon Publishing crew, who provided excellent support in bringing this book to life.

Chapter 1

JOSHUA GRAYSON felt a deep-seated trepidation he couldn't shake. He recognized his time was almost up, with little time to rally. Even the conference venue, Rode Hoed, a clandestine wooden church tucked behind three seventeenth century canal houses in the historic Amsterdam city center, couldn't capture his attention.

He stood in front of a narrow gothic second floor window, away from the growing pre-conference happy hour crowd, staring at the canal in front of the building. The window was a good vantage from which to observe people and the occasional boats that passed.

His thoughts were interrupted by a familiar voice bellowing, "A cure for cancer!"

Joshua turned to see his portly, wide-eyed partner leisurely ambling toward him. "Yeah, Graham, I've heard the rumor. Tantalizing to think about, but I don't believe it. Do you?"

Graham Roseboro knocked back his bourbon and shrugged, "It doesn't matter. If we can get an investment in the company, we'll make a killing on the expectation alone.

I haven't seen any execs from their team, and I'm reading every badge. Have you been able to network in?"

"No. I've never heard of the company; only found some vague references online, and I don't know who's providing the funding. It's like a ghost ship that emerged from the fog." Joshua looked over the crowd, a mix of biotech executives being hunted by venture capitalists and journalists. He recognized the typical nodding heads, polite grins, and arched eyebrows.

Roseboro scanned the cocktail hour participants spread across two adjacent rooms, occasionally raising his glass and waving to other attendees. He spoke quietly under his breath as his eyes continued to sweep the crowd, "I've been meaning to talk to you, and this is a good place to do it. We started Tremont Ventures together; you led us to years of great results, and we've moved into the big leagues. But your returns have been weak over the last couple years. I want you to know I'm on your side, but you're walking a tightrope. The other partners are getting very impatient, and together we don't have a controlling interest anymore. You need a huge win, and getting an investment in this, as you call it, 'ghost ship' company could be it."

Joshua stepped into Roseboro's gaze, a head taller at six feet, "It's called venture capital for a reason; it's high risk. You're the managing partner, and you know what I've brought to the partnership. Be firm and vocal. Take my side and lead." Roseboro diverted his eyes and waved to a lady across the room. Joshua subtly shook his head, "Just say it, Graham. Cochran is working the other partners to push me out. And as you say, together they can do it, according to the new partnership agreement."

Roseboro was silent and wouldn't make eye contact. Joshua paused to calm himself before he continued, "I warned all of our partners about Cochran. He has no track record, and to be factual, his father bought his partnership with a big investment in our last fund. He's a partner not based on talent, experience, or a strong track record."

"Cochran knows you voted against him becoming a partner. That's the reason for his actions." Roseboro nodded toward the exit and put his hand on Joshua's shoulder. "Come on, they probably have our table ready by now. Let's go and welcome our guests."

After descending an open staircase, they continued down a short hallway and stepped into the old wooden church. Joshua looked up and surveyed the historic place: a traditional vaulted ceiling of aged wood three stories high, no religious artifacts or murals, a broad open center area with two levels of balconies on both sides supported by white pillars. He expected the old church to have baked-in scents of aromatic oils and incense, like the older churches he'd visited in the U.S. But after almost 400 years of church services and meetings in Rode Hoed, he caught only the smell of clean linen.

He followed his partner toward their table, surrounded by red cushioned chairs a couple rows off the stage. Joshua looked up and traced the two large crystal chandeliers halfway down the height of the room, which provided elegant lighting to the thirty or so tables with white linen tablecloths. Additional seating was on the first floor, under the balconies, as well as on the second level. In the front of the room, instead of an altar, was a raised stage with a large banner above that read WORLD BIOTECHNOLOGY CONFERENCE below a large video screen.

As the people in the crowd found their tables and settled into their seats, a tuxedoed man appeared at the podium and cleared his throat, "Esteemed colleagues. Welcome to Road Hoed, which in English means 'The Red Hat.' We're very excited you could all be here to open the conference and what I believe will be an evening you will long remember." He stepped back until the clapping subsided, "As you have undoubtedly noticed, due to the overwhelming interest in this conference's opening, including many from the media, we have expanded the capacity by adding video screens in the adjoining rooms, where I understand we have standing room only."

After the applause that followed, and some perfunctory acknowledgements, he remained still until the room went silent. "Tonight, I have the distinct honor of introducing our keynote speaker. She is a top researcher in the area of oncology, and a graduate of the University of Oxford Medical School. She completed her postdoctoral research fellowship in applied and experimental oncology at the Karolinska Institute, in Stockholm, where she won the prestigious Crafoord Prize for her work in advancing cancer genome sequencing. She moved into the private sector several years ago and is currently the founder and chief executive officer of Golden Helix Therapeutics B.V., where she's rapidly made a name for herself in the field of biotechnology. I know you're all very interested in what she has to say tonight, so I'll spare you any further suspense. It is with great pleasure that I introduce our keynote speaker...Dr. Amaline Currie."

A slender woman in a royal blue dress, emerged from offstage and moved swiftly towards the podium, her blunt bob gently tapping her chin with every step. There she stood rigidly and scanned the room, pausing for a few moments at each section of the crowd, as if taking mental pictures.

Joshua leaned back in his chair. He'd heard hundreds of speakers over the years, and rarely did they live up to the advanced puffery. This ought to be interesting, he thought.

Dr. Currie tapped on the mic and smiled, *"Goedenavond,* good evening. I feel honored to be chosen to give the keynote address tonight to such a highly esteemed group. It's unusual for me to speak to such a large audience, so please bear with me...I'm a bit nervous."

She paused at the polite clapping before clearing her throat. "It's said that, in 1953, Francis Crick barged into a local pub in Cambridge, England, and announced that he and James Watson had just discovered the secret of life. He went on to celebrate the fact that they had unraveled the structure of DNA. I'm sure that was quite a party, especially considering that Watson's life code of conduct was to avoid boring people.

"This is, of course, not a pub, but tonight I want to share with you what I believe to be equally important news. News that I'm very confident will have profound effects on medical science for generations to come. After a great deal of hard work, my team and I have developed the means to correct DNA that has coded incorrectly. As you know, such incorrect replications can lead to gene mutations, and ultimately diseases such as cancer. I call this new tool 'DNA Restore.'"

The room exploded with a loud, sustained buzz. Dr. Currie stepped back from the podium with a gracious grin until the crowd noise subsided. "I'll discuss the key scientific details of this new therapeutic platform tonight, but several papers on the subject will be uploaded to the conference website if you wish to delve into it more deeply. To put this tool into simple terms for the media attendees, this new technology operates like a spell check for DNA. It analyzes a DNA strand, compares it to a benchmark strand, and if it finds a mutation, suggests corrections to medical geneticists working with oncologists, physicians, and other specialists. Corrections are implemented by introducing a functional, therapeutic gene to replace the mutated gene, thereby restoring the DNA to its original or desired state. If you look at the screen behind me, you'll see a video illustration of how DNA Restore works."

Joshua sat forward, crossed his arms, and concentrated on the screen. On cue, his mind began to generate questions, only interrupted by the buzz of the crowd. Above the podium, a DNA Restore logo appeared on the screen as a woman's voice began to narrate the video.

"The occurrence of gene mutations in humans is a natural process. Not all mutations are bad, and usually they have no adverse effect. Often the human cell is able to self-repair many of the DNA errors."

The video displayed a ladder representing a strand of DNA replicating itself alongside the original but with the color of one step of the ladder changed. *"As a cell copies its DNA before it fully divides, a 'typo' can occur. In some cases, the typo or mutation can create a variation in a gene that can cause disease, wherein the cell cannot repair itself. This is where DNA Restore provides a solution."*

The tall, thin man sitting next to Joshua leaned in and whispered in a Dutch accent, "I think we are witnessing history tonight."

Joshua responded with a slight headshake, and scanned the other tables where he saw similar dialog occurring.

The complexity is incredibly immense, he thought. I can't imagine it being 'solved.'

The video concluded with a step in the ladder corrected by the DNA Restore therapy and depicting two identical twisted ladders with the DNA Restore logo between them. The crowd noise reached a crescendo and reverberated off the church ceiling, creating a loud echo.

Dr. Currie retreated and held her hands on her trim waist, as she waited patiently until the noise subsided, "DNA Restore has vast implications for the treatment of cancer and other gene-related diseases. Eighteen months ago, the Brazilian Ministry of Health approached us to assist them in addressing a significant rise in the incidence of cholangiocarcinoma, commonly known as bile duct cancer or BDC for short, which has a very high mortality rate. Working with the ministry in a highly confidential manner, we quickly moved into accelerated human clinical trials in several hot spot areas.

"So far, those trials have already shown excellent results, with over ninety percent seeing some level of remission. The Brazilian Ministry has strongly encouraged us to make this information public, as there are other countries with similar issues. You are the first to hear this news."

Joshua's eyes widened, and he sat forward in his chair. He loosened his tie and tugged at his shirt collar. He was bombarded with thoughts, *Ninety percent? How can that be? This is a quantum leap in science!*

The crowd rose to their feet and clapped vociferously. Dr. Currie tried to continue but eventually gave way to the audience reaction, stepping back from the mic and holding her hands against her cheeks.

Joshua remained at the edge of his seat, mulling over the staggering implications of Dr. Currie's presentation.

A late attendee sat in the empty seat next to him and asked in a German accent, "My plane was late. Did I miss anything?"

"Not too much…maybe just a cure for cancer."

Chapter 2

As Dr. Currie made her final remarks and the crowd gave a standing ovation, Joshua stood, exited the ballroom, and moved to the reception area. Minutes later, the doors opened, and sound waves swept tsunami-like through the room. Joshua felt the vibrations hit his chest.

Graham Roseboro burst out of the ballroom, navigating the foot traffic like a husky fullback looking for daylight, and joined him. "Wow, how do we—"

The man's gaze was diverted as Dr. Currie exited at the far end of the reception area and walked briskly away, with a small entourage.

Joshua felt a yank on his lapel as Roseboro pulled him along, muttering, "Gotta catch her."

They moved forward, alternately speed-walking and jogging as they pursued the doctor. As they came within earshot, Roseboro called loudly until he caught the doctor's attention. She came to a stop and turned around slowly. The men closed the gap quickly, and as they approached, a man stepped in front of Dr. Currie.

Roseboro put his hands on his hips and caught his breath. He shifted to his left so he could make eye contact with her. "Hello, Doctor, my name is Graham Roseboro, and this is my colleague, Joshua Grayson. We're partners with Tremont Ventures, in Boston, and are interested in speaking with you about funding your future clinical trials and commercialization efforts." They presented business cards.

Joshua heard the doctor speak to the man in front of her in Dutch, "*Hassan…het is oké, stap opzij.*" The man moved enough for her to make eye contact. She looked at the cards and responded, "Hello, Mr. Roseboro and Mr. Grayson. Nice to meet you."

Roseboro stuttered forward. "Ah, yes, very sorry to catch you like this. I tried to reach you before the conference to schedule a meeting but wasn't able to connect with you or your people. First, let me say congratulations on your work. It's quite amazing, and I would love to learn about your therapy in more detail. Do you—"

She held up a manicured index finger. "Gentlemen, thank you for the interest, but we have ample funding at this time." Dr. Currie smiled at them and began to turn away.

As she pivoted, Joshua blurted, "Doctor, can I ask how you were able to bring your technology forward so quickly when the current leading genome editing tool is said to be years away from human clinical trials?"

She stopped, turned, and stepped toward Joshua. "Mr. Grayson?"

He nodded. She stepped in closer. He considered her attractive, lean like a runner, maybe early-forties, with piercing blue eyes framed by thin, arched brows. Joshua noticed a small hourglass-shaped birthmark on her temple near her right eye, which she touched while she spoke to him.

"What's the technology you're speaking about?"

He took a half-step forward. "The CRISPR technology. It's useful to snip DNA but not very good at replacing a faulty gene."

She grinned. "It's come a long way since 2007, when it was brought into the mainstream. Like Moore's Law, where transistors on a microchip double every two years, our advancement of gene editing follows a similar path. Much careful work has been done with CRISPR around genetic disorders, and we're starting to see the benefits, which are, and will, be extraordinary. Very recently, it's been used to create a CRISPR drug, which is injected into the blood of people born with transthyretin amyloidosis, a disease that causes fatal nerve and heart disease. In three trial patients, it nearly shut off the production of toxic proteins by their livers. This will save lives. We've also been part of advancing the technology with our work, and are also saving lives, as I mentioned in my speech. That's our singular goal."

Joshua leaned forward, eyebrows raised. "If that's the case, I'd be very interested in learning more about your technology, including the gene delivery vector you're using."

"I sincerely appreciate your interest. Maybe another time. Unfortunately, I'm late for an interview." Dr. Currie gave the men a polite smile, turned, and exited.

Wide-eyed, Roseboro whispered as he watched her walk away, "You need to birddog her. If this technology works as she says it does, her company is going to be worth tens of billions overnight! As we just spoke about, this is your chance to get on one of your winning streaks and shut down the talk among the other partners. I'm going to mingle. I'll see you later."

Joshua moved to a nearby sitting area and plopped onto a leather club chair, phone in hand. Before he could check his messages, a friendly voice drew his attention.

"Joshua Grayson?"

He looked up to see a bright-eyed, gray-haired gentleman staring at him. A smile crossed Joshua's face. He stood and shook the man's hand.

"Dr. Lange. Very nice to see you. It's been a while since we've spoken."

"Nice to see you, too, Joshua. Yes, it's been a while. Since our company was sold and your firm got rich, I haven't heard from you!" He laughed softly and gestured to the ballroom with his thumb. "Quite an announcement, huh? What do you make of it?"

He sat back in the chair as the doctor sat on an adjacent tawny leather couch and responded, "It's a colossal leap in science if it's as effective as presented. The Brazil results are startling."

Dr. Lange sighed. "It was quite extraordinary. The idea of being able to fix gene mutations has long been a holy grail of medicine. Although technology is moving more quickly, it's hard to believe the science has progressed to that level.

We'll see what the research shows, but I have my doubts." He tilted his head slightly, and his voice changed from professional too personal. "Joshua, is everything alright? You look a little piqued and green around the gills."

Joshua saw the concern in his eyes. "Sure, just tired and fighting jet lag from the overnight flight."

Dr. Lange started to speak, then paused. "Well, it'd be good to catch up sometime soon. When you have time to talk, give me a call." He stood and handed Joshua a business card. "These days, I have more time on my hands. I'm now what they call," he snickered and drew quotation marks in the air with his fingers, "a consultant."

His animated gestures reminded Joshua of his father. The thought further triggered a memory of pitching to his father on the sidewalk in front of their house when he was young. He could still vividly see the look on his dad's face when he occasionally skipped the ball into his shin - eyes open wide, teeth clenched, with a subsequent short dance.

He brought his attention back to the doctor, "What're you working on now?"

"I'm toying around with applying artificial intelligence to the drug discovery process. Looking to accelerate development to bring products to market faster and reduce the cost materially. A win-win for all."

Joshua grinned. "So, something simple! A.I. is all the rage now. Sounds like you're on the leading edge. Let me know if you need any funding."

"You're at the top of my list. Maybe I'll hit on something as my final hurrah."

"I think you have a lot left in the tank."

Lange put his hand on Joshua's shoulder. "Sorry to run, but I'm off to meet a colleague." He started to walk away, but after a couple of steps, he stopped and turned to Joshua and added, "You take care, and I hope to hear from you very soon!"

As the doctor disappeared around the corner, Joshua skirted the crowd and walked from the building into a cloudless, dark blue evening with Amsterdam lit up before him. Just outside the main entrance was one of Amsterdam's 160 canals. He walked over a nearby bridge as a tour boat passed underneath, slowly making its way south.

The Venice of the North moniker is clearly appropriate, he thought.

He walked slowly toward his hotel along the canal as he digested the events of the day and took in the scenery. Locals were walking in groups, ducking into local restaurants and bars. Joshua caught the skunky odor of potent cannabis from a nearby coffeehouse named Mellow Buzz. Out of curiosity, he poked his head into the place and saw a long bar with a half-dozen round tables arrayed around the place, roughly half-filled. A smiling woman behind the bar waved him over and gave him a menu. It read: *"Top shelf - weed, hash and marijuana,"* then listed various options below, such as: *"Purple Haze, Pineapple Chunk and White Widow."* Joshua coughed as a nearby patron at the bar exhaled. He covered his mouth and nose and handed back the menu.

"No, thank you."

Following the canal, he passed the Anne Frank House, crossed over a couple of bridges, and finally one spanning the Singel, the oldest canal in the city. He'd read about the famous canal at the hotel. The Singel encircled the city as a moat back in the Middle Ages, until 1585, when the city grew and canals were expanded to allow for movement of goods, and for defense.

After a short walk, he entered his boutique hotel, housed in another seventeenth century building. He gave a slight wave to the front desk clerk as he made his way through the colorful lobby fitted with two crystal chandeliers, a turquoise wallpaper backdrop, and an empty birdcage hanging near the front desk, then continued down a hallway to the lift.

He entered his room and shed his clothes, shoes, and socks in a trail on the floor before dropping onto a large, cushioned armchair facing the window. He rested his feet on the sill and checked voicemail. Joshua stood and paced while he replayed the third message several times.

"Hello, Joshua. This is Uncle Pete. I'm not sure you'll get this message, but I thought I'd try. Your Aunt Sara has passed away. The funeral is scheduled for eleven o'clock Thursday, at Saint Aloysius, in Bishop Creek. It'd be great if you're able to make it…I hope you're doing okay and that you get this message. You can call me if you need any details…okay, hope to see you there."

He fell back into the chair and recalled his aunt's wavy blonde hair and incandescent smile, her fondness for stale orange circus peanuts, and endearing penchant for dropping unexpected curse words into a sentence so deftly, it was often a sentence or two later before it registered with the listener. He remembered being eight or nine years old, running around the front yard of the farmhouse with his cousins in a summer sun-shower, faces to the sky and mouths open, catching sweet-tasting rain. Aunt Sara and his Mom sang songs as they sat on the edge of the wrap-around porch, feet dangling just above the grass.

She was front and center, consoling him when his parents died in a car accident just before he left for college, leaving him with no immediate family. Aunt Sara stepped in to try and mend the enormous hurt he felt when his cousin Jake didn't attend the funeral. He was in Florida with his school buddies, celebrating his high school graduation, and couldn't get back in time.

Emotions and memories raced through his mind. Despite the fallout with Jake, his leaving and disconnecting from the family, Aunt Sara unfailingly sent him an encouraging Christmas card every year. He counted off fifteen years since he saw her last and recalled her final words to him. "May God bless you and do wonderful things through you. Remember, your family will always love you."

He briefly debated whether to attend the funeral, but quickly concluded that his aunt deserved more respect than for him simply to move on as if nothing had happened. As if she meant nothing to him. The city lights blurred, and his cheeks grew warm. He slowly closed his eyes as his chin dropped to his chest.

Chapter 3

The rental car exited the freeway in Effingham and slowed to a stop at the end of the ramp. Joshua shut off the navigation and turned left. Located in south-central Illinois, the small city of just over 12,000 was promoted by the local Chamber of Commerce as the "Crossroads of Opportunity." Two major highways intersected in the city, I-70 running east to west for over 2,000 miles, the other, I-57, running from to Chicago to the bottom of Illinois.

Joshua navigated the car past the 198-foot-high structure locals claimed to be the largest free-standing cross in the United States. He noted the small city hadn't changed significantly; perhaps some modest growth except for the local Walmart, which had at least doubled in size since he'd visited last. On the way out of Effingham, he passed Cruisers Drive Thru Restaurant, which he and his cousins frequented regularly during teenaged summers.

The surroundings rapidly changed from gas stations, small chain hotels, and fast food joints to flat farmland bounded by a mix of asphalt and gravel roads. Traffic dissipated, stop signs replaced traffic lights, and the landscape more fully depicted the area. His memory served him well, directing the Toyota Camry along the back roads east toward Bishop Creek, a small farming enclave named after Samuel Bishop, the village's first settler in the 1830s. He drove in silence, as he had since renting the car at the Indianapolis airport two hours earlier.

Fields of corn stood tall in rows along the route, ready for harvest. Signs jutted from the end of the rows, advertising seed producers. Traditional mainstays, like Pioneer, Monsanto, and DeKalb, with its unmistakable bright yellow corn cob with green wings logo, were well-represented. Alongside familiar brands, new seed companies had come on the scene, providing strong competition. Joshua could see the stalks of the newer brands stood noticeably taller than the older standbys.

Too perfect; must be GE, genetically engineered, he surmised.

The route took him through the town of Teutopolis, known locally as T-Town, where his cousins attended high school. Just outside of town, he recognized a rusted Bierman's Welding sign on a worn white corrugated steel building, a childhood landmark that confirmed he was heading in the right direction.

After crossing railroad tracks and motoring a few miles, he turned left at the small, faded green street sign atop a tall steel post that read *"Rural Route 3"* and headed toward the steeple of Saint Aloysius Church, the highest, most prominent point in the small farming community. A quarter-mile down the road, Joshua pulled the car onto the shoulder, leaned forward, and rested his head on the steering wheel.

A question ran through his head several times: Am I really going to do this?

Half a dozen deep breaths later, he directed the car back onto the road, and continued a short distance to the church. Joshua scanned the area as he pulled into the parking lot. Not much had changed. The modest white-weathered stone statue of St. Isidore the farmer remained in place, standing on the side of the church facing the road. On the pedestal under the statue was a prayer to bless the crops and harvest.

Everything seemed smaller but remained in place. To the east of the church stood a small white box building, housing Bishop Creek Grade School. In-between the school and church was a basketball court, the site of many summer pick-up games under a hot sun. North of the court was an assembly hall, which served as an indoor gym for the school and hosted countless wedding receptions. Mature trees stood between and beyond the buildings, dressed in shades of gold, burnt orange, and crimson.

Joshua quietly entered the weathered red-brick church through the large, ornate wooden doors located near the building's cornerstone, "1893" impressed in the concrete. Many people were in attendance, wearing a mix of well-worn suits, dresses, and occasionally bib overalls. The voice of a solo female singer from the elevated choir loft at the back of the church echoed greatly, to the extent that the words became unrecognizable as they reverberated off the walls and ran into each other.

He genuflected haltingly before entering an empty pew at the rear of the church, holding his hand in front of his nose against the strong smell of incense. It was unclear whether it was from this funeral service or baked into the place from generations of funeral masses and over a hundred years of stations-of-the-cross services.

As he sat and surveyed the building, it occurred to him he hadn't been in a church since his parents' funeral. Growing up in the Irving Park neighborhood on the northwest side of Chicago, he attended Catholic masses every Sunday with his parents. Sitting in a church triggered ambivalent memories of deeply ingrained rituals and Sunday suppers.

The murmurs halted when two altar boys carrying tall candle holders followed by a bald, elderly priest in a white robe walked slowly up the long center aisle and found their places on an elevated platform. The priest stood at the rear of the altar and spoke in monotone.

"Today, Lord, we commend the spirit of our sister Sara to you."

Gentle sobs echoed from the finely painted ceilings and old stained-glass windows. A bronze casket on a cart, partially covered by a white linen cloth with a scarlet cross, stood in front of the raised altar. He looked up at the time-worn statues of saints, which stood overlooking the congregation on platforms attached to large white Doric-style pillars.

Joshua wore a blue Brooks Brothers suit and burgundy silk tie, drawing semi-discreet stares from other attendees. He looked toward the first pew, where five men wearing dark suits stood, heads bowed.

Regret ran through his mind, As hurtful as it was for Jake to miss Mom and Dad's funeral, was that enough to cut him, my cousins, and my aunt and uncle out of my life?

As the service ended, rays of sunshine refracted through the stained glass casting a rainbow of colors through the church. The priest rose and concluded with a final remark in a gravelly voice. "I have been asked to announce that the Grayson family will be having a collation at their home immediately after this service, and they invite you all to attend."

Six men surrounded the casket and slowly rolled it down the center aisle to the sound of "Ave Maria" played on the organ. Just outside the main entrance, they lifted the casket and placed it gently in the rear of a waiting hearse.

Joshua slid out of the pew and out a side door, exiting the church on the opposite side of the hearse and funeral procession. Outside, he expelled the church air from his lungs and drew in a deep breath of crisp, cool, late October air.

Bending at the waist, he put his hands on his knees, fighting nerves. Joshua drew a deep breath, and exhaled slowly through pursed lips. He stared at the Camry in the parking lot. A notion crossed his mind, No one has seen me yet.

He shook off the thought and walked toward the far end of the church, scanning the landscape as he advanced. Minutes later, the hearse came into view. It moved slowly, making its way to the church cemetery fifty yards from the building. The priest led a stream of people walking behind the vehicle, heads bowed.

Joshua joined the tail of the procession and stared at the dense trees in the distance, a couple hundred yards beyond the graveyard. His aunt and uncle's farm was on the other side of the woods. He remembered the woods fondly, having explored them with his cousins for many years. They hunted bullfrogs along the "crick," in local parlance, and when they had success, his aunt would serve fried frog legs with dinner. In their teen years, they would occasionally raid a wedding reception at the church, fill a jug or two with beer from a keg, and disappear into the woods, spending the night at a place they called "the opening." There, they talked about girls, laughed, and shared their dreams around a roaring campfire.

The crowd arrayed around the gravesite. Joshua hung his head as the priest concluded the brief graveside service.

"And I heard a loud voice from the throne saying, 'Behold, the dwelling place of God is with man. He will wipe away every tear from their eyes, and death shall be no more, neither shall there be mourning, nor crying, nor pain anymore, for the former things have passed away.'" Amid muffled crying, the priest ended with a short benediction, "Sara, may you always walk in sunshine. For the happiness you gave us, will always be with us. It broke our hearts to lose you, but you did not go alone. A part of us went with you the day God called you home. The Lord be with you and may you rest in peace."

After most of the people paid their respects and the crowd thinned, Joshua moved forward and joined the receiving line. At six feet and 190 pounds, he was the smallest of the Grayson men. His cousins were all at least six-foot-two and heavier, with physiques developed by years of farm work. His uncle, in his early sixties, was the leanest of the group and looked the most fit.

He reached cousin Jake and extended his hand. "Hi Jake. I'm so sorry about your mom."

Jake's eyes grew large, and he took a step back before nodding, his face pale, tired blue eyes showing red around the edges.

Joshua worked his way to his other cousins and expressed his sympathies, receiving quiet nods and handshakes. Pete was off to one side, speaking with an elderly couple, nodding occasionally. It had been years since he'd seen his uncle, but he immediately recognized his chest forward, reverent posture. When he finished the conversation, he made his way to the men, his head down and shoulders slumped. Pete stopped in front of Joshua, looked him in the eye, and shook his hand.

"It's been a very long time Joshua."

Chapter 4

Joshua stepped out of the Camry and surveyed the old homestead that had been in Aunt Sara's family since the mid-1800s. The farmhouse was washed out white, looking pale and in ill health. It had a hard edge to it, as if mourning for Aunt Sara's touch. The green shutters were giving up, loosely attached to the clapboard. Paint was peeling in places, rotted wood evident around a few windows, and the green tin roof had faded. The porch swing remained in place under the wrap-around porch, which was missing some gray flooring planks; like a grand old ship, worn down by time and use, on its last voyage.

An old hand-operated water pump, the only source of drinking water for the home, was visible in the side yard, bisecting a row of bushes a tin cup hanging from a nearby branch. The circular gravel driveway led to a white, two-car detached garage that was leaning to one side.

The contrast between Joshua's memories of the days of his youth and what he saw saddened him. He reasoned perhaps his memory was exaggerated by many fond summers spent on the farm. The environment was much different from city living, and he treasured the space, freedom, and brotherhood.

Neighbors and relatives filled the house, offering their sympathies and telling stories. One neighbor had a large group of women in stitches in the kitchen when she told of the time Sara had worn sunglasses to an extended family reunion. "We're talkin' second and third cousins once removed here," she said before noting Sara only realized at the end of the day she had only one lens in the frame.

The table in the dining room was overflowing with food: cold cuts, ham, bread, coleslaw, homemade sweet pickles, jams, ambrosia salad, and cakes. Father Vonderheide, who presided over the funeral, made an appearance as well, saying a short grace before filling a plate with food and sitting at the kitchen table.

Joshua followed a short line of people and slowly worked his way around the table. Concluding the circuit, he looked for a place to sit and eat, but the house was full, so he began to make his way through the kitchen toward the back yard picnic table. Skirting the mob of neighbors, he bumped into a petite blonde woman and excused himself.

She looked him up and down. "Nice suit. You're not from around here, are you?"

"It's that obvious?" She chuckled, and he continued. "I haven't been here in years but spent a lot of time here growing up. Sara Grayson was my aunt."

"Are you Joshua?"

He nodded, and she threw up her hands and spoke in a high-pitched voice over the crowd noise. "I'm Shelby, Jake's wife. I've heard a lot about you and your summer adventures with the boys. Good to finally meet you." She grabbed his elbow and yanked. "Come on."

She led Joshua through the crowd to his cousins, who were gathered near the fireplace in the living room, surrounded by their families and neighbors. "Jake, look who I found!" Shelby gave him a proud, toothy smile.

Jake turned toward his wife, finished a conversation with a neighbor, and edged over to her. He held the hands of two children, one on each side. Looking at Joshua, he held up one hand, then the other.

"This here is Henry and Dixie."

Joshua put his plate on an end table, crouched down, and shook hands with Henry and Dixie. Loose from his father,

Henry took the opportunity to run off. Shelby waved goodbye, crossed her hazel eyes, and chased Henry into the dining room with Dixie in tow, her short, sandy blonde hair bobbing as she juked her way through the crowd.

"I had no idea Aunt Sara was so sick. The news stunned me."

Jake looked down and fidgeted with his wide navy and gold striped tie for a moment before raising his sunken blue eyes to meet Joshua's stare. "It happened quickly. One month healthy, the next she was in the hospital with the doctors treating the cancer. They were talking about some options, but it moved too quickly, and there was no time."

"What type of cancer?"

"Bile duct."

"That's very rare." His mind jumped to Dr. Currie's speech in Amsterdam.

"Yeah, that's what the doctors said—" Jake abruptly cut the conversation short, turned, and walked away. "Well, thanks for coming. I gotta go help Shelby."

Joshua started to speak, but before he could say a word, Jake waded into the crowd. He frowned and turned to his eldest cousins Cole and Jesse, standing nearby.

"Hi guys, sorry to have to meet on such a sad occasion."

Cole gave him a questioning stare. "What's your name again?"

"I deserve that. How're you doing? Are you still living around here?"

Jesse nudged his brother aside. "No, Cole and I live an hour and a half away in St. Charles, near St. Louis, with our families. We run a distribution center for a couple big grocery chains."

The men briefly introduced their wives and six children, three boys for each couple. Joshua stared at his older cousins, who were a year apart. He looked up to them when he was younger. Other than a little age beginning to show on their faces and a few pounds emerging around their waistlines, they looked like a pair of linebackers wearing identical gray suits. He tried to keep the conversation going to ease the tension.

"How's your dad doing?"

Cole pursed his lips and shook his head slowly. "Dad's beat up pretty bad. He'll be alone in the house now. We've been sort of rotating staying with him since Mom passed…I guess thanks for coming. We need to say hello to some of the other people." The group moved en masse to the adjacent dining room at the front of the house, leaving Joshua behind.

He fought a strong urge to leave as they turned their backs to him. Sadness settled in deep, and a reflexive thought ran through his head, *I'm truly alone in this world... and it's my doing.*

He looked out a window at the rear of the house and picked at the food on his plate. Blaine, the youngest brother, was standing in the back yard, holding court with his friends, including several girls who seemed to laugh at everything he said.

Joshua made his way out to a picnic table, with his plate of food and a cold bottle of Busch. Blaine joined him just after he sat down, two girls tagging along. He stood a half-head taller than his brothers, with shoulders broad enough to cause any man to think twice about tangling with him. His physique, long, dirty blond hair, and green eyes reminded Joshua of Thor, the hammer-wielding god of thunder.

Sitting across from Joshua, scowl on his face, Blaine spoke in a rowdy voice. "Hey Joshua, where have you been? We don't even know where you live, if you're married, have a family, or what you've been doing. You basically went off to college and disappeared. Like we never existed. That's low, man."

"Yeah, I know. I'm sorry. I got a non-verbal butt-kicking from Jake, Jesse, and Cole already."

"I ain't gonna do any butt-kicking, man. Just catch me up."

Joshua grinned weakly and looked down at his plate. "Thanks. I'm not married, except to my job. I co-founded a venture capital firm in Boston, and I've been investing in biotech companies for the last ten years. But lately that's not going so well." He took a bite of his sandwich.

One of the girls on the bench next to Joshua narrowed her eyes. "Venture capital. What's that?"

"My company invests in new companies that are trying to come up with the next big drug or way to cure a disease. If it all goes right, we sell our stock for a big profit a few years later."

Blaine ran his hand through his hair, pulled it back off his face, and put on an exaggerated grimace. "Well, you ain't a freakin' Patriots fan, are you?" The group laughed. Blaine handed him another beer, tapped the neck of the bottle with his, and raised it solemnly. "To Mom."

The afternoon wore on, and the sun dropped in the sky, falling behind the oak trees on the periphery of the back yard. As the last guests left and neighbor ladies finished cleaning up the place, Pete strolled out to the picnic table and sat quietly with the group, listening to the conversation before Blaine left with friends.

Eventually, Shelby, Cole, and Jesse made their way to the table. Jesse and Cole hugged their dad. "We're gonna take off and get the kids home."

Shelby hugged Pete as well and kissed him on the forehead. "We're heading out, too. Jake's feeling sick and doesn't look well. I think he's got a bad case of the flu." She walked over to Joshua. "Nice to finally meet you." She hugged him and gave him a wink. "Don't be a stranger."

Twilight set in, and the night sky began to take shape. "I should probably get going, too, Uncle Pete," Joshua said. "I have a hotel room booked at the airport and a flight home tomorrow morning."

"Tomorrow's Friday. Why don't you stay the weekend? Cancel your hotel, change your flight to Sunday, and stay here. It'd give us a chance to catch up. It doesn't seem right for you to leave so quickly after being gone so long."

"Things are very challenging for me at work right now." The shift in the conversation to work brought a change in his countenance from casual to serious.

Pete looked him in the eye. "I could really use the company."

"It's been nice to see everyone and pay my respects, but I have serious problems at work I need to deal with this weekend." He paused, looked at his uncle, and noticed the crowd thinning. "How about I cancel the hotel, move my flight to tomorrow afternoon, and spend tonight here?"

"Sure. We can have a big breakfast before you take off."

Within the hour, everyone had left the farmstead and quiet settled in. They sat across from each other and ate leftovers at the picnic table. Midway through their sandwiches, Pete went into the house and brought out a half-gallon jug, and filled two small green juice glasses.

"How about a little dandelion wine?"

Joshua raised his glass. "To Aunt Sara."

They sipped the straw-colored liquid. Joshua's face puckered, providing welcome comic relief. Stars began to dot the big country sky. They sat quietly, breathing in the fresh, cool evening air.

"I don't think I ever asked you why you and Aunt Sara moved to the farm from Indianapolis. You went to college there, had a good job and family nearby. I know it was in Aunt Sara's family, but that's a big jump."

Pete looked in the distance as he spoke. "Sara wanted us to consider taking it over when her uncle died rather than selling it to another family. The farm was in her family for decades. I sensed she really didn't want to uproot us, but we needed to at least consider it. Cole and Jesse were young, and we had a lot of friends in Indy." His eyes slowly closed. "But I remember clearly the first time I set foot on this land. It just called me. I think your aunt felt it, too. I've farmed this land for over thirty years now. It hasn't been easy making a living, but we got by, we had each other. I know every inch of the property and have zero regrets. It's part of me now."

Pete paused, cleared his throat, and looked Joshua in the eye. "We're very thankful you could be here. I realize it's not easy for you to be with family and attend a funeral after what happened to your parents and falling out with Jake. Memories can be wonderful, but also very painful."

Joshua looked up at the sky. "A day doesn't pass that I don't think about my mom and dad. I almost turned around a couple times on the way here, not wanting to relive that time in my life and recognizing the fact that I didn't keep in touch with anyone. For fifteen years! What kind of person does that?" He drained his wine. "It's clear to me I needed to do this not only for Aunt Sara, but also to reconnect with you all. Hopefully to start mending relationships, at least try."

"It's never too late to reconcile, son. Your cousins are like your brothers. Give it some time."

The men sat quietly, a soft autumn wind tossing their hair and rustling the trees. Pete clasped his fingers together, sinewy forearms resting on the table. "I once saw an elderly preacher on TV who'd just lost his wife of sixty years. The interviewer asked him how he was able to deal with the loss, and I'll never forget his response." His lip quivered for a moment. "He said the antidote to grief is gratitude. I believe he was right. I'm just grateful and very blessed to have had Sara in my life for so many years. She was a gift from God and touched so many lives."

Joshua turned his head, and his vision blurred as he fought back tears. He sniffed and looked Pete in the eye. "I still carry the heavy pain from my parents' accident; it hasn't faded. I don't know how to find peace. I learned to push it to the back of my mind by throwing myself into school, and later into work. I didn't have closure, a chance to say goodbye, and now the same with Aunt Sara."

"Be right back." Pete went into the house and returned with a flat cardboard box. He set it on the table in front of Joshua. "I'm not sure when I'll get to see you again, so I want to give you something that's very special to me."

Joshua opened the box.

"That leather portfolio was given to me by my brother, your dad, as a gift shortly before the accident. He carried it for many years, and I mentioned to him how much I admired it. When I first saw you at the funeral the gift came to mind—you're his spitting image. The portfolio is made of the same leather as baseball gloves. It's always reminded me of carefree days of playing baseball with your dad. Just like you two used to do."

Joshua brought the portfolio to his nose and inhaled deeply. Musky-cured-leather.

The wind picked up and brought an increased chill to the air. Pete arose from the table and cocked his head. "I hope this is the extent of it. There's been a lot of cancer in the area over the last year, so I'm praying it's a coincidence. But it feels like a plague!"

Chapter 5

Joshua arrived at the Tremont Ventures office in Copley Square before seven o'clock Monday morning. Sitting back in his pleated leather desk chair, he yawned as he ran his fingers through his hair and surveyed his office. On the wall was a picture of him with the mayor of Boston, and another of him shaking hands with the CEO of a biotech company on the day of its IPO.

Alongside the photos was a framed copy of a *Boston Magazine* article naming him one of the up-and-coming "30 under 30" professionals in the Boston area. On a bookshelf stood two pictures, one of Joshua with his parents at his high school graduation, and another of him in a Boston College baseball uniform.

"Joshua."

"Whoa! Hutch, don't sneak up on me like that. Come in. What's up?"

Hutch Brown, one of the Tremont partners, sat on the opposite side of the desk. "Before the partners meeting, I have a couple of questions for you on your portfolio companies and thought it might be more efficient to discuss beforehand."

"Sure."

"Of the eight companies you're responsible for, only one has sufficient cash to last more than a year; the others will run out within the next four to six months. They're all behind plan, and I don't see anything on the horizon that'll provide a near-term remedy. We haven't budgeted further funding, and if other investors come in, our position will be diluted, and the valuation may even decline."

"Hutch, we've slowed the burn rates, and three of the companies will receive NIH funding coming in the next quarter—"

Hutch interrupted him. "Taking risk is obviously part of what we do, but you can't miss on eight of eight. If you want my opinion, I think you spend too much time working. That's not healthy. I know you coach baseball for inner city kids, but that's not enough. You need to take a vacation, get out with friends and reset. Also, this feud with Cochran isn't healthy for you either. You should push the reset button, however you do that." He stood and walked out of the office.

Joshua started to stand but fell back into his chair. His gaze turned to his leather messenger bag nearby. He retrieved his father's portfolio and held it to his nose. He opened it, and tucked inside a leather divider with an embedded red Rawlings logo was a picture of his father and uncle. Mid-twenties at a beach, bare-chested, standing shoulder-to-shoulder and smiling broadly.

An hour later, he poured another cup of black coffee and was off to the meeting. In short order, Tremont's four other partners made their way into the large conference room, tall coffees, laptops, and reports in hand. Graham Roseboro opened the meeting with a summary from the World Biotechnology Conference.

"All in all, the conference was a success. Joshua and I were able to get some good networking in, and I think we have a couple of potential investment opportunities. Also, importantly, two of our portfolio companies presented, and that may bear fruit in the form of pharma collaborations. But the highlight of the conference was a keynote presentation by Dr. Amaline Currie. She presented a potential cancer breakthrough using gene editing technology."

Tremont's newest partner, Jeff Cochran, rocked back and forth in his chair, his large size stress testing its tensile strength. "Is there an investment opportunity?"

Roseboro pulled a document from a manila folder and laid it on the table. "The science is deep and complex, very leading edge. We know DNA copies itself in each new cell and uses many levels of proofreading sequences and error correction to ensure perfect DNA replication; very complex processes that are not fully understood. Dr. Currie claims to have found a process that mimics natural error correction and can correct damaging DNA mutations. In simple terms, she called it 'spell check for DNA.'

"Joshua and I managed to have a very brief meeting with the doctor about a potential investment. Her response was that they weren't currently looking for funding. Not really a surprise."

Lewis Mulligan turned to Joshua. "You have some experience in this space. What do you make of it?"

Cochran interrupted and answered the question with a matter-of-fact tone. "We all know cancer is largely hereditary, so this seems like another expensive, high-risk bet."

Joshua turned to Mulligan and spoke slowly. "First of all, cancer is *not* largely hereditary. It only plays a major role in, at most, ten percent." He saw Cochran's face turn red out of the corner of his eye. "The science is incredibly daunting, and it's a stretch to think there could have been such rapid progress to the point of commercialization. It's like moving directly from a rotary phone to a smartphone. Also, we should note this treatment is currently only focused on BDC, which is a rare form of cancer with about eight thousand people in the U.S. diagnosed each year. So it's a small segment, but obviously if this approach works for other cancers, it's revolutionary. I ran into Dr. Martin Lange at the conference. He knows this subject very well and had his doubts based on the information he'd seen. That said, the results from a trial in Brazil are incredibly strong. But this is all very new, and I'm sure that it'll get more scrutiny and study going forward."

Cochran put his hands on the table, leaned forward, and sneered at Joshua. "I know Martin Lange. He's out to pasture! I can't believe you'd even think he'd be an authority on this subject, Grayson."

Joshua slowly turned his head and met Cochran's eyes, took a deep breath and willed himself to stay professional.

"He's a well-respected MD with a very strong oncology background and an excellent track record of commercializing new technologies. He's made this firm a lot of money by taking on CEO roles for our portfolio companies or troubleshooting issues."

Cochran stood up and talked down at Joshua from across the table, pointing his finger at him. "You're stuck in the past, and that's hurting this firm!"

Roseboro raised his voice. "Whoa, guys, relax. Jeff, sit down, and let's get back to the agenda."

Joshua felt electricity running up his back, and his pulse quickened. He forced himself to look at Mulligan. "We have some information, and there are a lot of people digesting it now with a strong critical eye. The announcement shocked everyone. That said, it would take a lot of guts to make a big announcement at the conference without some very strong data. As I mentioned, the technology is being used in Brazil, with reportedly astounding success. The global cancer drug market is over one hundred billion dollars and growing with the aging of baby boomers. If we have a chance to invest, we should look at it seriously."

Cochran laughed loudly. "That's all you have, Grayson? We send you to friggin' Amsterdam, and that's it? We expect more."

Roseboro slammed his mug on the table, splashing coffee on his papers. "Stop, Jeff! Clearly, you two have some personal issues, but they don't belong in this meeting. Let's focus on the opportunity. Is this an investment we want to pursue? If so, who's going to chase it for us?"

Cochran looked across the table with a smug look. "Anyone but Grayson."

Joshua leaned forward, eyes narrowed, and barked. "You take it. Show us what you can do!"

Cochran scanned his partners around the table; all eyes were on him. "Yeah, okay. I'll take the lead and show you how it's done." He sat back in his chair, folded his arms across his chest.

Roseboro looked to his right. "Okay, let's get to portfolio reviews. Joshua, you're first."

Joshua took the top file on a small stack and opened it. "Let's start with BioSymbiosis. The company has recently made some progress working through a set of compounds it licensed from big pharma. Its technology is showing promise, but —"

"You gotta be joking!" Cochran shouted.

Roseboro half-stood up in his chair. "Did everyone have a bad weekend?" The chatter around the table grew. Roseboro threw up his hands and spoke over the group. "Okay, we're going to skip the meeting this week. This isn't productive. Everyone can read the portfolio updates and ask questions individually as needed."

Joshua stood tall, chest forward, and glared at Cochran. He picked up his laptop and files and started toward the door. As he did, Cochran moved around the conference table and stepped in front of him, a good three inches taller and thirty-plus pounds heavier.

Cochran beckoned the other partners, "Let's end this now! We need to move on from Grayson."

Roseboro raised his voice. "Stop! This isn't the time or place to discuss partnership matters."

Joshua tried to step around him, but Cochran pushed him away from the door with his shoulder, causing Joshua to step backwards to catch his balance and dislodging the files from his hands. Joshua shoved him back and stooped over to pick up the folders.

Cochran raised his fists chest high, moved forward, and grabbed Joshua by the shirt with his left hand. For Joshua, there was no hesitation. Instinct took over. Software triggering keen muscle memory rippled through his body. Joshua hit him with a right hook to his jaw. The blow caused Cochran to release his grip as he backpedaled, trying to catch his balance. His head hit a wall, and he slid to the floor, red-faced and mouth open in a frozen stare.

Chapter 6

After working from his condo for the remainder of the week at the request of his partners, Joshua returned to the office the following Monday. He was seated at his desk when Roseboro walked in, closed the door behind him, and sat in the chair across the desk.

"Well, I hope you've had a chance to cool down. You knocked out a tooth, bruised his jaw pretty good, and gave him a mild concussion. Hurt pride is probably the thing that stings him most, though."

"I'm not proud of my reaction, but I was defending myself." Joshua stood and paced. "It was pure instinct when he came at me fists up and grabbed me." He looked down and shook his head. "I competed with him for investment opportunities when he was at Quotient Ventures for a few years and won all of them. Then he was voted in as a partner after his father invested in the new fund. I think he was a marketing major in college. What qualifications does he have? He's been here for almost a year and hasn't won any new business. I warned you all about him. He's a buzzword factory, spitting out words without a lot of content depth, just like his comment about cancer being hereditary. You're the managing partner. It's your responsibility to ensure the partnership is healthy."

Roseboro hung his head. "I'm not sure how we got here. Maybe it's my fault."

"Graham, it's hurtful that you act like he's the one who wasn't at fault. You've known me for years." Joshua swiveled back and forth in his chair as his feelings swayed between anger and despair. "He made it physical when he pushed me back to prevent me from leaving the room, then grabbed my shirt. Would you let someone do that to you?"

"I've never been in that situation." Roseboro shrugged. "I'm not someone who gets physical. I'm not an athlete like you. But I'm here to tell you that resorting to physical violence has put you in a bad spot. Long and short of it is, Cochran has agreed not to press charges, provided you leave the firm by the end of the month."

"Are you kidding me?" He stabbed a finger at Roseboro. "He's delusional if he thinks I'm going to leave the firm I co-founded to avoid him pressing charges. He was the instigator. Maybe *I'll* press charges!"

Roseboro stood, walked to the wall adjacent to the desk, and gazed at the pictures. He straightened a frame and stared at the photo. Joshua observed him in silence, stone-faced.

"Those were the days, Joshua. You were at the top of your game. We disagreed at times, but you were so good at recognizing patterns and working through the logic of a business proposition. It was challenging to even talk to you, because you were so obsessive and unwavering about your positions. But, incredibly, you were right on virtually everything. The Grayson computing engine at work."

Joshua's brow creased as he squinted. "Hmmm. You're speaking in the past tense. Maybe you and the other partners are looking for a reason to push me out. After founding the firm with you and the success we've had? If that's the case, it's incredibly disappointing."

"I'm sorry, Joshua. Just to be clear, I'm on your side. But this situation makes it even more difficult for us to include you as a partner in the new fund we've been planning. It seems inevitable we'll lose either you or Cochran over this rift. Your track record has been weak over the last couple years, and now this. If this altercation gets out in the market, it could hurt our fundraising ability, and tarnish your reputation as well. Why don't you take another couple days off and think this all through? I'll meet with the other partners today or tomorrow and put this to bed. We can't go on like this, and frankly, it's not fair to you."

He stared intently at Roseboro, wrung his hands, and felt a chill. "I don't think the situation is that dramatic, and two days isn't going to change anything. If our partners are choosing to bet on Cochran, that's a bad bet. Ultimately, you'll also find me competing against Tremont, and I don't lose often." He turned his gaze to the pictures on the wall. "Pass along the message not to be indecisive, just make a decision."

Roseboro stood expressionless.

"I'll take a couple of days, Graham, but I'm not the one who needs to think things through - and by the way, if our partners want me out of the firm, it's going to be very costly. If it moves that way, no games; just give me a package you'd want for yourself."

Roseboro walked out and closed the door softly. Joshua tucked some files in his messenger bag and left the office. He took a short walk to the Charles River. Across the river on the Cambridge side, people jogged and biked on the path along the shoreline to start their morning. To the south, a few rowers were out for a morning workout. Traffic was getting heavy as Boston came alive for another day.

During nice weather, Joshua always walked to work. After several spectacularly successful years, he bought a condo relatively close to the office in the affluent Back Bay neighborhood. The walk was normally twenty minutes at his usual pace. This morning, he slowed his stride, taking notice of each building, coffee stand, and store on the way home down chic Newbury Street. He'd lived there for several years but never paid attention to the numerous nineteenth century buildings and had never stepped foot in the nearby Boston Public Garden, considered a treasure in the heart of Boston.

Joshua stopped for a coffee and continued his walk taking in the window displays of the numerous high-end retailers along the street lined with mature trees: Cartier, Chanel, Tiffany & Co, Barneys New York, Louis Vuitton, and Emporio Armani. He was quite accustomed to the Boston accent and local phrases, but every so often a word caught his attention as a daughter asked her mother if they could get a frappe. Joshua still called it a milkshake.

His condo was on the top floor of a six-story, Federal-styled brownstone built in the late 1800s. Two bedrooms and 1,500 square feet of living space. An old girlfriend, Lisa, an interior decorator, helped him outfit the place and made it his retreat from the world. As they were putting the decor together, he often had the impression she was viewing it as her place, too. He liked Lisa, but she moved to the west coast to pursue an opportunity to work for a large home furnishing company before their relationship tipped to serious. That was over a year ago, and he hadn't had a relationship since. He pondered it further, concluding he'd managed to disconnect from family, colleagues, and college friends. Not a healthy pattern.

The one remainder from the relationship was his Abyssinian cat. Lisa talked him into adopting him for company. Joshua named him Ernie after Ernie Banks, "Mr. Cub," his father's favorite baseball player. He liked the ruddy-colored short hair and long, muscular body that reminded him of a wild bobcat.

*   *   *

Monday moved slowly as rain pelted the windows. The daily ESPNews loop played over and over on the television, filling the living room with noise and keeping him company.

Joshua sat on the couch with his laptop and scrolled through a large contact list, making a short list of people to approach in the event he was ultimately to leave Tremont. He ran across names of college friends, but he hadn't stayed in contact with most of them since he left school over a decade ago.

Mid-afternoon, he curled up on the couch, changing the channel until he found a movie, and quickly fell asleep with Ernie by his side. A couple hours later, his phone rang and woke him. He checked the Caller ID: unlisted, 217 area code.

"Joshua, it's Uncle Pete. Jake hasn't been feeling good, and the doctor wants to follow with some tests because he has decreased appetite and some abdominal pain. Your aunt had similar symptoms."

He sat up. "What? I know he wasn't looking or feeling good at the funeral, but I chalked that up to emotions."

"I'm worried. I'm calling to let you know, but also because you might be able to help us to make sense of all of this with your medical background. Based on experience, I'm concerned this might be more than a small hospital in a farming area can handle. I'm out of my wheelhouse here, Joshua. Can you help?"

Joshua stood, combed his hair with his fingers, and paced. "I wouldn't jump to conclusions. BDC is rare, and also the average age of people who it affects in the U.S. is seventy years old. It could be many other things, like an infection, digestive condition, or even grief and stress from the loss of Aunt Sara."

There was silence on the other end of the line. Joshua heard a long exhale before Pete spoke. "Well, he's seeing his doctor; that's good. I'm sure they're doing tests to determine the cause. Let's see what the tests show."

Joshua followed up. "Is he seeing the same doctor as Aunt Sara, or is he seeing his regular physician?"

"I'm not sure, but I'll find out. I pray it's nothing." Pete's voice wavered. "We just buried Sara…I'm starting to feel like the biblical Job. Praying on my knees this is a temporary illness for Jake."

"Uncle Pete, I'm here for you and the family. I'm happy to speak with the doctor, but if this doesn't go away soon, I think we need to bring Jake here to Boston. The hospitals and medical care are world-class. I'll make all the arrangements, and he can stay with me."

"I'm not sure if his health insurance would cover it."

"Let's worry about that later. I'm going to try and reach him. But in the meantime, can you email me Jake's doctor's name and contact information? Also, Aunt Sara's doctor's name, if it's different."

Pete sniffed and cleared his throat. "Sure, and I'll get in touch with Sara's doctor and let her know you'll be in contact."

"How's Jake handling this?"

There were several seconds of silence on the other end before Pete's voice cracked. "He's downplaying it, calling it the flu. But I can tell he's scared, mostly for Shelby and the kids."

Joshua paced around the room as they ended the call. He flopped on the couch and closed his eyes.

Chapter 7

The weather improved in Boston overnight. Rain gave way to a soft glow as sunshine threatened over the horizon. For Joshua, autumn was the ideal time of the year - requiring a light jacket in the morning, then discarding it in the afternoon. Tree leaves were well into the annual process of turning an array of colors, plus baseball playoffs and the football season were underway.

He tossed and turned all night, unable to shut off his mind, whirling between the situations with Tremont and Jake. A midnight sleep aid was ineffective. He sat in bed, Ernie at his feet, amid papers, his laptop, and phone. Early morning he checked his messages. The first email was from his uncle from very early that morning.

"Spoke with Dr. Kaymer. She sent you the medical records for your Aunt Sara and is available for a call this morning at ten o'clock central time. I'll text you the number. Let me know how it goes."

He began to review the files, taking notes, jotting down questions, and reviewing medical reference books as he went along. A web search provided a profile of St. Anthony's

Memorial Hospital. Modest in size at 133 beds, it was the largest hospital in the area and an accredited general acute care health facility with national accreditation for breast and rectal cancer.

As the appointed time approached, Joshua fed Ernie breakfast, then sat at his dining room table in a pair of gray sweatpants, Sam Adams Boston Lager T-shirt, and Boston College hat worn backwards. He put a spiral notebook and pen in front of him, and dialed.

A soprano voice with a touch of a soft southern accent answered. "This is Megyn Kaymer."

"Dr. Kaymer, this is Joshua Grayson calling to follow up on your discussion with my uncle, Pete Grayson."

"Yes, I understand you have some questions about your aunt. Are you a physician?"

"No. I majored in biochemistry as an undergrad, then attended medical school but left after two years and currently work as a venture capitalist."

There was a pause on the other end of the phone. "Mr. Grayson, do you mind if we FaceTime or have this discussion on Zoom? Ever since the pandemic, I've become so used to seeing the person I'm speaking with...of course, if that's okay with you."

"Well, I just woke up after a restless night, haven't showered or shaved, and I'm dressed in my workout clothes. But if you can bear the sight of me, that's fine." He heard a laugh on the other end. "Let's hang up, and I'll FaceTime you."

Joshua took a quick look in the mirror, shrugged and spoke out loud, "You asked for it!"

"Hi, Mr. Grayson, that's better. Thank you for indulging me...and you look fine. So, how can I help you?"

Joshua gave a polite chuckle. From the vantage point of a small two-by-five inch screen, she had a great smile and seemed about his age. "Are you attending to my cousin Jake?"

"No, is he a cancer patient at the hospital?"

He gave her a confused look. "I thought you were evaluating him. He hasn't been feeling well, with some abdominal pain and loss of appetite. My uncle must have been mistaken. But I do have a few questions, if you don't mind?"

He took her silence as tacit assent. "First, I'm curious as to why it was suggested my cousins go through genetic testing for a disease that's not known to be hereditary?"

She paused and tilted her head, causing her raven hair to fall to one side. "Well, the testing was triggered by the fact that there has been an increase in that type of cancer in the area over the past year, and we're gathering as much local data as possible to try and determine causation. It's commonplace to test family members to create a more robust picture of the situation. For example, your aunt had mutations in several genes. How does that compare to her family and others affected by the disease? That data may be able to help us diagnose and treat patients more quickly and effectively in the future. By the way, the Illinois Department of Public Health requested the tests - voluntary, of course - and is paying for them."

"BDC is rare."

"Yes, and it typically develops very slowly, with the average age of onset around seventy. Your aunt was sixty-two, so a bit young, but it was only about forty days from diagnosis to her passing. She only showed symptoms a couple weeks before diagnosis. So, that pattern is an anomaly we're very, very concerned about. By the way, we've seen some younger individuals in their fifties contract the disease, which is also a cause of concern. How old is your cousin?"

"He's thirty-six, my age." Joshua walked to his picture window as he spoke. "Have you heard of DNA Restore, a gene therapy developed by a biotech company in the Netherlands? The therapy is focused on BDC."

"Thirty-six is way outside the norm! It would be a very rare anomaly if it was BDC." The doctor shook her head. "To answer your question, no I'm not aware of the DNA product. Did you say gene therapy?"

"Yes. The company is Golden Helix. I'm in the business of knowing all the biotech companies, but this was a big surprise to me as well. The early results in Brazil are very strong."

She looked away in thought before turning back to make eye contact. "Interesting. As you probably know, gene therapy has a somewhat challenging history in the U.S. An area like hemophilia seems to have some positive response. But addressing cancer is a daunting task."

Joshua returned to the table. "Yes, I'm not entirely clear on the details. That said, can your hospital handle these cases effectively if my cousin were to have BDC? Wouldn't a large regional specialty hospital be better equipped?"

Dr. Kaymer cleared her throat. "Yes, a larger specialty hospital has more resources. There are larger, specialty hospitals in Chicago, St. Louis, and Indianapolis, all within a four-hour drive of Effingham."

"Are there any other clinical trials that would potentially address the cancer?"

She turned her head as someone spoke to her, and she held up a finger. "There are some that are focused on cancer with a potential application. That might be a possibility, but they don't specifically focus on BDC. I gather the historic low incidence rate doesn't warrant the required investment."

"I'm curious, Doctor. If this incidence rate spike is relatively recent, doesn't it seem like something has changed or been introduced in the area to trigger it?"

She looked over her shoulder again. "I know the Department of Public Health is focused on those questions. They're better equipped to investigate this situation. Sorry, I'm being paged, so I'll need to hang up—"

"One last question, please, Doctor. The survival rate for BDC?"

He saw her countenance change. "Historically, two to thirty percent, depending on the location of the cancer…locally, we haven't had anyone survive."

* * *

Joshua stepped out of his brownstone and walked down the block, looking up at the colorful leaves on the trees lining the street. He gave an occasional nod at neighbors passing by as he made his way to Newberry Street, where he stepped into the Thinking Cup, a favorite café complete with an alluringly bakery display case filled with decadent, heart-stopping pastries.

The crowd was surprisingly light, so he was quickly able to order his usual Stumptown Coffee, imported from Oregon, a chocolate croissant, and find a small table in the corner. He dialed Pete as he finished the croissant and heard the connection, but the response was slow.

"Uncle Pete, it's Joshua. Have I caught you at a good time?"

"Sure…I was just going to take an inventory of all I need for planting next season. Did you speak with Dr. Kaymer?"

"Yes. We spoke briefly, but Dr. Kaymer said she hasn't seen Jake. Are you sure he said he was going to see her?"

Pete raised his voice. "That's what he said. I know he's stubborn and all, but he's all about taking care of his family, so I can't imagine he wouldn't visit the doctor and at least get checked out. Shelby knows how to handle him and is very tough. I expect she'd handcuff him and drive to the doctor's office if needed. Maybe he has an appointment coming up. Well, I need to call him or sic Shelby on him."

Joshua stepped out of the café as Pete spoke and took in the fresh air. "Good idea. Dr. Kaymer and I discussed Aunt Sara's circumstances and the local BDC situation. Hopefully, Jake's fine. But if he shows *any* - and I mean *any* symptoms - then we need to move fast, based on how quickly it affected Aunt Sara and others locally.

"Also, I don't think St. Anthony's is the best place to be treated. It's small, with a limited oncology group. There are other highly rated hospitals with leading-edge therapies and deep resources, plus strong track records and outcomes. There are several not too far from Bishop Creek: Indianapolis, Chicago, or St. Louis…or here in Boston."

"Thanks for speaking to the doctor, Joshua. I'm sure you're right. But first we got to get him in front of a doggone doctor!"

"Hello? Uncle Pete?"

Joshua heard a heavy sigh and what sounded like a metal-on-metal crash. He waited for a response. Half a minute later, he heard his uncle's serious bass voice.

"Yes, let's see what happens here. Jake's way too young to have the same cancer as Sara. He's…" Pete's voice paused. "He's one tough son of a buck."

Chapter 8

The Amsterdam biotech cluster, located in the eastern section of the city and adjacent to a multi-century historic area, housed the highest concentration of life science companies in the Netherlands. Based on the number of biopharma jobs, patents, and venture capital invested in the area, it was one of the largest biotech hubs in Europe, and growing. The development of new companies was largely fed by technology originating from twelve universities but primarily driven by two: the University of Amsterdam, and the Vrije University Amsterdam.

The Golden Helix offices sat on the northern edge of the cluster. The building was contemporary, a concrete base supporting four large rectangular glass boxes in a staggered arrangement, each cantilevered over the floors below. Unlike most of the buildings in the cluster, it stood alone, surrounded by grass fields and small irrigation canals.

In the only office on the top floor of the Golden Helix building, Dr. Amaline Currie sat alone behind her glass-topped, stainless-steel desk, eyes closed, a metronome in front of her, with its weighted arm moving back and forth.

At eleven o'clock, her phone sounded a soft alarm. She swiftly silenced it and the metronome, rose from her desk, pushed open two doors, and stepped into a large conference room. Talking quieted as she entered.

Dr. Currie sat at the head of a large conference table made of wood from an old Dutch windmill, six well-dressed men and women in front of her, three to a side, with a man joining the meeting by videoconference via a screen on the wall at the end of the table.

After all attendees provided updates for their respective areas of responsibility, Dr. Currie scanned the group, ultimately focusing on the face on the video screen: a gray-haired, box-bearded man wearing reading glasses balanced on the end of his nose.

"Dr. Telling, what's the status of the DNA Restore trials in the U.S.? The application was submitted fifty-seven days ago. The Brazil trials are showing excellent results. In the U.S., reports show that there are similar small, but growing, BDC issues, which, so far, cannot be treated effectively with existing solutions. We have a treatment that works. One that can save lives. Can't we get a Fast Track designation, like the COVID mRNA therapies?"

The distinguished-looking gentleman spoke with a British accent and addressed the doctor in a professorial manner. "Dr. Currie, the U.S. is an entirely different matter than Brazil or the scale of COVID-19. The FDA is slow to move when it comes to gene therapy products like DNA Restore, given bad past experiences dating back to the 1990s. It recently granted 'Breakthrough Status' for a therapy to reduce the risk of heart failure in patients with a deficiency of a very specific enzyme, which is in Phase One clinical trials, but it has only recently approved gene therapy products. They tend to move slowly in this area, given the very high complexity of the therapies."

"Is there anything further they need? Are we ready to go once we get the approval?"

"I'm in regular contact with the FDA and…no new requests. We're also planning to be ready to start the trials once we get the approval. But it's also my understanding that it will be restricted to a single site or a small number of sites."

Currie asked for specifics. "How many hospitals have you surveyed? Obviously, focus on those that have the highest need. We want to be ready in advance so we are prepared to commence immediately when the FDA approval comes."

She saw him stiffen; he stammered something under his breath and coughed. "We have two interested and will be meeting with other hospitals in the coming weeks."

"Dr. Telling, let's move quickly to line up hospitals in the affected areas, expecting that we'll receive an approval. I know we have a lot going on in Brazil, but our ability to move quickly can save lives."

Dr. Currie returned to her office and walked to a paneled wall on the far side of the room, where she waved a card in front of a small scanner, causing the adjacent panel to pop away from the wall. She opened the panel door, stepped through the doorway, and closed it behind her.

Just inside was a sitting area with multiple screens, some dark, others showing empty desks, one showing words being typed on a computer screen. On the other side of the room was a twin bed, a bookshelf holding a set of colorful matryoshka nesting dolls, several books by Ayn Rand, and a black-and-white picture of a middle-aged man in a lab coat. She opened a small refrigerator, selected a cup of yogurt, banana, and bottle of orange juice, retrieved a spoon from a nearby drawer, and sat at a small table.

After a few bites of the banana, she withdrew a world map from the table drawer and spread it out in front of her. Across the top of the page was the title "Colangiocarcinoma Trending," with a key of colors corresponding to the incidence rate per 100,000 people. Three countries in red were areas characterized as having a high, but stable, incident rate: Thailand, China, and South Korea. Brazil was light red showing a declining trend. Several yellow countries noted as stable: Japan, Singapore, United Kingdom, and France, with only the United States showing growth in incidence over historical levels.

As she studied the map, a digital ringing came from a screen in the sitting area. Currie rose and made her way to the chair across from the screen and picked up a remote. With the click of a button, a conference table with four white-coated men and women filled the screen. On the wall behind the table, a sign read "CDC - Centers for Disease Control and Prevention," with a tagline underneath - "CDC 24/7 Saving Lives. Protecting People."

"Hello, Dr. Currie. We appreciate you making time for us."

The doctor sat tall and responded quickly. "My pleasure. I'm here to help."

"As we briefly discussed with you in Amsterdam, we're interested in working with you to develop a thesis around the cause of the increase of BDC in the U.S. As you know, we've experienced an uptick in the disease, and we're struggling with identifying the source. Have you explored the potential sources in your research?"

"Unfortunately not. If you were to ask me, I would only be able to provide you with a listing of the general risk factors such as obesity and diabetes, which I believe have doubled in frequency over the last twenty years. Or I could cite the aging of the U.S. population, plus smoking and alcohol use, and similar behavioral actions. The focus of my research has been identifying the genetic impact of the disease, and not the source."

She took a breath, realizing she was pontificating too much. I'm talking to experienced scientists, she reminded herself.

Currie reset her tone. "As we continue to receive data, I expect that this will provide valuable information that could be helpful in learning the source. I believe you know that we've applied to the FDA for approval to bring our DNA Restore to the U.S., and that application is currently being reviewed. That could help outcomes. In terms of data, perhaps more disparate data from the U.S., combined with that from Brazil, would accelerate our learnings here. Hold on a minute."

Currie opened her phone, rolled through a listing of Brazilian contacts, and jotted two names down on a sheet of paper. Ruminating further, she shuffled through her contacts and added two other names.

She re-engaged. "A couple of things may be helpful. First of all, I can send you two names from ANVISA, the Brazilian regulator, who have done significant research into the local cancer and have a good-sized database. That, combined with yours, may bring some interesting findings. Also, I believe adding analytics and artificial intelligence teams around that data may prove useful. I'll also send you a couple of names there as well; one person based in the Netherlands, and the other a professor at MIT."

One of the CDC members responded. "Thank you, we'll speak with the people you suggest. We understand that you have a company to run and are very busy, but would it be possible for you to come to the U.S. and work with us for a few days on this subject? You're closer to this disease than many scientists, and we're hoping your knowledge and experience can help accelerate our work. I'm afraid time is of the essence on our end."

Currie sat still, reviewed her schedule, and weighed taking a few days to assist the CDC, and perhaps meet with the FDA while in the U.S. "I understand your urgency. I'd be happy to assist you but would need to move my schedule around. Would it be possible to also meet with your FDA colleagues on the same trip? That would be helpful to my work. I'll need to get back to you on potential dates. Please send over any data you have, so I can review it in advance."

She ended the call and returned to the bookshelf, took the framed picture of the man in the lab coat, and sat at the table. She kissed the picture, set it down in front of her, and finished her yogurt.

Chapter 9

Joshua stepped from a cool, early afternoon rain into the Boylston Café and was met with the aromas of dark roast coffee and bacon. The café was a local hangout for the Boston venture capital and biotech crowd. The walls were filled with biotech-related artwork by local artists. In the entry area hung: a watercolor painting of the DNA helix, a line drawing of test tubes, and large abstract oil painting of a collage of cells.

At the door, he shook his travel umbrella outside, rolled it up, and scanned the place quickly, catching the eye of Graham Roseboro sitting at a corner table. He navigated through the lunch crowd, waving to several patrons along the way.

Joshua sat across from him. "I guess I'm still banned from the office?" He rolled his eyes at Roseboro.

Roseboro shook his head. "Come on…how're you doing?"

"Well, let's see…beyond this riff with Cochran, you know my aunt passed away, and now my cousin, who's my age, isn't feeling well, and there's a fear he may have the same cancer that took the life of my aunt." He paused to gain his composure and spoke softly. "So Graham, my world has been shaken big time."

They ordered and engaged in local chit chat before Joshua steered the conversation to the topic they'd been dancing around. "I sense from some of the comments and vibes I've been receiving, our partners want me to move on from Tremont. The situation with Cochran being another reason for me to leave."

Roseboro was silent and sipped an iced tea.

Joshua looked down at the table and fought back emotions before looking Roseboro in the eye. "I hope you've given them some perspective. If you exclude the gains from the investments I've led since the firm started, Tremont's results would be at the bottom of the lower quartile for VC firms. Basically, we wouldn't be in the position we're in currently where we're expanding. And frankly, the others wouldn't be partners at Tremont, because we wouldn't have been able to access funding based on historical results without my contribution. I'm sure that data will concern investors in the new fund we're planning if I'm no longer a partner. On top of that, there would be a need to bring in at least one additional new partner, probably two, to source and manage new investments for the fund."

He paused for a moment and saw he'd drawn the attention of other patrons. He lowered his voice before continuing to make his case. "Even the investments I currently lead still have good upside potential, which shouldn't be discounted. Unfortunately, the technologies have taken longer to develop than the original plan." He took a bite of his sandwich and stared at a blank-faced Roseboro. "I've invested an incredible amount of time in building Tremont, and maybe I'm reading things wrong, but if not, I think you're all being very short-sighted."

Roseboro put down his sandwich, swallowed, and ran a napkin across his mouth. "I can't dispute anything you've said, but I'm very sorry to say, the ship has left the harbor. We've been outvoted, and unfortunately, the firm is moving forward without you. The partners believe it's best, reputation-wise, to split amicably with a common story line, which is: you want to move on to another challenge. Basically, everyone agrees to protect each other's reputation."

Joshua grimaced, and his eyes turned steely. "I can't begin to tell you how much this hurts. Why don't you outline in writing how to split, and we can talk from there. Again, give me a deal you'd accept, Graham." He gritted his teeth. "Disappointing."

"I'm sorry, Joshua. I fought it with everything I have, even making the case you just laid out, to no avail. I also noted the fact that for many venture firms and biotech CEOs, you're the face of Tremont." Roseboro put his sandwich on the plate and dropped his napkin on top. "Just know I'm around to help you in any way I can."

Joshua rose from the table, dropped his half-eaten sandwich on the plate, and growled, "This is bush league." He left the café shaking his head and stepped into a cool November breeze on a dreary Boston day. Gray nimbus clouds moved in from the west, and with them the earthy scent of imminent rain.

* * *

As he walked down Boylston Street toward his condo, his phone rang. He slowed his walk and sat on the stairs of the Boston Public Library.

"Dr. Lange, thank you for returning my call. I have a personal situation I'd appreciate your thoughts on."

"Sure, glad to assist if I can."

"An aunt of mine passed away recently."

"I'm very sorry to hear that, Joshua."

"Thank you, she meant a lot to me. It's the circumstances of her death I wanted to speak with you about. She died from BDC, which came on rapidly. More specifically, she passed away a month-and-a-half from diagnosis, no prior indications. I understand this is a relatively rare form of cancer that primarily affects older people, say an average age around seventy. She was a healthy sixty-two. Also, I understand the incidence rate has grown in the farming community where she lived, and I hear it's even affected younger people. My aunt's son, who is my age, isn't feeling well. If it's BDC, I'm not confident a modest-sized rural hospital can handle it, and I'm looking for a little guidance in the event we need to move quickly."

The doctor spoke sympathetically. "A month-and-a-half from diagnosis is scary, but I wouldn't jump to conclusions. Yes, cancer is a genetic disease, but keep in mind that inherited gene markers showing cancer susceptibility play a role in only about five to ten percent of all cancers, and even if there is a predisposition, it doesn't necessarily mean cancer will occur."

Joshua replied, "Yes. It's too bad DNA Restore isn't available, given the results we heard in Amsterdam. If it's needed, any suggestions for treatment places in the Midwest? I'm not sure my cousin will agree to Boston."

Dr. Lange responded quickly. "Well, the jury is still out on DNA Restore, although the results seem remarkable. In terms of hospitals, Northwestern and University of Chicago immediately jump to mind. In the St. Louis area, Washington University – Barnes Jewish; I have an old friend there. But I'd push to bring him to Boston and get him into Dana-Farber, at Harvard, at least for a consult. We have plenty of connections there. In the meantime, send over the information and test results from the local doctor, and let's see what we have."

Joshua looked up at the overcast sky as he replied, "If it looks like there could be an issue, I'll push for him to come to Boston. Given my aunt's experience, this could move quickly."

As the conversation wound down, misty rain began to fall, creating thin streams of water that ran down Joshua's face and dripped off his nose and chin. He realized he'd rushed out of the café without his umbrella.

How apropos, he thought.

He sat staring at the ground until he finished the call, then resumed a slow, wet walk home.

* * *

At his condo, he checked his messages: no email, no voicemail, no texts. He filled Ernie's water bowl, then slumped in a leather recliner in his wet clothes.

He considered his plight, I've failed, my reputation will take a hit, how do I come back from this…why is work top of mind? Why do I care so much about reputation? Is my job 'me,' or am I more than a venture capitalist? Isn't family more important?

Joshua put on dry clothes, dried his hair, and retrieved his family photo album on the way out of the bedroom and relaxed on the couch. He opened to the first page and was met with a picture of him with his parents at Disneyworld in front of Space Mountain. He smiled as tears rolled down his cheeks. He flipped through the pictures. There was a photo of his mom giving him a big kiss on the cheek as he tried to pull away, which triggered a grin. There were several pictures of his aunt and uncle's farm, a few others with him shoulder-to-shoulder with Jake. Mouths gaped in smiles.

There were fewer pictures of his father, but in each of those he saw a glint in his eye, as if he was saying, "I love you, you'll be fine." He ran his sleeve across his eyes.

Joshua dialed his phone and waited for several rings before it was answered.

"Jake, it's Joshua. Your dad gave me your number. How're you feeling?"

There was a long pause on the other end. "Doin' fine."

"He said you've had some tests done…Are you worried?"

"Yeah! Who wouldn't be?"

"I'm going through a tough time at work. Looks like I lost my job today. It would probably be good for me to get away from here for a while. Mind if I join you at your next doctor's appointment?"

Jake responded in a cavalier tone, "Nah, I'm good. Shelby's gonna come with, just some sort of bug."

"I'm thinking of spending some time at the farm anyway, to get a break and spend more time with you all. You're the only family I have, and I'd like to be there with you. I can help with some of the medical stuff. I've been around it for years." The line remained silent. "Jake, I want to be there to support you, whatever you need. I'm very sorry for how I've acted, but I'd like to turn the page and be a part of your life."

"Yeah, I'll call if I need help."

The phone went silent. Joshua looked at the screen…the call ended. He closed his eyes and rubbed his temples with his thumbs.

Chapter 10

A couple days later, Joshua visited a local biotech company he invested in on behalf of Tremont. He sat in a tiny makeshift conference room in the Boylston Street offices of Elypsis BioPharma and concluded a discussion with the Founding CEO.

Joshua stood. "I wanted to meet with you in person to tell you how much I've enjoyed working with you and your team. Your therapeutic technology will be a hit and advance the science. I wish you all the best in the future, and feel free to call me if I can be of assistance. I'll keep you updated on where I land next."

He shook hands with the CEO and started to turn to leave before stopping abruptly. "Does anyone on your staff have experience with bile duct cancer?"

The CEO pondered the question briefly. "Well, if anyone does, it's Dr. Grimes. He's our local savant. Have a seat. I'll have him stop in and see you. Thanks for all your support the last couple years…you take care, Joshua."

Minutes later, Joshua stood and offered his hand as a small, lean, middle-aged man with unkempt salt-and-pepper hair entered the room. "Hello, Dr. Grimes, I'm Joshua Grayson. Nice to meet you."

Grimes bobbed his head, haltingly offered a fist bump in return, and sat at a small conference table, where he awkwardly started the conversation. "Something about BDC?"

"Yes, in a small farming area in south-central Illinois. There's been an increase in that type of cancer. Unfortunately, it's impacted my family, and I'm struggling to understand the cause. I know it's rare."

Grimes rocked from side to side in his chair, apparently waiting for more information. Joshua complied. "The local incidence rate has apparently grown enough for the Illinois Department of Public Health to recently take notice. The onset seems to be unusually quick, and I believe they've had young people affected. The survival rate is effectively zero. My aunt died forty days after diagnosis. I'm worried about the rest of my family. I'm also wondering what's causing the cancer. It seems to have just emerged out of nowhere."

The doctor continued to rock back and forth as Joshua spoke, so he rambled on, imagining he had to feed the computer with more data to get a response. "The cancer isn't known to be hereditary, so maybe it's triggered by environmental factors. It's an agricultural area where they use pesticides and fertilizers, so chemicals can't be ruled out."

Grimes stopped nodding. "Correct. I follow your logic so far. Continue."

"Maybe lifestyle elements or a change in dietary patterns? But I know the area, and things change very slowly there. I'd say possibly related to epigenetic tags from past generations increasing the likelihood of occurrence, but prior generations didn't have similar incidence rates. I know in some countries, parasite infestations cause inflammation in the bile ducts, but—"

Grimes stopped head bobbing and blurted out, "Dietary, remote possibility it's chemical."

"Why?"

"Virtually everything you mentioned is a potential cause, but it would likely take significant time to trigger a change in the incidence rate. Ask, what would be the most likely pathway to quickly turn off tumor suppressor genes or activate cellular oncogenes?"

Joshua spoke his thoughts. "Chemical exposures generally require long, repeated contact, usually at high levels to have an effect. Dietary the same, I think…but in that case you're ingesting the source."

Grimes stood. "Inventory what changes in chemical use or dietary intake have occurred over the time period. Think broadly. For example, dietary could include water." He turned to leave, stopped abruptly, faced Joshua, and bowed deeply before departing.

Joshua walked out of the building into a blustery wind and shivered. As he walked to his condo, the prospect of how to move his career forward, family reconciliation, potential medical issues with Jake, along with the dramatic quiet that had fallen like a dark cloak over his life all ran through his mind.

He calmed himself by inhaling deeply and exhaling slowly. He focused his thoughts and counseled himself, *What first? What's most important? Give it time, don't vanish. If anything, use this time to reconnect.*

Inside the foyer of his building, he picked up a FedEx envelope at the bellman's desk and opened it in the elevator. The return address was Tremont Ventures, Boylston Street,

Boston. Inside, he found a document entitled "Separation Agreement." Quickly scanning the pages, he found the large, bold signature of Jeffery Cochran on behalf of Tremont Ventures on the last page made with a red Sharpie. Above it, a yellow Post-it note with a large, exaggerated arrow pointing to the place intended for Joshua's signature.

As the elevator doors opened on the sixth floor, he hit the lobby button. Once on the ground floor, he walked with purpose, flung the front doors of the building open, and speed-walked, eyes focused only on his next step.

Fifteen minutes later, he burst into the Tremont office and smiled meekly at Emmie Rooney, the firm's long-time receptionist, as he rushed down the hallway and barged into Roseboro's office, finding him at his computer. Joshua tossed the document on the desk in front of him.

"What's this?"

"Looks like the separation agreement we talked about."

"Why is Cochran involved in this? Do you think that's productive? Do you think he has even a clue as to what I've done here? Do you think he'd be fair? And he signed it with a red Sharpie! Have you read it?"

Roseboro gave him a dazed look. "It was delegated to Hutch, who I guess gave it to Cochran. But we were all supposed to review and approve it before it was given to you. Also, I just found out Cochran is in touch with the police about the incident. Piling on, if you ask me." As Joshua turned and walked briskly toward the door, Roseboro added, "Cochran isn't in."

Joshua stopped abruptly and spun around, red-faced and jaw clenched. He spoke in a careful, controlled tone. "Let's handle this between us. I expect we'll be able to work it out fairly, given our history. I'll get a redlined version back to you. I'm sure Cochran was one-sided just to try and stick a dagger in me. I warned you about this. It could get ugly very fast."

"You're right, letting Cochran handle this makes no sense. I'll find out what's going on, and let's get it done quickly. That would be best for everyone."

Joshua moved to his office, where he found all his personal effects in boxes stacked next to the door. He slammed his hand against the doorframe and sprinted to Cochran's office, finding it empty. He paced back and forth for a short while before emptying the contents of the trash can over the desk. Scanning the room, he moved back to the desk, took a letter opener from a steel mesh cup full of pens, and plunged it into the front of Cochran's black leather chair.

Breathing hard, he walked slowly to the reception area, where Emmie was dabbing at her eyes with a tissue. Joshua put on a forced smile. "It'll be fine." The inflection of his words made it sound more like a question. "These things happen in business. Can you just please have all my things moved to my condo today, if possible? We'll stay in touch, and reach out if I can ever help you."

He hugged her, and as he turned to leave, Jeffrey Cochran entered the office, briefcase in hand. Heat flashed through Joshua's body, and he quickly joined him in the reception area as Emmie ran down the hallway.

Cochran, seeing his nemesis, quickly shifted from bug-eyed to a furrowed brow and broad smirk. "Cleaning your crap out, I guess?" He laughed.

Joshua edged closer to him and felt his stomach tighten. "How's your jaw? Most men know how to fight their own battles. You hide behind others. Going to the police for a small scrap you initiated and going to the partners to push me out was gutless. You feel entitled coming from a family with money, and you've probably always picked on others because you're bigger than them. I've always hated bullies and stood up to many—they all back down just like you. All words. I competed with you before you joined Tremont and beat you every time. I voted not to bring you on board because you're not smart enough and don't know the business; the others will see they made a terrible choice in short order."

Cochran scowled and began to walk away slowly. "I have no time for you. I'm busy making money for this firm, unlike you. We'll scrape you off the bottom of our shoe and move on like you were never here."

Joshua took another step forward, his hands squeezed into fists. "Why don't we just step into the alley behind the building, just you and me alone, and settle this right now? I barely clipped you with that punch, and you went down like you got hit by a truck. So, now's your chance…"

Cochran took a step back and stood as tall as he could, like a peacock showing its plumes. His eyes scanned the room actively as he very slowly moved toward the hallway.

Just then, Roseboro burst into the room and stepped between the men, putting his arms out to hold them apart.

Cochran moved forward into Roseboro's hand and howled, "You're lucky, Grayson."

"Guys, stop! Jeff, go back to your office. Joshua, go on home. You and I are going to handle things between us fairly and equitably. You have my word."

Joshua glared at Cochran. "Anytime, anywhere."

* * *

Retracing the route to his condo, Joshua's emotions fluctuated from embarrassment by letting his pride and anger override his professionalism to wishing Cochran had taken him up on his offer to fight it out. The image of Cochran's laughing face, and the way he stepped forward into Roseboro's hand, pumped adrenaline through his system. Rain started to pelt him hard. He slipped into the Thinking Cup and ordered an espresso. As he waited for the rain to abate, he scrolled through his contacts, stopping at Bill Gilchrist, an old college baseball teammate.

The place was crowded, a mix of professionals and students from local universities looking to escape the downpour. He managed to find a high-top seat at the window and left a message for Gilchrist.

"Billy, Joshua Grayson here. Long time no talk, my fault. Hope you're doing well. Hey listen, can you give me a call? I need your legal help. I'm getting forced out at Tremont, and I need you to look at the separation agreement for me. Long story, I'll share it with you over a beer. Give me a call back when you have a chance. Talk to you soon."

As he continued his walk home, he raised his head as the sun peeked through the clouds. He pictured his aunt dancing in the sun showers at the farm…the smile turned to a frown when he recalled the reality she'd faced in her illness: limited options, and limited hope.

Chapter 11

Dr. Currie sat in a low back, rounded swivel chair upholstered in indigo blue cashmere, one of four grouped on the opposite side of her desk. Behind her was a window running the length of the office facing the city. She watched Hassan stand from a nearby chair, button his gray sharkskin blazer, and step forward to set expectations for the *Time* magazine reporter who was just shown into the office with a photographer. He moved with an athletic stride. The overhead lighting highlighted scars on his dark tawny face and the black furrowed eyebrows over his deep-set brown eyes.

"Hello, my name is Anas Hassan. I'm the Director of Communications for Golden Helix. Before you begin, I want to inform you that Dr. Currie is a person of few words." He paused, interrupted by the rapid clicking sound of the photographer's camera. Slowly, he turned his head, stared at the man with a penetrating gaze, and spoke sharply with a Spanish accent. "Sir, please stop the photos and let me go through the rules." The man held the camera at his side.

Hassan stared at the man, who gave a slight nod, acknowledging his acquiescence. "Firstly, in terms of photos, refrain from taking too many, as the shutter clicking sound is distracting. Also, as agreed, Dr. Currie will have final say on the photos used. No more than three, the rest to be destroyed."

He turned to the reporter. "Secondly, regarding the interview, Dr. Currie is a very private individual, so we expect the focus to be on Golden Helix. Lastly, the interview will last no more than one hour, after which we've arranged a tour of the Golden Helix building for you." The *Time* correspondents signaled agreement.

The middle-aged veteran reporter stepped forward and shook Dr. Currie's hand. "It's a pleasure to meet you, Doctor, and congratulations on your success with DNA Restore. I've never been to a biotech company, but the architecture of your building is incredible, and exactly what I'd expect." She added as she moved to her seat, "And the view out of your window is spectacular!" Currie gave her a smile and polite thank you in reply.

The reporter turned on her voice recorder and placed it on the round coffee table between herself and the doctor. She took a sip of bottled water and cleared her throat before she launched into her questions.

"Dr. Currie, to begin, I understand and very much respect that you're a private person, but the world is very interested in getting to know you at least a little bit personally. You've jumped onto the world stage so quickly." Currie watched the reporter's eyes dart quickly back and forth between her and the reporter's notepad.

"Can you give our readers a little glimpse into who you are? I take it you were raised here in the Netherlands?"

"Yes, I was born in the Netherlands and spent most of my childhood here. As I began to progress in school, my parents felt it was necessary for me to attend schools abroad in order to get a well-rounded education, and my father was able to move freely with his job, as he worked for the government's foreign service."

"That sounds exciting and challenging. I believe that you're an only child?"

The doctor shifted in her chair. "Yes."

"Doctor, you speak excellent English. How many languages do you speak?"

"Six languages, fluently."

"Out of curiosity, what are they?"

"Dutch, English, French, German, Russian, and Swedish."

"Wow, very impressive." She paused after jotting notes on her pad and looked up wide-eyed at Currie. "I think you even noted them in alphabetical order." She laughed lightly.

Currie smiled and shrugged. "Habit, I guess."

"Are you married? Have any children?"

Hassan stepped forward and began to speak, but Currie held up her hand and answered, looking off in the distance and rubbing the birthmark on her temple. "No to both questions."

"The news you delivered at the Amsterdam biotech conference was shocking. Do you really believe your company has found a cure for cancer?"

"I truly wish that was the case. What we have is a platform that we believe has the ability to correct many forms of cancer. We have very, very high success rates so far in reducing, bile duct cancer or BDC for short, in our trials in Brazil. I believe that we can apply our technology platform to other forms of cancer over time. We'll learn from the clinical trials and continue to refine and improve our technology."

"How high are the success rates? And why the focus on BDC?"

"The success rates, defined as an alleviation of symptoms and no recurrence, are over ninety percent so far after almost one year of trials. To put that into perspective, the standard of what success is in clinical trials is historically around ten percent. We're in the process of expanding the trials to the U.S., where they are starting to see, in some areas, an increasing incidence rate of BDC. We're hopeful that we have a solution that can help many people in the U.S. We expect the FDA to approve the trials, but that remains to be seen.

"We focused initially on BDC because the health care authorities in Brazil asked for assistance, as they saw dramatic increases in the frequency of occurrence. We were able to isolate gene sequence defects quickly. That allowed us to clearly target those defects for correction, which is done through our DNA Restore platform."

The reporter glanced at her notes. "Golden Helix is a private company. It seems like the owners are in line for a big financial return at some point. They must be very happy."

"I hope that's the case." Currie's eyes looked upward. "I feel very grateful that we have been able to fund our work, which is starting to bear fruit. Hopefully, it's a win for all."

"You mentioned that you're looking to conduct trials in the U.S. Can you elaborate on that further? I believe our readers would be very interested in more detail."

"Yes, we've petitioned the FDA to start a Fast Track designation for BDC, as well as a small trial in the U.S. The situation is much, much smaller than the size of the COVID pandemic, for example, but the The Centers for Disease Control and Prevention has seen an uptick BDC in some areas. It's also not nearly the scale of Brazil, fortunately. We feel that if the FDA allows it and strong results follow, like our experience in Brazil, it will provide experience and confidence with our DNA Restore therapeutic platform generally. That may allow us to accelerate our ability to bring new cancer treatments to people in the future."

Currie sipped her tea before continuing. "I've also been consulting with the CDC on the BDC situation and trying to assist them where we can. If we're approved, we'll have the trials locally, if possible. It's a burden and high cost for many people in rural areas to be able to travel long distances for care. Also, the costs can be very high to get care in big cities. So for that reason, we're focused on putting the affected people first, bringing our platform to them locally. The hospitals would need to meet certain requirements, of course, but where needed we'll bring financial assistance and experts to assist them in meeting those requirements."

"I think that's unheard of, and very magnanimous and inspiring!" The reporter scanned her notes and moved to another question.

"Other than your work fighting cancer, are there any other causes close to your heart?"

Currie tilted her head, closed her eyes, and sat silent for an awkward moment, a noticeable contrast to her prior quick responses. "Yes. I started an orphanage here in the Netherlands several years ago. I was very close to someone who was raised in an orphanage, and when that person died, I channeled my focus and resources there as a way to, as some people say, 'pay it forward' for other children in the same situation."

"That's wonderful. How many children are at the orphanage?"

"Currently, forty-seven. The facility is in the Dutch town of Bronkhorst, which is on the border of the Netherlands and Belgium. It's very rewarding to be involved in the children's lives."

They continued the interview for the balance of the hour, focusing on future clinical trial roll-out plans, next cancer targets, and a range of questions around how DNA Restore differs from current alternatives. As the time moved toward the hour mark, Hassan stepped forward and noted only a few minutes remained.

"Dr. Currie, I'd like to ask you some quick final questions that only require short answers, what we call a 'lightning round.' Hopefully, this will interject some fun into the article for the readers, so please just respond with the first thing that comes to your mind.

"Okay, here we go…how many hours do you sleep each night, on average?"

"Six."

"What's your favorite book?"

"Atlas Shrugged."

"Favorite meal?"

"Kobe beef stuffed with foie gras and gold-leaf, covered in caviar, lobster, and truffles."

The reporter stopped and opened her eyes wide at the answer before continuing. "What's the quote or motto that you live by?"

"The question isn't who's going to let me, it's who's going to stop me."

Currie's answers were immediate. The reporter's eyes again opened wide as she asked her final questions. "What do you do for fun?"

"Work on scientific problems."

"Your favorite song?"

"Rhapsody in Blue."

"What inspires you?"

"Finding solutions to complex scientific problems."

The reporter closed her notebook, leaned forward, and extended her hand to Currie. "Thank you very much for your time, Doctor. I know the world will be very interested in learning a bit more about you, your work, and of course, best wishes for much success."

Hassan stepped back into the conversation. "When will we receive a copy of the article? And when will it be published?"

She looked up at Hassan and replied as she packed her briefcase. "We're going to fast - track this, so within the next two weeks, it should be completed. We're aiming to have it in next month's magazine, with the doctor on the cover. As soon as we have a final draft, we'll send it to you."

He escorted the two visitors to the door, where he handed them off to an employee for a building tour. He took the reporter's seat across from Currie.

"Hassan, how do you think it went?"

He ran his fingers through his black, short-cropped hair and considered the question for a moment before rattling off thoughts in staccato. "Very well…clear and succinct…some personal information…clear path forward."

Chapter 12

Effingham's St. Anthony's Memorial Hospital, an affiliate of the Hospital Sisters Health Systems, based in Springfield, Illinois was housed in a six-story brick building with an ornate concrete façade over a pillared rotunda main entrance. The hospital, with 133 beds and 700 employees, serviced the Effingham area, but also more broadly the south-central Illinois region, covering an estimated 200,000 people. Late afternoon, Joshua entered the main entrance and stepped into a reception area. There he scanned the high walls covered in warm green and brown Italian marble. Having been involved with the medical and biotech community in Boston, he felt like he'd stepped into a time machine that dropped him in the 1950s. It reminded him of the look and feel of the Catholic church he attended growing up in Chicago.

He asked the receptionist, an elderly woman with gray hair pulled into a bun on top of her head, if she could let Dr. Kaymer know he arrived. He received a very professional, "Yes, young man, please have a seat" in response. He smiled and wandered through the small gift shop adjacent to the lobby for a few minutes before sitting and scanning through a brochure providing a history of the hospital: built in 1875, destroyed by a fire in 1949, and rebuilt in 1954.

Every so often, he looked at the receptionist. She sat upright and answered the phone in an exaggerated professional manner. Soft music played in the background, a muzak rendition of the Rolling Stones' "You Can't Always Get What You Want."

Half an hour after his arrival, the sound of hard-soled shoes on the tiled floor drew Joshua's attention away from a dog-eared article on "Self-Tanner Tips" from a worn, very dated edition of *WebMD* magazine. A woman in a white lab coat exited one of the hallways and walked toward the reception area. As the figure drew closer, Joshua stood and walked toward her. She held an open file in her right hand and was reading it as she walked.

Joshua stood in her path and adjusted his navy blue blazer. "Dr. Kaymer? I'm Joshua Grayson."

She raised her head, brushed back her shoulder-length dark hair, and replied with a slight southern accent, "Nice to meet you." The doctor led him just past the lobby elevators, a bank of vending machines, and into the café. He bought two cups of coffee, and they sat at a table in the corner of the cafeteria, where they would have a modicum of privacy.

Joshua jumped immediately to questions. "I'm worried about my family and the incidence of BDC in the area. It's affected my aunt, and maybe now my cousin. Why isn't the CDC all over this?"

Dr. Kaymer sat back in her chair and raised her eyebrows. "You're preaching to the choir here." She squinted her eyes and raised her voice slightly. "As I mentioned on our call, the Illinois Department of Public Health is looking into the issue. I suggest you call them. They're engaged, but there's no simple, quick solution, as much as we want it. The CDC isn't likely to get involved in a small local issue unless the state requests it and it's broad."

Joshua sipped his coffee as the doctor spoke but kept a quick pace of questions. "I was speaking the other day with a senior research scientist at a biotech company in Boston. I explained the situation and asked him for his thoughts on the root cause of the spike. His response was, it's likely dietary or, much less probable, chemical. Are you aware of local changes that might fit in those categories? Even, for example, the water supply for the area?"

"No. We're focused on treating the disease here. Once again, if you want more information on potential causation, you should contact the IDPH directly." She shook her head and glowered at him with her hazel eyes. "Mr. Grayson, we've already discussed much of this on the phone. Frankly, I think you ought to slow down on the coffee. I feel like I'm spinning my wheels here."

"Do you have a contact at the IDPH, then? How about the CDC?"

The doctor paused, crossed her arms, then answered slowly. "I have someone at the CDC from a prior inquiry. But not from the IDPH. The CDC contact is Edwin Boechenhold." She found the information on her phone, jotted it on a napkin, and handed it to him. Joshua tucked it in his blazer pocket.

"What about treatment options? This cancer appears to be aggressive."

"Depending on the case, surgery is the main treatment protocol, combined with adjuvant radiation or chemotherapy. Again, I mentioned clinical trials to you on the phone, but it's way too early to tell if those therapies are efficacious. Financial resources can be challenging for local patients, and they are, let's say, homebodies, tied to their land and routines. The trials tend to be in big cities, none in the U.S. focused on BDC, which, as you know, is a rare form of cancer. Plus, the trials take time, which is a challenge on a number of different levels."

Joshua looked down and stirred his coffee.

This is a waste of time, he thought. Things move in slow motion here. That's dangerous!

His stomach churned. "As we discussed on our call, my aunt passed away forty days after diagnosis. Is that about the average you're seeing?"

"The local average is around sixty to seventy days from diagnosis. So roughly two to three weeks longer than your aunt, but still extremely quick based on history and very concerning. Historically, some BDC patients live for years. I do believe your aunt waited a couple of weeks before we tested her."

He peppered her further. "I understand my cousin Jake's genetic test came back with one of the same markers my aunt had. Is that the case?"

"I can't speak to you about a person without the their consent."

Joshua leaned over the table, wearing a frozen smile. "Come on, Dr. Kaymer, let's not dance here. It's my cousin, and I obviously know he has a common genetic marker."

The doctor stood, looked down at him, and called him out. "Mr. Grayson, this isn't Boston. It's bold of you to presume I'd provide private information without permission and break the law. You work in or around the medical community, so you certainly know about HIPPA." She paused briefly and raised her voice, turning heads. "I'm not about to shortcut the law, and I'm not someone you can push around." She turned abruptly and walked away.

* * *

Later that afternoon, Joshua pulled up next to a dusty, rust-covered red Chevy Suburban in the driveway of a modest-sized brick ranch. The home was surrounded by an acre or so of lawn, with kids' toys arrayed in the front yard. The rear of the property abutted a narrow line of woods with planting fields beyond. As he strolled toward the front door, admiring chalk drawings on the driveway, it opened, and Shelby stepped out.

"Hey, you didn't need to dress up for dinner. We're just havin' chicken."

"Thanks for the invite. Are you sure Jake's okay with it?" He tilted his head and raised an eyebrow.

"Yeah. And if he isn't, you and I'll have time to get to know each other." She waved him forward. "Come on, now."

Entering the door, he gave her a bottle of Niemerg Red from a local winery. The smell of fried chicken met him as they ventured into the kitchen. Jake was at the counter, making coleslaw, his head nodding to Van Morrison's "Wavelength" playing softly in the background on a turntable. The open floor plan had a welcome feel, enhanced by family pictures and walls painted with a warm golden straw color.

"Hey Jake, look who I found in the driveway!" Shelby lifted her hands toward Joshua like a model showing a new car.

Jake turned his head briefly before returning his attention to the coleslaw. Shelby stood, hands on hips, and stared. "Hey, where are your manners? Aren't you going to say hey to your cousin?"

Jake muttered, "Hey" as he continued chopping cabbage.

"Well, okay, have it your way." Shelby retrieved two beers from the refrigerator and motioned Joshua toward the couch in the adjacent room. "Joshua and I are just going to get to know each other."

"Jake, I didn't know this was going to be a surprise for you."

Joshua paused and stared at his cousin. He could still see the teenage Jake. The ember still glowed, but it had faded. He felt a swell of emotion.

Shelby turned her eyes to Jake as she spoke with a raised voice. "So, why do you live in Boston?"

Joshua turned his attention to Shelby. "I went to college in Boston because I had a baseball scholarship. It was a rough time in my life, my parents had just died. It was also a chance to escape everything. Looking back, it was a stupid thing to do, at least how I went about it."

"Why?"

"I just completely disconnected from everyone. Put school and then my job first. I pushed all those feelings to the back of my mind. Which, by the way, isn't an emotionally healthy thing to do, I'm learning."

She looked at Jake, dish towel over his shoulder, wearing an empty stare, still busy in the kitchen. "Your turn to ask me a question."

Joshua took a gulp of beer and rubbed his chin. "Okay. Where did you get your name? Maybe you grew up near Lake Shelbyville?"

She laughed hard, snorted, and laughed harder. "Nooo, my father wanted to name me after his favorite car! You know, the Shelby Ford Mustang?"

He shook his head and gave her a blank stare.

"Really, you don't know it? It's a high-performance Mustang version. It was big in the late sixties and early seventies."

Jake finished the preparations, put the food on the table, and added an extra plate. "Come on, before the food gets cold."

At the table, Shelby said a short prayer, and they served themselves.

Before taking his first bite, Joshua started the conversation. "I don't see the kids. Where are they?"

"They're at my mom's. Jake and I wanted a little time to ourselves." Shelby looked Joshua in the eye. "I hear you're having problems at work?"

"Yeah. Looks like I need to find another company to work for; it's sort of political. The firm hasn't been doing well, and my partners are pointing at me as the reason, which is somewhat fair. I also got into a little scuffle with the new partner, which didn't help."

Shelby's eyes grew large. "Like a fight? What happened?"

Jake mumbled under his breath. "I'll tell you what happened, the guy got his butt kicked." He looked up from his plate briefly before re-engaging with his meal.

"It wasn't a big deal. We had a new partner trying to make his mark. He and I had some history competing against each other. He held a grudge and pushed my buttons, and it got a little physical." He quickly transitioned the conversation before he took another bite of chicken. "So, how did you two meet?"

"No, Mister, you don't get away that easy. What did he say or do to start the fight?"

Joshua shook his head as he chewed and swallowed. Shelby stared at him, eyes bulging. "Okay, okay." He held up his hands in surrender. "We were in a partners meeting, and the guy was relentlessly giving me a hard time. We decided to end the meeting early. I started to leave the room, he stepped in front of me and pushed me with his shoulder."

Jake laughed and spoke softly as he chewed. "That ain't good."

"I pushed him back and picked up the files he knocked out of my hand. I guess he didn't like me pushing him, so he put up his fists and started coming at me." He took another bite of chicken and smiled at Shelby.

She put her hands on the table and leaned toward Joshua. "If you don't swallow that fast and finish the story, you're going to have another fight on your hands."

Joshua looked at Jake, wide-eyed, drawing a smile. "Okay. Well, he moved closer to me and grabbed me by the shirt."

"Oh man, not a good move," Jake muttered.

"So, I hit him in the jaw, he went down, and I walked out."

Shelby sat down and put her hand over her mouth.

"It's not that bad; he's fine. I shouldn't have hit him. It was just reflex."

Joshua shrugged, swept up coleslaw with his fork, and asked a question before depositing it in his mouth. "Now, tell me how you two met."

Shelby dropped her fork on the plate, put on a wide smile, and began an animated recollection. "I was at the state fair, you know, in Springfield, with my two college roommates. It was at the end of a long, hot day, and we were thinking of heading home but decided to sit down and listen to more music before leaving. It turned out we sat down where the state fair karaoke contest was being held." She laughed and stared at Jake, who rolled his eyes.

"So, we're close to the stage, and listening to a couple of bad singers when we see this hot, good looking cowboy strut onto the stage." She paused and looked at Joshua. "Wasn't Jake. It was one of his buddies…so he sings a song, and after he's done, some guys push Jake onto the stage, and the music starts. He's singing 'The Time of My Life,' one of my favorites. He sounded pretty good, but something was missing. It's a duet, so suddenly I find myself standing, walking up on stage and singing with him!"

Shelby crinkled her eyes. "Funny thing is, we won the contest! Got a trophy, and I think two hundred and fifty bucks. Married six months later!"

Jake looked her in the eye. "You made us better when we were singing, and it's continued ever since."

Shelby sat on Jake's lap and kissed him. "Before I start crying again, please tell me a story from when you guys hung out during the summers."

Joshua cleared his throat dramatically and gave her a broad smile. "On the plane to Boston after the funeral, I was thinking about some of the fun we had growing up. I miss those times." He paused for a moment, then put on a big grin. "One summer we had a big family reunion at the farm, and while everyone was playing games, Jake and I took Aunt Sara's brother's video camera and filmed a tour of some…well, let's call it 'animal life.'"

The comment caught Jake in the middle of a gulp of beer, and while he tried to contain it, the liquid came back out of his mouth and nose, and Shelby jumped for cover. He tried to speak but just couldn't gain control, which triggered irrepressible laughter from Joshua.

"Let me in on it, boys!"

The coughing and laughter eventually subsided, and Jake continued the story. "My Uncle Paul showed the video later that night to the whole family, must'a been twenty people, most of them young kids…" He and Joshua laughed again. "The video went from the little kids playing duck-duck-goose to a big ol' pair of pig gonads, and then it cut to a couple of pigs doing the Humpty Hump!"

Shelby's eyes narrowed. "The what?"

Jake looked at her wide-eyed and said very slowly, "They were makin' bacon."

Shelby buried her head in her napkin and shook with laughter.

Tears rolled down Jake's face. "Man, I haven't laughed this hard in years."

They reminisced a bit further over apple pie and coffee before Jake said goodnight and Joshua moved to the door. "Thank you for the invite, Shelby, I needed it. I know Jake has a doctor's appointment tomorrow, and he hasn't been feeling good. I'm glad he's seeing the doctor, but if this doesn't go away quickly, I think he should see someone at one of the large hospitals in Boston. I can get him an appointment and take care of all the details."

"You're scaring me. Sara passed so quickly, we hardly had a chance to say goodbye. She was the heart of the family. A wonderful woman of faith."

"Sorry, I tend to think too far ahead. But I think it'd be a smart option."

Shelby spoke confidently. "There are a lot of people praying that Jake's situation is nothing major. I believe it's God's timing that you're here, Joshua. Jake needs you, we need you." She gave him a hug, then asked him to wait. She turned, walked across the room, took a picture off a shelf, and handed it to Joshua.

Joshua smiled. The picture showed him and Jake around eight years old, standing side by side, broad smiles and arms over each of the other's shoulders.

Joshua closed his eyes and said, "I'm glad to be here, too."

"He's a tough guy, Joshua. I'm sure he'll be up tomorrow, eating a big breakfast and feeling better…stayin' at Pete's?"

"Yep. Thanks for sharing the picture. I had a great time."

He directed the rental car slowly along the roads of Bishop Creek, illuminated only by moonlight and his high beams, navigating toward the well-lit St. Aloysius steeple.

The car moved slowly as Joshua focused on the farmhouses. He noted most were set well off the road, like his uncle's. They stood alone, diminished by the scale of the surrounding land. Each home had mature trees that provided shade during the hot summers. Many of the fields were harvested, providing him with the opportunity to see the lights in the rooms at the front of the houses. He wondered what their lives were like.

As he turned down the lane and moved slowly to the farmhouse, he saw a light on in the front of the house. Entering the kitchen, he found a note and photograph in the center of the table:

Joshua – Welcome. I'm out until late. Take your old room. See you in the morning.

P.S. Found this picture of you and your aunt the other day.

He stared at the photograph. He was in his mid-teens, standing next to Aunt Sara, who had her arms around him with a big, magnetic smile. Tucking the picture in his shirt pocket, he made his way to a room at the east end of the second floor, turned on the light, and got settled.

Through his teen years, he spent summers on the farm. As an only child, it was his parents' way for him to have a bigger sense of family. He shared the room with Jake and Blaine. The two double beds were still in the same place, probably the same mattresses, he figured. Over an old bureau, he recognized a sign next to the mirror:

I believe in the future of agriculture, with a faith born not of words, but of deeds, achievements won by the present and past generations of agriculturists; in the promise of better days through better ways, even as the better things we now enjoy have come to us from the struggles of former years.

Future Farmers of America

Before turning in, he checked his phone and found a text from his Boston neighbor, looking for Ernie's cat food, plus two voicemails. The first was from his legal buddy, Bill Gilchrist, wanting to discuss the Tremont separation agreement. The second turned his stomach.

As he replayed the message, papers could be heard rustling for quite a while before a voice was heard. "Yeah. This is Sergeant Slocum, Boston PD. I need to advise you we have an assault and battery complaint that's been filed here by a Jeffrey S. Cochran against you regarding an altercation that occurred recently. The complaint has been turned over to the court, and you'll be served with the complaint in the coming days, with instructions."

Joshua slammed the phone on a side table, flopped onto the bed, closed his eyes, and put his hands over his face.

Chapter 13

The following evening, gravel crunched under the tires of Joshua's car as it moved down the lane. The sun was beginning to set, and he could see the light on in the kitchen, soft smoke plumes coming from the chimney intended to ward off the effects of an unusually cold early November day. He entered through the screened-in porch at the rear of the house, as everyone did, and stepped into the kitchen.

Pete was at the stove, stirring a big cast iron pot, and spoke over his shoulder. "Did you get the cheese and cornbread?"

"Yep, got everything on your list. Smells great. I'm hungry."

Pete dished out two steaming bowls of chili garnished with sharp cheddar cheese, sour cream, and, on top, a sizable piece of cornbread. "Let's eat," he said as he brought the bowls to the table. He interlaced his fingers in front of him and looked at Joshua. "I hope you don't mind if I pray before we eat." With a nod from Joshua, he closed his eyes, bowed his head, and said a brief prayer aloud.

As Pete stared into the bowl and stirred his chili slowly, he asked, "So, did you hear anything about Jake's doctor's appointment?"

Joshua swallowed. "The doctor wants him to have some tests done. Shelby's pushing him to go to Boston with me for another opinion, if needed."

Pete's eyes remaining focused on his food. The room fell quiet. Joshua turned his attention to his bowl, glancing at his uncle every so often. He was now in his early sixties, but his appearance hadn't changed much over the years. Pete wore a perpetual five o'clock shadow, that accentuated his square jaw. Time had touched him with gray accents around his temples, and he now carried reading glasses between buttonholes in his shirt. Joshua peered down and saw a red handkerchief hanging out of the rear pocket of his jeans, something he'd always done.

As Pete walked to the stove for a refill, he spoke over his shoulder. "Makes me angry and sad that we didn't have any options for Sara." He filled his bowl and started to talk but stopped to compose himself. As he walked slowly back to the table, he asked Joshua, "What options are there?"

"It depends on what the issue is, of course." Joshua told himself to keep it simple and don't get too far ahead. "If it's BDC, there are traditional treatment options, like chemotherapy, radiation, and surgery. There may also be other clinical trials for cancer available, but not specifically for bile duct. On the outskirts, there's a Dutch biotech company called Golden Helix with a new gene therapy targeted specifically for this type of cancer. I saw a presentation at a conference, and the treatment has been doing very well in Brazil, so that would be a very positive development. But it generally takes quite a while to get an approval in the U.S."

Pete raised his voice. "Yeah, but they moved quick on the COVID vaccines. Why couldn't they do that for BDC? They could use the results from Brazil, right? If it was needed, could we get Jake to Brazil for the new therapy?"

"Uncle Pete, I wish everything moved more quickly and we could bring Jake to Brazil if needed. Unfortunately, it's all very complicated. In this case, BDC only effects a very small population annually, and it's rare compared to the million-plus people who died from COVID.

"Also, I don't know that BDC is growing that quickly across the country. Even a FDA Fast Track emergency authorization for drugs to treat serious conditions needs a lot of data to determine safety, and that takes controlled testing through clinical trials. I think the COVID vaccines were tested on over forty thousand people, and then there was a waiting period to see if there were issues. Ultimately, the FDA had to weigh the risks and benefits after analyzing all that work."

Pete poured coffee for each of them and wore an expression that he was deep in thought. As he put the carafe on a trivet, he asked, "So the trials are basically experiments?"

"In a sense, but first they go through a series of scientific studies, usually first with animals that have anatomical commonality with humans, then the results are reviewed by the FDA to make sure the treatments are reasonably safe to even consider testing on people."

"Sounds like something to consider and follow just in case. Judging from Sara's medical bills, I'm sure it's expensive…enough to take your breath away. Are those trials covered by insurance?"

Joshua gave a half-shrug. "I'd guess they're covered, and the sponsor of the trials usually absorbs much of the cost because they get the benefit of the results. But there are risks, and there could be travel involved, which could be costly."

Pete stared out the kitchen window and sipped his coffee. "Nothing like the beauty of a sunset after a long day of work."

"You know, Uncle Pete, it could be my memory, but you seem calmer and less on edge than you were when I used to spend summers here."

Pete put his cup on the kitchen counter. "It's true, I had a quick temper. I was unhappy for many years. One particularly tough day, as I stared at myself in the mirror, I realized I wasn't the man I wanted to be, or one my father would be proud of. I was overweight and, frankly, drinking too much." He shook his head. "I just wasn't proud of where I was in my life and the example I was setting for my boys.

"I thought about that for days before sitting down with your aunt and pouring my heart out. She'd been waiting for that moment for years. Sara told me the emptiness in my life was caused by having what she called a God-shaped hole in my heart. I'm hard-headed, so it took some time for me to see it, but she was right."

"How did you see it?"

"Well, I actually heard it."

Joshua sat back in his chair, arms crossed. "What do you mean?"

"I began to attend church with your aunt, prayed, and read the Bible for no reason other than I wanted to. One day, probably a year or so later, I was having a very tough time. It looked like the harvest was going to be terrible, and I was worried about paying bills and taking care of my family. I was driving through Bishop Creek, thinking about my troubles, and I heard God speak to me. He said, 'Trust in Me.'"

"Audibly?"

"Well…I'm not sure. I heard it in my mind very clearly, and it definitely wasn't from me."

Joshua sat up straight and put his forearms on the table. "Didn't that scare you?"

"No, the opposite. I felt immediate peace and knew without a doubt things would be all right. It affirmed to me I was on the right track."

"Hard for me to imagine what that must've been like."

"Had the same experience not too long ago when your aunt was very sick. I felt like I'd failed her. I was standing in church alone, and everyone around me was singing. Those thoughts of failure and inadequacy were whirling through my mind, and I heard God's voice again, so very clearly, same experience. Again, three words." He wiped away welling tears with his hand and paused to gather himself, "He said, 'I made you.'"

Pete took a sip of coffee and regained his composure. "Those three words re-enforced that everything was going to be okay, that I wasn't alone and could withstand the pain and soldier on."

Joshua sat and listened intently. "It'd be nice to get an audible affirmation that I'm on the right road."

"What's on your mind?"

Joshua stared at his empty dinner bowl and considered the question. "My world is upside down. Worried about Jake. Have to go to court because I punched out a partner at my firm. Then I lost my job. Don't have any close friends. Can't sleep, and can't keep my mind quiet."

"That's all?" Pete grinned. "Let me ask you this: What's most important in your life?"

"Good question…I'm not sure."

"What's important commands your actions. It sounds to me like work has been the most important thing for you. Could be the challenge, or maybe the pay. So your decisions are influenced by that, and also your time. Something you should think about. At the end of your life, what do you want to have accomplished? Or what do you want your legacy to be? I'm sure you've heard the question: What do you want written on your tombstone?"

"I don't think about things like that."

"You're in a challenging time, but you're young, with a lot of life ahead of you. I believe it's something your dad may have challenged you with if he were here. He had the same talk with me, by the way. It did me good."

Joshua leaned back in the kitchen chair and looked up at the old plastered ceiling. "How did you answer my dad?"

"Like you, I couldn't, at least not right away. I had to think about it for a while. You should, too. Call it finding for your true north."

"My dad was a man of few words. I remember asking him once if he had any words of wisdom for me. He said two things: 'Follow the golden rule,' and 'Everything in moderation.'" He paused and laughed softly. "And he also said to never touch a public toilet seat and use your foot to flush."

The men chuckled as the radio station gave the local news. Pete stopped abruptly and turned up the volume.

"The Illinois Department of Public Health is now looking into the growing incidence of cancer in the Effingham area. The investigation is in the early stages, reviewing potential causes. The current focus appears to be on the large Steuben Printing Company that closed within the last two years, and an investigation of potential leakage of heavy metals, ink, and other solvents is underway. We're tracking this story and will provide our listeners with updates as the investigation progresses."

Quiet fell on the room as a commercial played. Pete squeezed his eyes shut.

Joshua felt a tightness in his chest. A short time later, he spoke softly. "Hopefully Jake's okay, but if the tests show anything, we need to act urgently, as if it's BDC." He held back sharing his further thoughts with Pete…

A thought ran through his mind, Aunt Sara passed on day fifty-four from when she first felt the symptoms. If Jake has BDC, it's day eight!

Chapter 14

Dr. Currie sat at her desk, jotting notes on the weekly staff meeting agenda with her Mont Blanc pen. She ruminated on her enduring question - how to accelerate the introduction of DNA Restore across countries, and broaden the scope beyond BDC?

A few minutes later, a soft computer alarm sounded, letting her know the senior staff meeting would start shortly. She used the time to scroll through her email. The last email caught her attention, she read it quickly before leaving for the meeting.

Dr. Currie pushed open the two large room doors from her office and stepped into the conference room on cue. The picture window captured the sunset above the Rembrandt Tower, the tallest building in Amsterdam, and provided the room with a subtle glow. A dozen people sat arrayed around the conference table.

She stood at the end of the conference table, her blue eyes traveling from attendee to attendee before she raised her hands in front of her, as if in prayer. She turned and paced slowly back and forth. After a few passes, she stopped, clasped her hands behind her back as if they were bound, and systematically looked each attendee in the eye as she spoke slowly in quiet tones, with conviction.

"I understand that you are working hard. Is it your best?" She paused after catching the eye of each person. "I implore you to keep our mission in mind always. While we have our health, there are people dying from a cancer that we have proven we can stop. Even cure!

"Just before I left my desk, I received an email. I'd like to read part of it to you. She read from her phone. 'BDC took a special person from my family, and now another much younger member is not doing well, and we're scared it could be the same disease. When do you expect DNA Restore to be available in the U.S.? Are there other options?'"

The room was quiet. Currie shrugged. "How do I respond to this person? How many others are in the same situation?" She sat at the end of the table and turned her attention to the opposite end of the table. "Dr. Telling, where are we with the U.S. FDA application?"

Telling looked over the reading glasses perched on the end of his prominent hawkish nose. "As you know, we've gone back and forth with the FDA for months on our application to conduct clinical trials for DNA Restore. The process was moving slowly, largely because of the prior COVID crisis, which consumed resources. When we look at the average timeline for a priority review for a new drug or therapy, it's on average six months. However, given the growing BDC incidences in the U.S. with high mortality levels, we shifted our strategy and submitted a request for a Fast Track Designation for DNA Restore, which is being reviewed now. This is the same process used to review the COVID vaccines and bring them online for emergency use. This would not be a formal approval, but rather an approval to start clinical trials early based on data."

Currie interjected. "How quickly can we expect an answer? What's the latest status?"

Resting his chin on his hand, Telling deliberated for a moment and cleared his throat. "The Fast Track option is for emergencies, the definition of which is subjective. The FDA protocol is they will review and decide within sixty days. We are using the strong results from Brazil to make our case. The other side of the matter is, while BDC is growing, it's still very, very small in terms of population. Also, this is a gene therapy product, for which the history is limited, and there have been some negative events in the past. That said, a small number of very specific gene therapy products have been approved in recent years with an abundance of caution. Hopefully, that bodes well for us."

The news brought applause and broad smiles from meeting attendees. Currie let the celebration go for a while to drive some positive energy among the leadership team. As the noise wound down, she raised an index finger. "Team…let's be ready to move forward assuming we receive the designation, and be prepared to implement. Let's target hospitals where BDC is growing. Educate them on our technology, the Brazil successes, and perhaps they can also lobby the FDA."

* * *

Early morning in Bishop Creek, the screen door from the back porch slammed shut, drawing Joshua's attention. He looked out his bedroom window at the front of the house, and saw Pete jogging past the garage and up the lane toward the local road.

As Pete disappeared from view, he sat at a small desk and checked his email, deleting most of them. Midway down the new messages, he found an email from Dr. Currie.

Dear Mr. Grayson, I am very sorry to hear about your loss. Please accept my sympathies, and I hope you and your family will remember only the fond memories. Regarding your question about DNA Restore. We are only live in Brazil for trials with high levels of participation, and we are trying to move as quickly as possible to the U.S. The affected Brazilian people are still suffering greatly, and we are focused on further increasing our capacity there.

For the U.S., we have submitted a Fast Track application to the FDA. That may take almost two months for a decision. If it's approved, it will still take some time for rollout. In terms of other options, I'm afraid they are the standard protocols that have been in place for years. My great hope is that your younger family member does not have BDC.

Kind regards,

Dr. A. Currie

Joshua leaned back on the back legs of his chair and looked at the ceiling, hands clasped behind his head. As thoughts ran through his mind, a knock on the door caused him to bang his knee hard on a leg of the desk.

"Arghhh!"

"Joshua?" Pete poked his head in, sweat beading on his forehead, hair matted. "Saw the light on. Breakfast in ten?"

Joshua rubbed his knee. "Sure." Before heading to breakfast, he finished checking his email and found a note from Bill Gilchrist:

Joshua, received the copy of the police complaint you sent. We need to respond within thirty days. Let me know what day and time work for you, and we'll talk. I'll need to involve another attorney, one who handles these matters for our firm. Back in town soon?

Bill

He read, shaking his head. He'd forgotten the police situation, and emotions came flooding back. He slammed his laptop shut. The room was awash with sunlight and the familiar smell of bacon. He made his way down the old, oak staircase, through the dining room, and into the kitchen.

Pete tended a skillet on the stove and spoke over his shoulder. "Your plate's on the table, eat up."

Joshua yawned and rubbed his knee, sat and waited for his uncle to join him. The radio played country music just barely above the sound of the sizzle from the stove.

"So, you run, huh?"

Pete turned his head and gave a nod. "For years now. It's peaceful and makes me feel good…alive. Plus, it keeps my weight down." Pete filled his plate, sat across from Joshua, and deposited a forkful of scrambled eggs into his mouth. "Want to join me tomorrow?"

Joshua rubbed his eyes as he spoke. "Sure. I have a lot on my mind. Exercise may help me sleep better."

"Great. We're on." They plowed through their meal. "Happy to talk more, but I'm off to town. Come along if you want."

"Sure, it'd be good to get out." Joshua returned to his room, threw on jeans and a Cubs hat. As he changed, he received a text message. He dialed his phone. "Hi Martin, just read your text. I'm curious about your comment about the Tremont news you mentioned."

"Good morning. I read the press release that came out yesterday about you leaving your firm. I found it surprising."

Joshua's eyes narrowed. "I wasn't aware of a press release, and we haven't finalized anything at this point."

"Well, good for you to read it. Call me later if you want to talk."

He opened his laptop and searched Tremont Ventures news.

FOR IMMEDIATE RELEASE

Tremont Ventures to Raise New Fund (Boston, MA)

Tremont Ventures has announced its intention to raise a new fund to invest in early stage biotechnology and medical device companies. The firm notes that the target size is $400 million and will be Tremont's fourth fund.

Graham Roseboro, the VC firm's Managing General Partner and co-Founder, remarked, "We're seeing tremendous investment opportunities within the life science sector, and as we finish investing our current fund, we aim to capitalize on the opportunities we continue to see daily."

The firm also announced the hiring of two new associate partners, Sonny Atella and Wilma Payton, both coming from other life science focused venture capital firms. Tremont partner Jeffrey Cochran commented on the new hires. "Sonny and Wilma are two up and coming, well-respected investors with strong market knowledge. We welcome them to Tremont and expect big things from them." Cochran also noted that current partner and Tremont co-Founder, Joshua Grayson, will not be involved in the new fund.

Joshua slammed his hat on the floor before taking a deep breath and chastised himself, I have issues, but nothing like what Jake or the community may be facing.

Chapter 15

The following morning, Joshua slept in late and found a note from Pete on the kitchen table on top of the local newspaper.

Joshua,

If you're going to run with me, you need to be up early! I'll give you a break today. I'm heading out to help our neighbor Ted Westendorff with some fencing. Should be back around lunchtime. I picked up a newspaper when I was in town yesterday and thought you might be interested in the front-page article.

- Pete

He picked up the *Effingham Daily News* and read the headline: "Illinois EPA Looking into Printing Sites." He poured himself a cup of coffee and sat at the kitchen table.

The article provided the background on Steuben Printing Company. Its primary production site was a large 13,000 square foot building in Effingham, built in the 1950s. In the mid-seventies, the company added another smaller 5,000 square foot site in nearby Teutopolis to handle overflow. At one point in the sixties, Steuben was the largest printer in southern Illinois in terms of volume. Failure to keep up with technology ultimately triggered its failure, which fell at the feet of the second generation owner Karel Steuben II.

Steuben Printing was ultimately liquidated through the bankruptcy process. Karel Steuben owned the company via a shell corporation and had no personal liability for the company debts and didn't contest the bankruptcy. There was no remediation of the sites as part of the bankruptcy case, due to the fact that at the time there were no known remediation issues or claims.

Joshua took a look at the recent photo of Steuben at seventy-three years old: a full head of thick, gray hair slicked back, wearing dark Celine style sunglasses and strutting with a much younger lady on his arm. He was reported to live in the largest house on nearby Lake Sara. Joshua pictured him as a Jack Nicholson wannabe.

The reporter described the situation as HAZMAT central, a very surreal scene in a small city like Effingham. No remediation findings were released yet by the Illinois EPA. It was also nmentioned that the city had hired a professional engineering firm from St. Louis to provide guidance and support. According to the article, there was no activity yet in Teutopolis. He read the last line twice. "For now, local authorities are requesting residents within the Effingham metro area to boil drinking water or use filtered water until the water system can be thoroughly checked."

He finished his coffee as he considered the question, Is this the source of the local cancer? He recalled the conversation with Dr. Grimes in Boston and the two words he blurted out in their meeting: dietary or chemical. A couple of questions came to mind, Could the chemicals used in the printing process have made their way into the water supply or soil? But wasn't all drinking water treated to purify the water?

Joshua moved into research mode…

* * *

Early afternoon, Pete walked through the rear screened-in porch, and stepped into the kitchen. He wore a well-worn green mesh ball cap with a Repking Seed label on the front, which he hung on a hook as he passed the refrigerator. He pulled his red handkerchief from a rear pocket and wiped sweat off his brow and the back of his neck as he walked to the sink. Joshua sat at the kitchen table quietly, laptop open, a pad of paper in front of him. His eyes were focused on the screen, pen in his hand taking notes.

Pete dipped a large orange plastic cup into the five gallon bucket of drinking water near the sink and took several large gulps before he sat at the table. "What're you up to?"

Joshua's head stayed down over the keyboard, but his eyes rose to meet Pete's stare. "I don't know. Maybe chasing something that doesn't exist."

Scratching his chin, Pete drew back his head. "What're you talking about?"

"The paper you left on the table." Joshua pushed away from the computer. "It says the Illinois EPA is looking at the site of the former Steuben Printing Company in Effingham for potential pollutants that were released into the soil, and maybe into the groundwater, for fifty years! Just to be clearer, they may have allowed poison to get into the soil, and it's highly likely it found its way into the water system. That could be the source for the cancer in the area. They also had a facility closer to Bishop Creek in T-Town…by the way, the authorities suggest boiling or filtering drinking water until they can ensure the system is safe." He gave his uncle a 'can-you-believe-it' stare.

Pete crossed his arms. "There's nothing we can do now. The authorities are taking care of it."

"Yeah, but if there are pollutants, they're in Effingham, not Bishop Creek. That's over ten miles away. Do you believe that could pollute the water here? I don't know if that's the case. You've also mentioned there have been others who've had BDC even further away."

Pete sat and contemplated the question. "Honestly, I don't know. My guess is it does, otherwise what would be causing the cancer rate here? If the source isn't the water, what would it be? It seems to make sense. I'm not sure if our water is from the same aquifer or not. I'll let the pros handle it." He gave Joshua a questioning stare.

"Do you have the well water tested every year? Apparently, chemicals from fertilizer and all the 'cides'" Joshua read from his notes. "Pesticides, herbicides, insecticides, and fungicides can leach into the water."

Pete gave a thumbs up. "Good call. It's been a long while since I've had the water tested."

Joshua gave Pete a questioning look. "I have a hard time believing it's the water. I've done some research. The city drinking water in Effingham comes from surface and ground sources, including the Little Wabash River and Lake Sara. Then it goes through a process of letting sediment settle, adding chemicals, filtration, and then disinfection. The Illinois E.P.A. also requires annual testing for contaminants. I read the last several annual testing reports on the drinking water quality in Effingham. There weren't any contaminants over the E.P.A. regulated levels. Other towns, like T-Town, undergo the same process."

Pete stood, sniffed the water in his cup, paused, then drained it. He smiled and put the empty cup in front of Joshua and winked.

Joshua grimaced. "When I was running with the 'in crowd,' my dad used to tell me to always drink upstream from the herd."

"That's a wise saying. Passed down from your grandfather. Very sad you never met him. A smart and wonderful man." Pete arched his back, weariness written on his face. "I'm tired. Gonna shower. Hey, by the way, Jake's back at work in case you haven't heard." He took a few steps toward the stairs, then turned around. "How long have you been sitting there?"

"Since breakfast."

"Well, it's after noon. I know you have all the right intentions, but I think you need to get away from the screen for a while and get some air. If anything, it'll clear your head." He turned and headed to the shower.

Joshua toyed with his pencil for a minute before he decided to take Pete's suggestion and walk the property. The temperature was in the low fifties, but the intermittent breeze made it feel cooler and was strong enough to dislodge leaves. He walked through the back yard to a trash pit near an old stone chicken coop.

Trash was burned at the farm and food waste fed to the hogs or, in the current case with no livestock, thrown into a nearby compost area for use in the garden. He remembered the relief the fire gave him and Jake in the winter when they were assigned trash-burning duty during holiday visits.

Beyond the coop, a long path led to the woods and, ultimately the creek. He remembered feeding the chickens when he was very young. In his teen years, they'd lay on the coop roof, shot BB guns, and shared stories. Joshua recalled his cousin Cole joining them with a bow and arrow. Instead of shooting at a target, he shot an arrow straight up, causing major commotion to find cover. Fortunately, it landed safely just beyond the water pump in the garden.

Instead of tromping through the woods, he turned right and moved up a gentle slope to a modest-sized pond. It triggered memories of swimming there on hot summer days. Cousins Jesse and Cole used to tease them relentlessly, swearing the pond was home to large snapping turtles, which caused serious concern among Jake, Blaine, and himself. As he surveyed the pond, his phone vibrated in his rear pocket. The screen noted Gilchrist.

"Hey Billy, how are things?"

"Not too bad, working too many hours and missing old pals like you."

Joshua laughed and sat down on a step of an old metal frame that once held a diving board. "Yeah. We get wrapped up in work, and it pulls us into a perpetual cycle. I'm going through the wash cycle right now!"

"Ha…I know it well. Hey, the reason I'm calling is about your court case. They've moved it to this coming Monday. Is that a problem for you? The attorney I have handling the case believes it's beneficial to get it done quickly. He thinks it'll be brief, but you need to be there."

"I'm out of town right now, visiting family downstate Illinois. But it sounds good to get past this bogus legal situation. Can you send me the details, and I'll make plans to fly back?"

As they concluded the call, Joshua slowly moved downhill past the smokehouse toward the screened-in porch at the rear of the farmhouse. His eyes followed the line of an old twenty foot rusted antenna connected to a triangular metal structure that ran up the chimney and reached above the roofline. He laughed, remembering that he and Jake used to climb the support and taunt Blaine from the rooftop.

Virtually everywhere on the property held a fond memory.

Chapter 16

Joshua leaned against the white ceramic kitchen sink early morning, dressed in a pair of shorts, Boston College sweatshirt, and white Converse Chuck Taylors. Pete entered the room ten minutes later and opened his eyes wide when he saw Joshua.

"Whoa!" Pete held his chest and feigned a heart attack.

"You're late! I'm a man of my word, but do we need to run on Saturday? That just doesn't seem right."

Pete dipped a cup in the water bucket. "Yeah, Saturday, too! Hydrate up. Gonna be a painful one." He grinned from ear to ear. Joshua loved the smile and reciprocated. Pete threw an arm around him and pushed him toward the rear door. "Let's see what ya got!"

A jog around the block was a roughly four-mile loop that started at the top of the lane, ran right along roads that bounded the farm property, looped past a long line of woods, and passed St. Aloysius and its small school before returning to the road that led back home.

The sounds that disturbed an otherwise quiet morning had a cadence, a staccato as feet met the road, and punctuated by heavy exhaling every fourth beat. Joshua looked at Uncle Pete moving effortlessly in front of him, bursts of mist coming from his mouth every so often, eyes focused on the road ahead. Joshua wore a pained face but pushed on, a stitch in his side and sweat beading on his brow, despite the cool early morning air.

Fifty minutes later, the duo slowed to a walk as they completed the run at the farm mailbox. Pete watched Joshua finish, bend forward, place his hands on his knees, and breathe heavily.

He limped past Pete and whispered, "Piece o' cake."

They chuckled and walked slowly toward the house. Joshua felt the mutual camaraderie and appreciated the moment. He held his hands on his lower back. Halfway to the house, he veered off into the nearby cornfield, crouched, and picked up a handful of dark black dirt. He opened his hand and stared at the soil, raised it to his nose, and inhaled slowly. He glanced at Pete as he rubbed the dirt between his hands and let it fall gradually to the ground.

Pete joined him. "What do you think?"

"Fresh, clean earth."

"That's right. Healthy organic soil, ready to produce food, as it has on this ground for over a century." Pete pointed at the soil. "Do you know that soil is alive?"

Joshua shook his head, and Pete continued. "It's amazing. One tablespoon has more organisms than there are people on Earth!" Pete raised his eyebrows. "It's mind-boggling to also consider it takes a minimum of five hundred years to form an inch of topsoil. A very valuable commodity, wouldn't you say?"

"Yeah, I had no idea. I think people, at least here in the U.S., take it for granted—kind of a shame."

"I see your point, but not everyone takes it for granted, Joshua. Any idea who the largest private farmland owner in the U.S. is?" Joshua shook his head. "Bill Gates! It's true. Something like 270 thousand acres over at least ninteen states. As the saying goes, they don't make any more land."

They stepped into the kitchen and hydrated themselves. As Joshua finished his water, he addressed Pete. "Well, I'm afraid I'm going to miss running with you for a while. I need to get back to Boston for a court date on Monday. But before then, I'm going to meet Jake, Shelby, and the kids at the hospital. There's a fall festival this afternoon, and I have an afternoon flight tomorrow." He felt guilty leaving Pete alone. "I hope you don't mind if I come back to spend more time here once I get things settled in Boston."

Pete gave him a playful punch in the shoulder.

* * *

The hospital parking lot was half-full when Joshua pulled into a space. Corn stalks and pumpkins welcomed the community to the annual autumn event. He could see a Ferris wheel in motion beyond a tall hedgerow of holly at the rear of the hospital.

He made his way along a sidewalk toward the fair area, looking for familiar faces. The weather had grown much warmer since the morning, and he relished the idyllic autumn afternoon. He passed young teenage boys struggling with the high striker game, hitting a lever hard enough with a large wooden hammer to cause a weight to ring a bell ten feet above. The central grassy area was filled with tables and a row of food and drink vendors. Off to the side, a small local band played classic rock tunes.

Joshua ducked under a big tent and scanned the crowd. Seeing a familiar face sitting alone at a table on the other side of the tent, he walked over.

"Dr. Kaymer, hello. Where's your lab coat?"

"Oh, it's handy, just in case it gets chilly later. I also use it as a bathrobe, you know."

"Touché!" He laughed with her. "I'm supposed to meet my cousin Jake and his family here but just got a text that they're running late."

"I'm supposed to meet some people here, too, but it looks like I'm being stood up."

Joshua slipped his hands in his pockets and glanced from side to side before turning his attention back to her. "I think we may have gotten off on the wrong foot when we met. It's Megyn, right? I'm sorry I came on strong. I've been under a lot of stress lately." He casually checked out her left hand resting on the table…no ring.

She smiled. "It's okay. We're all under stress around here. How about we start over?"

Joshua felt his face blush and a smile crossed his face. "Are you hungry?"

"Yes, I could eat." They walked slowly side by side along the row of food vendors, scanning the options. Occasionally, they made eye contact, and Megyn waved to people as they passed. She wiped her brow with the back of her hand, took off her sweater, and tied it around her waist.

Joshua couldn't think of what to say to fill the void, so he went with, "I love the smell of fresh cut grass." She simply grinned. He chided himself, Gee, that's a good conversation starter!

As they passed the last vendor, he slowed and asked, "I think that's it. So, what do you feel like? I've always loved the local sausage. I can't get anything close to it in Boston. I also hear the corn is incredible."

She chuckled. "Sausage? Really? How about we go there?" She pointed to a booth with a large banner above the counter reading "Effingham's Best!" They returned to a shaded table with two baskets of food and lemonades.

Joshua cut a piece of fried fish, dipped it in tartar sauce, and followed it up with a few bites of corn on the cob.

He raised his eyes and met hers. "Excellent choice! This is perfect."

"Fried catfish, but the best part is the cornbread coating. It has an incredible, unique flavor you can only get locally. I used to crave it to the point of tears when I was away from home." Her eyebrows did a little dance as she talked.

"I've been here now for almost two weeks, and aside from the health issues, it's been nice to be back. It's been way too many years."

"How long are you staying in the area?"

He poked at his food and shook his head. "I don't know. I plan to be here as much as possible, but I'll probably need to shuttle back and forth. I have a flight to Boston tomorrow. I need to take care of a few things."

"What about work?"

"That's evolving right now…I'm staying with my uncle at his farm in Bishop Creek and can work from there or head back in Boston if needed."

Megyn flipped her hair back and put it in a ponytail. "Do you have a specialty focus in your work?"

"Biotech, generally, but I'm focused mostly on drug discovery. I have a biochem background, plus two years of med school. In med school, I got to know several of the local venture capitalists at conferences and ultimately realized my interest was more on the intersection of business and biochemistry. Being part of new innovations and solutions seemed very interesting. Ultimately, I co-founded a VC firm with another person I knew fairly well."

Her mouth fell open. "That's right, you mentioned you left med school! That's unusual, but…I think brave. Following your instincts."

After lunch, they walked the grounds slowly. Halfway through the amusement area, Joshua turned to her. "Have you ever been in a batting cage?"

"I don't think I've ever swung a bat. I'm more of a runner. But I'm game!"

She put on a batting helmet. Joshua helped her pick out a bat, gave her some basic instructions, and positioned her near home plate. The first ball loaded and shot forward. She swung, hit the ball, and raised her hands over head in victory.

"You're a natural!"

Nine swings later, she exited the cage, rubbing her hands and laughing. "Your turn. See if you can beat that."

"Oh, you're competitive! Well, I haven't done this in a while." He stepped to the plate, took the bat off his shoulder, and took a couple of slow practice swings. He cocked the bat back and focused on the machine. The balls loaded, and the first shot forward with a sizzling sound. Joshua's bat moved quickly along a long arc and met the ball with a loud crack, sending a line drive into the left side of the net. The scene repeated itself over and over before he left the cage, walking through a group of young boys gathered around the net.

Megyn gestured toward the boys. "Looks like you have some fans!"

"I played baseball in college, so I've done this a lot, but it's been a while. I didn't realize how much I miss it." He felt a big smile spread across his face.

"What position did you play?"

"Shortstop. Swinging a bat brings back great memories. Makes me feel like a kid again. I should do it more often."

They moved to the beer tent, where Megyn found a table with her hospital colleagues. Joshua turned to her. "Well, thanks for having lunch with me. It was fun, and maybe we can do it again sometime. I'll make a round to look for my cousin."

Megyn stopped him. "Why don't you join us until your family arrives?" Her co-workers waved them over. "Come on."

Joshua took orders and bought a round of beers for the table. He returned to a serious conversation. A middle-aged man, whom Joshua took to be one of the more senior members, was speaking.

"The accelerating cancer rate needs to be treated like an epidemic, with federal presence!" He looked at Joshua, standing steps away from the table with a tray of beers. "I'm sorry, this isn't the place for this discussion."

Joshua handed out drinks. "No apology necessary. I appreciate your passion. My aunt was one of the recent victims. Have you come up with any thoughts on the cause?"

"Sorry to hear that. The most logical source in my view is the water supply. You may have seen in the news there was a large printing company that used to be in the city and chemicals were disposed of improperly for decades. It was closed down a few years ago, but who knows if any chemicals made it into the water supply. Thank God they're investigating it."

"Yes, I saw the news. My aunt lived in Bishop Creek, where they use well water. We should probably have it tested."

The man nodded solemnly.

Chapter 17

Upon entering the Boston Municipal Courthouse, Joshua immediately saw Bill Gilchrist and his associate standing near a security checkpoint. They made small talk as they climbed the stairs to the third floor, where they found a quiet corner.

Gilchrist's associate led the conversation. "The purpose of this hearing is to decide whether this case will go to court. We've argued that you're an upstanding professional in Boston, have never been involved in a situation like this, and you regret it occurred. You just need to appear contrite and regretful that the situation escalated to the point it did. I spoke with the D.A., and we'll be okay. They don't want cases like this clogging up the court system. Plus, you weren't the only person at fault here."

As the men entered the courtroom, Joshua scanned the room and saw Cochran with Graham Roseboro alongside him. Roseboro caught his eye and motioned for him to meet in the back of the room.

Roseboro ambled up to him, smiled, and extended his hand. "How're you doing?"

Joshua left him hanging and gazed over Roseboro's shoulder at Cochran, who wore a satisfied grin. "What are you doing here, Graham? Supporting your guy? You're making the separation situation tougher to conclude."

"No, I'm only here to see you. I haven't been able to get a hold of you, and I wanted to speak with you to see if we can finalize the separation agreement and move forward."

Joshua ground his teeth. "Trust me, I have a lot going on right now. We sent you a proposal. Are we good to go with that?"

"The partners think it's too rich."

"Graham, do you remember when you canned me at our lunch? I told you to give me a deal you'd want for yourself." Joshua turned his head away for dramatic effect before looking him in the eyes. "Is this what you would expect and accept? I think it might even be actually less than the partnership agreement requires." He saw surprise in Roseboro's eyes.

Roseboro replied. "This was reviewed by our law firm, in addition to the partners."

"You didn't answer my question, Graham!" Roseboro was flummoxed and didn't respond. "Look, you guys want me out, you need to increase the payout significantly. By the way, the press release throwing me under the bus doesn't make me want to cooperate. I thought we were going to be professional about our split. That'll cost you. A little respect, please."

The bailiff called out, "Case number one-four-seven, City of Boston versus Joshua P. Grayson."

He turned to Roseboro, his eyes narrowed to crinkled slits, turned and walked away.

The prosecutor read the charges and noted the city felt successful completion of anger management classes, and Joshua paying any out-of-pocket medical expenses incurred by Cochran, would be appropriate given his clean record. Joshua's attorney agreed, and the judge quickly approved the agreement.

In his peripheral vision, Joshua caught sight of Cochran, fists in front of his face, claiming victory. He slammed his eyes shut and stuffed his hands into his pockets.

* * *

That evening, Joshua sat at his dining room table with a cold, half-eaten microwaved burrito and Ernie the cat sleeping peacefully on an adjacent chair. In the background, a classic rock station played Jethro Tull's "Thick as a Brick" at a low volume. With the ouster from Tremont, he turned his attention to the future and compiled a short list of VC firms to contact for possible partnership opportunities. He managed to schedule a meeting with a partner of a local venture firm the following day, but gloominess hovered over him. As he thought deeper, he knew the emotion he felt was embarrassment, and hurt pride.

Joshua covered his face with his hands and asked himself, How did I get here? How do I handle this?

His thoughts were jarred by his cell phone vibrating. He found the phone under a folder.

"Hi, Uncle Pete. How are things?"

"Joshua, I'm calling to tell you Jake is feeling sick again. He's in the hospital overnight so they can monitor him and do some tests." Pete paused. Joshua heard him sniffing on the other end of the line.

"Uncle Pete, I want to get Jake to Boston for testing. They have world-class medical facilities here. I'm going to make this my whole focus, and I'll bring everything I have to make sure he's going to be okay." He wiped pooling tears from his eyes. "How are Shelby and the kids doing?"

"Ummm...not so well. Shelby's parents are with them."

The line was quiet for a while before Joshua heard his uncle's quavering voice. "I'm scared I'm going to lose my son right after Sara's passing. I'm not sure if I could survive it."

Joshua consoled Pete as best he could, left a voicemail for Dr. Kaymer, then, given the late hour, sent an urgent email to Dr. Lange:

Martin,

Can I please take you up on your offer to help me get my cousin Jake a consult at Dana-Farber ASAP? He seemed to recover after an initial scare, but now he's in the local hospital with symptoms similar to those my late aunt had, and you might recall she passed away from BDC.

- Joshua

He closed his eyes and ran his fingers through his thick ash brown hair. He felt prompted to pray, something he hadn't done since high school.

"God, please protect Jake and his family. I pray that he'll be fine…Help me find a solution if this is cancer…Amen."

Joshua and Ernie made their way to the bedroom at midnight. He took a sleeping pill, as he did when his mind raced. Ernie crashed on a beanbag chair.

* * *

Tuesday afternoon, Joshua found himself at a coffeehouse in Cambridge with the managing partner of a large Boston-based venture capital firm. He was on edge. It was his first exploratory job meeting since his jettison from Tremont, which still wasn't resolved.

Joshua shifted in his seat as the conversation turned from small talk to job opportunities. "Tim, I've had a lot of success in the biotech space for years. I know the market, the people, I have deal flow, and I'd be interested in bringing my experience plus a portfolio to your firm."

Tim set his coffee cup on the table. "Unfortunately, Joshua, we're not looking for a partner right now, or actually any additional headcount. But we might need consulting help in the future, like due diligence on new opportunities or another set of eyes on our existing portfolio companies. I know you have a strong track record in drug discovery. Would you be interested in helping us in a consulting capacity?"

It was what he generally expected, but it hurt. More than anything, it was embarrassing. He hid his feelings and answered nonchalantly.

"Sure, Tim. Give me a call if you have a need or things change. I know it's all about timing. I may just take my existing accounts, find funding, and work them. That may be the best approach for now."

Joshua saw the look in Tim's eye it read; No way are you going to raise millions to make that happen, Grayson, but I understand you need to maintain your hope and pride.

"Hey Joshua, what happened at Tremont? I hear you got physical with Cochran. Is that true?"

Joshua squinted. "That's the word that's circulating, huh?"

Tim gave him a wide-eyed nod.

In Joshua's eyes, Tim looked like a schoolboy confirming a rumor and wanting a blow-by-blow. "It was nothing." But inner curiosity got the better of him. "What did you hear?"

"The story I heard, you had a squabble with Cochran, and when he turned his back to walk away, you punched him, caused a concussion, and knocked out some teeth. Cochran's a big guy, played football at Boston U, and you were a jock at Boston College. Must have been some melee." He cackled, and his eyes grew big asking for details.

"That sounds like it came from Cochran's mouth, so not factual." He fought the temptation to give a narrative like a schoolboy. "The incident isn't something I'm proud of, or something I want to talk about." Joshua guzzled the rest of his cold-brewed coffee and set the cup down gently. "We've known each other for years, Tim, and worked together on a couple of deals, so I think you know me fairly well. I guess I'll leave it at that…thanks for the time. I appreciate it." Joshua dropped a ten dollar bill on the table and left the café.

Halfway across the Harvard Bridge, he received a ping. He stopped, put his elbows on the railing, and brought up the text:

[Dr. Lange] Dana-Farber appointment Thursday 3 p.m. Call you tomorrow with more details, including where to send the local test results. They may repeat them. Best, Martin

[Joshua] Thank you very much!

[Dr. Lange] By the way I had a call with an old friend, Jerry Ackerman, in Salina, Kansas. They seem to be having similar BDC growth. I'll send you his phone #, it might be worth a conversation.

[Joshua] Thats's odd. I wasn't aware that there were other areas with the same issue.

Chapter 18

Joshua covered his eyes as sunlight reflected brightly off the glass panels of a fourteen-story modern building in the Back Bay area. Jake stopped and looked the building up and down before they entered under a Dana-Farber Cancer Institute sign.

They crossed the entry area and caught an elevator. During the ride, Joshua gave Jake an overview of what to expect. "We're going to the biliary tumor center to meet with one of the specialist doctors. You're in very good hands here. This hospital is a teaching affiliate of Harvard Medical School. It's one of the top hospitals in the country. If you have any questions, just ask. They'll probably do some tests as well."

Jake plodded off the elevator on the seventh floor, shoulders hunched and eyes staring straight ahead. Joshua had a hand on Jake's shoulder to direct him, and tried to relieve the stress. "Too bad the Red Sox didn't make the playoffs, or we could take in a game. It's not Wrigley, but it's a very historic park. What do you say we do it next spring?

Maybe Shelby could get away for a weekend, too? I might even be able to find a date, although no promises!"

Jake's stomach growled audibly. "Wish I could have had something to eat...I'm not sure my insurance is gonna cover this."

"You need to fast for the procedures, we'll get a bite later. Don't worry about the insurance. I have a doctor friend who knows someone and got us this appointment. Just leave it to me."

They flipped through sports magazines and watched a lame afternoon talk show in the waiting room for close to an hour before being escorted to a patient room. Jake donned a gown and perched on the end of the examination table. They sat in silence after a nurse shuffled in, checked his vital signs, and took some information.

In short order, the door opened, and a white-coated doctor stepped in and addressed Jake. "Nice to meet you, Mr. Grayson. I'm Dr. Voss."

"Good to meet you, too." He pointed toward Joshua. "That's my cousin, Joshua."

Joshua raised his hand. "I'm a friend of Dr. Martin Lange's. He helped set this appointment up." The doctor gave him a slight nod.

"Well, Mr. Grayson, I've received the latest test information and notes from your local doctor, and I've had a chance to review everything. The liver and gallbladder function tests are slightly outside normal ranges, as is the bilirubin. The ultrasound images of the bile duct area show some potential narrowing in the distal section, but again, just outside what we'd consider normal. Unfortunately, we don't have a time series, so we can't discern changes."

The doctor had Jake lay back, then he pressed around his abdomen, checked his lymph nodes, eyes, and listened to his lungs and heart.

"I'd like to do some further tests. The last were done over a week ago, and I'd like to see if there's been any change. We also want to take some cells and fluid from the bile duct area to see if we can determine if there are any issues."

Jake gave the doctor a bug-eyed look. "How do you do that?"

"ERCP. It's a procedure using an endoscope. We sedate you and pass a long, flexible tube down your throat and into the bile duct. There, we can inject dye to see the duct more clearly and take cell and fluid samples. Also, if we find a narrowing or blockage, we can place a stent to help keep the area open. It'll be painless for you."

"But I have a flight home tomorrow."

The doctor smiled and put his hand on Jake's shoulder. "We're all ready for you, and we'll get everything done today and we'll share the results with Dr. Kaymer and take it from there, okay?"

"Sure, Doc, thanks."

"Do you have any questions for me?"

Joshua moved next to his cousin. "If the tests show further degradation, what would the next steps be?"

"Based on the rapid onset being experienced in the area, as I understand it, we'd move quickly to resect the affected area and be prepared for further targeted therapy."

Joshua asked a follow-up question. "Are you familiar with the DNA Restore platform? Does that sound like a viable option if it's BDC?"

"It's not available in the U.S., so it doesn't look like an option. If the tests show cancer, we're left with the traditional treatments, and we'd need to move very quickly."

* * *

Later that evening, the men stepped out of Dana-Farber to a dark sky. Jake took a moment to take a few pictures of the Boston skyline, with a full moon in the background. Joshua breathed the cool night air in and out quickly, trying to purge the antiseptic smell from his nose.

He gave Jake a nudge in the appropriate direction. "Come on, let's get some dinner. I know a good Italian place around the corner. It's late, and we haven't eaten all day. Sound good? Feel up to it?"

Jake's stomach growled. "Yeah, I could eat. I think the drugs are finally wearing off."

It was a short walk to Classico Italiano Ristorante. Inside the reception area, the hostess welcomed them and sat them at a table near a fountain. At nine o'clock, the place was almost empty; just one couple sharing a key lime pie.

Soft Italian music played in the background as a hostess appeared and placed a basket filled with fresh bread in front of them. Joshua picked up the cruet on the table and poured olive oil on a bread plate, dipped a piece of bread in the oil, and took a bite. Jake followed the same routine. They sat in silence for a short while, sipping on water and eating bread.

After downing several ciabatta rolls, Jake stood and wandered slowly around the place, focusing on signed photos of celebrities, including: Marlon Brando, Robert De Niro, and James Gandolfini. On the other side of the restaurant, a man was mopping the floor.

As Jake scanned the wall of memorabilia, the waitress arrived. "Hi, late dinner, huh? The chef is closing the kitchen, so we only have osso buco, gnocchi, and lasagna available for you. Is that okay?"

"Sure, that'd be fine. We'll have a lasagna and osso buco, with two Sam Lagers. We haven't eaten yet today, so this should be quick!"

After casing the place, Jake wandered back to the table and took a seat across from Joshua. "Pretty cool place, they even have a few olive trees inside. I have to sit down; I'm getting dizzy."

"Jake, you need to take it easy after the procedure. Drink some water and take it slow—including eating. You probably shouldn't drink beer either." Joshua snickered. "Guess I'll drink yours too."

Blaine swallowed another roll. "Beer is like water to me." He smiled for the first time that day.

The meal arrived. Before they dug in, Joshua raised his beer. "Jake, I'm very sorry for the past. For everything. I have a bad temper, and I tend to hold grudges. It's gotten me in trouble over the years, and I'm realizing it's not a healthy pattern. I know it wasn't possible for you to get to my parents' funeral in time. Losing my parents was traumatic, and it still affects me. I'm recognizing I haven't let anyone get close to me since the accident.

"I just lost my job. Had to go to court earlier this week for that scrap I mentioned over dinner at your place. I'm struggling to hold things together, and I don't know where I'm going in my life at this point. I don't have any close friends, which is my fault because I've put work ahead of everything, including relationships with family. I've already wasted many years, and I feel very alone. I know I can't make up for lost time, but I really want to try. I'm turning the page and working on getting my priorities in the right order."

Jake raised his glass, looked away, and drew a deep breath before looking him in the eye. "We've missed a lot of years together. But it ain't all your fault. It's my fault, too. You and I used to talk about living together after high school or going to college together. So when you went off to Boston on a baseball scholarship, it hurt. I felt like you left me behind, and I held a grudge for many years, which isn't fair either." He paused to control his emotions. "I also should have done whatever it took to be with you at your parents' funeral. It's easy to make excuses. So if you need me to forgive you, Joshua, I do, and I hope you forgive me."

They tapped mugs, drank half of the beer, and resumed eating. They made small talk, catching up on the years they'd missed. Some topics were emotional, while some drew uncontrollable laughter. As they finished dessert and Joshua paid the check, Jake turned serious.

"This was good, and thanks for caring enough to bring me here to the highly rated hospital. I'm glad you're in our lives again. I need you in my corner more than ever. I don't get scared easily, but this situation scares me. If I have the cancer, I need to beat it. I have to be around for Shelby and the kids. That's all I care about."

"I'm in your corner a hundred percent, Jake."

Jake looked him in the eye. "I have a very big request, Joshua." Tears pooled and began to roll down his face. His voice shook. "Please take care of my family if I don't make it."

Joshua looked away for a moment to compose himself, determined to stay positive. He turned to his cousin. "Jake, you're going to be okay." He used his napkin to wipe his eyes. "But if it comes to it, I'll be fighting by your side with everything I've got. That's a promise."

Chapter 19

Sicut patribus, sit Deus nobis.
The rocky nook with hill-tops three
Looked eastward from the farms,
And twice each day the flowing sea
Took Boston in its arms;
The men of yore were stout and poor,
And sailed for bread to every shore.

Joshua read the first stanza of the poem by Ralph Waldo Emerson nested in a wooden frame on the office wall. He recognized the Latin phrase as the motto of Boston, translated as, "May God be with us as He was with our fathers." One thing he loved about Boston was its deep history. He imagined the land and population, largely farmers like his uncle, working hard to feed their families—deeply rooted in their land, moral, noble, righteous, and virtuous. Those same farmers, stout and poor, taking up arms to fight for freedom.

"Mr. Grayson, Mr. Gilchrist will see you now."

He turned to the receptionist, who led him into Bill Gilchrist's well-appointed office overlooking Boston Harbor. Gilchrist met him at the door with a handshake and half-hug. They caught up and reminisced for half an hour about their time together on the Boston College baseball team.

"So Joshua, down to business. As you noted, the separation agreement is one-sided. I hope you don't mind, but I took the liberty of flipping the tables on them. The Tremont partner agreement gives you more protections than you think. As a founding partner, they can't just let you go, even given the situation we addressed in court recently. So I've shot a hot flare over, and let's see what happens."

Joshua sat back in the leather chair in front of Gilchrist's large desk and gave a long exhale. "Thanks, Billy. I knew I could count on my double-play partner. It's a tough situation, and I don't want to hurt the firm I helped build. That said, it puts me in a challenging spot, so a little hard ball is probably needed." Joshua rubbed his reddened eyes.

Gilchrist came around the desk and sat in the chair next to him. "Everything else okay? You look beat."

"A lot going on. Besides the Tremont situation, I reunited with family back in Illinois. But the occasion was the funeral of my aunt." He paused to collect his thoughts. "She died from cancer, and one of my cousins, who's my age, hasn't been doing well. I brought him to Dana-Farber for a checkup the other day. The results were negative, but I worry about him. He has a great wife, and two young kids." He rubbed his forehead.

"Sorry to hear that. I hope he's fine. How about we get a bite to eat?"

* * *

As they finished lunch and exited the restaurant, Joshua's phone rang. He pulled it from his pocket but didn't recognize the number. He took the chance it wasn't a pesky solicitor or robo call. "Hello?"

The response was a bass voice. "Hello, is this Joshua Grayson?"

"Yes."

"This is Jerry Ackerman. You sent me a message, and I'm returning your call."

Joshua put his hand over the phone and whispered to Gilchrist, "I have to take this." Gilchrist gave him a thumbs up, and they continued walking toward the law office. "Thank you for returning my call, Mr. Ackerman. Martin Lange suggested I speak with you about the incidence of BDC in your area. I have family in a farming area in Illinois, and they seem to have the same issue. He also mentioned you were supporting a CDC review of the situation. Is that the case?"

"Well, yes, we have a growing problem, and we've worked with the Kansas Department of Health and Environment, but they escalated it to the EPA, who also brought in the CDC."

Joshua interjected. "That sounds serious, but also odd that the CDC would become involved in something that seems very local. Did both agencies engage?"

"Yes, they moved quickly and are now in the lead. What makes it unusual is the incidence rate of younger people has skyrocketed, relatively speaking. As you may know, it's a disease that primarily affects the elderly."

Joshua looked at Gilchrist and opened his eyes wide. "I understand this is early, but do you have any ideas about the source?"

"At this point, we believe it's localized based on the cancer incidence rate within, say, a thirty-mile radius. Here in Salina, we have multiple potential sources. Shilling Air Force Base is in the southern part of the city, and we know there was an accident there several years ago where toxic chemicals, used to clean planes, leaked into the soil. However, we estimate it would take almost one hundred years to reach the water supply. The area was remediated to the tune of ninety million dollars. We also have the Saline River, as well as the Smoky Hill River in the area. We're checking the water quality, but the rivers run well beyond the area including into Colorado. So that's where we are at this point. It's early, and the CDC is bringing in other scientists to help accelerate the investigation."

Joshua whispered to Gilchrist to go on to his office and he'd follow shortly. He sat on a stonewall surrounding a small park, as Ackerman spoke. He pondered whether there was a similar pattern to the situation in Effingham. When Ackerman concluded his overview, Joshua thanked him for his time, promised to stay in touch, and asked him who the name of the CDC lead was. Ackerman promised to text him.

He resumed his walk to the law office when he heard a ping halfway down the block. A text:

[Jerry Ackerman] CDC contact is Edwin Boechenhold.

[Joshua] Thank you. Much appreciated.

Joshua recalled the same CDC name given to him by Megyn Kaymer. No time like the present, he thought.

He dialed. After several rings, he was about to hang up when a voice came on the line.

"Hello, this is Edwin Boechenhold."

"Mr. Boechenhold. My name is Joshua Grayson. I've been in touch with a couple of people you know related to areas that have seen a material increases in BDC."

"Who might those people be?"

"Dr. Megyn Kaymer in Effingham, Illinois, and Jerry Ackerman in Salina, Kansas."

"How can I help you, Mr. Grayson?"

From the sound of his voice, Boechenhold was a bureaucrat, and Joshua figured it wasn't likely he'd give much information.

He bluffed. "I'm a biochemist that's been asked to join the Illinois investigation, and I'd like to understand the big picture here, so I can leverage that information and be efficient in my work. It was suggested I give you a call." The other end was silent, and he could picture Boechenhold thinking on the other end of the line. Joshua paced back and forth on the sidewalk as he waited for an answer.

"Mr. Grayson, I would have expected you've received the big picture." Joshua shook his head as the phone went silent. But surprisingly, Boechenhold continued. "Let me just tell you, our investigation is in an early phase, but we expect there are other areas with similar issues, and that is why we're involved."

Joshua suddenly felt cold and sat down on a low rock wall that surrounded an oxidized-bronze statue of a revolutionary soldier. "I wasn't aware of that. How many other areas? I know both Effingham and Salina have had environmental problems. Is that the likely cause?"

He heard Boechenhold exhale deeply. "I tell you this in confidence. In a nutshell, it's odd that these problems are occurring at roughly the same time in different areas. We believe environmental problems are the likely source, as both Salina and Effingham have clear toxic chemical issues.

That said, we're also not ruling out, for example, bioterrorism. But we need your help, as well as other scientists, to determine causation. At some point, we'll connect the science and medical groups to share findings and identify the source or sources. I hope you're able to provide a clear answer for us quickly."

Joshua interjected before the man hung up, "How many areas are affected so far?"

"We don't know for sure at this point. But they seem to be small Midwest farming towns."

As the call ended, Joshua put his phone down on the rock wall and rubbed his eyes. His thoughts were interrupted as his phone vibrated and fell off the wall.

"Hello...hello?"

"It's Uncle Pete. I want to let you know I'm at the hospital. Jake's not feeling good. They're doing more tests."

The line went silent. Joshua rubbed his forehead. "Should I catch a flight?" He could hear a hospital page faintly in the background.

Pete replied in a subdued voice, "I don't think you need to do that; it could be nothing. Just wanted to let you know."

Joshua stood and walked toward the sidewalk. "I'd rather be with my family than sitting in Boston, wondering what's going on and struggling with my job issues."

"Joshua…you don't need an invite. You're always welcome."

Chapter 20

Joshua entered the farmhouse kitchen late evening, Ernie in one arm and his luggage in the other. He found Pete at the old oak kitchen table, a Pabst bottle in front of him, staring out the window. As Joshua moved closer, he saw Pete's reddened eyes and red handkerchief on the table rolled into a ball. Pete half-smiled but didn't speak.

"Uncle Pete. I'd like you to meet Ernie." He held up his cat. "I hope you don't mind that I brought him. I thought he could keep us company. He's also a good hunter, in case you have a mice issue." Joshua smiled but only got a perfunctory nod. He put Ernie on the floor and sat next to Pete. "Any news on Jake?"

Pete mustered a soft, "Yes, he's home." He took a sip of beer. "Our neighbor Butch Hartke is in the hospital now. Sounds like the same issue, he's my age."

Joshua searched for something comforting to say. "I'll visit Jake tomorrow, and maybe see Dr. Kaymer as well. Is there anything I can do for you?"

Biting his lip, Pete stood and moved to the sink, where he poured out the rest of the beer and put the bottle on a stack of dishes. "Pray. Please pray for Jake and his family. Also Butch Hartke." He moved slowly toward the dining room, turned, and gave Joshua a slight wave before continuing up the stairs.

Joshua brought his suitcase to his room and made a bed for Ernie before returning to the kitchen. It wasn't like Pete not to have a clean kitchen. He always washed the dishes immediately and put them in the cabinets. The drinking bucket by the sink was empty. Joshua walked outside to the water pump and filled it under starlight.

* * *

At dawn the following day Joshua waited for Pete in the kitchen in his running gear. He didn't show.

Understandable, he thought. He's been through hell, and it keeps on coming.

Ernie entered the room and quickly found a bed in the corner of the kitchen on some laundry.

Since his last visit, he felt a down-shift in the mood, as if Pete was throwing in the towel. He searched the kitchen cabinets for a small jar but couldn't find one. Looking in the garbage, he found an empty mayonnaise jar, went to the sink, and cleaned it well. He walked through the rear porch and continued to the water pump, where he manually pumped until water filled the jar, then sealed it.

Climbing into his rental, he started the engine and noted the time, seven-thirty. A quick search on his phone noted the Effingham County Health Department wasn't open until eight o'clock. He turned on the local T-Town classic rock station and drove slowly up the lane bound for Jake's house.

The country roads and landscape captured his attention. Not a soul around, radio playing songs he'd heard in high school, and the the treetops were lighting up. Running over a small bridge, he eyed Jake's house. In the driveway sat a blue Nissan Sentra and a children's bike. He parked behind the Nissan, walked to the door and heard voices inside. He knocked softly. The door opened half a minute later.

"Whoa, Joshua. This is a surprise." Shelby held Dixie in her arms. "We didn't know you were going to be in town."

"Well, I heard about Jake and wanted to be here. I know he just got home from the hospital yesterday, but I wanted to stop in and say hi. Sorry if I'm early."

Tired of wrestling with her daughter, she put down Dixie, who ran off. "Yeah, false alarm, I guess. But you missed him. He went off to work an hour ago."

Joshua raised his voice in surprise. "What?!" His eyebrows drew together. "He went to work? Why would he do that so quickly?"

Tears welled in Shelby's eyes. "He's a stubborn guy, Joshua, but as he says, he doesn't make money unless he's working, 'cause he's paid by the hour." She sniffed and rubbed her eyes with her shirtsleeve.

He spoke softly. "I understand. I'm just worried about him. Will you tell him I stopped by and plan to be around this week or longer?" He turned and started toward the car before he paused and turned back to Shelby. "Shelby, I know Jake is a proud man. a good husband and father. Between you and me, if you need financial help, please let me know. I'm happy to help." She started to speak, but he interrupted, "You don't need to say anything. Just know I'm here to help if needed."

Joshua routed the rental to the Effingham County Health Department and was waiting at the door when the first employee arrived shortly after eight o'clock. He followed a middle-aged, heavy-set lady in and stood at the counter while she turned on the lights, started a large coffee maker, walked to the counter, and jokingly looked around the room before saying, "Number one, please."

Joshua took the hint and looked around himself with his hands in a salute over his eyes.

She laughed. "What can I do for you, young man?"

He put the water sample on the counter. "I'd like to have this water tested for contaminants, please." She provided him with a label, on which he put his name and phone number, then stuck it over the Heilman's label. He gave her thirty dollars cash for, as the lady called it, "the big shebang" covering the broadest level of testing.

Joshua leaned in over the counter. "Have you had any failed water tests in the area over the last year or so? I know the Illinois Health Department is checking the water locally to see if the printing factory chemicals may have made their way into the water."

The lady bobbed her head. "Sure, we've had some, particularly lately. Sounds like you've heard about the Steuben Printing water pollution. That's a terrible shame, and the former owner doesn't seem to care, but that's been his M.O. since his father died. But the town water gets tested each year and is in compliant with the US EPA drinking water standards." She gave a look around the office, even though there was no one else there, leaned forward and added. "But the tap water regs haven't been updated for almost twenty years. If you look at those limits, you'll see there are elements linked to cancer and other diseases that aren't on the list. In farming areas, there are pesticides, fertilizers, and even animal waste." She put her hand over her mouth, as if she was telling a secret. "I've made my view known…I only drink bottled water." She bent forward, eyes wide open.

"That's interesting," Joshua responded. "Maybe they haven't changed the regulations for the last twenty years because there was no need?"

The clerk pulled back her long, frizzy, peroxide hair and held it back with a clip. "I don't think that's the case. The *Chicago SunTimes* just had an article on this very issue. Basically, there are something like one hundred town drinking water sources in the state that show contamination." She paused and held up a finger. "Hold on, be right back." She went back to an office and returned a few minutes later with a copy of the *SunTimes* article. "Here, you can have this copy. I think you'll find it very enlightening." She gave him a questioning eye, then added, "I need my job, but sometimes I just want to scream —what's going on here?!"

Joshua left and sat in his car, reading the *SunTimes* article, entitled "Will Your Water Make You Sick?" The article introduced the term "forever chemicals," being contaminants that have been linked to various cancers and other health issues. Also, a class of chemicals called PFAS—perfluoroalkyl and perfluoroalkyl substances—was highlighted. It noted PFAS chemicals are used for waterproofing and providing stain resistance to products like non-stick pans, waxes, and firefighting foam. It also mentioned local authorities note they see trace amounts, but they also can't determine how the chemicals are getting into the water systems.

Reading further there was no agreement locally or nationally on a threshold level for PFAS. Some residents in the City of Rockford were required to drink only bottled water seemingly attributed to three hazardous waste sites being cleaned up under the Federal Superfund program. Lawsuits were on the uptick across state and federal levels.

Joshua considered the information and thought, There are just too many variables to sort through here…BUT! How would Bishop Creek well water be impacted?

Chapter 21

Wednesday, mid-morning, Dr. Amaline Currie stood at a large window in the reception area of Building 21, the headquarters for emergency operations for the Centers for Disease Control and Prevention. Her eyes moved left to right and back as she surveyed the manicured grounds surrounding the building, located just northeast of downtown Atlanta.

Passersbys took notice of her business attire, a flattering celestial blue double-breasted suit jacket and pencil skirt, with Louboutins accentuating her athletic figure. She turned to sit and found eyes on her, both men and women, as they passed. Sitting in an armchair she checked her messages for a minute before looking from up her phone as her name was called.

A short man in a white lab coat, light blue shirt, thin red tie, and brown suit pants approached her. "Dr. Currie. I'm Edwin Boechenhold. I'm running point for the BDC investigation."

Currie was half a head taller than him, and noted his weak handshake. He had thin, light brown hair brushed forward, was in his mid-forties, and she thought, He's a long-time mid-level government employee.

"Nice to meet you," she managed.

He stepped back and gestured awkwardly toward a hallway—a half-bow and outstretched left arm. "We're incredibly grateful you could make time to provide us with some input on your research and help us focus on targets that could be the underlying cause of the growth in BDC. It's quite a challenging situation." He continued speaking as they made their way into a large ground floor laboratory, where he gave a tour and made introductions to everyone they ran into. Despite his position and awkwardness, she appreciated that he was obviously proud of his role.

She tugged on Boechenhold's lab coat to get his attention. "May I have a quiet place where I can study the data you've accumulated? I want to make the most of my time here, and I'm also transitioning from Central European time."

"Yes, of course. We have a conference room ready for you. We've provided you with our findings to date, research results, and a current action plan. Also, a pot of hot water and an assortment of tea, as requested. We'll debrief at six p.m., and please don't hesitate to ask if you need anything."

Currie poured a cup of hot water and searched through the tea before retrieving a small case from her satchel. She extracted a tea infuser, filled it with Tieguanyin Oolong Tea, and dropped it into the cup.

She began systematically pouring through black binder after black binder, taking notes as she went along. Every hour on the hour, Boechenhold poked his head in the room and checked in. Currie's response slid downhill, changing from a polite "doing well, thank you" to eventually not looking up from her reading and flicking the back of her hand at him.

At the appointed time, Boechenhold and several white-coated associates entered the conference room. Dr. Currie rose from her chair. "I've read through over half of the information you've gathered; it's quite expansive. I can imagine the source of the increase in BDC is somewhere within these binders.

"It appears the focus is on chemicals getting into the water system or soil and finding its way into the food or water supply. I do see, however, many of these small towns have some industrial businesses, which likely use toxic materials such as zinc, cadmium, lead, and chromium. As we know, regular exposure to toxins can be a cause of genetic changes, which can trigger cancer. However, it's not clear to me the areas noted had a chemical leakage of some sort. Also, I see agricultural products noted as being a potential source. I've studied plant morphology and note GE crops have been around for over twenty years, are well vetted by your FDA, and in almost all processed food. I would put this as a low probability bucket."

Boechenhold spoke out. "Yes, however, even if there are chemical toxins in each area, many, many other cities in the U.S. also have them but do not have the escalation of BDC! Have you reviewed the Agronos file yet?"

"No. I'm not familiar with that name."

One of the other white-coated staff members spoke up. "It's a fertilizer that's been in the market for over a year. The challenge here is the regulation of fertilizers. This fertilizer is manufactured in France. When the product is imported to the U.S., it may require approval from the U.S. Department of Agriculture, or the Environmental Protection Agency, and maybe the state's Department of Agriculture. That is, I would say, confusing and a potential slippery slope. Most fertilizer is nitrogen, phosphorus, and potassium, plus micronutrients like zinc and other metals. But there are regulations around concentration limits. What is troubling, in my view, is the high level of nitrogen in that fertilizer. We've contacted the manufacturer on the topic, but they've been slow to respond."

Currie questioned. "Has there been robust genetic testing across all the towns for all those diagnosed with BDC? That would be valuable. I know the CDC also has a branch in Brazil. Has there been information sharing with Brazil you can use to enrich the data?"

Boechenhold shook his head. "Unfortunately not. Data in general has been sporadic between affected towns. We're currently trying to coordinate that information and add to the database we've built. I'll follow up and check on the status of the Brazil data…this snuck up on us and a lot of innocent people."

Currie stood and walked around the table arms crossed. "I have contacts in Brazil if needed. It's close to midnight European time, but is it possible for me to stay longer tonight? I must leave tomorrow afternoon and would like to review the Agronos data and the rest of the information before I leave."

Boechenhold surveyed the room and a young lady raised her hand. "Happy to stay for a couple hours."

As the group left, Currie opened the Agronos binder and worked her way through the material over the following hour, taking copious notes and jotting down a series of questions. She concluded by reviewing the last binder. The first page noted: "External Sources." She read through the first few sections before realizing they were random inputs from concerned citizens. Currie picked up speed, as many of the comments were repetitive.

As the time moved to eight o'clock, the volunteer stepped into the room. "Dr. Currie…You must be exhausted."

"Yes…a long day."

As Currie packed up, the staff member asked her to sign a *Time* magazine cover with her "speech heard around the world." She obliged with a courteous smile and added, "We have a lot more work to do here."

* * *

The following morning, Currie was up early, sitting at the desk in her hotel room on video calls to Golden Helix leaders in the Netherlands, six hours ahead of the eastern U.S. The primary focus: preparing to launch DNA Restore trials in the U.S., under the lead of Dr. Telling. The goal was to ensure the organization was positioned to move quickly, with the expectation that an FDA emergency approval would be granted.

At quarter to eight, she stepped out of the Four Seasons Hotel into crisp, cool weather and a waiting car. Her phone never left her ear, speaking in Dutch, then switching to English for the following call. As the car moved forward, she took in the skyline and Atlanta's urban Piedmont Park northeast of the city.

Between calls she commented to the driver, "I like your city, and the park looks wonderful."

The driver spoke over his shoulder. "Yeah, nice except for the traffic; it can be brutal." He chuckled. "Some days, you might move faster riding a bike."

She gave him a smile in the rear-view mirror and added, "In the Netherlands, almost everyone rides bicycles. Amsterdam has something like 800,000 bikes!"

The driver raised his eyebrows and mouthed, WOW!

At the CDC she convened with a large group of scientists mid-morning around a large round conference table. Edwin Boechenhold began the discussion by introducing Dr. Currie and asking her thoughts based on her review the prior day.

The meeting took her by surprise. She took her time to organize her thoughts for a few moments, and took a couple sips of tea before speaking. "Firstly, let me say you are a very impressive group of scientists. So, I'm not sure I can add much value to your work, but I came here to contribute, because this is a serious threat to people's lives.

"I went through most of the information yesterday, and as you know, it's quite challenging because it's a very diverse set of data. Narrowing multiple potential triggers to identify the source of the BDC is very difficult, and of course, time is of the essence.

"My primary thought is: why aren't we leveraging the experience of Brazil? I called the person leading the BDC fight in Brazil this morning. They've gone through the same process, attempting to identify the source, and have been collecting data for almost two years. We can learn from them. I also suggested on a recent call that utilizing artificial intelligence may accelerate the process, taking into account numerous variables. I'm not clear if that is in progress."

A thin man with wide green eyes asked, "Well-said, Dr. Currie. But did you see anything in the data that led you to believe it could be a source?"

"Well, yes. I've heard several people suggest the Agronos fertilizer, and I would put it at the top of the list given the high nitrogen component, and the fact that it is sold in the areas where BDC is elevated. On my call to my Brazilian contact, I asked about Agronos, and she said yes, they have the same product in Brazil. I mentioned it's under scrutiny here in the U.S."

The connection to Agronos triggered chatter in the room. She stepped back from the table and waited until the discussion subsided. "My view is that we follow our scientific discipline: observe, identify the variables, research, develop a hypothesis, then design an experiment and draw conclusions from the results." She paced back and forth, making strong eye contact with the members. "I see value in animal trials on the Agronos fertilizer, but also other common potential sources with Brazil. Time is of the essence to save lives, acknowledging trials may take months to show conclusive results."

Chapter 22

Joshua trailed Pete to a single-story whitewashed building. The sign on the roof over the door read: "Repking Seed and Supply - Teutopolis, IL." Behind the store, a tall, rust-red barn stood with silos on both sides, and beyond the barn was a short string of grain hopper cars on a train track.

Inside the door, Joshua found a display of product catalogs. As he browsed through them, he heard footsteps and heavy breathing. He turned and saw a husky man with a crew-cut and horn-rimmed glasses stacking baling wire on a shelf.

Joshua cleared his throat and caught his eye. "Hey, what're the bestsellers here?"

The man turned, hitched up his pants, and stepped toward Joshua. "Depends on the crop. We have over twenty producers, and they control around seventy percent of the global seed market. The most popular crops round here are field corn and soybeans. But we also have sweet corn, wheat, flax, sorghum, rapeseed, and alfalfa." He looked Joshua up and down. "You new to town?"

"Actually, I'm just here with my uncle. He's putting in his order for next season. Thanks for the information." Joshua wandered over to Pete, who was laughing with a bulky man and a skinny elderly gentleman on the other side of a retail counter.

Pete made introductions, turning to the larger man. "Ted Westendorff, this is my nephew, Joshua.

"Joshua, Ted is a very good friend, and the first person I met when we took over the farm years ago. He's also Jesse's godfather." They shook hands and exchanged pleasantries. Joshua noticed Ted was clearly shy, but also personable, given his warm smile.

As the men said hello, Pete looked at the man behind the counter. "Clem, this is my nephew, Joshua."

Joshua stepped forward, reached over the counter, and shook the man's hand.

"Clem's the owner of Repking Seed and has been selling me seeds and everything I need for many, many years. He's taught me a lot along the way, too."

Clem smiled under his bulbous nose, showing off a couple of missing incisors. "We like to treat our customers right, don't ya know. Good man, your uncle."

Joshua looked over Pete's shoulder. "So, what're you ordering? Don't you basically just buy what you bought last year, assuming the seed produced a good crop?"

"Yeah, usually. But there are other things to consider, like the demand for the crop, which affects price when you sell. Every little bit helps small farmers like me. A move in crop prices can cause a loss and ruin the year. Plus, you need to consider things like crop rotation to keep the soil fertile."

Clem put his pencil behind his ear and elevated his voice. "You also want to consider other seed products that might be new to the market."

Pete put up his hand. "Don't start in on me again, Clem."

Clem turned to Joshua. "Look, I'm an old coot, but your uncle is what we call an 'old school farmer,' a real throwback. More and more farms are using things like soil health and moisture sensors linked to mobile apps, drones to check crops, and them GE seeds, to keep away pests and give growers bigger production. But not your uncle…no, siree."

The comment brought Joshua's mind back to his conversation with Dr. Grimes in Boston. "Clem, can you tell me if there have been any GE seeds, fertilizers, and other chemicals that have been new to the market in, say, the last two or three years?"

Clem took off his tattered DeKalb hat and ran his fingers through what hair he had left. "I'm sure there have been. Likely the big four seed companies, since they own over sixty percent of the market, so it's tough to compete with them. Most seeds sold for the main crops are GE nowadays. I'd have to go through all the purchase orders over the last few years to see."

"Do you think you might be able to get a list for me? Or I'd be glad to put the list together, if you can give me the information to sort through."

Clem paused in thought for a minute, his forefinger to his chin. "Well, it'd be a lot of information."

"I'm pretty good at digging through data."

"Tell you what. Let me talk to Sandy, she's our accounting clerk, and see if she has the information or can help you put it together. Mind telling me what you want it for?"

"I do a lot of financing of biotech companies, and I'm interested in the agri-biotech market and want to learn more about farming, and get an idea of the newest advances."

Clem pushed a pad of paper in front of Joshua, plucked a pencil from behind his ear and put it on top of the pad. "Gotcha. Write your number down, and I'll have Sandy give ya a call. She's not in yet."

Pete completed his seed order, and they walked over to nearby Brownie's Tavern for an early lunch, taking a booth near the front window. A middle-aged woman in a bright yellow apron made her way to the table, order pad in hand.

"Hey there, Pete. Haven't seen you here in quite a while. How you doin'? Sorry to hear about Sara. Too much of that going around here these days."

"Thanks, Beth. This is my nephew, Joshua."

She playfully rearranged her hair and gave Joshua a wink. "Boy, he's a looker, Pete. Single?" She paused. "Okay, okay…the Friday special is smoked brisket, comes with a side of slaw and corn on the cob, local grown! The good stuff."

Joshua looked up from the worn, laminated menu. "Sounds good. Support the local farmers and economy."

Beth beamed. "Oh, yeah. The beef and corn are local, can't keep enough in house. Sometimes we'll get other produce, too. Haven't you seen all them blue signs in town—

'Buy Fresh, Buy Local?' It's a big push around here. We want to support our community."

Pete pulled her attention away from Joshua with a wave. "We'll take two specials and a couple iced teas."

As they spoke, Blaine walked through the door and slid into the booth next to Joshua, ramming him playfully with his shoulder. "Hey, saw you two through the window. What're you doin' in town?"

"Put in my seed order," Pete mumbled.

Joshua responded to Blaine's shoulder shot with an elbow to the ribs. "Shouldn't you be working?"

"Lunch break."

"So, you work here in T-Town?"

Blaine stood up and saluted. "Yep, first shift supervisor for Midwest Plastics up the street, past the high school. Just pickin' up some grub for the crew." He stood and strutted to the cash register as a large carton was placed on the counter. On his way out, he lifted his chin toward his dad and cousin as he backed out the door.

The men began to make short work of lunch as Joshua received a call. "Hello, Joshua? This is Sandy at Repking

Seed and Supply. I'm available whenever you want to stop over and start going through the POs."

"That's great. I'm finishing my lunch and I'll be over shortly." He turned to Pete, "I have to stop at Repking Seed when we're done." He glanced at Pete's plate and laughed, "Must be good corn. I don't think I've ever seen a corncob so clean."

Pete licked his fingers. "Well, I was taught never to let food go to waste." He wiped his hands with a wet nap. "Why do you really want to go through Clem's POs? I can't believe you want to do it for fun."

Joshua put down his brisket sandwich. "You're right. I'm wondering if there are any new products here that might be connected to the BDC situation. Could be fertilizers, insecticides, or other chemicals. Some pesticides in the past have even been connected to non-Hodgkins Lymphoma." Pete gave him a skeptical stare, prompting a response. "Probably nothing, but it shouldn't take long, and it'll let me check that off the list in my head."

"You have a list in your head?" Pete laughed and stood. "If you want to do something valuable, you can check off something from my list, like fixing the house doors; they need to be adjusted so they can shut properly."

Joshua listened as he took care of the bill. "Okay, Uncle Pete. I don't think this'll take long. I'll catch a ride home with Blaine and start working on the doors."

They made their way back to the seed store. Pete conversed with Clem and another customer, while Joshua met with Sandy in an office at the rear of the building. She was in her mid-twenties, and had a quick wit.

"I do have a lot of the information on products, but you'd have to dig through that!" She smiled, pointing to a large box sitting on a dented tan filing cabinet with papers flowing over the top. "Those are our POs for roughly the last four years."

Joshua laughed with her for a moment. "So, you don't have any product information on a computer? I can't get the information in an Excel file?"

"Excel?! My uncle likes the old 'tried-and-true' ways, as he calls it." She threw her hands in the air.

He scanned the office. It seemed to function more as a storage room than a place of business. The paint on the walls had faded to a spotted diarrhea motif; it was challenging to deduce the original color. Peppered on the walls were promotional calendars from agricultural product companies, the oldest dating to 1994.

Joshua pulled the large box off the cabinet and set it on one side of a metal desk. He looked at Sandy and stuck his tongue out the side of his mouth and held his lower back. "Killer! You need to move into at least the twentieth century here!"

"Talk to Clem! That's a big challenge."

Alongside a steel table, he found an empty box, which he set on the other side of the desk. Sandy moved a chair between the boxes so he could pull from one box, review the PO on the desk, and deposit it in the empty box.

He stepped back, gave a thumbs up, and looked at Sandy. She nodded in agreement.

"Sandy, what do you think of GE crop products? I understand they're good sellers."

She raised her chin and folded her arms. "Probably eighty percent or more of seeds we sell are GE. They're good sellers, but at what price?"

Joshua drew back, sensing he'd hit a nerve. "What do you mean? They've been around for a long time."

"I fought with Uncle Clem about stocking those products. They've been around for many years, but I'd rather stick to things that are natural. We probably won't know for decades if GE crops aren't good for us. Why gamble with your health? Can you undo it if you're wrong? We have to stock 'em, because if we don't sell them, we're out of business. Nothing's natural anymore. The FDA recently approved genetically modified farmed salmon for human eating. The fish grows twice as fast as other farm-raised salmon. Would you eat that? Maybe a better question: Would you even check the label before buying it?"

"When you say it like that, no, I guess not."

Sandy sat in the desk chair and frowned. "Did you hear some supposed scientist in China genetically engineered twin babies? Now human beings?"

Joshua shook his head and gave her a surprised look.

She stood and walked to the door, stopped, and whirled around adding, "I don't want to get preachy, but where does it stop? Can we do better than what God gave us?"

Chapter 23

The following day, late morning, Clem greeted Joshua with a salute as he walked through the store and into the office. He restarted poring through purchase order after purchase order, a spiral notebook and large cup of weak coffee in a white Styrofoam cup at his side. For the most part, the information was in chronological order, dating back four plus years.

He worked his way through two years of the oldest purchase orders and hadn't identified any new chemicals or GE seeds and related products. It reaffirmed to him things changed slowly in the area, and he began to wonder if this work was the best use of his time.

As Joshua made his way through the newer two years, he came across multiple orders from new suppliers: Shea Seed, Gelden AgriCo, Johnson & Dore, BioMaïs, and Ritaglia Ag. The POs noted GE, genetically engineered, in the descriptions alongside the SKU number. The introduction of multiple GE products struck him as unusual based on the prior years. He made a note to discuss the anomaly with Clem.

He recorded the information on his laptop: company name, dates, products ordered, and any other descriptive text that might be relevant. Reading over the remaining documents, he found several additional entries for new chemicals and GE products.

With the data in hand he sought out Clem and found him leaning on the order counter, doing a crossword puzzle. "Clem, can I bother you for a few minutes?"

Clem looked up over his reading glasses just below the bridge of his nose. "Only if you help with eight across."

Joshua laughed. "Sure."

"Something that baffles understanding and cannot be explained. Seven letters and has a 'g' in the middle." Clem slid the puzzle in front of him.

"Enigma."

Clem slapped the counter. "Shoulda got that." He looked up from the paper. "You're a regular enigmatologist!"

"A what?"

Clem dropped the pencil and stared at him for a moment, then stood straight, chuckling. "Ha! I got a word you don't know!" He swaggered a little and puffed out his modest chest. "It just happens to be someone who's good at crosswords, puzzles, logic games, and such."

"I'm pretty good at puzzles, but you got me, Clem. Actually, when I start a puzzle, I can't stop until I solve it. That can drive a person crazy." He grinned at Clem as he thought about the genuineness of the man. He was who he was, absolutely no pretense. "Hey, how about I take you to lunch?"

"Now you're talkin'. Andy, come take the counter." A large, portly man wearing a polo shirt with a T-Town High School "Wooden Shoes" patch waddled around the end of the counter. Clem dropped his pencil and pointed at the man. "And don't mess with my puzzle while I'm gone."

At Brownie's Tavern, the men sipped on lemonade and waited for their meals. "So, Clem, thanks for letting me go through the POs. I have some questions for you."

"Shoot, son."

"In the last couple years, it looks like you ordered new chemicals or GE products from multiple different manufacturers: Shea Seed, Gelden AgriCo, BioMaïs, Ritaglia, and Johnson & Dore. Does that sound about right?"

Clem wrinkled his face under a battered St. Louis Cardinals hat and thought for a short while. "Off the top of my head, yeah."

"Something strikes me here, Clem. For the first couple of years, there were no POs with GE products. Then suddenly I see many in a year or so. Why?"

"I don't rightly know. We've had some products for many years, probably around early 2000s or so. I guess the companies found some new crop genes. Sometimes they're called GMOs, genetically modified organisms."

Joshua reviewed his notes. "Yes, GMOs, or GE…I can't tell what the products were from the POs. Most of them were SKU numbers, with a GE prefix. Can you help me identify the products?"

"Sure, Shea Seed is alfalfa, BioMaïs is sweet corn…" Joshua reminded him of the other suppliers. "Yeah, Gelden is what they call a GE organic fertilizer. Ritaglia is a fungicide from Italy. Johnson & Dore is a field corn seed, not a big seller, but enough to keep it in the batting order." He gave Joshua a wink. "But not batting cleanup."

As they spoke, the waitress brought their orders. Joshua popped a couple of French fries in his mouth. "Where's the alfalfa sold?"

"Some are kept local, but most is sold at market. It's forage for cattle mostly, like dairy cows. The GE piece gives it resistance to herbicides and insects, so when chemicals are sprayed to kill off weeds and insects, it won't hurt the crop. Sells okay, use is growing slowly."

Joshua added the information to his notes. "What about BioMaïs?"

"Sweet corn didn't sell much in the first year. But it's been catchin' on in the last year. They also have a hybrid sweet corn product, but it don't sell nearly as well."

"Hybrid is not GE, right?"

Clem nodded, swiping his napkin across his mouth to clear the barbeque sauce from his lips. "It's cross-breeding two different types of plants. Natural process."

"What about Johnson & Dore…field corn? What's field corn?"

Clem dipped a French fry in mayo and deposited it in his mouth. "Yeah, a decent seller. Most corn you see growin' is field corn. It's not eaten like sweet corn; it's ground up for cornmeal, corn starch, corn flour, made into corn syrup and such like that."

Joshua watched Clem eat awkwardly. Without his two lateral incisors, he sometimes bit into his food from the side of his mouth. "Can you give me someone to contact at these companies?"

"Yep, we'll stop at the office."

After lunch, the men strolled to the seed store; it was a ten-minute, slow walk. Along the way, Clem received no less than half a dozen honks or hellos from passersby. In the office, Clem ruffled through an old rolodex containing his contacts.

"Thanks for all the help, Clem." Joshua offered his hand.

"Anytime, son, and thanks for lunch. I think Sandy's gonna miss you, though!"

"Tell her thanks for me. I like her a lot; she definitely has some spunk!"

Clem gave him a pat on the back as he left the store. Joshua pulled out of the lot, exited T-Town, and navigated toward the hospital. His mind started to generate question after question. He scolded himself and thought, I have to stop this. It's stuck in my head, and probably a waste of time.

On the open road, he lowered the window, found a local classic rock station, turned up the volume, and hit the accelerator.

* * *

Joshua walked into the main entrance of St. Anthony's Memorial Hospital, passed the receptionist and stepped into the cafeteria. There, he found half a dozen people sitting at tables in the circular seating area just outside the food counters. A few were eating a late lunch, while others sat talking, coffee cups in hand. He looked closer and saw a wide range of emotions: red eyes, tears, laughter, and numb faces.

He put his phone on the table, checking email, texts, and his calendar. Without a job, his world went dramatically silent, as if a switch was flipped. He closed and rubbed his eyes.

"Joshua."

"Whoa!" He flinched and held his hand to his chest before looking up at a smiling Megyn Kaymer. "You scared me." He gave a long exhale. "I was deep in thought."

She gave him an apologetic smile. "Good thing I know CPR. I think you're safe here…What're you thinking about?"

"I was counting the days since my cousin started feeling ill. You remember my aunt passed away roughly fifty-four days after her first symptoms." He felt a wave of emotion but stuffed it back down and took a deep breath.

"You know both our hospital and Dana-Farber tested him, with no clear evidence of any cancer, right? We're monitoring him, and I also understand he's back at work."

He stared at her as she spoke. She was beautiful even without makeup or accouterments, which took his mind off the discussion for a moment. "Yes, but the biopsies here and at Dana-Farber were both inconclusive. That doesn't make me feel confident. I'm not going to wait for this to play out. I need to put him in the best position possible to survive if he ends up with BDC."

"Joshua, we've had BDC patients here, as you know. None of them have had the strength to work. There was no progress; just a progressive, quick downward slide. Your cousin is back at work! That's very positive, right?"

Her pep talk drew a modest smile. Joshua leaned forward with his elbows on the table, hands clasped and replied, "No offense, Megyn, but I'm not going to relax. Inconclusive means there wasn't enough information to diagnose or rule out cancer. Based on the local experience, that's enough to stay on high alert. My uncle just mentioned another farmer in Bishop Creek was diagnosed with BDC. There's no sign this is letting up or it's an anomaly."

Megyn softened her tone. "Yes, that's right, it could be the levels from the testing weren't high enough to give a clear result. So, we plan to take a follow-up test in the coming week until we get something definitive. We're not letting this go until there's clarity." She looked Joshua in the eye. "What else can we do?"

"Find the source and a solution. You remember med school and the focus on the scientific method?"

"Of course, but isn't that what's happening here with the Steuben Printing investigation?"

Joshua massaged the back of his neck as he spoke. "Yes. But I've spoken to the contact you gave me at the CDC, and he notes there's another town in Kansas with a similar situation. They have environmental issues and growing

BDC, and he inferred there could be more towns. The odds of this all happening at roughly the same time is improbable in my mind. If we're following the scientific method, I think we need another hypothesis."

Chapter 24

Joshua's head rose off his pillow in response to a couple of quick, light knocks on the bedroom door.

"Come on, Joshua, Sunday, no running today. I want you to go to church with me."

He groaned and sat up in bed, eyes half-open. He saw Ernie curled up at his feet, fast asleep. "Okay…quick shower."

Fifteen minutes later, Joshua stepped into the kitchen, hair wet and shoes in hand. Pete put a coffee in his hand, and a short time later they were heading up the gravel driveway. The truck turned left onto the local road and then right onto Rural Route 3. Joshua looked toward the St. Aloysius steeple in the rear window.

"I thought we were going to church?"

Pete gave a slight grin. "We are."

Twenty minutes later, a modest-sized white A-frame building with a Victorian red roof came into view. As they drew closer, Joshua saw a cross on a cupola on the roof above the main entrance. He scanned the area as they followed a line of cars into the parking area, passing a wooden sign that read "Christ's Chapel." The church was tucked away between a deep, tall stand of mature white oaks to the north and lazy flowing creek on the south side.

Joshua looked at Pete quizzically. "I don't get it."

Pete pulled into a spot, opened his door and replied, "I hope you will. Think about this as a continuation of our conversation about finding purpose in your life."

Just inside the entrance, Joshua surveyed the place. The space looked like a modest school auditorium outfitted with rows of cushioned folding chairs on each side of a middle aisle. He noticed there were no pews, no kneelers, no incense smells, no holy water, no statues, no crosses, no other religious symbols. He followed Pete in a row midway down the main aisle.

At the end of the aisle stood a raised stage where several musicians started to play music as the entry doors closed. The song was contemporary, led by guitars, keyboard, and drums. A talented young woman led the singing. The congregation stood and sang the words displayed on a screen above the stage.

Joshua glanced at his uncle, who was singing and occasionally dabbing at his eyes with his red handkerchief.

The leader sang in a soulful soprano. Joshua wasn't familiar. with the songs, but he followed the lyrics and found them poetic and uplifting. Following several choruses, the musicians stopped playing, and the congregation continued a cappella.

After three songs, a middle-aged gentleman wearing a blue sport jacket took the stage and stood behind a modest podium in the middle of the stage. "Welcome, everyone, it's nice to see you all this morning. Don't let the gray skies fool you, it's a wonderful day! This morning, we're going to continue our study in the book of John, but before we start, let's pray."

The crowd bowed their heads and closed their eyes as the pastor prayed before launching into his message, focused on John 3:16, the Bible verse made famous by cardboard signs in the end zones at NFL games. The pastor began by asking for those in the congregation who knew the verse to raise their hands. Many hands were raised, prompting a thumbs up from the pastor.

Joshua gave Pete a questioning look, he handed him a card he received on the way in. He pointed at the card and whispered in his ear, "You're going to want to keep that."

Joshua took the card and read the message several times.

John 3:16

For God so loved the world that He gave His one and only Son, that whoever believes in Him shall not perish but have eternal life.

It struck Joshua as odd that he'd never read the Bible, or even parts of it, despite attending church regularly until he went off to college. He could recite prayers he was taught that were deeply embedded in his memory, but that was it.

The pastor had a down-to-earth way about him, focused on communicating clearly and simply. He categorized the verse as the cornerstone of Christianity and a beautiful way of laying out the message of the Gospel in one sentence. "If you're going to memorize scripture, this needs to be at the top of the list! But…this also needs to be embedded in your heart."

After the service, Pete introduced Joshua to several of the locals. The conversations were generally focused on Butch Hartke, the incidence of BDC, and the source of the cancer.

As they left the parking lot Joshua started a conversation. "Thanks for taking me, Uncle Pete. I would say I enjoyed that, but I'm not sure that's an appropriate thing to say."

Pete sat quiet for a while before he turned and looked him in the eye. "I'm not an evangelist, although I have a strong faith. Giving you the card in church was more my style, although I'd be happy to talk about the message…I hope this might prompt you to consider taking a closer look."

It was quiet in the car for a few miles, with the only sound being an oldies radio station broadcast from nearby Newton. Joshua turned down the volume. "If you attend that church, which is, I think, Protestant, why is Aunt Sara buried at St. Aloysius, which is Catholic?"

"I attend both churches. I go to St. Aloysius once or twice a month, and I also attend Christ's Chapel every week. St. Aloysius is part of the family heritage I want to respect. It's also a large part of the Bishop Creek community, and it's filled with wonderful people. I find myself getting more spiritually fed at Christ's Chapel at this time in my life. I'm a simple guy, Joshua, I just need clear and simple Bible-based messages." He smiled and added, "By the way, your Aunt brought me to the church years ago. She had to drag me there the first few times. But she was persistent, and I, as they say, eventually saw the light."

Joshua looked out the window over the empty fields. "We went to the local church growing up. It wasn't a big part of my life, more of a Sunday ritual. How about you and my Dad? Did you go to church?"

"Yep, every Sunday. Rain or shine. Sun or snow."

He looked closely at his uncle, his face was etched with worry. Joshua assumed it was from years of tending crops, following the agricultural cycle for decades. His hands were rugged from fixing machinery, mending fences, pouring concrete, repairing barns, and whatever else was required. He felt his father's presence in him, which evoked memories and emotion.

"Do you like farming, Uncle Pete?"

"It's not an attractive life to many. Sad to say, suicide among farmers is becoming way too common. It's very hard to provide for a family. Costs continue to climb, the price for seed over the last ten years has tripled because there's less competition, and also the costs of research for genetic engineering have to be included in the price.

"In the early 1800s, ninety percent of families lived on farms. That's roughly when Bishop Creek was founded." Pete took his eyes off the road and looked at Joshua for a moment. "Around here, holding on to family land from generation to generation has a strong pull. It's an unwritten obligation, a source of pride, but it can also be an albatross. For me, though, there's something noble about it, something rich in spirit, in kinship with the land and a community of like-minded people. A hard but peaceful way of life in many ways."

* * *

Back home, they sat at the kitchen table, sipped coffee, and picked at a cinnamon coffee cake. Joshua sat back on the rear legs of his chair and stared at the old plaster ceiling, while Pete held Ernie on his lap.

"Joshua, something's obviously on your mind. You're quiet and counting the cracks in the ceiling. Might be helpful to talk."

"I'm wrestling with this BDC situation. I know Jake is back to work, but something keeps gnawing at me." He sat forward and stared at Pete, who raised the palms of his hand, as if to say, "What gnaws at you? How can I help?"

Joshua ran through the pieces of the puzzle in his mind and then spewed them out as a long, run-on sentence. "The local printing plant with the leakage of chemicals that may have made its way into the water or soil and somehow ingested in some manner by locals and triggering cancer. The Illinois Department of Health is investigating. Then there's Salina, Kansas, with a similar chemical-related situation. They also have a growing occurrence of BDC. Now a person at the CDC, a national agency, notes there are potentially more Midwest farming towns with the same situation. All this has been occurring over the last year or so, and while it's a pattern, the absolute number victims is still small relative to other cancers and severe illnesses, so it doesn't get the same level of attention. Some people I've spoken to relate it to the prior COVID pandemic, expecting it to recede. But it doesn't strike me as similar."

He paused and rubbed his eyes. "This is a challenging puzzle, and I just can't let it go. Could it be bioterrorism? I thought maybe some new GE crop, but there are protocols and controls around the introduction of new crops and fertilizers. I reviewed four-plus years of new GE products introduced in the area. Those products are relatively recent. By all standards, this situation is an anomaly. It also occurs to me that change is slow here, and in small farming towns generally. So what's triggered this?

"I'm going to St. Louis tomorrow. An acquaintance of mine, Dr. Martin Lange, has a contact at Barnes Jewish Hospital. I want to see if they're seeing an increase in BDC patients, and also learn how they're treating them. It's a highly regarded hospital, and if needed, that might be a good option for treatment."

Ernie purred as Pete leaned forward, worry in his eyes, his voice unsteady but firm. "You do what you need to do to protect our family and friends, like Butch Hartke.

Chapter 25

It was mid-afternoon when Joshua pulled into the parking garage of Barnes Jewish Hospital. The hospital was set on 164 acres in St. Louis, along with the Washington University Medical Campus.

He managed to find his way to the reception area for the cancer center, signed in, and sat in a leather wing chair. A few minutes later, the receptionist approached him.

"Mr. Grayson, Dr. Simon is ready to see you. Please follow me."

The receptionist led him past a well-appointed conference room to a corner office where a plaque outside the door read, "Dr. Richard Simon, CEO, Alvin J. Siteman Cancer Center." He was met by the doctor just inside his office door. Dr. Simon was a short, bespectacled, heavy-set man with a welcoming smile.

"Hello, Mr. Grayson, nice to meet you. Our mutual friend, Martin Lange, says you're someone I should make time for." He shook Joshua's hand and pointed to a short tan leather chair. "Come on in and have a seat."

"Please call me Joshua, and thank you for making time to see me on such short notice. I don't want to take up a lot of your time, but I have two subjects I'd like to speak with you about and get the benefit of your experience." The doctor gestured for him to continue.

"First, are you aware of the growing rate of BDC in a rural area in south-central Illinois?"

"No. BDC is a rare disease. It's been in the scientific news recently because it's the focus of a potential new breakthrough therapy developed by a European biotech company."

"Yes, the DNA Restore therapy from Golden Helix, in Amsterdam. There appears to be a rural BDC hot spot a couple hours from here in the Effingham, Illinois area. I'm interested in the subject for a couple of reasons, the primary one being I have family in that area. My aunt passed away recently from BDC, and my cousin, her son, may have the same disease. He's struggling with something, and they've been running tests."

The doctor's brow wrinkled. "Sorry to hear that. How old is your cousin?"

"Thirty-six."

"Highly unusual for someone so young!"

"Yes, it is. So, from a personal perspective, if it comes to it, and assuming a DNA Restore trial isn't an option, I'm concerned about my cousin being treated in a small, rural hospital. For the sake of precaution, I'm looking ahead. If it's confirmed by test results, my understanding is, they'd likely surgically remove a segment of the bile duct where they believe the cancer is confined to."

The doctor took some notes on a small notepad before looking up. "Yes, I believe it's the suggested protocol."

"I know I'm putting you on the spot here, Doctor, but do you believe that procedure can be done at a rural hospital?"

"I don't know the hospital well, or its capabilities, but I'll tell you it requires great skill, because the operation can be very extensive. It could, for example, require partial removal of the liver, maybe lymph nodes, gallbladder, and even part of the pancreas or small intestine. We have surgeons here who have extensive experience with such complex surgeries."

"He's being monitored closely. I just want to be proactive in the event we need to act quickly. My cousin also visited Dana-Farber for a consultation. I live in Boston, so that could be a possibility, but it's a good distance from here. All that said, he's back to work."

Dr. Simon leaned forward in his chair and rested his hands on the chair arms. "A couple of things come to mind. Firstly, your cousin can come here. We're a highly-rated cancer center, and we're much closer than Boston. In terms of alternatives, I have two. We can consult, or it may be possible we can supply the surgeon to the local hospital. We don't do it often, but it's something we've done."

Dr. Simon made another note on his notepad and set it on the table beside his chair. "Joshua, you mentioned a couple of reasons. What's the other?"

"The other is more of a nagging question I can't shake…what's causing the cancer? I have this tendency not to let puzzling things go until I find the solution. You have young people being affected by a disease that's historically limited to much older people. The onset is extremely rapid. My aunt passed away forty days after diagnosis. So, I'm being drawn in, sorting through that puzzle using the resources I have."

The doctor stared at him with wide eyes and shifted in his seat. "That's startlingly fast. It typically has a long timeline, even years." He paused for a moment. "I imagine the Illinois health authorities are on top of the situation."

Joshua leaned forward. "They are now."

"Joshua…I believe you know we're a teaching hospital for Washington University School of Medicine. So in terms of resources, given your humanitarian mission, let me offer you access to various medical research databases, and I can also arrange to have you speak with specialists, if you think that would be helpful."

Joshua stood. "Thank you very much for your time, generosity, and support." He passed along a business card. "By the way, out of curiosity, how do you know Dr. Lange?"

"We went to med school together. He also saved my life late one night after a sudden cardiac arrest. I owe Martin a great debt."

* * *

Late that night, Joshua directed the rental car down the lane and parked behind his uncle's truck in front of the farmhouse. As he entered the kitchen, Pete was just sitting down at the table with a leftover drumstick and glass of milk.

Pete turned his head toward Joshua. "Long day for you, huh? Just got home myself."

Joshua took a plastic cup off the counter and dunked it in the water bucket near the sink. He raised the cup to his mouth, paused, looked at, and smelled the water before he gulped it down.

"Where were you?"

"Just came from church. St. Aloysius, that is..."

"At ten o'clock? Big bingo game?"

"No. Do you remember years ago, when we had severe droughts every year? We held weekly prayer services to pray for rain."

"Sure."

"Now we have weekly prayer services to pray the cancer that's plagued our community would stop and the people affected would be cured."

* * *

The route from Effingham to St. Louis is a one hundred mile, one-and-a-half-hour straight shot southwest on I-70. Like much of downstate Illinois, the route takes travelers past numerous farms, small towns, and signs for fast food. The following day, Joshua joined trucks and cars on the route for the second day in a row.

Just before noon, found him sitting on a cushioned folding chair in a small, stuffy office on the Washington University Medical Campus. "Professor, I understand Genetically Engineered crops have been in the food chain for a number of years, as far as I can tell, without incident. I also know biotech companies have been trying for decades to produce pharmaceutical proteins and vaccines through plant or crop modifications, but I don't think anything's been approved by the FDA. I'm wondering whether it's possible for a genetically modified plant to trigger disease, specifically cancer, in humans?"

Across the desk, over the top of several piles of paper, an elderly man with short gray hair and Coke bottle glasses considered the question while leaning back in his chair and looking at the dull white ceiling. He spoke in a gruff voice. "I'm not sure if you're speaking of some random occurrence or so-called 'pharming,' that is, pharmaceuticals produced by plants. As I routinely ask my students, first give me your thoughts on the subject."

"I'm thinking of GE plants, but I hadn't thought of pharming." Joshua paused for a moment to consider the professor's comment. "I have a biochem degree, a couple years of med school, and have invested in numerous biotech companies. Based on everything I know, it's my understanding DNA and RNA from any food, genetically modified or not, does not enter the human genome. There's no evidence GE plants would cause cellular, genetic changes in human cells that would trigger cancer.

"Also, while it's true proteins in GE crops are digestible, there are many digestible proteins in a non-GE diet, and there are no examples of any of those increasing cancer risk. There's also a lot of genetic variability in non-GE plants."

The professor was silent, still looking upward; Joshua took it as a sign to continue. "I know GE crops go through a review following international guidelines. They test health and safety, comparing the crop to a non-GE plant. In that process, they look at safety implications of genetic modifications on DNA, RNA, resulting proteins, and so forth. I know the FDA considers GE crops generally safe. Given the many years the crops have been consumed by people with no link to cancer, I have to assume there is, in fact, no link…am I missing anything?"

The professor smiled and turned his gaze to Joshua. "That's quite a question, Mr. Grayson. You're asking me if, in the whole realm of science, something could be missing?"

"Point taken. Okay, how about in your experience?"

The professor sat up in his chair and turned to face Joshua. "Better question. First, let me mention a few things. GE crops have been approved in the U.S. since the 1990s. More than ninety percent of the corn, soybeans, cotton, canola, and sugar beets have some genetic modifications. Most are used for animal feed or to make ethanol. Some make their way into processed foods. In fact, it's hard to find a processed food *without* a GE modification.

"That said, I'd say the research and testing work done by companies such as biotechs, and even large agricultural companies, hasn't been as robust as many independent scientists would manage the process. For example, data on trials in rats and other surrogate animals have been subject to quite a lot of criticism.

"Corporate research indicated things like PCBs, DDT, and even Agent Orange weren't harmful to humans. There have been companies that run testing for, say, ninety days and pronounce it efficacious. However, when the testing cycle is run for twelve months, the results showed quite the opposite.

"There've been many other studies that offer similar results. One study found the presence of pesticides associated with GE food in the blood of people. There are studies that have linked glyphosate to a disease like Alzheimer's. Remember, cells in a petri dish can have quite different behavior than cells in a human body."

"So not as unequivocal as I suggest?"

The professor nodded and took a sip of tea before continuing. "Some, including renowned scientists, say, as you suggest, there's absolutely zero chance GE plants could cause a disease such as cancer, even considering the complexity of that group of diseases. But I would not rule it out."

"What about GE fertilizers, insecticides and similar products? Would that have a similar potential impact on plants?"

The professor looked at him over his round glasses. "Hmmm, one level further away from the plant itself. My suspicion is that it'd be less likely to impact the plant, but that's purely a guess."

"Professor, are there any GE products that aren't processed that might go from farm directly to human consumption?"

"Well, you'd have to research that a bit. But I believe some apples and potatoes may fit that description. Same thesis."

Joshua stood and thanked the professor.

"My pleasure, young man. If you're interested, I have a listing of studies done in this area, including pharming-related, which I've compiled over time." He searched through the piles on his desk and found it as he finished his sentence. "Ah, here you go."

Joshua left and made his way to the Bernard Becker Medical Library. Campus activity was winding down, with trails of students following well-worn paths to their dorms.

He found a table in a corner next to a floor-to-ceiling window on the third floor, where he set up shop, focusing on the listing of articles the professor provided. After several hours scanning articles, he stopped for a quick dinner of Fig Newtons from a vending machine near the restroom.

Back at his work area, it became challenging for him to stay focused as he reviewed page after page of academic text. Hours later, his phone vibrated, rousing him. Joshua picked his head up off the table and rubbed his cheek to get feeling back. He yawned, and glanced at his phone—a text.

[Blaine] Where you at? Dad's?

[Joshua] Washington University Medical Library. Back later.

As he finished the text, he sat up, a computer screen in front of him and papers arrayed on the table. The library was largely empty, owing to the fact that the time was approaching eleven-thirty.

He returned his attention to the listing of studies on pharming, using plants to manufacture and deliver pharmaceuticals. The list had checkmarks for most of the studies, and a small set of printouts was clipped to it.

Joshua moved to the last page and quickly scanned it from top to bottom; more of the same, he figured. As he began to drop the packet of reference information onto the table, he hesitated. Returning to the last page, he scanned the studies more slowly and stopped three-quarters of the way down and found:

Currie A., de Wit A.J.C., Johansson E.; *Lakartidningens: Journal of the Swedish Medical Association.* E/N-cadherin recognized as a feature of aggressive cancer tumors, switch mediation by plant ingestion shown to be effective in lab rats. [PubMed: 1503958]

He searched for the paper in the database of clinical studies, as an announcement was made over the loudspeaker that the library would close in fifteen minutes. He managed to find and print the article as a librarian approached and instructed him gruffly to pack up and leave.

Joshua slung his messenger bag over his shoulder, tucked his hands in his pockets, and exited the building. A cold breeze and bright full moon met him as he walked toward the parking lot, where his car and a black pick-up truck with its engine running were the only vehicles in the lot.

He started his car, turned on the overhead light, opened his messenger bag, and found the printout of the Swedish medical journal article. He scanned it, searching for a biography of the authors. Finding nothing except the same abbreviated names, he started his ninety-minute drive back to Bishop Creek—Route I-64 to I-70 East, reversing the trip to St. Louis he started almost twelve hours earlier. The St. Louis Arch and city lights eventually vanished in his rear-view mirror, with only sparse truck traffic keeping him company on the road.

Despite being mentally and physically exhausted, his mind churned with thoughts… A. Currie? Can it be the same person running Golden Helix? The date of the article would make her over fifty years old, which can't be the case. I met her in person at the conference. She's much younger. What about the remediation issue from the printing company dumping chemicals? How far would that reach? Hot spot areas in Bishop Creek? Most of the scientific literature says it's not GE crops. Could GE fertilizer have an impact? Not clear.

Joshua caught himself fading and pulled off I-70 in Greenville, Illinois. He stepped into Love's Travel Store, which had quite a few patrons considering it was after midnight. He purchased a large Monster energy drink and soft pretzel.

In his car, he alternated chugging the energy drink and eating his pretzel to the sound of hard rock playing over the radio. Feeling growing a surge of energy, he backed out of his parking spot and was blinded briefly in his mirror. He turned his head, looked out the rear window, and saw a black pick-up truck behind him.

He wondered, Is that the same truck from the library parking lot?

Chapter 26

The next afternoon, Joshua returned from a grocery run with a cheeseburger and locally famous crinkle-cut fries from Cruisers Drive Thru. He pulled in front of the farmhouse. As he exited the car, he saw Pete's pale blue pickup in front of the equipment barn. He walked over, opened the large wooden door, and stepped inside. On the near wall, tools and other necessities were hung—an old pickaxe, spade and shovels, several rolls of barbed wire, and baling twine among it all. Overarching it all was the smell of wood, straw, oil, and gasoline.

"Uncle Pete?"

With no answer, he followed the sound of a local country station and made his way past an old planter and grain cart. As he stepped into the center of the barn, Pete slid out from under his International tractor.

"Joshua!"

"What are you up to?"

Lying on his back, Pete wiped grease off his hands with an old, well-used rag and looked up at Joshua. "Just an oil change." He stood and dropped the rag onto an overturned metal barrel. "You look perturbed. What's up?"

Joshua sat on a metal stool and leaned back against a workbench with a sigh. "I'm frustrated because I think the health authorities are on the wrong trail for the source of the BDC. They've been looking at environmental issues, but in my mind, given that they're seeing more in other areas, the odds are it's not environmental."

"I think they're the experts, aren't they?" Pete picked up the rag off the barrel and threw it across the barn. He sat on the lowest step of the tractor, put his head in his hands, and sat quietly for a while. "Sorry, I'm just frustrated…" He caught Joshua's eye. "I'm sure they're working their way to find the source."

"Yes, the CDC is looking into the situation, and it seems like they're making it a priority. Of course, I'm not working with the CDC, but if they're looking in the wrong area, they could be wasting time and risking lives."

Pete gave him a sympathetic look. "Not sure what you mean by 'wasting time.' Isn't that what they should be doing? Testing possibilities until they find the source?

"I hope they move quickly. Maybe you should volunteer to help them!" Pete picked up his phone. "My phone's been pinging away. Solicitors don't give us much rest these days." He put the phone to his ear, Joshua saw his face go flush. "It's Jake. He's at work and in a lot of pain. We need bring him to the hospital." The men jumped into the old pickup and took off up the lane, spitting out gravel.

Pete navigated the country roads at high speed. Joshua looked at his uncle, who was rubbing tears from his eyes. The two didn't speak until they arrived and found Jake sitting on a curb, head between his legs, outside the main plant entrance.

* * *

Late the next morning, Dr. Kaymer entered the hospital room with another physician. Jake was lying on a bed with an IV, and Shelby was holding his hand. Pete, Blaine, and Joshua stood as they entered.

Dr. Kaymer acknowledged the group, and spoke quietly to Jake and Shelby. "This is Dr. Riemann. He's a gastroenterologist and handled the biopsy procedure you went through yesterday. He took several samples from your esophagus and bile duct areas during the procedure. We rushed them off to a lab to get the results as quickly as possible." Pausing briefly, she cleared her throat and delivered the results. "I'm very sorry to say the labs show the bile duct cells are cancerous. They appear to be confined to a distal bile duct near the pancreas."

Jake closed his eyes and dropped his chin to his chest. Shelby hugged him and stuttered, "It'll be alright." Pete and Blaine moved in to comfort them.

Dr. Kaymer whispered to Joshua. "I'll be back in a little while."

Joshua's only thought, Day twenty-four, thirty days to find a cure.

* * *

That evening as Joshua lay in bed, his head swimming, emotions coming and going, his phone rang. He checked the Caller ID; it read "Martin Lange."

He sat up against the headboard. "Hi, Martin."

"Joshua, I just want to let you know I've scoped out a couple of limited animal trials for the GE products. But I only have capacity for two, maybe three trials at one time. I expect they'll each run for at least three months, likely longer."

"That's good news, and very generous of you. Obviously, we want to move quickly, but without jeopardizing the validity of the trials."

Lange replied confidentially. "I'm sure we can handle it. But you need to determine which products you want to test. If it's indeed one of the products triggering the cancer, your selections have immense importance. Meaning, pick those with the highest probability to the extent you can."

Joshua sighed. "Of course you're right. We need to pick the most likely candidates to test first or potentially risk lives if we're wrong, given the timeline of the trials."

"Give it some careful thought. I'm ready when you are; just need the product names and a supply of the products. The sooner, the better." There was a pause on the other end. "How are you doing, Joshua? You don't sound like yourself. Everything okay?"

Joshua sat up and threw his legs over the side of the bed. "We just found out a couple hours ago my cousin, who's my age, has BDC. He's scheduled to have surgery tomorrow or the following day. I've imposed on your friend, Dr. Simon, for a favor. My cousin is resistant to traveling, so we're trying to coordinate borrowing an experienced surgeon from his team."

"Oh no! I'm sorry, very sorry, Joshua. This BDC is becoming a menace. Do you want me to call Richard? I'm happy to do it."

"No, he offered and is just trying to find an opening to supply the surgeon."

"Well, Joshua…I'll wait to hear from you. Best wishes to you and your family. Please don't hesitate to call me if I can help in any way."

* * *

Early the next morning, the faded blue pick-up truck moved slowly toward the local road. In the cab, Pete and Joshua rode the country roads in silence, leaving Bishop Creek, marked by an old familiar sign that someone had peppered with buckshot—"Good-bye, Godspeed, Come Again."

At the hospital they met the whole family in the surgical waiting area. Family members rotated in to wish Jake well and reassure him. Eyes red and swollen, Shelby put on a strong face as she sat quietly with her children on a waiting room couch.

Joshua entered the room with his cousins. Cole stepped in and put a hand on Jake's shoulder. "The gang's all here. Everything's going to be okay."

Jesse leaned in and hugged his younger brother. "Gonna be alright, Jaker." Jake gave a half-hearted grin.

Jake turned to Joshua and spoke in a brittle voice. "Remember your promise." Joshua gave him solemn nod.

Pete joined them, wearing a somber expression. "Boys, let's pray. Oh, dear Lord, we ask that you guide the doctor's mind and hands, and that this surgery would be a cure for Jake's condition. Lord, we know you work all things for good. It's a challenge to see that now," he paused, his voice wavering, "but we trust you, and give thanks for all our blessings. Please be with Jake and our family now. Watch over us and strengthen us all. In Jesus's holy name, I pray."

The men responded in unison, "Amen." Pete kissed his son's forehead and whispered in his ear. He stayed with Joshua as Shelby re-entered the room with the surgeon.

"Hello, Mr. and Mrs. Grayson. I'm Dr. Beckman, from Barnes Jewish Hospital, in St. Louis. I'm going to be doing your surgery today. What we're going to be doing is removing a cancerous area at the distal portion of your bile duct, where the imaging and cell tests indicate cancer and a narrowing of the duct." He held up a hand-drawn picture and pointed at different areas as he spoke. "The bile duct has branched tubes that connect the liver and gallbladder to the small intestine. Depending on what we find, we may take out more of the duct or surrounding areas, including possibly parts of your pancreas, small intestine, liver, or gallbladder. The idea is to get everything while we're there and stop this cancer in its tracks."

Jake took a deep breath and slowly exhaled. "Okay, Doc."

"I think you've been through this with your doctors and signed the patient consent forms, but do you have any questions for me about the operation itself?"

Jake and Shelby shook their heads.

"If not, then I'll get ready and the anesthesiology team will be in to see you shortly. The surgery should take two to three hours."

Dr. Kaymer walked into the waiting area, where Joshua intercepted her. "Coffee?" They made their way to the café and sat at a quiet table with their Styrofoam cups. "Megyn, the U.S. trials aren't running yet. Have you heard anything about getting Jake into the Brazil DNA Restore trials? It's more urgent now. We need a back-up!"

"I've put in a call to the contact I was given at Golden Helix to check about Brazil but haven't heard anything back yet. It turns out I know one of the doctors at one of the Brazilian clinical sites from my time at Penn. He was there at the same time on a research sabbatical while I was doing my fellowship. I have a call in to him as well."

"Thank you very much, Megyn. Will you let me know as soon as you hear something?"

"Of course. I'll follow up closely." She tilted her head to one side. "Joshua, are you feeling okay? You look pale."

Joshua rubbed his eyes. "Lack of sleep. I have a lot on my mind. How quickly do you think we'll know whether the surgery was successful?"

She gave him a questioning stare and finished her coffee. "Do you need me to prescribe you a sleep aid?" Joshua shook his head. She hesitated but continued. "Based on the imaging tests, it looks like we should be able to get the whole affected area by surgery, which is why we moved quickly. If we don't, I'm not sure. We've seen how this cancer can be very aggressive, so we'll have to wait and see."

* * *

The surgeon appeared hours later, Shelby and Pete moved into the adjacent hallway to speak with him. Pete returned to the waiting area minutes later and updated the family. "The surgery went well, the surgeon thinks he got everything. Jake is resting in recovery, Shelby's with him. It'll be a while before he can see visitors, and the doctor suggested everyone head home and come back later tomorrow. I'll stay and make sure Shelby gets home safely. Cole, you take Dixie and Henry with you to Jake's house."

Joshua felt the anguish in the room. He tapped Blaine on the shoulder, and they headed to Bishop Creek. Back in the quiet farmhouse kitchen, Blaine took a mound of pizza dough out of the refrigerator and, like a professional, began to roll it out on a large butcher block carving board, adding flour as he went.

"Get the pizza stone on the top of the fridge, hit it with some olive oil, and get the fixings from the fridge."

Joshua complied and pre-heated the oven. He raided the refrigerator, fetching a Mason jar of tomato sauce, cheese, sausage, and a green pepper and onion, which he chopped.

Blaine prepared the pizza, put it in the oven and said over his shoulder. "How 'bout a couple cold ones?"

Joshua walked onto the screened-in porch and returned with two cold bottles of beer from an open case of Pabst. He raised his bottle. "To Jake and a quick recovery."

Blaine raised the bottle and drained it.

They sat at the kitchen table in silence for a while before Joshua tried to veer away from Jake's situation. "Do you remember when I used to visit with my mom and dad? We'd arrive late on a Friday night, and your mom would make pizzas? Boy, were they good."

Blaine was quiet, stood, and kept moving, setting out plates, napkins, retrieving the pizza cutter and a jar of oregano.

Joshua stood and moved toward him. "Are you okay?"

"Why our family?" Blaine brushed back the hair from his face. He squeezed his hands into fists and hit the countertop. "We're good people. People don't get better than Mom…" He teared up and rubbed his eyes with his shirtsleeve. "And Jake. He's a good man, with a great wife and family." Blaine turned, put his hands on the kitchen counter, and dropped his head. Joshua put his arm around his cousin's shoulder.

Blaine left after a quiet dinner. Joshua slowly climbed the stairs, turned on the overhead light in his room, and sat at the desk. Scrolling through emails, he stopped to read one from the Effingham County Health Department.

Dear Mr. Grayson,

Attached, please find your well water analysis report for the sample you provided. In sum, the water sample meets Illinois drinking water standards. The contaminants listed in the report are well within acceptable limits.

If you have any questions, please feel free to call our office or stop in to speak with one of our Certified Water Specialists.

Sincerely,

The Effingham County Health Department

* * *

Martin, I'm going to Fedex the following to you for the trials to get things moving.

(1) Agronos - fertilizer.

(2) BioMaïs - sweet corn.

(3) Johnson and Dore - field corn.

I think those would be the quickest because we have the outputs. The others are a GE fertilizer (Gelden) and alfalfa (Shea Seed), so I'll need to track down farmers who use those products and send you samples of the output. Let me know how much product would be needed. If you can't handle all, then please use the order above.

I owe you big time for this!

Thank you, Joshua.

He shut the computer and flopped on the bed. His thoughts drifted back twenty years. He and Jake were lying on the same bed, laughing, no cares, and boundless dreams.

Chapter 27

As was his early morning ritual, Joshua checked emails from bed. One email, flagged as urgent, caught his attention.

Mr. Grayson,

We expect to receive FDA emergency authorization in the U.S. for DNA Restore in the very near term, and will be starting up Golden Helix human clinical trials in the coming weeks. I am writing to you to let you know that we may be interested in engaging a financing partner to fund the trials, an investment of $10 million. You expressed an interest in funding our commercial efforts at the recent Biotech Conference. If that's still the case, please let me know.

I'm aware that you are no longer with your VC firm, but I prefer to work with you, as I appreciated your thoughtful questions at our brief meeting. So perhaps this is an opportunity for you to continue with your old firm or a new company. However, this opportunity is available only for a very limited time. We have sufficient funding, but another financing source may prove useful.

Please let me know your answer within the next three days, 21:00 CET/ 14:00 your local. If yes, I will have Dr. Wilfred Telling call you to discuss this further.

Sincerely,

Dr. Amaline Currie

Chief Executive Officer

Golden Helix Therapeutics, BV

Joshua reread the email several times. He sat up, a blank look on his face as he digested the message.

He considered the offer and thought, Excellent to have another option. But why me? What do I do with this? Maybe an opportunity to close things out with Tremont?

He texted Graham Roseboro.

[Joshua] You want in on Golden Helix? Dr. Currie offered ME a funding opp, $10 million. Not sure what I want to do with it. Let me know if Tremont is interested. Quick fuse.

After a brisk morning run, Joshua and Pete departed for the hospital. En route, Joshua checked his cell phone and found three text messages from Roseboro:

[Roseboro] Yes!

[Roseboro] Call me!!!

[Roseboro] Is this a joke?

He turned off the phone and put it in his coat pocket as they pulled into a parking spot next to Blaine's bright red pick-up truck with a sticker on the rear bumper: "For Airbag Test - Keep Tailgating."

They entered the hospital room and found Shelby, Blaine, and Jake in a conversation.

Pete moved bedside. "How're you doing, son?"

"Feeling stronger today."

As they engaged in small talk, Joshua stepped into the hallway and called Roseboro, who answered on the first ring. "What's the deal with Golden Helix?"

"Yeah, Graham, how are you doing? Just returning your call."

"Uhh, sorry. I'm just excited to hear about the opportunity. How are things with you?" After a long pause, "Joshua?"

"Here's what I know…" He walked through Currie's email and the need for a quick turnaround.

"I've already spoken with everyone at the firm, we're in for the ten million. Could do more, but we'd need investor approval."

Joshua leaned against a wall and gathered his thoughts. "Okay, but I'm not sure what I want to do here. Remember, Dr. Currie gave me the opportunity; not Tremont." As he spoke, he heard an echo on the line. "Did you hear me?"

"Yes. What do you mean? Huge opportunity, of course we'd need to understand the terms and do some due diligence, but—"

"Graham, what I mean is…I'm not sure whether I want to pursue it with Tremont. Do I work with you, someone else like my next employer, or no one? I met with Tim Montgomery at Vector Funds the other day for lunch. He's been calling me about Golden Helix. I'm out of a job at this point, remember, and I'm not sure my reputation is intact after the press release you guys put out and the word being spread about the reason for my exit. I received a separation agreement that's one-sided after giving a good piece of my life building the firm, and I had to go to court despite the fact that I defended myself…so I have a lot to consider, and I'm disappointed at how I've been treated."

"We want you back at Tremont. Sorry, I should have led with that…the others agree; we were short-sighted and…by the way, I didn't know about that addition to the press release; it was added after I reviewed it."

"Graham, let's make this easy, since there are only limited hours left before I need to answer Dr. Currie. I'm done at Tremont. No way can I work with you and Cochran. You've shown your spots. I'll give you the opportunity because I think you may be the only firm that can execute in a short timeframe. But I want to close everything out at once, including my separation from Tremont. So I propose this: you sign the severance agreement as marked up by my attorney. It's fair. You pay me a four percent referral fee on the Golden Helix deal, half upfront, the other half at close, plus two percent of the carry. If not, I move on."

"The separation agreement you marked up is one-sided, and the fees you propose are insane."

"I'm sure Cochran has been trying to get to Dr. Currie, but as expected, he's failed because you're talking to me. I need to get back to her by two o'clock tomorrow afternoon. You have until one o'clock. I'm not afraid to walk away from this opportunity or contact Currie for an extension and pursue another funding source. You think about it and get back to me. Clock is ticking."

Chapter 28

The following day, after a long visit at the hospital, Pete and Joshua sat quietly on the farmhouse porch swing. The air was cool, and the only sounds to be heard were crickets and the creaking of the swing as it swung gently back and forth.

Joshua looked at his uncle's silhouette; it appeared like his father was sitting beside him. He scanned the sky. "I've missed the quiet here. I didn't realize until now how loud my life has been. I wish I could rewind the clock. I'd love to bring frog legs home for Aunt Sara to cook. She got such a kick out of it. Her laugh was so buoyant. I can still vividly picture her smile and wide open eyes."

"I miss her so very much, Joshua. I can still feel her presence, it's still so recent. She gave me more than I could ever give her…I don't know who I am without her. Your aunt was one of a kind, full of life." He laughed lightly. "You know, she tried her hand at watercolor painting, and her work was stunning. They were in high demand at the church fundraisers. Her talent hangs in many of the homes in Bishop Creek. We didn't have money or time, given the work on the farm, to travel, so she would decorate our dining room like a Paris bistro and make a French meal for dinner."

Pete stared at the faintly visible, crescent moon and took a deep breath. "She'd have a record on the phonograph and a bottle of French wine." He looked at Joshua and laughed, a tear rolling down his cheek. "I have no idea where she found French wine around here. Sometimes she'd meet me at the door with a picnic basket, and we'd find a place to have dinner and watch the sunset. Once in a while, she'd bring poetry and ask me to read it to her."

"Did she have a favorite?"

"Not really, but I did. I remember the refrain:

'My home, my home

Right where it stands;

Built by generations,

Gentle souls with calloused hands.'"

Joshua listened quietly and played it over in his head. "Sounds like Bishop Creek. Robert Frost or Walt Whitman?"

"No. Sara Grayson."

"Really?!"

"Sure, she had a book full of them." Pete paused. "For years, I wasn't good to her; just an angry man overwhelmed with work and trying to provide for our family. But…she marched on and stuck with me. Faithful to the promises we made to each other. In the end, my anger and selfishness were no match for her love, her gentleness, and strong faith. The Good Book says faith can move mountains, and it did."

The swing creaked like a metronome for a while before Joshua cleared his throat and spoke. "I wasn't able to say goodbye to my parents, and it's been an open wound I've ignored for years. I also regret, from the deepest part of me, not being able to say goodbye to Aunt Sara." Tears filled his eyes. "She was my only connection to family for so many years, and she's the one who brought me back here…what a great gift."

"Just like her. She loved you, Joshua." Pete lowered his head. "I'm praying fervently that Jake comes through this illness and is healed. Time is so precious, and sometimes it takes moments like this for us to recognize it.

"I see you searching like me. I hope you find your path earlier in life than I did. Sara used to tell me I needed to find an anchor. I thought it was her; she told me it was God…" He stopped and cried silently.

Joshua put his hand on Pete's shoulder. "Thank you for sharing with me, Uncle Pete."

Pete composed himself and gave a long exhale and spoke calmly. "Did you know Joshua was one of the Bible's greatest warriors?"

"No."

"Well, he led the Israelites into the Promised Land after Moses died. God put him in the right place at the right time, and he was never defeated. I think God brought you back here at this time for a reason, too. It's times like this when you find out who you are."

"I do think we're in a war, Uncle Pete…I'm not completely sure who the enemy is, but I'm ready to fight."

* * *

Mid-morning the following day, the fields of Bishop Creek wore a low layer of fog. Joshua drove slowly toward T-Town and took in the scenery. Twenty minutes later, he pulled into Repking Seed. He waved at the clerk stocking the shelves as he entered and continued to the rear of the store.

"Good morning, Clem."

Clem looked up from his crossword puzzle. "Hey there, Joshua. Want to look at my POs some more?" He gave a hardy laugh and slapped his thigh.

"That sounds tempting, Clem, but no. Just want to ask you a question."

"Oh, you know you gotta pay the price first." He looked down at his puzzle. "Thirty-four across. Capital of Peru. Ends in an e."

A broad smile crossed Joshua's face. "I think you have the 'e' wrong. The capital of Peru is Lima. L–I–M-A."

Clem pushed his T-Town baseball cap up off his forehead with the eraser end of his pencil. "Dog-gone it." He dropped the pencil. "Whatcha got?"

"Do you carry Agronos fertilizer?"

"Yes."

"I didn't see it in the POs I reviewed."

Clem reached into a drawer under the counter and with two hands pulled out a six inch stack of papers, put it on the counter, and started ruffling through them. "It's in here somewhere."

Joshua let out a forceful breath. "So you don't keep it with the other POs?" He paced back and forth as Clem looked at his POs page by page. He stopped and stepped to the counter. "Clem, no need to go through those. Just tell me how long you've sold the product."

Clem looked up with a confused look. "Well, I'd say in the last year and a half. It's getting more popular, and recently they've had trouble producing enough supply. I have an order in, and it's backlogged."

"Do you know how I can find out where the different GE seeds and fertilizers we discussed are sold in the U.S.? I tried all the companies you gave me but just got people reading from a script. I got bupkis!"

"Seeds and such are usually sold through national distributors who sell to my place and other sub-distributors. There are fewer and fewer seed stores these days, because the whole industry has consolidated. I believe the largest four seed suppliers control over sixty percent of the market. They buy up competition and basically call the shots."

"So I'd need to call the distributors to find out where seeds are sold?"

"Yep. The big boy seeds are sold everywhere. The small guys, like some of the ones we talked about, usually hire a private company or two to coordinate distribution in the country. They usually sell through independent agents or sometimes in small areas through farmer-dealers. Take another look at the contacts I gave you. You should be calling the distributors, not the companies. Those contacts would know where and who is selling the seeds for their products."

"Thanks, Clem. Sorry to bother you. That's clearer."

* * *

Joshua followed a lady with a tray of food into Jake's hospital room and found Shelby, Pete, and another man at the end of his bed, talking. Pete turned and waved him over. He chuckled and pointed a thumb at Jake.

"Best leave him alone, he's not happy about the food here…Joshua, you remember Ted Westerndorf, don't you? I believe I introduced you to him at Repking Seed."

"Yes." He stepped forward and shook Ted's hand.

"Good to see you again, Joshua."

The nurse set the tray in front of Jake on the bed table. "Enjoy," she mumbled as she left the room. Jake sat up and surveyed the lunch: a small broiled chicken breast, vegetable mix, roll, and small sugar-free strawberry Jell-O cup. His face went from a half-smile to a rigid expression and wrinkled nose.

"Come on!" The group had a hardy laugh as Shelby walked over to see if she could pacify him.

"So Joshua, I was talking to Ted about his winemaking exploits. He's a big home winemaker, and he's even won some regional contests!"

Ted blushed. "Well, it's a fun hobby."

"That sounds interesting. When you think of wine, Sonoma or Napa come to mind, not Bishop Creek! Do you grow the grapes?"

"I do now. Takes three years after planting the vines before you get grapes you can make wine with. I planted an area of Concord grapes. They're native, have good pest resistance, and can take the cold weather. So far, so good. Why don't you come over with your uncle sometime, and I'll give you a tour and," he winked, "we'll do some heavy sampling."

A short while later, Jake closed his eyes to nap, and the group left the room. Joshua checked his phone just outside the door. Three text messages from Roseboro.

[Roseboro] Separation agreement is ok, but the referral fees are too high. Move it to two percent for each of the referral and carry and we have a deal.

[Roseboro] Okay?

Finally, half an hour after the previous text:

[Roseboro] Ok your terms, let's get this deal done. Please confirm ASAP.

[Joshua] Good. I'll let Golden Helix know and we'll get details on pricing, etc. Sign the severance agreement and return it to my attorney ASAP. He'll also send over a Referral Agreement for the Golden Helix opportunity, sign and fax to him ASAP as well.

He checked his text message to ensure it was sent. The history noted it was sent three times.

Joshua thought, Odd, I know I only sent it once.

He responded to Dr. Currie with a brief email.

Dr. Currie,

Thank you for the opportunity to finance the U.S. trials. Tremont Ventures would like to provide the $10 million subject to pricing and due diligence. Can we arrange a time to discuss the details?

Kind regards,

Joshua Grayson

As he walked toward the reception area, his phone rang. He didn't recognize the number, but answered.

"Hello, Mr. Grayson. My name is Dr. Wilfred Telling. I work for Dr. Currie and am the person in charge of the DNA Restore trials. She asked me to call you to work out details for an investment to provide financing for our U.S. trial rollout. Assuming we get the go ahead."

"That was fast! I just sent a note to Dr. Currie a few minutes ago. At this point, we're looking for the details of the investment terms, plus the firm would need to conduct due diligence."

"Right, right, of course. It may be best to meet in person. I'm currently in Wisconsin. Shall I come down to your location in Illinois, and we can discuss the details?…Hello, Mr. Grayson?"

"Sure, that would work." He hung up.

After the call concluded it struck him, *How did he know I'm in Illinois?*

Chapter 29

Early Saturday morning in Amsterdam, Dr. Currie stood at the large window in her office wearing a lilac-colored cashmere sweatsuit, the sky was a lazy blue, with thin ribbons of clouds to the north. Although she was born Dutch, she spent as much time in other countries as she had in the Netherlands. But while she could have located Golden Helix anywhere, she chose the country of her birth. It felt right to her.

She inserted a pod in her coffee maker, and when the cup was filled, she sat down at her desk and took a sip. As usual, she checked her email first. Scanning the long list of emails, she noted one marked urgent from Dr. Telling.

Dear Dr. Currie,

I am pleased to report I've just received word of the FDA's approval to commence limited clinical trials in the U.S. under a Fast Track authorization. I've attached a copy of the approval for your information and reference.

We're of course ready to deploy, trucks are on the move to deliver supplies to the locations of participating hospitals, and training has already occurred.

Three of the hospitals have patients enrolled. The locations are as follows:

1) Davenport, Iowa

2) Salina, Kansas

3) Fond du Lac, Wisconsin

I fully expect that we'll commence trials within the next three weeks in those locations. Future locations may be possible if other BDC areas arise.

In your service,

Dr. Wilfred B. Telling

Her expression changed from nonchalant, business as usual, to a wide smile. She sat in silence, staring at the screen for several minutes. Currie opened a black Moleskine notebook and stared at a picture of a Anton Currie in his lab coat. She added an entry.

My Love,

Today we have achieved victory with an approval of DNA Restore in the U.S.!!! I wish you were here with me to celebrate our grand achievement.

All My Love,

Amaline

Twenty minutes later, Currie sat at a corner table at De Koffie Salon, sipping on an espresso. The shop had just opened, and only one other patron was in the café. She finished the espresso as Anas Hassan entered and ordered on his way to the back corner table.

"There's news?"

Currie fought back a smile and restrained herself from speaking too loudly. "We've received FDA emergency approval, and the trials will begin in the U.S. soon. The U.S. opens the rest of the world."

Hassan sat slack-jawed for a moment, his eyes fluttering before his face regained its usual ambivalent look. "That's excellent news. What's next?"

Currie rubbed the birthmark near her right eye as she considered a response. "We continue to expand where the treatment is needed. As you know, we have started developing applications of the technology for other genetic diseases. Also, we've just received confirmation a U.S. venture capital firm will invest ten million dollars in the company. That'll also be helpful to our efforts."

"Yes, more capital is good. How is the cooperation going with the CDC? Perhaps your involvement accelerated the approval?"

"The FDA is a different department, so I don't believe it was a factor. The Brazil results have been perhaps better than we even imagined, and there are limited options for patients. The results drove the approval. I'm happy to be part of the direction for the CDC investigation to find the source of the cancer."

"Yes, I'm quite sure you're leading them in the right direction. What country is next?"

"Likely China. Not on the same scale as Brazil and U.S.A. at this time."

Hassan rubbed his goatee, clearly in thought. "I grew up knowing only poverty and bloodshed. It truly was fight or die. I was moved back and forth between countries with different families and have no place I can call my home. This is a dream come true, and perhaps a home for me. We have quite a lot of work to do, but the doors are now opening."

Currie replied, "Yes, Hassan. You have done well and been an important part of this journey, watching out for our best interests and handling logistics."

Hassan bowed slightly.

Currie waved at the barista and held up her empty cup, and caught Hassan's eye. "We're dealing with things well to this point, and it's nothing we can't handle. For now, let's enjoy the victory."

* * *

Mid-afternoon, Currie called Dr. Telling, who answered on the first ring.

"Hello, Dr. Currie. I assume you received the good news!"

"Yes, indeed! This happened more quickly than I ever expected. Very good work! This will save lives, as we well know." She paced back and forth in front of her desk. "Do you know why we were approved so quickly?"

"My belief is that it's twofold. Firstly, the data from Brazil is extremely strong, and I know they sent people from the clinical review board to Brazil to see firsthand, as well as to closely scrutinize their data. Secondly, the BDC incidence is growing rather quickly here in the U.S., and the cancer is quite aggressive, with a very, very high mortality rate.

Traditional surgery has only proved to slow down the mortality rate and not cure the patient."

Currie sat behind her desk and leaned back in her chair. "That's quite sad. Similar to Brazil before we were able to assist. What are the next steps?"

"The FDA has seen and approved our protocols, so we need to put those in place with the local clinicians. The hospitals have ample patients in our initial three areas, so we should be able to bring our treatment online quickly. I also expect the FDA will be in early to confirm we're following our protocol and meet Good Clinical Practices standards."

"Dr. Telling, where are we with the other areas where BDC is growing? Will we also be able to add more trial sites as we move forward?" There was a quiet pause before Currie heard loud hacking on the other end of the line, causing her to take the phone from her ear, put it on her desk, and hit the speaker button. When the noises stopped, she spoke. "Dr. Telling, are you alright?"

There was some residual coughing on the other end of the line before Telling spoke. "Yes, yes…please excuse me, I was taking a sip of tea but swallowed wrong." He cleared his throat. "To your question. Yes, we'll be able to expand to other sites with FDA permission. My take, for what it's worth, is that if we're getting the same results as we've achieved in Brazil, we'll be given a quick approval to expand."

"That's certainly what I would expect. How many other potential sites are there?"

"I've been conferring with various U.S. departments on the matter. The BDC growth seems to have caught them by surprise! So, we're investigating multiple areas. I'm traveling to the sites where there's a growing need."

Currie took a map of the U.S from her desk drawer and put it in front of her. Multiple areas in the Midwest were circled. "Where specifically?"

"They all seem to be what the Americans call the 'Heartland.' It covers the center of the U.S., something on the order of one million square miles. I've been getting well-acquainted with the area." Currie heard Telling chuckle.

She shook her head and raised her voice "Specifically?"

"Ah, yes. Mostly small farming towns, such as Faribault, Minnesota, North Platte, Nebraska, and Ste. Genevieve, Missouri. I have to say, the people are wonderful; hard working, focused on the simple things in life, and friendly. I guess you'd call them the 'salt of the earth' types."

Dr. Currie finished jotting down the last town and concluded the call. "Dr. Telling, thank you for the update, and very good job getting the approval before we expected. Do you need anything further?"

Hearing a "No," she concluded the call and searched for the towns. She highlighted each before returning the map to her desk drawer.

Chapter 30

Late Monday morning, Joshua sat on the edge of the farmhouse porch and spoke to Pete, who stood in front of him, arms crossed.

"When I visited Washington University in St. Louis and spoke with Dr. Simon to discuss Jake, I also did some research on GE products and spoke with a professor about pharming. That's p-h-a-r-m-i-n-g. Meaning, delivering pharmaceuticals through plants. It got me thinking about the GE plants around here. Most are produced for cattle or processed for various foods, but the GE sweet corn around here isn't processed; it goes directly from field to mouth. I don't believe there are other similar crops.

"The many years of GE crops in the food chain say the cancer can't be caused by the produce, and science says the same. There's no evidence that any consumed plant would cause changes in human cells. But my gut tells me I can't rule out the corn."

"I thought you said the CDC knew the source?"

"They think they may have the source, but I haven't seen any confirmation or action yet. It troubles me that the

Agronos fertilizer, they suspect, is new to this area, so it would be hard to believe it could have that quick of an impact on people. But they have many experienced scientists reviewing it."

Pete covered his eyes with a hand. "Did you call the producer of the corn seed?"

"I expect that the authorities have already addressed it. What would I ask them?"

"Make them aware of your concern. Even if there is a question about it being the source, we need to pass on the word to avoid it. We're not going to let people get sick if there's a possibility the corn or another crop is causing the cancer."

"The local farmers wouldn't be happy. It's just speculation." Joshua sat forward.

Pete brushed the comment aside. "Everyone is putting orders in now for next season, and more and more farmers are planting GE products, so we need to move quickly."

"You're thinking about speaking with Clem at Repking Seed?"

Pete nodded.

"Those seeds are a big money maker for him and the farmers planting those seeds. It could be a hard sell to him without proof."

Pete rubbed his forehead. "What does your gut say?"

Joshua looked up at the gray porch ceiling and paused for a moment. "My thought originally was, it had to be the water. But I had a sample from the well tested, and it was okay, no contaminants. Beyond that, I don't know for sure, but I can't pinpoint anything else that could be the cause, other than a new GE crop, and the corn seems the most likely. I'm trying to test the crops with a scientist I know well. But that could take months and may not show anything."

Pete stepped in closer and pointed a finger at him. "I'm not going to look back and say, 'I should have'…I'm starting with our family, and then I'm going to have a word with Clem. It's a small price to pay, if it's true. Let's spread the word."

* * *

Late afternoon, Joshua sat in the hospital reception area and looked at the elderly woman, gray hair pulled into a bun, sitting very upright at the hospital reception desk. The Rolling Stones' "You Can't Always Get What You Want" played in the background. He grinned—same lady, same muzak, new day. The sound of the entry door drew his attention, where he saw a tall, lanky man wearing a navy blue pin-striped suit enter the building and walk towards him.

"You must be Mr. Grayson. I'm very sorry I had to delay our chat; we had some minor issues that needed attending to at another clinical trial site." He shook Joshua's hand vigorously.

"Yes, please call me Joshua." He led Dr. Telling to a table in the hospital cafeteria.

The doctor stood tall, removed his reading glasses, pulled a handkerchief from his suit coat, and wiped his brow before he set his gangly frame in a chair across from Joshua. "We're grateful that your firm is looking to partner with us as we bring our initial product into the U.S. We're excited at the prospects it brings for many afflicted people."

Telling spoke like a salesman, and Joshua vehemently disliked being sold, but his instinct was to trust the doctor. "How did your visit go with the hospital yesterday?"

"Oh, fine, fine. Well-run, strong staff. That Dr. Kaymer is a tough, smart physician. Focused keenly on patients. We're only allowed a limited set of trials, so we're trying to be fair from a geographic standpoint. We also need to see which hospitals are interested and have a strong need in order to make that decision."

Joshua rested his hands on the table. "One of my cousins is Dr. Kaymer's patient. He had an operation for BDC. It looks like he's going home today."

"Oh? I'm very sorry to hear that. I mean, I'm sorry he had to have surgery…not that he's Dr. Kaymer's patient."

Joshua acknowledged him with a grin. "I understand. My cousin has had a couple of scares, but the recent surgery seems to have gone well. That said, the BDC rate is so high here, it's challenging not to be on edge."

"I certainly hope the surgery was a smashing success. Good that we're looking to bring DNA Restore to the States."

Telling put his briefcase on the table and sorted through a multitude of files before pulling one out and laying it on the table in front of him. "So, getting down to business, these are the terms I've been given about the investment." He balanced his reading glasses on the end of his nose. "Tremont Ventures may participate in the Golden Helix Series C preferred stock at a twenty percent premium to the previous valuation, which was established one year ago. There would be a maximum two days' due diligence in Amsterdam, with funding within two weeks after that review is completed. Also, Dr. Currie has made it a condition precedent that you participate in the on-site due diligence."

"That sounds fine to me, but it's not my decision. I'll relay the terms to my counterparts at Tremont."

The doctor popped a Tic Tac into his mouth, swirled it around, chewed it, and swallowed. "Okay, but I should also tell you that, per Dr. Currie, these terms are non-negotiable. Take it or leave it." He handed Joshua a term sheet with all the requisite information.

"Understood."

"I'm not a financial person, far from it, but the terms sound very reasonable to me, given the technology and experience-to-date in Brazil." Telling gave him a wink.

"Given that this is a take-it-or-leave-it offer, I expect a quick answer. Should I call you?"

"Yes, please do, and I'll relay the decision."

"Okay, perfect." Joshua leaned forward and squinted. "Out of curiosity, Doctor, has anyone from the CDC approached you concerning potential sources of the BDC? Maybe even about the situation in Brazil?"

"No, not me. Dr. Currie has been conferring with various governmental parties in Brazil and here in the U.S. trying to assist. She's an expert across a number of scientific areas, including oncology, genetics, plant morphology, and who knows what else. She's invested a lot of time to support those efforts."

"That's good to hear." Joshua paused. "Sorry to pepper you with questions, but what prompted your company to focus DNA Restore on BDC? It's such a small market."

Dr. Telling clasped his hands together in front of him on the table. "Well, I don't know the full history, but I believe it was initiated by the Brazilian government. Apparently, one of the scientists there was aware of DNA Restore being developed at Golden Helix and asked if it could be tested on BDC. As it turned out, it's certainly been an incredibly fortuitous event!"

As the meeting concluded, Joshua messaged Megyn Kaymer, "Meet me in the café?" Several minutes later, he received a thumbs up emoji, followed by, "10 mins."

He sat so he could see the reception area. There, he saw people coming and going, saying goodbye or hello. Hugs, kisses, and handshakes, sometimes the trifecta. He gazed at an elderly gentleman sitting on a chair, looking anxiously at everyone who passed by. He imagined his father sitting in the chair. Without thinking, he stood and walked over to the man.

"Hello, sir, my name is Joshua. I see you looking for somebody. Can I help you?"

The man looked up. Joshua could see the confusion in his eyes. "No, I'm waiting for my daughter."

"Can I call her for you?"

"She'll be along soon." He repeated it three times, then looked past Joshua, scanning people coming and going.

"I'm waiting for someone, too. Do you mind if I sit with you?" Joshua sat in the adjacent chair and spoke with him until his daughter arrived, then made his way back to his table as Megyn stepped into the cafe.

She joined him, her hands folded on the table. "So, your cousin is doing well and—"

Joshua raised his hand. "Megyn, I just wanted to say hello and thank you for putting up with all my questions, talking about clinical trials and…well, everything. I want to see how *you're* doing."

She tilted her head and sat back in her chair. "Oh. Well, it's definitely a challenging time, but I came here with eyes wide open. The people are wonderful, and I want to make a difference in the community."

"Why Effingham? You could practice anywhere with your credentials."

She sat forward, put her elbow on the table, rested her chin on her palm, and looked him in the eye. He felt uneasy as she read him. "I'm sorry if I'm being too personal. I thought I'd just see how you're doing and get to know you better."

Megyn smiled. "No, you're not being too personal...I'm touched. It's been a while since anyone genuinely asked me that question. I'm so used to being 'on.' So okay, I'm from the Springfield area and wanted to be relatively close to home because my parents are getting older. When the local cancer incidence rate spiked, it felt like I was being called to practice here. No regrets, but it's been a full-out mission."

"What were you like as a girl growing up in Springfield? Do you have any hobbies? What's your favorite color? Favorite book?"

She laughed hard at his burst of questions, clearly ramping up his more-than-professional interest in her. "Hobbies? Hard to fit them in, but I guess I'd say running, and I enjoy writing poetry and short stories. And no, I'm not going to recite one for you now."

"Fair enough. What were you like when you were in...eighth grade?"

Megyn scrunched her face and made him laugh. "I was fairly quiet, a good student, and loved science. Oh, and I was a cheerleader for the basketball team."

"Favorite book?"

"*A Tree Grows in Brooklyn.*"

"Favorite color?"

"I'll go with periwinkle."

He smiled. "Well, I'd like to take another swing in the batting cage with you when you have time. Or get a bite to eat. You know, everyone needs to relax and laugh…it has therapeutic value. Just let me know when you have some free time."

"Sounds nice. I'll let you know."

His mind refocused as he walked through the parking lot and thought, Here I am, talking to Megyn, looking for a date, I have no job, Jake had surgery, and there's no clear understanding of the source of the disease.

We're in the eye of the hurricane.

Chapter 31

Joshua pulled into Jake and Shelby's driveway. He could see strong emotion in Jake's eyes as they parked. He leaned on Joshua as they slowly made their way into the house. Blaine pulled into the driveway and followed them, carrying Jake's suitcase.

The children corralled Jake's legs. Blaine peeled Henry off and began to wrestle with him. As Jake moved to the couch, Shelby stepped into the kitchen, turned her back to the group, and cried hard into a dishtowel. Jake settled in with the kids, while Joshua made his way into the kitchen and put his arm around Shelby, who sobbed quietly.

"He's home, Shelby. I know it's been very tough on you and the kids. But he's home!"

She stuttered and wiped her eyes. "I'm happy, Joshua…" she said while dabbing at her eyes with the towel. "But I don't want it to come back. I'm going to worry—"

"I understand. But for tonight, enjoy Jake and the kids." Joshua gave her a wide, cheesy smile that made her laugh. She punched him in the shoulder.

Henry raised his voice in the family room. "Daddy, can you read to us?"

Dixie echoed her brother as she ran out of the room, returning with a well-worn book.

"Yes! I missed reading to you while I was away." The children sat close at his side. "Once upon a time in a rickety old castle lived a giant Ogre named Uncle Blaine." Henry and Dixie laughed hard and pointed at Blaine, who put on an exaggerated frown. Shelby joined them, towel in hand.

Joshua gave Blaine a look and motioned to the rear door. They stepped outside and sat in silence in two Adirondack chairs on the patio. Their breathing created light puffs of mist.

He looked at Blaine staring off into the distance. "What're you thinking about?"

"Nothin'. Glad Jake is okay and home from the hospital. Guess I'm worried the cancer will come back. First Mom, now Jake. Butch Hartke, too…it's really unbelievable." Blaine turned and looked at a flock of birds on the adjacent field, stood, picked up a rock, and threw it toward the birds, scattering them. "They ought to be down south by now…" He turned back to Joshua. "Hey, did you hear about old Karel

Steuben? He got arrested in Vegas, and then he comes back to Effingham and the city is suing him for the cost of the printing company cleanup. People are getting sick, that SOB is enemy number one!"

Joshua sat forward. "He doesn't seem like a good guy for sure. But I'm convinced the printing company pollution isn't the reason for the cancer. There are other places with the same issue that's occurring around the same time. Too much of a coincidence."

"What is it, then?"

"Not sure yet. We're looking at some of the new GE seeds."

Blaine asked, "Who is 'we?'"

"I have a doctor friend who's taking a closer look with some animal trials. So, like your dad told everyone, let's stay away from the GE products until the source is found." Joshua looked up and saw the stars beginning to appear. He added, "Hopefully, Jake's surgery took care of the issue."

They sat in quiet for a while. "Hey Blaine, I have to go out of town for a few days on business. Keep an eye on things, okay?" He zipped up his jacket and tapped Blaine on the shoulder. "By the way, did you notice a black pick-up following us here from the hospital?"

Blaine looked at him and crossed his eyes. "Plenty of black pick-ups in these parts, cuz. Why do you think someone would follow us?"

"I don't know, but I think I've seen the truck before. I've been poking around, looking for the possible source of the cancer in the area, so maybe someone doesn't want me digging into things. Also, I got a call from someone who knows I live in Boston but knew I was here."

Blaine gave him a faux serious look, bug-eyed, with his mouth wide open.

Joshua stared back at him. "No, really. I picked up a cheap second phone and new laptop yesterday. If I'm being followed, it's probably from the GPS in my cell phone, and I've been hearing an echo on my phone. My computer's been slow, too."

"You're one paranoid dude. You watch way too many spy flicks. This is Bishop, yo! I think I need to go inside and make you one of those tin foil helmets!"

Joshua laughed. "Hope you're right."

* * *

Late evening, Joshua sat at his makeshift desk, with Ernie sleeping near his feet. He opened his laptop and provided Gilchrist, Dr. Lange, Dr. Kaymer, and family with his new phone number and email, with instructions to keep it confidential. Blaine responded with a GIF of a smiley face with the eyes rolling around in opposite directions.

Sipping a beer he re-engaged with the information he'd gathered at the Washington University Medical Library. He questioned himself, I'm caught in this maze, trying to find my way out. Maybe there is no exit, no solution; just a circular problem that'll drive me insane. Maybe it's best to let the pros handle it.

Joshua convinced himself at least to satisfy his curiosity about "A. Currie," one of the authors of the Swedish Medical Journal article he printed. Accessing the Washington University Medical research environment via a virtual private network connection provided by Dr. Simon, he began. He searched the scientific database for "A. Currie," and the only result was the article he printed. He tried the other author of the article "A. de Wit," and the only hit was a reference to the same article. Other iterations brought nothing further.

Shifting to Google search, he tried "A. Currie." He mumbled, "Come on, give me something."

In less than a second, numerous search results popped up. He scrolled through six pages. They were all related to Dr. Amaline Currie and her DNA Restore revelation. Pictures of her on the cover of *Time* Magazine and delivering her biotech conference speech, articles in the *Wall Street Journal*, multiple scientific journals and blogs.

He tried "A. de Wit." No results.

Joshua picked up Ernie and laid him on a cushion at the foot of the bed. He yawned, put an elbow on the desk, and propped up his head. As a last thought, he typed "Currie deWit."

He growled, "Come on, now" and slowly depressed the enter key.

The resulting text from the search was mostly in Dutch. He waded through page after page. The results showed pieces of each name separately. On the fourth search page, a headline caught his eye: *Drs. Currie and de Wit trouwen, onderzoekers worden verliefd*. He leaned in and clicked the link. A newspaper page popped up. In the middle of the page, he focused on a wedding picture of an older man and what appeared to be a young Amaline Currie in a modest wedding dress. The caption read, "*Onderzoek wetenschappers Anton Currie and Amaline de Wit trouwen.*"

Joshua caught a second wind. Over the next hour, with the help of Google Translate, he was able to put together a rough profile of Dr. Anton Currie, professor at the Karolinska Institute in Stockholm, where he overlapped with Amaline Currie. At the time, she apparently was a research assistant. He found limited research papers. A newspaper article reported Anton was arrested in London for protesting against stem cell and gene therapy prohibitions. He had at least three patents to his name related to: methods of delivery of molecules to cells, methods of producing a plant through cross breeding and related genetic components, and systems for delivering therapeutic agents to "particular" organs, cells, and/or tissues.

He uncovered a very brief obituary in a Karolinska Institute Newsletter, a short seven years after his marriage to Amaline de Wit. Elbows on his desk, Joshua rubbed his eyes and attempted to sort through the data in his mind.

Joshua whispered, "What does this all mean, if anything?"

He flipped off the desk light, pet Ernie as he made his way to the bed, and dropped backward onto the mattress. He turned off the reading light and closed his eyes. Just before he fell asleep, his new phone vibrated on the nightstand.

[Blaine] Followed you to Dad's -- 34G456 -- Missouri plate of the black pick-up following you. Got your back.

Chapter 32

Joshua put his hand over the phone as someone shouted, "Grayson!" He shielded his eyes from the reflection off the glass of the Golden Helix building and saw Graham Roseboro standing in front of the main entrance, waving him over in an exaggerated manner. Joshua raised his index finger and turned his back to him.

"*Hallo?*"

Joshua put the phone back to his ear. "Professor Johansson?"

"*Ja.*"

"My name is Joshua Grayson. I'm a venture capital investor doing some research on the work done by Dr. Anton Currie."

The professor was quiet on his end for a while. "Oh. Investor?"

"Yes, Professor. My company is looking to invest in agricultural biotechnology companies, and I know Anton Currie was an active researcher in that area. I've reviewed his work, but I thought it would be helpful to speak with someone who worked with him. I'd like to understand more about his research."

"*Ja, Gol'd morgon.* We worked together on some research at the institute. Anton, he was interested in finding…" He paused for a moment. "Sorry, I don't speak English often, so excuse my 'Swenglish,' please. *Ja*, he looked for how to trigger genetic changes in plants, and later animals. He worked many years to develop a…eatable vaccine for Hepatitis B, and later HIV. Interesting science, but it did not lead to anything of use. He was very frustrated. I moved on to other areas of interest. He continued his focus after we didn't collaborate any more. I was at his funeral, very sad. He was a nice man. Determined to help people."

"Do you know where his research ended?"

"No. He did not publish anymore. He continued his work outside of the institute and married one of the oncology research fellows, who is now very famous. You know the name Amaline Currie?"

"Yes, I do. Do you know who funded his research when he was outside the institute? I can imagine money would be needed."

"No. I don't know about funding. But yes, it's important. Perhaps the government gave some funding. That is possible."

"Do you know if Amaline Currie continued the research?"

"I assume so. They were very passionate, or you might say even obsessed about it. Anton talked about changing the world. Amaline, she was very smart and private. They left the school together. I believe they did that so they could continue their research and own intellectual property rights themselves, not the institute. Anton, changed after we worked together and he began working with Amaline. We lost touch. I didn't know her well. I don't believe anyone did."

Joshua heard his name called again, looked over his shoulder, and saw Roseboro speed walking toward him. "Do you know anyone else who might know more about their work?"

"No, sorry."

"Okay, Professor. I thank you very much for your time. If you think of anything else about Anton Currie's research, I'd greatly appreciate it if you'd contact me at this number."

Roseboro gave him a stark stare and pointed at his watch. "Come on, we don't have a lot of time to get this done."

As they approached the entrance, Joshua scanned the group, which included several people he didn't know. "I see a lot of hired guns, Graham…where's Cochran? I thought he was in charge of the Golden Helix relationship?" Roseboro looked at him out of the corner of his eye and mumbled, "He has a different skill set."

Joshua started to respond but bit his tongue.

The group was led in silence to the second floor by the Golden Helix CFO, a tall woman with a leather portfolio tucked under her arm. They entered a large, well appointed conference room. The CFO made a round of fifteen stacks of files, each with a subject placard, neatly arrayed around a large conference table. In the center were three thermal insulated coffee dispensers, cream and sugar, a case of bottled water, two carafes of orange juice, glassware, and bite-sized stroopwafels.

After making her way around the files, she moved to a corner of the room. "The information you should need to complete your review is here." She pointed to a paper next to a phone. "If not, here is a listing of people who are available to answer questions by topic. Please do not hesitate to call them. They are expecting to hear from you."

Roseboro rubbed his hands together. "Will Dr. Currie be available to meet with us?"

The CFO turned to him and gave him a blunt, "No."

* * *

After a long first day of due diligence and dinner with the group, Joshua sat in his Amsterdam hotel room, a darts tournament playing on TV as he checked his messages. As he began to fade, he sent an encrypted email to Dr. Lange.

Martin,

I am sending the attached file (BDC data) to you for a couple of reasons. First, for your review and thoughts, and secondly, for safekeeping. It also supplements the package of GE sweet corn, field corn, and Agronos fertilizer I sent you. I'm very curious to see the test results on those samples. The consensus at the CDC seems to be focused on the Agronos product.

As you know, my cousin recently had surgery to remove a cancerous section from his bile duct. Thanks to you and your colleague Dr. Simon, we were able to utilize a surgical specialist from Barnes Jewish Hospital to perform the operation at a local hospital in Effingham. By all accounts, it was successful.

While all this has been going on, I've learned that there are similar BDC hot spots in similar small farming towns beyond Salina.

In my meeting with Dr. Simon, I mentioned the situation, and he was kind enough to refer me to one of the professors and allow me to use the Med School facilities for research. The key information I've gathered to date is in the attached file. I'm also pursuing some other open questions.

As crazy as it may sound, I think my communications are being accessed, which is the reason for the new phone and email. It's a very strange feeling. If that's true, I believe it may be associated with the questions I've been asking. I want others to have this information, including my legal friend Bill Gilchrist, who's copied on this email. That said, I expect it's probably nothing.

I'm in Amsterdam for a couple days for due diligence on Golden Helix for a potential investment by Tremont. Any thoughts on next steps, etc. are welcome.

I'll keep in touch.

Best, Joshua

* * *

The following morning was cold, and the strong wind and drizzle made for a miserable start to the day. That said, the group was surprised to see many cyclists still in the bike lanes as the team Ubered to Golden Helix. Joshua was impressed at the resiliency of the local Amsterdam populace.

Due diligence was a slow task, reviewing lengthy technical documents, legal opinions, asking questions, and requesting more data. The group was effectively quarantined in the conference room and showed little sign of jet lag or fatigue as they moved into day two, after which the group needed to conclude with a quick "Yes" or "No" on the investment opportunity.

Joshua was assigned to review the management team with Roseboro, while hired specialists focused on the scientific, financial, and legal details. It was a precondition that Joshua be part of the due diligence team, but it was clear to him he wasn't to be relied upon, given his recent ouster.

While Roseboro looked at the curriculum vitae's of the management team and scientific staff, Joshua prodded the lawyers for information on the Golden Helix intellectual property, patents, trademarks, and copyrights. As expected the patents were strong and owned by the company. Much of the underlying technology was attributed to Dr. Amaline Currie. Before he could get into detail, Roseboro pulled him away and told him he wasn't privy to the legal or other information, since he was no longer employed by Tremont.

After some back and forth on the topic, Joshua gave up and moved to a corner table away from the main group. There, he used the time to call the seed distributor contacts Clem provided.

He dialed the first number. "Hello, is this Eric Brummer?"

"Yes. Hold on, it's hard to hear you, I'm at a plant. Let me step into my car." Joshua heard a door slam, which triggered quiet on the other side of the line. "Who's this?"

"My name is Joshua Grayson. Clem Repking from Repking Seed in Illinois gave me your name. I have a question for you about the areas where the products you represent are sold."

"Sure, shoot."

"I think your company handles several GE products. Shea Seed alfalfa, Gelden fertilizer, and Johnson & Dore field corn."

"That's right. Shea and Johnson & Dore are across the U.S.; they've taken up well. The Gelden product is only sold in the western U.S. and a few areas in the Midwest, but they're in the process of being acquired by one of the big four manufacturers. I don't know who the buyer is."

Joshua jotted a note and looked at his list. "Do you know anything about Ritaglia? It's a fungicide. Also, BioMaïs sweet corn?"

"We don't distribute Ritaglia. All I know is, it's new to the market, and it's Italian. I don't see it making a dent yet, and I think it's the company's first product introduction in the U.S. Same with the sweet corn, it's a very small, new product and isn't large enough for us to handle." There was a pause and Joshua only heard muffled dialogue. "I'm sorry, I need to run. Feel free to call me later if you have any other questions, and say hello to Clem for me."

Joshua jotted notes, and dialed the next number as he stood in front of the conference room window.

"U.S. Agri, can I help you?"

"Yes, Phil Coventry." Joshua waited half a minute before being connected. "Hello Phil, my name is Joshua Grayson. Clem Repking from the Effingham, Illinois, area gave me your name and number."

"Sure, good guy Clem. What can I do for you?"

"I understand you handle the U.S. distribution for Ritaglia and BioMaïs products, and I'm interested in which markets the products are sold. Clem didn't know."

"Both Ritaglia and BioMaïs are relatively new to the U.S. Ritaglia is a new fungicide imported from Italy. BioMaïs has two types of sweet corn, a hybrid and a GE product. It's a Belgian company. Both companies are interested in testing the market before they invest more significantly. I think they're only in a few countries, but I'm not sure outside the U.S. Our company specializes in assisting the placement of new products in the U.S."

"Where are the products sold? Can you give me specifics for each product?" Joshua flipped open is notebook and picked up his pen.

"We've started with towns across the Midwest for both companies."

"The two BioMaïs varieties of sweet corn?" Joshua heard chuckling on the other end.

"They were pretty specific about the markets they wanted to be in, sort of dipping their toes in the market, I guess."

"Is that common?"

Coventry spoke matter-of-factly. "Maybe fifty-fifty. Clem's area is obviously one, but I don't have the list of other markets handy. Can I email that information to you later today?"

* * *

Mid-afternoon, the Golden Helix CFO entered the room and surveyed the group. Graham Roseboro stood up as the she spoke.

"Mr. Grayson, Dr. Currie would like to meet with you."

Roseboro looked at the CFO with hopeful eyes but returned his gaze to the file in front of him as Joshua left the room. On the way out the door, Joshua looked over his shoulder and felt a wide grin grow as he saw the dejection on Roseboro's face.

Joshua was ushered into Dr. Currie's spacious top floor office. She was seated in a grouping of four chairs with a table in the center. Sitting next to her was a dark-skinned man with a fine, closely trimmed goatee.

"Mr. Grayson, thank you for interrupting your review. Let me introduce Mr. Hassan, our Director of Communications."

Hassan stood, and they shook hands. Joshua noticed Hassan's firm grip and piercing eyes. He spoke with what seemed to be a slightly truncated Spanish accent. "Nice to meet you, Mr. Grayson."

Joshua sized him up, as was his long-standing habit when meeting someone for the first time. Athletic build, his serious eyes indicated he was cerebral, probably a man of few words. The scars on his left hand, chin, and another inch-long scar just under his right eye signaled he'd either been around violence or was in an accident. The watch on his right wrist, scars, and a coffee cup to the left of the plate in front of him indicated he was probably a southpaw.

Dr. Currie motioned for Joshua to sit across from her, as a secretary served them coffee and tea.

"It's nice to see you again, Dr. Currie, and thank you for the investment opportunity."

Currie responded in a slow, deliberate pace. "Yes, nice to see you again as well. While you're here, I thought I'd let you know I'm very sorry to learn your cousin underwent surgery to address BDC. It's a terrible disease. Hopefully, the surgery will suffice to cure him."

Joshua tensed slightly at the unexpected dialogue. He recalled their first meeting at the conference, noting she had an odd way about her. It could be her English or the fact that she didn't interact with people much, he thought.

"Congratulations to you doctor, I understand the FDA deems BDC an emergency. I didn't think BDC was that broad in the U.S." She gave a nod in reply, and Joshua followed with a question. "How did you learn of my cousin's health issue?"

"Dr. Telling informed me. He was very concerned and wanted to make sure your cousin was taken care of if needed."

Joshua looked into her intense eyes, finding them hard to read. She had a penetrating stare and crisp, measured diction. He turned his head slightly to look at Hassan out the corner of his eye and met his stare. He was calm, with no expression.

He returned his attention to Currie. "That's certainly very much appreciated, Doctor."

She sipped her tea from a blue Delft coffee cup and held a companion platter below the cup, and squinted as if processing his response.

Joshua sipped his coffee and shifted in his chair. "Thankfully, my cousin seems to be doing fine now. I appreciate your concern. It's a strange circumstance that BDC is so much on the rise. My aunt died from it recently. Do you have any idea what the cause of the increase in the U.S. could be related to? It baffles me, but I understand from Dr. Telling you're helping the authorities try to find the source."

Currie set down her tea and leaned forward. "It's certainly perplexing. I've been actively assisting both the Brazilian government and U.S. CDC on this topic, but to date there hasn't been a link or even a clear short list of potential sources other than environmental issues, generally. I assume many other qualified people are studying the problem and looking for the source. While we're actively assisting, we're keenly focused on helping the affected people. You speak with many scientists in your line of work. What do you think could be the cause, Mr. Grayson?"

Joshua shook his head. "I don't know, it's very puzzling. Could be chemicals or the water source. Maybe the overuse of pesticide. There are many possibilities, so I don't know how the CDC and others go about isolating it. It's a very sad situation for a lot of good people. But it seems to be confined to small rural areas, as far as I can tell. Thankfully, DNA Restore has already saved a lot of lives in Brazil and will help people in the U.S."

Currie leaned back in her chair. "It's indeed challenging, but hopefully we'll find the trigger soon. It's good we could help you with this investment, which will make you very rich, I assure you." She smiled. "That's, after all, the goal of a venture capitalist, no?"

He forced a smile. "Yes, and again, thank you very much for the opportunity."

Dr. Currie stood and extended her hand. "I wish you and your family the best. I'll let you get back to work."

Joshua stood, shook her hand and Hassan's, and made his way out of the office.

Chapter 33

The following morning at Amsterdam's Schiphol airport, Joshua sat with Roseboro at a table, sipping coffee. The central plaza was busy, people shopping, buying tickets and descending down escalators to trains that would take them across Europe. Others moved through long ticket and baggage check lines. The traffic wasn't unexpected for the third busiest airport in Europe, but it was quite a transition from its original purpose: a military base built in the early 1900s.

"So, Graham, do you need me for anything else?"

"No, we're good. The data looks compelling, as expected. We'll pull it all together for a final review. Assuming it all lines up, we should meet their closing deadline." He stood, shook Joshua's hand, and added, "But stay available in case we need you to run interference for us."

Joshua stood, threw his messenger bag over his shoulder, and extended the handle of his suitcase. "I'm going to take an extra day here in Amsterdam to see the sights and clear my head...maybe find a job." He grinned, unable to resist the jab.

With a quick wave, he walked to the other side of the terminal and purchased train tickets to Antwerp and Brussels. He checked his email as he walked away from the ticket counter.

The first message was from Megyn Kaymer:

Joshua, I finally managed to speak with Dr. Pilla in Brazil. He indicated that there is high demand for participation in the DNA Restore trials there, but he'll put your cousin on the waiting list as a placeholder - using an anonymous name, as you requested. Hope all is well.

Megyn

The second was from Dr. Lange:

Joshua, I reviewed your information with much interest. I'm engaged in the GE trials here. Hope to know something, albeit very early stage, in the next months. Will keep you apprised. Take care of yourself.

Best, Martin.

Tickets in hand, he took the escalator down one level, moved into the crowd, and waited for the train. A group of students squeezed by, causing him to step back and bump into a tall blonde woman in a jean jacket. He apologized and looked down the track—nothing but dim light turning to darkness.

As it grew closer to the arrival time, people moved back and forth, positioning themselves to board: business people, small families, and others he couldn't place—college students or maybe recent graduates looking to backpack across Europe and find purpose in their lives. He smiled longingly for a moment at the freedom they enjoyed before texting Bill Gilchrist.

[Joshua] Billy, did you get the copy of the information I sent to Dr. Lange? I just finished the due diligence, and received some interesting information last night from some agri product distributors. Some products seem to generally align geographically with the BDC areas. I'm going to dig further while I'm here and one company is relatively close.

BioMaïs is based in Belgium. I'm on my way to visit the them. More later. -J"

Joshua was tucking his phone into his jacket pocket when it rang.

"Joshua…where you at?"

"Blaine. I'm waiting for a train to Antwerp."

"You remember that black truck that was followin' you? I saw it a couple times around Dad's place. Then yesterday I saw it at The Blacktop. You know that place?"

"No."

"It's a bar in Dieterich, bunch of locals drinkin' beer and shootin' pool. So, I pulled into the lot and parked. I go inside, and I spot a new guy sitting at the bar. I sit a few stools away and order a beer. He's staring at his mug and eating a burger. After a while, he looks over at me, and his eyes get big. He finishes his food quickly and starts walking out. So I follow him to the parking lot. I say, 'Hey you, that your black pickup?' He keeps on walking. But I keep after him, and he tells me to back off before I get hurt."

"Not a good idea Blaine. You really shouldn't—"

Blaine's voice grew stern. "Yeah, well, I did. I move in closer; he's a pretty big guy, you know, but heavy 'round the middle. He says something like, 'Sorry, one too many beers.' But I say, 'What's your business here?'"

"Blaine!"

Blaine grew animated and continued. "He says, 'Best you turn around and go party with your homies.' Said he don't want trouble but glad to oblige if that's what I have in mind. He moves to try and shove me, but I step to the side, put my foot in his gut, and push him onto the hood of an old Buick. I think it was old Bernie Brumleve's car. When he got up, he reached into his jacket." Blaine stopped talking.

Joshua looked at the phone to make sure there still was a connection. "Well?"

"Then I friggin' clocked him."

"You what?!"

"I knocked him on his butt, and I reached in his coat to see what he was goin' for, but I didn't see a gun or knife. He starts kickin' at me. He gets up…and we go."

"What happened?"

"He's pretty strong, you know, but slow, so I'm workin' him over good. I hit him with a left hook, it glanced off his jaw, but he fell down. When he started to stand, I landed a big uppercut to the middle of his jaw, and he fell, hit his head on the front bumper of the car, and dropped hard. He got up pretty quickly, came hard goin' for my gut, but before he could grab me, I put my arm around the guy's neck and flipped him over my hip. He didn't get up 'cause he was tryin' to catch his breath. Then the police showed up and broke it up. Guess someone called them."

Joshua spoke loudly, drawing stares from the people waiting for the train. "Why would you do that? It may make things more dangerous for the whole family!"

Blaine raised his voice. "Why? Why? 'Cause I want to send the guy a message not to mess with my family! The local deputy is a bud of mine. I figured he'd have to show some ID, and maybe that would scare him off, too."

Joshua looked down and kicked the concrete. He exhaled slowly and spoke in a contrite voice. "Okay, what happened after that?"

"The cop on duty was Clay Probst. I dated his sister for a while. He breaks things up, the sheriff comes and asks the guy for his ID, 'course he knows me. They take us into the station, and he asks what happened. The guy says it was just a misunderstanding, he doesn't want any problems, he's just passin' through town. They take down his info, give us a talkin' to, and then they let the guy go."

"Blaine, please keep your eyes open. Gotta go, talk to you soon."

Joshua dropped his head and closed his eyes. A short time later, he felt a tap on his shoulder.

"*Heer, gaat het?*"

He opened his eyes to see a young woman backpacker. "English?"

"Are you okay?"

Joshua bobbed his head and gave her a slight grin. He watched her walk away, shook his head, and answered her question aloud to no one in particular, "I don't know."

In short order the train headlight grew brighter, and as it moved forward, people positioned themselves to board. Joshua's arms felt heavy as he stepped toward the entry door with his luggage. He shivered, zipped up his winter jacket, and breathed deeply.

* * *

The trip to Antwerp, Belgium was crowded, as Joshua imagined it was every day. The car was clean and quiet. He sat in a seat near a window and watched the landscape pass for a while, flat land, farming areas, and small towns. Bored, he turned his attention to the other passengers. Virtually all his car-mates had earbuds in place and eyes focused on their phone or laptop.

Several seats behind him and across the aisle sat the tall blonde woman in the jean jacket from the station platform. He glanced her way, caught her eye before she raised her phone, and texted. A short while later, out of the periphery of his eye he thought he saw the women taking a picture in his direction, but when he turned his head, she was looking out the window. The rhythm of the ride and general fatigue eventually lulled him to sleep.

Two hours later, a voice on the speaker made an announcement in Dutch, which jarred him, and he felt panic and thought—Did I miss my stop? He felt great relief when he heard the next stop—Antwerpen Centraal.

Joshua followed a mass of people off the train. He watched the blonde lady walk in the opposite direction as he moved forward. The cool November air was refreshing as he walked toward the old, ornate, stone-clad terminal. The interior was striking, a domed ceiling with a pleasant blend of old world and modern design, quite a departure from the typical U.S. station. Just like Schiphol, he thought, Clean and well-maintained.

Shortly thereafter, he was Ubering over a bridge spanning the Scheldt River. The car moved south down Beatrijslaan along the waterway in a heavy industrial area.

The driver turned into a parking lot marked as number "23" where a two-story concrete building stood. In the lot were a few cars and several bikes.

Uncertain he was in the right place, he asked the driver to wait as he walked to the entrance. Seeing a small BioMaïs sign over the entrance door, he waved the driver on and stepped into the facility, triggering a loud ring. A tall, lithe man in army green overalls opened the door after a second ring.

"*Ja?*"

"English?" The man gave a slight nod. "I'd like to speak with the person in charge."

"That is me."

"My name is Joshua Grayson, I'm a venture capitalist from the U.S., and my company is interested in investing in new agricultural companies. I know your company because your sweet corn product is selling very well in my country. I'd like to meet the owner of BioMaïs." Joshua handed him a business card.

The man paused to read the card and put it into the large pocket at the front of his overalls. "Owner is Sweden company name of Beskära."

"So I should speak with someone there about investing in the company?"

He eyed Joshua up and down before responding, "Yes."

"Can you give me a name, and contact information so I can speak with someone at that company?"

He waved Joshua into the entry area. "Wait here."

The man turned and walked the length of the building toward a suite of offices. As he did, Joshua stepped into the production area. It was dimly lit and quiet, with a fresh sweet smell in the air. The only sound he heard was the echo of a machine working in the distance. Shelves were filled with burlap bags, and leaning against the far wall was a long row of pallets.

A couple minutes later, he turned to explore further and faced the man he'd met earlier.

The man scowled. "You were to wait at the entrance!"

"I'm sorry. While I'm here, I just wanted to see the facility. You don't have a lot of activity here."

"It is the down season now. Come, we don't have visitors here. It is dangerous." He pulled Joshua by his coat sleeve before letting go as the two moved forward.

At the front door, Joshua was handed a Beskära business card. He scanned it, only one name—H.M. Krupp. "What's your name?"

"Hugo."

"Hugo, another reason I want to speak with someone is because there seems to be a high rate of cancer where your sweet corn is sold in the U.S. So, I want to alert someone in your company of that situation so it can be looked into. Have you heard that before?"

The man pushed Joshua out the door. "Our products are inspected and approved by many, many people."

As the door slammed shut, Joshua added loudly, "I'll call Mr. Krupp, but please make others in the company aware."

Joshua stepped into the lot, phone and a train ticket to Brussels in hand.

* * *

Inside the Belgian Federal Public Service Economy building at Vooruitgangstraat 50, Brussels, Joshua took in the old stately interior: stone walls, globed ceilings, and finely-detailed woodwork. Reviewing a building map, he veered to a hallway on his right, climbed one flight of stairs, entered an office, and approached a lady in a bright yellow dress behind the counter.

"Hello. Is this where I can get information on corporate records?"

The woman smiled. "Yes."

Joshua took his Rawlings leather messenger bag from his shoulder and withdrew a manila folder. "I was able to check on the Business Hub Database online and found the company I was looking for, but it didn't give information on the ownership of the company. Can I find that information here?" He handed the printout to the lady.

She flipped through the papers. "Perhaps, but there may not be more information than is in the database. The manager is often a shareholder, but that may not be the case."

"I understand I may be able to see a copy of the articles of association for the company."

"I can look to see if it's available. BioMaïs, SA, correct?"

"Yes, please."

"This may take some time. You may have a seat or come back later." She pointed to a row of chairs against the near wall.

The lady returned in fifteen minutes with three pages in hand. Joshua met her at the counter. "That's all?"

"Unfortunately so." She handed him a copy of the corporate articles of association and motioned to a series of computer terminals. "You can use the computer terminals if you want further information on any EU companies."

Joshua flipped through the pages and found one owner, Beskära Holdings AB, a Swedish corporation. He sat at one of the terminals and searched for Beskära Holdings AB, which turned up the name of a manager, H.M. Krupp. The same as the Belgian entity but little else, and the same name on the business card he was handed in Antwerp. Frustrated, he approached the lady again.

"Is there any way to obtain information on ownership? I placed a call for the manager Krupp earlier, but it was a law office."

"Unfortunately, there are no obligations or authorizations required for an EU mother company like this Beskära Holdings unless it had regulated activities, like a bank. Company privacy is protected very closely in the EU."

"One last question: Can you give me the names of two or three local law firms that are most active in incorporating companies? Preferably in this building."

A few minutes later he was on the third floor. Tired, he stopped for an espresso at a counter in a small café. He swiveled his head as he sipped his espresso and watched people in business attire entering offices or walking in small groups toward the elevator.

On the far side of the floor, a tall blonde woman caught his attention. He slung his bag over his shoulder, and, luggage in hand, began to walk toward her as she reviewed a listing of floor occupants.

He spoke loudly as he moved. "Hello! Are you following me?"

Joshua picked up his pace as the woman turned and quickly walked down the nearby staircase, a jean jacket tied around her waist. Joshua ran to catch her. He moved quickly down the staircase, banging his luggage into the wall before dropping it and having to stop to retrieve it. On the ground floor he ran out the main entrance of the building. She was nowhere in sight.

He retraced his steps to the reception area of the law firm of Peeters & Maes, sat, and put pressure on his temples to sooth a tension headache.

This is real, he thought.

Twenty minutes later, he stood to leave as one of the lawyers, a middle-aged man with long, copper brown, slicked back hair and rimless glasses, walked into the area.

"I'm Marc Peeters, how can I help you?"

"I'm looking to find the ultimate ownership of a Belgian company by the name of BioMaïs. I haven't been able to find it online or looking at the articles of association. I'm wondering if I could engage your firm to track down the ownership."

"Sure, that's possible, but I have to tell you the EU is not yet as transparent as, for example, the U.S. But perhaps we can find out more information through our legal network."

"Fair enough. You're hired."

Chapter 34

The KLM Airbus landed at Boston Logan International Airport eight hours after taking off from Brussels. Sluggish from the trip, Joshua slowly navigated immigration, baggage claim, customs, and exited the building, where he found a dark blue BMW waiting for him. He opened the rear passenger door, threw in his luggage, and plopped in the front seat.

"Hey, Billy, thanks for picking me up."

Bill Gilchrist eyed him and pulled away from the curb toward route 1A South. "You look beat. Let's get you home, and we can debrief on everything if you feel up to it."

Joshua sank down in his seat. "You got the file I sent you?"

"Yep. How's your cousin?"

"He seems to be doing okay…" Joshua's voice faded as he composed himself. "He has a wonderful family."

"I want to help where I can, whatever you need."

After the twenty-minute ride, Joshua picked up Ernie from a neighbor, and he and Gilchrist sat in the living room of Joshua's flat. They walked through the materials he'd compiled. Joshua stood and paced in front of the large windows as he spoke.

"It seems like I've touched a nerve somewhere, given the surveillance by the man in the black pick-up, the blonde lady following me in Belgium, and I believe someone hacked into my cell phone, and maybe my computer, or at least my email. So while I have a new phone and laptop, I'm still concerned."

"Yeah, you mentioned it in your email to Dr. Lange…Seriously?"

Joshua stepped into the kitchen, returned with two bottles of beer, and sat across from Gilchrist continuing his thoughts. "So I've learned there are other rural towns in the Midwest with high growth in BDC. Based on what I know, the towns have environmental issues that could have caused the cancer. But it's not plausible to me that multiple discrete locations had the same experience within, say, a year.

"I also had the well water in Bishop Creek tested, and the larger town of Effingham did the same, and both came back negative." Joshua paused and sipped his beer. "Then I started to think more about GE crops and related products. Could they be the source? GE products have been around for a long time with no issues. Then I went through the new GE product introductions in my family's area over the last four years and identified new products that were introduced in the last year and a half. Coincidence?"

Gilchrist set his empty bottle on the coffee table between them, "Do you truly believe a new crop could be the source? They get screened, don't they? If there was an issue, the company would be basically out of business…who would ever trust them?"

Joshua pondered the questions as he finished his beer. "They do vet new products, and the history is good. So I may be chasing the wind, but I asked Dr. Lange to put together some animal trials to test three of the local new GE plants. One a sweet corn, another a fertilizer that seems to be a high focus, and the last a new field corn product which is in most of the food we eat.

"While I was in Europe for the due diligence on Golden Helix, I took the opportunity to go to Belgium, where the GE sweet corn company BioMaïs is based. I was able to get information on the companies, including ownership for the GE field corn and fertilizer, but not the sweet corn." He yawned loudly and rubbed the back of his neck. "I didn't get a great reception. But they didn't have any business people there. Actually, I thought the guy I met was going to get physical."

Gilchrist leaned forward, wide-eyed. "You're kidding, right?"

Joshua shrugged, leaned back on the couch, and put his feet on the coffee table. "I definitely wasn't wanted there, but like I said, it was a workplace, kind of a warehouse, not the main office. At least it didn't seem like it." He yawned. "Have you ever heard of the term pharming—p-h-a-r-m-i-n-g?" Gilchrist gave him a questioning stare, prompting Joshua to continue. "Basically, it's GE plants designed to deliver pharmaceuticals. So when people eat the plants, they're getting medicine, too. The idea is to be able to bring better health to people cheaply, particularly those in impoverished areas. Think about growing fields of corn or wheat that can deliver vaccines to people in Africa. Inexpensive and something that can be more broadly available in countries around the world.

"I discussed it with a professor at Washington University in St. Louis. He gave me pages of research on the subject, and in one of the last pages I stumbled across information that the Golden Helix CEO's husband, who died years ago, seemed to be heavy into research around pharming. He was focused on developing an edible vaccine for Hepatitis B and HIV. But I spoke with a professor at the Karolinska Institute in Stockholm who said, in the end, the vaccines didn't amount to anything. The professor also mentioned that he left the institute with Amaline Currie shortly after they were married. Apparently, the professor never heard from them, and they didn't publish any of their work."

"I'm not sure what that means, or if it matters?"

Joshua rubbed his eyes. "I just thought it was interesting their backgrounds were similar. Dr. Currie's husband was focused on pharming instead of something more…" He searched for a word. "Let's say 'traditional,' like his wife." He leaned back against the couch. "Sorry…I think I just need a good night's sleep. My brain's just jumbled."

"What about Dr. Lange? Weren't you speaking with him about all of this? What does he think?"

"I've only sent him the same information package I sent you and also the products for the trials. He thinks given the quick trigger of the cancer, a limited clinical trial on mice or swine might give a quick read on whether there are potential issues."

"This is incredibly serious stuff. I mean…" Gilchrist stood and walked to the window, looking down at the quiet street below as his voice faded. "Joshua, we have to bring it to the authorities immediately. If you're wrong, fine; no harm, no foul. If it's true, we need quick action to stop people from dying. Why don't you let me pull this together with what you already sent me. Also, I'll follow up with the Belgian law firm on the BioMaïs ownership; just give them my number. You need to watch your back and try to get back to a regular routine. What about the other GE crops? Do we need to pursue additional information?"

"I think we're okay with the other companies for now. Billy, I appreciate your support, but you don't need to get involved with this potential goose chase. I have time on my hands, you're a busy attorney."

Gilchrist moved to the couch. "Remember, I'm your double play partner…"

Joshua stood across the coffee table and fist bumped him.

"We're still a great double play combination, Josh. I want to help you; it means a lot to me. You focus on your cousin and let me do a little work here. I'll go to the authorities and take you and your family out of the equation. You should go back to your usual routine."

Joshua messaged his head with the palms of his hands. "This is moving fast. Feels like it's about to explode."

* * *

The following day, Joshua looked out a window in an office nook, bordered on two sides by mahogany shelves filled with law books. He looked down on Boston Common as Bill Gilchrist spoke on a speaker phone with the Belgian law firm. With the holiday season around the corner, he saw park workers stringing lights among the trees and a Salvation Army Santa ringing a bell on a corner. Joshua spent a lot of time in the park thinking through problems like the one he currently faced.

The history of the place ran through his mind…the oldest city park in the U.S. dating back to the early 1600s. A place where George Washington and John Adams celebrated the country's independence. A hotbed of the abolition movement in the nineteenth century and civil rights movement with Martin Luther King, Jr., drawing a large crowd in the mid-1960s. Fifty acres of history. Colonial to present day. It always inspired him. His thoughts triggered an adrenaline spike and warm sense of calm.

Gilchrist's voice brought him back to the conversation at hand. "So, you aren't able to find the ultimate beneficial owners of BioMaïs?"

"That's correct, Mr. Gilchrist. What we've found is a trail of holding company owners over multiple countries, but we haven't been able to find the names of any individual owners of those holding companies."

Joshua turned to Gilchrist and threw his hands up in the air.

Gilchrist leaned forward and hovered over the speaker. "Let me ask you this: Is it legally required to disclose the individual owners at some ultimate level?"

"Mr. Gilchrist, the legal landscape in the EU is changing to provide more transparency, but persons owning entities can still easily remain hidden by setting up trusts, using jurisdictions that don't require that disclosure, or having proxies involved. Those practices have been in place for many decades, even centuries, and will not change overnight."

He looked across the table at Joshua and shrugged. "So, in your view, it would be useless for Mr. Grayson to continue this search, is that correct?"

"Yes. We don't think it's a good use of his money to continue."

Joshua interjected. "Gentlemen, thank you for being honest. But if money was not a concern, do you think I'd be able to find out the ultimate ownership?"

"Unfortunately, no. If someone doesn't want to be known, it's perfectly legal and possible to avoid being known. Based on our research and experience, we believe that's the case here."

Joshua scratched his head. "I figured as much when I tried to reach H.M. Krupp on the Beskära Holdings business card I was given. He's an attorney at a law office in Stockholm. In your opinion, is what you found common? I mean, not only no name disclosures, but the use of an array of multiple holding companies across countries?"

"Mr. Grayson, the Dutch have a saying, 'In the land of the blind, the one-eyed man is king!' I am not a king, but the clear intention here is to keep ownership unknown. Keep everyone blind."

"Nothing on the Swedish company?"

"You mean Crop Holdings? No, nothing."

Joshua shook his head. "No, it had another name."

"Sorry, yes, Beskära. That's Swedish for 'crop.' I speak some Swedish, so I translated it in my head."

After they closed the call, Joshua stood and walked back to the window and silently panned the area. Gilchrist came alongside him and did the same.

He turned to Gilchrist. "Crop Holdings; makes sense, I guess." As Joshua spoke, his phone chirped. He picked it up off the table.

Gilchrist watched him shake his head. "What's up?"

"A text from Roseboro. They funded the deal with Golden Helix."

"Cool, you should be getting a nice wire transfer."

"He sent a link to the press release. It's full of Roseboro's name, and even Cochran is quoted, and he wasn't involved. What a piece of work." Joshua looked down, his slight smile turning into a frown.

"Let it go, Joshua. Let's get back to work pulling this summary together. Maybe the Feds will be able to make headway on the ownership piece. Have you heard anything further from Dr. Lange?"

"Spoke with him last night for half an hour."

"Did you talk about the information you put together?"

Joshua rolled his head, wincing occasionally. "Yeah, he received the information, and I told him we're putting together a packet to send to the authorities. We also talked about my instinct that someone's watching me. He didn't actually laugh at me, but he thought it better to be careful and on guard in any event. I asked him to put together a summary of the trials he's doing and any initial findings. He said he'd send it to both of us today so it can be included in the packet."

"Perfect! Let's get the packet together."

* * *

Late afternoon, the men sat at the conference table piled with papers, books, computers, potato chips, sandwiches, and empty paper coffee cups.

Gilchrist saved the document on his laptop and announced, "I think that's it."

Joshua paused before taking a bite of a stale half-eaten tuna sandwich. "Can you check the patents for BioMaïs in the U.S.? I tried online, but it was challenging to navigate."

"Sure, I can take a look if we can identify them. Why?"

"I'm interested in knowing who the owners of the patents are and seeing if there's any useful information, like links to the patents of Dr. Currie's deceased husband." Gilchrist made a note. Joshua sat back in his chair and rubbed his eyes with the palms of his hands. "It's been a long week. What do you think of the case, Counselor?"

"Incredible job getting this far. I think it's compelling, particularly for safety-oriented organizations like the FDA and CDC. I've also contacted the FBI and gave them an overview of what we're doing. They took it very seriously and want to meet on Friday."

"The FBI?! Why would they need to be involved?"

"If this is true, it's criminal and spans multiple states. Also, it could be considered a crime against the United States, or terrorism, all of which are within the bureau's remit. If they take it on, it's a virtual guarantee they'll get to the bottom of it all and you can offload it. They have big resources and smart agents. I'm planning to send this off overnight mail today to all the appropriate agencies once we get Dr. Lange's input."

He looked at Joshua, slumped in a chair. "You forget about this now. I'll take it from here. Get a good night's sleep, and I'll see you at my place tomorrow for Thanksgiving."

Joshua stared out the window, his mind moving from his Aunt to Jake, and ultimately to a somber notion…Maybe we're chasing an illusion.

Chapter 35

The day after Thanksgiving, Joshua and Bill Gilchrist sat at a table in the large conference room of Gilchrist & Girard, PLLC, along with another attorney. The office was largely vacant, given the long holiday weekend.

Gilchrist put a large coffee in front of Joshua and dropped a box of Kane's donuts on the table. "The meeting should be straightforward. We've added disclaimers noting we don't claim all the information we're supplying to the FBI and other agencies to be accurate, and we're sharing it with them as we believe it's in the public interest." He motioned toward his colleague sitting next to him. "I've asked our newest attorney Nancy, to sit with us and take notes. Anything new to discuss before the meeting? Any new developments?"

Joshua reached into the box and plucked out a Maine Blueberry donut, set it on a napkin, and turned to Gilchrist. "I did speak with Dr. Telling, the lead of the U.S. DNA Restore trials, just before my trip to Amsterdam. He told me a few of the U.S. trials are getting closer to starting, but not all. It's not clear whether the area where my family lives will be part of the trials. He expects it'll be a few weeks before everything's settled." Joshua crossed his arms.

Gilchrist wiped jelly off his lips with his tongue. "I guess that's normal protocol?"

"I guess. Selfishly I'm anxious for them to bring it to the Bishop Creek area."

Joshua's attention was drawn to the adjacent lobby, where two people entered the office. The first person was a barrel-chested man in a worn brown sport jacket with patches on the elbows, and the other was a younger woman in a blue suit, following closely behind. Gilchrist's associate met them and ushered them into the conference room, the man's gun visible in a holster under his jacket as he walked.

"Special Agent Dan Webber," the man said in a loud, bass voice, shook hands, provided business cards, turned, and pointed to his colleague. "Agent Hawickhorst, fresh out of Quantico."

Webber moved directly to questions. "Mr. Grayson, to lead off, I want to thank you for the information you've compiled for us. You've pieced together quite a diverse set of information, which, taken as a whole, is very interesting and potentially alarming. I'd like to start by asking you a few questions." The room was silent as he paused to open a notebook and find the appropriate page. "First of all, what caused you to believe there might be some relationship between locally grown GE field corn or sweet corn…or," he flipped over a page of paper in his file, "GE fertilizer, and the incidence of BDC being experienced in some Midwest farming towns?"

Joshua took a deep breath, and made eye contact with Webber. "When I learned of the high cancer rate in the area, it struck me as very odd. Things change slowly in the small Illinois farming community where my family lives, and tradition is sacred. I have an inquisitive nature, and I couldn't shake wondering what was causing the unusual growth of BDC in the area. Later, I found there was at least one similar issue in another small farming area in Kansas that started at roughly the same time, which I believe is very improbable. That drove me to consider environmental issues, like water sources, but again, those sources also seemed improbable. So, I dug deeper. I'm a venture capitalist focused on the biotech space, so I picked the brains of several scientists and others. My thoughts and findings are in the information we sent you."

Agent Webber grunted. "How did you find out about the other area? I missed that."

"I heard it from a scientist I know. He heard it from a contact in Kansas and made me aware. Then I confirmed it with a contact at the CDC."

Webber turned to Agent Hawickhorst. "We'll need those contacts." He shifted his stare back to Joshua. "Why did you send the information when you did, and not earlier?"

Joshua looked across the table at Webber's penetrating stare, accentuated by his green eyes and bushy brown eyebrows. "I developed as much as I could, shared it with Mr. Gilchrist for his thoughts, and we concluded the information was compelling enough to share with the authorities. Also, I hit roadblocks. We thought the authorities could navigate more quickly and speed up the process if needed."

"You actually didn't answer my question. Why not earlier? After all, people are dying."

Joshua sat back in his seat as Gilchrist leaned forward to reply. "Agent Webber, the information here is very disparate and—"

Webber raised his hand to Gilchrist, but his eyes didn't move from Joshua. "Counselor, I would like Mr. Grayson to answer."

Joshua sat tall and raised his voice despite Gilchrist holding up a hand for him to refrain. "Because it took time to accumulate the information, and I'm still not sure it all means anything."

"Fair enough. So where are you now in terms of your line of thought?"

Gilchrist intervened. "Agent Webber, for the record, Mr. Grayson is not making any accusations here; he is simply following the data and—"

Webber looked at the attorney and raised both hands. "Mr. Gilchrist, I just want to understand Mr. Grayson's thinking."

Gilchrist looked at Joshua and gestured to continue with a wave of his hand.

"Honestly, I'm not sure. I've been working to try and identify if it's any of the newer GE products. A scientist acquaintance of mine, Dr. Lange, is running a small set of clinical trials on three of the products in his lab in Research Triangle Park. I believe that was noted in the information you received. He's attempting to determine if any of those products produce cancer in mice." Joshua saw Webber was ready to ask another question and spoke first. "Of course we'll let you know the results."

That prompted a slight grin on Webber's face and caused him to review his notes. He raised his eyes to Joshua. "So what are your information gaps here?"

Joshua began to feel a bit of a kindred spirit toward Webber perceiving, the man is experienced, has the law behind him and appears to be a no-nonsense fighter. *This is the opportunity we need to determine the source.*

He leaned toward him, elbows on the table. "A couple of things. First is finding the ownership of BioMaïs, one of the seed suppliers. I tried to determine the owner but was stymied, no issues with the other producers. Also, it would be interesting to understand the patent estates for the GE products. Those areas may be quite challenging because of the international nature of the companies and fragmented requirements around public disclosure. It's a complex puzzle, and information isn't always readily accessible. For your information, there are other GE products that aren't being tested. Those will be next, but the animal trials would need to be designed."

Webber looked up from his notes, sat tall, and raised his chest, then gave Joshua a slight wink. "We'll be able to get answers. But we don't want to spend time chasing something that's half-cocked."

Gilchrist's eyes opened wide as he quickly responded, "Half-cocked? Are you kidding?"

"Whoa, whoa, whoa. Relax, Counselor. I'm not saying this is half-cocked. It's our job to test the hypotheses to make sure we're not wasting time and resources. In this case, we wanted to meet immediately because the information here is well enough developed to get our attention and we don't want to lose any time moving forward, given the stakes."

Both sides were quiet until Agent Hawickhorst looked up from her notes. "Mr. Grayson, we have a contact at the CDC, Dr. Rioux. We'd like to have him speak with Dr. Lange on this matter. Can you arrange that?" Joshua agreed and scribbled a note.

Gilchrist spoke in a moderated tone. "Agent Webber, before we move any further, I need to raise a serious issue mentioned in the materials. That is, the well-being of Mr. Grayson and his family. We have reason to believe they're being watched and potentially at risk. We need assurance they'll be protected."

"Yes. We need to take ownership from here."

Joshua crossed his arms and rubbed each one to ward off a chill. He looked at Webber and lifted his chin. "What does that mean exactly? What's going to be done to protect my family? We need to treat it like the risk is very real. We've seen a black pick-up truck with Missouri plates around my uncle's farm. My cousin had a run in with the driver and the police were involved. I've had some unusual issues with my phone, so I bought a burner phone. Also with emails. So, there's something going on here."

"Understood. Believe it or not, we have a bureau office in Effingham, Illinois, covering the south-central region of Illinois. I'm going to make them aware, have them check out the farmhouse, and meet your uncle in the next day or two. They'll also connect with the local police."

Joshua pressed his palms to his eyes and spoke. "Good, thank you. They should also meet with my cousin Jake and his wife at their house. They have two little kids."

Webber cleared his throat. "We'll have the agents meet with them and do a security check there. If anyone feels like they're in any danger, they can call day or night. The local agents will check in regularly until things become clear."

After the agents left, Gilchrist looked at Joshua, slumped in his chair. "Are you okay? You look beat."

"Billy, I don't know how we got here. It may be a small possibility, but we're talking about the lives of my family being at risk because of my pushing the buttons of a lot of people. What if someone gets hurt? What if I'm just plain wrong?"

Later that evening Joshua laid in bed and opened an email from Phil Coventry.

Joshua - sorry I'm late with this information. Below are the areas where the BioMaïs GE sweet corn is sold (first round):

- North Platte, Nebraska

- Salina, Kansas

- Davenport, Iowa

- Ste. Genevieve, Missouri

- Faribault, Minnesota

- Effingham, Illinois

- Fond du Lac, Wisconsin

- Marietta, Ohio

He forwarded the message to Bill Gilchrist.

* * *

The next morning, on a perfect late-November day, Joshua finished a run through the streets of the Back Bay, slowing his pace occasionally to appreciate the Christmas decorations. There was no wind, providing welcome relief from the recent gloomy weather. It had always been his favorite time of the year, reminding him of his parents and their seasonal rituals. He thought of them especially around Christmas, as he decorated the tree in his condo using family ornaments passed down over generations.

He bought a peppermint latte from a local food cart and sipped it as he walked the last leg to his condo. For the first time in months, he felt refreshed, more optimistic, and had uninterrupted sleep. Transitioning the investigative work to the FBI provided a satisfying feeling, as if a large weight was lifted off his shoulders. He breathed easily and slowed his pace, nodding at neighbors and wearing a sincere smile.

After a long, warm shower, he dressed and fed Ernie, who kept rubbing up against his leg. He stepped to his turntable, which he hadn't played for several months, and put on an Alice Coltrane jazz album. Halfway through side one, his phone vibrated in his pocket.

"Hi, Uncle Pete! How are things?"

He heard Pete clear his throat and take a couple of deep breaths. His voice was shaky and somber. "I want you to know Jake's been admitted to the hospital. He wasn't feeling good at work, so I picked him up and brought him in." He paused. "They're running tests now…and we're praying." There was soft sniffling on the other end. "I was hoping to bring him home after seeing the doctor, but they needed to keep him at the hospital. Shelby's devastated. Blaine's going to bring her to the hospital as soon as her parents arrive to watch the kids. Jesse and Cole are on their way."

"Hang tight. I'll catch the next plane out." He hung up and called Megyn Kaymer, it went to voicemail. "Hi Megyn, it's Joshua. I heard the news that Jake's back in the hospital. I'm catching a plane as soon as I can. Please call me when you get a chance. Did you hear from your contact?"

He found an afternoon flight, and on the way to the airport called Blaine. The voice on the other end wasn't as animated as usual.

"Hey, cuz."

"Your dad called. How are Shelby and the kids?"

"Shelby's putting up a good front, but dang, she looks like she's a sliver from cracking. The kids are crying a bit, but Shelby's mom and dad just got here, so they're distracted now. We're headin' over to the hospital."

Joshua felt the weight return. He shifted quickly back to action mode and paced back and forth as he spoke. "Blaine, listen. You're going to need to trust me. We need to be very careful. Do you still have someone following you?"

"Don't think so. I'm watchin'. It's pretty easy to spot someone around here, 'cause there ain't much traffic, you know."

"Okay, keep your eyes open. You handled the security at the farm and at Jake's place, motion sensors around the perimeter, doors and windows, right?"

"I called in my police buds; they said we don't need it…but yeah, it's taken care of…waste of money. You must like to throw away bucks."

Joshua found a center seat on a two-thirty afternoon flight to St. Louis. As he sat in his seat awaiting final boarding to be complete, his phone buzzed twice.

[Dr. Kaymer] Just heard. Yes!

[Dr. Lange] Trial update. Some early deaths occurring with the sweet corn. No other issues at this time, but it's early. I'll provide an update for the authorities. Good call Joshua. This could save lives.

Chapter 36

Early evening a midnight-blue S Class Mercedes with darkened windows pulled into the parking lot of a nondescript, two-story concrete building. Out of the rear door stepped a woman, cloaked in a black scarf.

She moved quickly from the car to the entry door of the building, which sat in the shadow of a large Monsanto agricultural manufacturing facility on the outskirts of Antwerp, along the west side of the Scheldt River. Above the door, a small sign read BioMaïs, within a purple outline of an ear of corn.

The place was quiet as she stepped inside, the workers having punched out hours earlier. In a second-floor conference room, a tall, wiry man wearing khakis and a light blue windbreaker was waiting for her. They sat across from each other at the conference table, where she flipped through the pages of a large black binder.

"Production looks good, Hugo. Is that the case?"

"Yes. Seed production is strong for both the maize F1 hybrid and GE seeds. We are ready to start building inventory for China, awaiting your approval. Do you want any changes in distribution in Brazil or the U.S.?"

Amaline Currie continued to leaf through the reports, her head still cloaked in the scarf. "Keep the GE and hybrid seeds selling in the current ratio and only in the same markets for now. Keep the prices at the same level so we can continue to get strong sales penetration." Her eyes narrowed. "Do you foresee any problems in doubling production in the next months?"

"Not at this time, Doctor. If it changes, I'll contact you immediately."

"We'll focus on China soon, so prepare to start production in anticipation of selling in the areas I provided to you."

"Yes, Doctor. The current prices are quite low in Brazil and the U.S. and will cause us to continue to lose money."

"No matter, in the end the money will be extraordinary, and you will be highly rewarded." She rose from the table. "Are the most recent Brazil and U.S. random GE seed samples in the laboratory as I requested?"

He stood and replied, "*Ja.*"

Currie walked to the end of the hallway, unlocked the laboratory door, and entered. The man remained in the conference room, quietly focused on paperwork.

In the lab, she found two sets of seed samples, set them in front of her, and retrieved a container marked "GE NewZoet Original," setting it alongside the respective sample seed counterpart. On a nearby laptop, she entered her pseudonym username and password, which gave her access to a testing log.

She prepared samples of random seeds from the current batch as well as the original GE seed and started the near-infrared spectrometer to analyze and determine if there was any variation between the original and most recently produced seeds. Quality control was paramount in her mind, providing consistency and predictability.

As the machine worked through its testing cycles, Currie withdrew a worn, black Moleskine notebook from her leather satchel. Clipped inside the front cover was a black-and-white picture of her husband with dark long hair in a white lab coat sitting in front of a large microscope with a wide, engaging smile. Turning the picture over, she read and re-read the words on the reverse side:

"Amaline, together we will achieve scientific greatness and the riches that come with it! It is our destiny.

To us, my love, Anton"

She paged through the book, scanning text and illustrations before stopping midway at a page dated over a decade prior:

October 23 - my findings are confirmed that plants including food crops can be modified via insertional mutagenesis. Need to test what the implications are for interaction of those foods with genes of the animal that ingests the crop, including human. Exciting! To be further tested.

It was the last written page in the notebook. Currie kissed the picture, closed the book, and tucked it in her bag. She stared at the NIS machine, as if hypnotized, until it completed the last testing cycle, whereupon the soft hum stopped.

She read the results showing comparative numbers, then added them to the log with a brief note, "no variation," before retracing her steps toward the entrance door.

As she passed the conference room and started down the stairs, the man stepped out of the room. "Madam."

Currie turned and saw the tall man walking toward her. "I forgot to tell you we had a visitor stop in recently, asking about the GE NewZoet product, and wanted me to tell the manager of the business there's a high cancer rate where it's sold in the U.S. so it can be investigated."

"Who was this visitor?"

He gave her the business card. She read it and glowered. Her eyes narrowed, and her lips tightened. She turned, moved quickly down the stairs, and left the building, phone in hand. The Mercedes accelerated out of the parking lot, starting the two-hour return to Amsterdam. Currie stared out the window and watched a barge slowly make its way up the river toward the North Sea as the sun fell off the horizon.

* * *

Early the next morning in her Golden Helix office, Dr. Currie sat in an armchair across from Anas Hassan and inspected her fingernails.

Hassan ran his fingers across his goatee. "How did the testing go? All is well?"

"Yes. The testing was fine, no variance." She added, "Anton was correct. The GE protestors are voices crying out in the wilderness. No one is listening. New ideas are protested as they challenge norms, but over time the protests fade. They always fade. The ideas become accepted, silently in most cases, and the norms and line of what's acceptable shifts. The majority become tolerant."

"That is so. He would be proud that you're continuing his science and fulfilling his dreams."

Currie stood and moved to the window and took in the blue sky and growing daylight. "It's my life mission. Anton's dream for us was scientific fame and the rewards that come with it. He was poor and never fulfilled his dream. I'm making it come true." She turned toward Hassan, jaw clenched. "But now we meet an obstacle that must be eliminated."

"*Sí.* Grayson is still searching for information. Now we know he visited BioMaïs in person after the due diligence, and also the EU business registry in Brussels. The investment offer did not dissuade or distract him."

"What do you make of it?"

"The local man in the farming town in the Illinois state indicates that Grayson is living at a farmhouse when he is there. We had access to emails and phone calls but that has slowed. He had the well water from the farm tested, which was reported to be safe to drink by local authorities. He has asked for distribution data on the sweet corn product. He has called Krupp for ownership information. He has been most days in Boston with his attorney, perhaps looking for a job, but taken together, this appears unusual."

Currie sat silently at her desk, eyes staring straight ahead. "He's obviously still working his way through sources that might be the cause for the local cancer."

"*Sí*. He is hunting."

Hassan withdrew a bound dossier from his messenger bag and gently placed it in front of her. Currie opened the title-less report. Across the top of the first page read "Joshua P. Grayson."

The summary page provided a range of information:

- Age: thirty-six years
- Birthplace: Chicago, Illinois (U.S.A.)
- Current address: 1226 Boylston St., Boston, MA (U.S.A.)

- Occupation: Co-founding Partner of Tremont Ventures (Note: he has left this company - Press Release, Appendix C)
- Family: Parents deceased (traffic accident)
- Marital Status: single
- Education:
  - Boston College (B.S. Biochemistry) plus
  - Tufts University School of Medicine - 2 years
  - Tufts University (M.B.A.)

She flipped through the other pages of the report: photographs of Joshua, his parents, his Boston condo, the Tremont offices, multiple pictures of the Bishop Creek farmhouse, multiple drone shots of the Grayson farm and general area, business associates, a credit bureau report, a rough personal net worth statement based upon bank and investment accounts and real estate data, copies of press releases, and articles that included his name.

Hassan remained expressionless, his finely-shaved goatee framing a small mouth.

"You have done well on short notice. As usual."

The man gave a slight bow.

"He was with a fat American at the recent conference, and they were interested in investing in Golden Helix. Chasing wealth." She grimaced and raised her voice. "I gave him the opportunity to invest and get rich, to get his job back. But he did not stop. Why? Money is the American's god! I don't understand.

"I have invested everything to make Anton's dream come true. I will not let him take what is ours. We are so close to untold riches and scientific glory. It is time to eliminate the threat. We may have waited too long."

Currie closed her eyes and rubbed her birthmark. "We cannot afford for him to continue." She stood, stared at Hassan, rage in her eyes. "Take care of him."

Hassan picked a piece of lint from his suit, and left the office, speaking into his phone.

* * *

After a quick lunch, Dr. Currie sat at her desk, reading a single-page memo, perfectly placed in the center of her black desk pad. She was interrupted by a knock on the door and swung her head toward the sound as it cracked open and a pair of eyes appeared around the edge.

"Excuse me, Madam. I've been instructed to inform you that you have received a call from the U.S. FDA. They said it was urgent."

Her eyes like slits, her brow wrinkled, she barked, "Get me telling immediately!"

The door closed quickly. Currie rose from her desk and walked to the window, where she pressed her forehead against the cool glass and closed her eyes.

Minutes later, the assistant's eyes reappeared. "Dr. Telling is on the phone. Would you like me to put him on the speakerphone for you, Madam?"

She turned and shooed him away with the back of her hand, walked to the desk, and picked up the receiver. "Telling, the FDA has called here to speak with me. You're to handle all these matters. We've provided them all the information they require, correct?"

Dr. Telling spoke defensively. "Yes, of course! They have all the information and have given us Fast Track approval for emergency use and trials. I've sent you a copy of the approval. We've also been communicating with the FDA weekly as we move forward on the trials."

"If we are cooperating fully, why are they calling me?"

"I have no idea why they would call you."

She tapped the index finger of her right hand on the desk. "What's your recommendation? Should I speak with them?"

"I would suggest yes. You should be very responsive. I can join you if you wish."

In a frustrated tone, she dictated, "You call them to find out the reason and resolve this."

"With all due respect, Dr. Currie, I speak with them regularly. If you don't want to damage the relationship, I believe you should personally return the call. This is a critical market."

She stood at her desk, rubbed her birthmark, and provided a guttural response. "*Jij stomme idioot van een man. Ik zal je kont afvuren!*" [You stupid idiot of a man. I'll fire your rear end] She followed with a text to Hassan. "Need you to return this afternoon."

* * *

Later that afternoon, Dr. Currie paced back and forth behind her desk. After several minutes, she stopped, clenched her jaw, and turned to Anas Hassan, who sat quietly and perfectly still in a cushioned armchair in front of her desk.

"I spoke with Telling. He returned the call to the FDA. They insist on speaking only with me. He was told it wasn't about DNA Restore, but other scientific questions they wish to know my thoughts on. I am scheduled to speak with them shortly…I've been consulting with the CDC. They know my thoughts and recommendations. What do you make of this?"

After a lingering pause, Hassan raised his head and angled it slightly. "It seems to be odd, unless perhaps the CDC and FDA don't share information or communicate well. If they do share information, as you expect, I don't understand why you'd need to be involved if Dr. Telling is the primary contact with them."

Currie's voice vacillated. "I'm concerned." She found herself in an uncommon position, a place of uncertainty. "I want you to sit with me on the call. Would this be related to Grayson?"

"He has gone to the farmer's house and will be taken care of in short order. The man we have at the farm town area hasn't seen anything unusual. His orders are to contact me immediately if he does."

Currie remained silent for a few moments. "Do it very quickly. I believe I must speak with the FDA people; we cannot afford to hurt that relationship and jeopardize what is due us."

"*Sí*. But do not start DNA Restore trials in the hospital near the farm relatives of Grayson, to maintain leverage if needed. We may need to draw him out."

She sat her desk, put the phone on speaker mode, and dialed into the scheduled call with the FDA. Hassan moved his chair closer, his elbows on the desk, hands clasped.

A beep opened the call. "Hello, this is Dr. Armond Rioux, representing the FDA. Dr. Currie and Dr. Telling, are you both on the call?"

Telling cleared his throat. "Yes, we are."

"Great. I'm here with a couple of associates who're focused on attempting to identify the root cause of the increasing frequency of BDC in the U.S. Dr. Currie, there's some thought that a genetically modified food source could be a cause. I believe you have extensively studied genetically modified plants in the past, which is also one of the reasons we thought your input might be particularly valuable to our efforts."

Currie sat back in her chair, rubbed her right temple, and looked at the ceiling. She replied in monotone, as if reading a scripted response, "Dr. Rioux, I assume that you know that I've been working closely with the CDC for quite a while on this subject, and also with the Brazilian government for over a year, but apparently not. I'm surprised you haven't spoken with that group. I was in Atlanta and spent two days going through data." She received a reassuring nod from Hassan.

She continued speaking matter-of-factly and with authority. "In short, there's no evidence that genetic modifications of plants would cause cellular changes in humans, because DNA and RNA from *ANY food source* does not enter the human genome. Also, I know your FDA process is quite thorough in approving all new products to ensure they're safe. So that possibility doesn't seem scientifically plausible. The CDC is focused on a high nitrogen fertilizer as the potential source at the moment. Perhaps a discussion with them would be the best course. I've always been open to assisting where I can help, but I would just be repeating myself here. We're quite busy attending to the people affected who are facing this dreadful situation. I can provide you with other names you may also want to query."

A deep voice came across the line. "Dr. Currie, this is Daniel Webber. Have you ever heard of the company BioMaïs? It's based in Belgium. Also a fertilizer called Agronos?"

Her hands shook, and she clenched them tightly. She sat up very straight in her chair, lifting her chest as if she were in a military march. "The names were mentioned in discussions with the CDC with a long list of other companies. The CDC was highly focused on Agronos which is a high nitrogen fertilizer, and I understand that the manufacturer has been slow to respond."

After a brief silence, Webber continued. "I ask because we've received information from an interested source. That source provided an inventory of GE crops that are being grown in the areas where the BDC rate is high in the U.S., and BioMaïs has a GE sweet corn product that seems to be popular in the affected areas. That said, we understand your comment about the CDC is also concerned about the Agronos fertilizer. We're speaking with them on this topic."

The call went silent. Currie sat with her elbows on her desk, chin resting on clenched hands as she listened to Webber. She broke the silence and spoke very slowly. "Once again...GE crops have been around for *decades and are part of most of the food we eat.* As I mentioned, scientifically there's no evidence that such crops can change human DNA or otherwise harm people, and they're thoroughly reviewed. I believe the science is very clear."

Telling chimed in immediately afterwards. "I agree."

With an extended period of silence on the other end of the phone, Currie looked at Hassan as she spoke into the speaker. "Unfortunately, at this time we're not in a position to help you further than what we already have. If I have other thoughts on this matter or believe there is someone else I think you should speak with, I'll certainly let you know. I'd also suggest you discuss this subject with the Brazilian healthcare service, which has been dealing with the same issue for almost two years. I can provide you with names if needed."

The call concluded, Currie peered at Hassan. She saw him looking down at his black European-styled loafers with his dark brown fiery eyes.

She stood, put her hands on the desk, and leaned toward him. "They're, as the Americans say, 'fishing.' Grayson is the rare American who is not influenced by money. I was foolish to give him a chance."

Chapter 37

Twenty long hours of flights later, Joshua, Jake, Shelby, and Blaine walked sluggishly, following signs that read *Esteira de Bagagens*, accompanied by a graphic of a suitcase. No airport shops were open. The place was quiet, not unexpected for early Sunday morning.

Jake sat on a bench near a small baggage carousel alongside Shelby, his head supported by his hands. Joshua and Blaine retrieved three suitcases once the baggage began to circulate.

The humid weather hit Joshua like a hot shower as they stepped outside. He flagged down the largest of three cabs lined up at the curb and handed the driver an index card with the address of their hotel.

As the car moved onto the highway, Jake and Shelby looked out the passenger side window wide-eyed as the taxi passed several churches and office buildings before driving over a bridge. Shelby had her nose pressed to the window as she looked down at a river paralleling the road.

"Jake, look at the boat over there. What's it carrying?"

"Looks like corn stalks."

The driver spoke over his shoulder. *"Cana de açúcar*...sugar canes."

Once over the bridge, the landscape became more rural with trees, winding roads, and scattered fields of crops. Every so often, a farmer could be seen in a field, getting an early start to the day. Jake and Shelby spoke quietly to each other.

Joshua glanced at Blaine, who was on alert, his eyes darting back and forth across the front passenger seat window, staring at, and sizing up, the driver every few miles. Joshua leaned against the car door. His eyes closed intermittently, only to be opened when the car hit a pothole on the pitted roads.

The taxi exited at a sign reading São Leopoldo, where it crossed a bridge over the Rio dos Sinos river and followed azure blue signs bearing a white "H." From what Joshua read on his phone, the city was a German settlement in the early 1800s located just north of Porto Alegre, the capital in the State of Rio Grande do Sul. The area was now largely industrial, with a population just over 200,000 and clearly a heavily religious area, given the numerous churches they passed.

A few miles beyond the bridge, the cab pulled up to a three-story, peach-colored building, Hotel de Esperança. Joshua paid the cab driver 160 Brazilian reais, and the group entered the hotel, luggage in tow. Fragrant multi-colored orchids welcomed them in the lobby. The reception furniture was clean but worn. Blaine helped Jake sit down in a wing chair, and Shelby took a seat on an ottoman next to him as Joshua checked-in the group.

With the elevators under repair, the group slowly climbed three floors before settling into adjoining rooms. The rooms were dated but functional, and most importantly, clean.

Joshua watched Shelby give Jake his medication before he quietly closed the common door. He and Blaine prepped for bed, which meant each of them quickly brushed their teeth, stripped down to their underwear, and dropped onto their twin beds.

As he laid down to rest and recover from the hours of flights, Joshua sent Pete a text:

[Joshua] Arrived. All is well. Thought you'd enjoy a picture of Blaine. Typical Blaine, dead asleep but with his mouth open.

[Pete] Good to hear. I'm sure you're all tired

[Pete] I meant to tell you not to worry about me. I don't think you needed to have security added to the farm.

[Joshua] I'd rather err on the side of caution

[Pete] Thanks

* * *

Two hours later, Joshua's phone alarm chimed softly. He turned it off after a few cycles and pried his eyelids open, eyes burning. Lightheaded, he slowly sat up on the edge of the bed for a few minutes to get his equilibrium. After a long shower and a change into fresh clothes, he left a note on the nightstand next to a snoring Blaine:

Meeting Dr. Kaymer's contact. Back in an hour.

The hotel reception area was very quiet, apart from some construction work being done on the entryway. He saw an elderly couple speaking to the person at the front desk and a man wearing light-green trousers and a blue floral button-down shirt in a lounge chair on the other side of the lobby.

Joshua walked across the room. "Doctor Pilla?"

"Yes. Mr. Grayson?" The doctor wore a big smile as he shook Joshua's hand.

"Thank you for meeting me at the hotel on a Sunday morning."

"*Bem vindo do Brasil*…welcome to Brazil." The doctor led him into the hotel restaurant and ordered lunch for them: *Salpicão*, Brazilian chicken salad sandwiches. "How was your trip?"

Joshua took in the smell of cooked beans and fresh fruit as he rubbed his eyes and stretched his legs under the table. "Long, but fine. Twenty hours, connections in Miami and Rio. Fortunately no delays."

"Well, you're here, that's the main thing. I've spoken with Megyn Kaymer, and we're all set. Your cousin is to be admitted into the trials. I have registered him as José da Silva." The doctor grinned. "The Brazilian equivalent of John Doe. But we'll have to retest him locally to make sure he's a good candidate for the treatment."

"We are very grateful, Doctor. Megyn speaks very highly of you. She mentioned this area has been suffering from high BDC rates for a couple of years."

Dr. Pilla nodded vigorously. "Yes. Fortunately, the DNA Restore treatment has had tremendous results, saving many lives." He sipped his espresso. "It's a very small world to reconnect with Megyn in this situation. She is a wonderful physician and person."

The waitress delivered the sandwiches with sides of beans and rice. Joshua didn't wait and took a ravenous bite immediately after the plate was set in front of him.

Dr. Pilla laughed. "Better than airplane food, right?"

Joshua nodded and smiled as he chewed.

Halfway through their meal, the doctor put his sandwich on his plate and provided Joshua with expectations for the following day. "Since your cousin had adjuvant radiation treatment after his recent surgery to kill any tiny deposits of cancer cells around the surgical site, and the resulting biopsies validated those areas were clean, we should be able to move directly to the DNA Restore treatment if the tests confirm he's a candidate."

Joshua replied, "I understand." He paused for a moment. "Doctor, I'm curious how the DNA Restore treatment moved from clinical trials to approval here in Brazil. It was incredibly quick."

Pilla responded with serious eyes. "Yes, it was very quick. It's currently still considered as a clinical trial, not formally approved. But not unlike the COVID pandemic, the government allowed an emergency approval given the early results and limited other options to help affected people. So basically the data is still being collected, and ultimately it will be reviewed for approval. With the very high survival rate, I can't imagine it not getting approved. Without DNA Restore, many thousands would have died."

"How did the trials start?"

"Golden Helix reached out to ANVISA, the Brazilian Health Authority, and suggested they had a potential solution to the BDC problem. So after due diligence and reviews, they were approved on a restricted emergency basis to start trials, and you've seen the results."

Joshua replied with eyes squinted. "I heard it the other way, ANVISA contacted Golden Helix."

Pilla shook his head. "No, the government was approached. In the end, we're all thankful it's saved many lives."

They returned to the hotel reception area after their meal. Joshua spoke with a tremor in his tone.

"Doctor, again, thank you very much for your assistance. This may be my cousin's only chance to survive this situation."

Pilla put his hand on Joshua's shoulder. "It's my great pleasure, Joshua. Let's pray this will be a cure. I'll meet you at the main entrance to the hospital tomorrow at eight a.m. sharp!" He flashed an infectious smile. "I'm looking forward to celebrating your cousin's recovery. We'll share a *Caipirinha* or two!" He waved and left the hotel.

Joshua sat on a loveseat in the corner of the lobby and called Dr. Kaymer. He was tempted to hang up, but before he could, he heard, "Joshua. Are you in Brazil?" Without hearing a reply, she repeated her question.

"Yes, we've arrived in São Leopoldo. I just met Dr. Pilla for lunch, and it sounds like we're all set for tomorrow. I'll keep you updated." He took a deep breath, recognizing his emotions were getting the best of him. "Well, I guess that's all."

"Wait. What's wrong?"

He felt a growing headache and closed his eyes. "Nothing's wrong. We're here and checked into the hotel."

"I don't know you all that well, Joshua, but I can sense something's bothering you…what is it? Maybe I can help?"

He paused, before responding. "Megyn. My family trusted me to make a life-or-death decision on the path forward for Jake. We could have taken him to Dana-Farber again for treatment. They're among the best cancer centers in the world…*the world*!

"Or we fly him, in a weakened state, twenty hours to southern Brazil, navigating two connections along the way to get a new treatment that's not even formally approved within the country. I didn't even consult you or Dr. Lange or the specialist at Dana-Farber." Joshua stopped there and kneaded the back of his neck as a tear rolled down his cheek.

"Joshua, I understand. But I do know you're very smart and have an incredible sense about you to be able to assess options. You've chosen to invest in companies when they were small and only had a vision…and you bet on them, and they were successful."

He interjected. "Yes, but that was only money, Megyn. Not a life. I'm okay with losing money, but not my cousin. Jake's life is likely resting on my recommendation."

Megyn's voice turned assertive. "Listen to me, Joshua. You're tired and jet lagged. Let me tell you what you saw in this situation. First, you saw a highly-regarded hospital surgeon from a top hospital operate on your cousin, and his conclusion was we got everything…But the cancer returned. Secondly, you know the history of DNA Restore in Brazil. It has an astounding record of dealing with BDC…something on the order of ninety percent. Lastly, you know time is of the essence and DNA Restore is not available in the U.S. yet."

He closed his eyes and replayed his thought process in his mind. "I'm still not sure, but thanks. Maybe some sleep will help."

"You need to believe in yourself and your decision. Your proposal was based on probability, which is what I would do in your shoes. Stay positive, your family is looking to you, Joshua."

Before returning to his room, he reviewed his email, stopping at a message from his condo building superintendent…

Mr. Grayson. It looks like you're away. I want to let you know that your condo was broken into yesterday.

Chapter 38

Joshua signed for the bill as the group finished their hotel breakfast—known locally as *café da manhã*, or morning coffee. Blaine devoured the homemade bread, cheese, ham, and fresh fruit. The rest of the group sipped coffee and nibbled on bread and banana coffee cake. Jake sat, eyes closed, and leaned on Shelby.

Blaine led the group out of the hotel at seven-thirty. They stepped into a comfortable seventy-degree morning and met the spicy and floral scent of orchids. Jake leaned on Joshua as they moved down the street, following the directions from a lady at the hotel check-in desk.

After taking two left turns, they walked slowly down the road toward the hospital. Across from the hospital were multiple single floor white buildings with alternating green and terracotta colored tiled roofs. The street was punctuated with Brazilwood trees and blooming begonias. Blaine walked ahead of the group.

As they caught up with him, Blaine stepped into the street and pointed to a large billboard on top of one of the buildings across from the hospital. The sign read: Funeraria Jed Lopes.

Blaine bellowed, "Can you friggin' believe that?! The guy is advertising funeral services across the street from the hospital." He looked down the street and pointed. "Look, more signs! That's just way wrong, man."

Located in the center of the city, Oncologia Centenário - Centro de Câncer was housed in a modern three-story white tiled building with a dark glass entrance. The group expressed surprise at the building, which wouldn't have received a second look in the U.S.

The group entered the hospital just before eight o'clock, and were met by a familiar antiseptic scent. Joshua was surprised at the modern reception area. The room was bright, as the entry wall allowed plenty of light into the area. It was relatively large with an off-white tiled floor with a small azure blue diamond-shaped mosaic in the middle of every four abutting tiles. The first impression of the interior, along with his constructive meeting with Dr. Pilla, gave him greater hope.

As Joshua stood at the half-round reception desk, he turned and saw Blaine helping Jake sit in a high backed chair next to Shelby. The crew looked quite fatigued, and Jake's face was pale with no emotion, as if he were sleeping with his eyes open.

At eight o'clock, Dr. Pilla promptly appeared from a nearby hallway with a warm smile on his face. "Welcome, gentlemen and Mrs. Grayson." He led them down the hall to a private room, where the doctor addressed a droopy-eyed Jake. "Let me describe the process from here. First, we need to recheck and confirm that you're eligible for the trials. Assuming the answer is yes, we'll profile your DNA for 'errors' across key genes. Once the errors are identified, we'll begin the DNA Restore process. That means we create a custom medication, which will be delivered by IV for two or three hours daily for one week.

"As we go along, we'll be checking your DNA to determine if the medication is working. Once your DNA is restored to the correct sequencing, you'll need to recover and have some testing for the following week or so to ensure your health and DNA readings are stable. Beyond that, there will be follow-up DNA testing with a descending frequency."

Dr. Pilla turned and faced Joshua, Blaine, and Shelby. "This initial testing is going to take perhaps a couple of hours. You can enjoy our small cafeteria or explore the area and return around ten o'clock to check on…Mr. José da Silva."

As tough as Jake was, Joshua saw uncertainty and a hint of fear in his eyes. He caught Jakes' eye briefly and gave him a slow, firm nod. A nurse in a crisp white uniform appeared with a wheelchair, and after a kiss and hug from Shelby, Jake was wheeled back down the hall, with Dr. Pilla in tow.

Outside the main entrance, the group sat on a bench next to a small garden. Blaine closed his eyes and angled his face toward the sky. Shelby dabbed at the corners of her eyes with a tissue.

Her voice trembled. "I'm nervous. What if he isn't eligible?"

Blaine held her hand and opened his eyes. "It'll be okay. It's all happened so fast. I mean, we're sitting in another country. But hey, on the walk over I saw a rooster and three goats walking down the street. That's a good omen in Brazil. Yep, I've read that." Blaine smiled wide at his weak attempt to reassure Shelby, but he knew, somehow, it had helped ease the tension when she elbowed him in the ribs.

The trio killed time walking slowly around the block, surveying the area under a warm, cloudless morning. They found it to be an interesting mix of medical facilities and residential homes.

They stopped at their hotel for coffee and *Bolinhos de Chuva*—deep-fried dough sprinkled with sugar and cinnamon—before returning to the hospital. After waiting for almost an hour in the small cafeteria, Jake emerged in a wheelchair, propelled by the same nurse.

Sitting around a cafeteria table, Jake took them through his experience. "Wasn't really different from a check-up. They took blood and basically gave me the once over. Checked my heart, and even my eyes."

Blaine smirked. "Did the doc make you turn your head and cough?"

Jake punched him in the shoulder. The levity reduced the collective stress for a short while. Later that afternoon, Dr. Pilla pulled up a chair and joined them in the cafeteria.

"Hello…we have the labs. They're positive." Shelby gave him a confusing stare, prompting the doctor to clarify. "Meaning that they meet all the trial criteria, so we can move forward immediately with the treatment."

They looked at each other with half-smiles. Jake sighed in reserved relief. "I need to call Dad."

Joshua dialed and handed his phone to Jake. Shelby sat by his side, hugging his arm as the men walked to the other side of the room to give him privacy. Jake spoke quietly, chin on his chest, nodding every so often. After a short while, he hung up, put the phone on the table, and wiped his face with a napkin.

Blaine pulled a chair next to him and put his arm over Jake's shoulders. "Gonna be okay, Jake, and we'll all be home for Christmas with the kids opening presents, eating candy canes, and laughing." Jake was stoic.

Joshua felt the emotional heaviness, but was determined to be firm and positive. He stepped in and crouched in front of Jake. "Are you ready to beat this thing?"

Jake visibly choked back tears and buried his face in Shelby's sweatshirt as she hugged him hard and cried. He spoke softly to her. "Shelby, I love you. I want to see Dixie get married and Henry grow into a good man…and babysit grandbabies with you."

As they composed themselves, Jake looked Joshua in the eye. "This is the only hope?"

Be confident, Joshua told himself.

"Jake, we spoke about this, it's the best route. I know we're in another country in an unfamiliar hospital, but the treatment is leading edge and the same treatment that's been emergency approved in the U.S. for clinical trials, so it went through a thorough screening. It's had great success here so far. So yes. YES!"

Jake pressed his lips together firmly and hunched his shoulders, as if preparing for a fight. He wiped his eyes and brow with his sleeve and stared off into the distance. Shelby grasped his hand. She leaned forward slightly as if to speak but withdrew, leaving him to his thoughts.

He squeezed her hand, looked at his family, and managed two raspy words, "Let's roll."

* * *

Late afternoon, after several tests and mixing the medication based on his genotype, a nurse inserted an IV needle into Jake's right arm and left the room, leaving behind a strong antiseptic odor. She returned shortly with an IV, checked the code on the bag, and compared it to the hospital bracelet on Jake's wrist. The medication was hung alongside Jake's bed, and the nurse connected it to his IV port. She flipped a switch, triggering a pump to start the flow of medication. They all watched quietly as a pale blue liquid flowed slowly through the tube and into his arm, the pump sound echoing through the room.

As the medication flowed, Joshua attempted to break the somber silence. "Shelby, I have a Blaine story for you, if you're interested."

She wiped her eyes with her shirt-sleeve, and forced a half-smile.

"Blaine brought a girl home for dinner one summer night. I know this is true because I was there." He turned and looked at Blaine with wide eyes. "There was a girl in high school he'd been dying to ask out for a year. It took him a long time to get the courage to ask for a date. Surprisingly, she said yes." Joshua stopped and put on a big smile before continuing. "On the day of the date, believe it or not, he washed and combed his hair and put on clean clothes before he went to pick her up."

Blaine sat up straight in his chair alongside Shelby. Joshua stood and acted out the scene as he spoke. "Blaine brought her home, ran around the car, and opened the door for her, introduced her to everyone. He even asked her how her day was—"

Blaine started to get restless. "Come on, bro." Shelby put her hand over his mouth.

"So, the girl, I forget her name."

Jake sat up taller in bed. "Amy."

"Yeah, that sounds right." Joshua gave Jake a thumbs up. "So, Amy sat down on the couch, and we're all talking to her. She's very nice. At that point, Aunt Sara asked Blaine to step into the kitchen…he came out maybe ten minutes later with this look on his face like he'd been kicked in the gonads!"

Shelby spoke over the men laughing. "Come on! What happened?"

Joshua batted his eyes. "It turns out old Romeo here asked out his cousin!"

Blaine stood, laughed, and punched Joshua in the shoulder—pretending it to be a playful punch, but with actual force behind it. He then added, "Second cousin."

There was a light knock on the door, and the group quieted quickly. Dr. Pilla poked his head in and looked at a pale-faced Jake. "How're you doing?"

"Feeling fine, I guess. I don't feel anything. Maybe just a bit warm."

The doctor stepped just inside the room. "You shouldn't feel anything, except perhaps some fatigue. It should take about two hours for the IV bag to empty. If you feel anything strange, ring the nurse button. The nurse can adjust the flow rate if needed. We're going to keep you here tonight, and maybe longer as a precaution, just to make sure you don't have any bad reactions to the treatment. Once we're sure you tolerate it well, you'll be able to leave the hospital and stay at the hotel after your treatments."

Joshua followed the doctor out of the room and watched him walk away down the empty hallway. He made a brief call to Pete to bring him up to speed, then followed with a call to Dr. Kaymer, who answered after several rings.

He stuttered briefly as he spoke. "Hi Megyn, it's Joshua. I want to let you know we're at the hospital and they've started the treatment."

"Good. So he met all the requirements for the trial…is everything okay?"

"Yes, but we're all a little on edge. The environment is so different here, and we're dead tired. Things are moving quickly. A few months ago it was life as usual, and now we're in Brazil and my cousin's life rests on a new therapy."

"That's jet lag, emotions, and lack of sleep talking. It's a different country, but the doctors are very capable. I know Dr. Pilla personally, and he's well-respected and experienced. The treatment is straightforward, and they'll be sending data to me daily so I can monitor things from here. If I have any questions or concerns, I'll call them and you immediately."

"Thank you, Megyn…I guess time will tell."

Chapter 39

The following evening Pete Grayson sat in the farmhouse kitchen, eating his dinner at the oak table as his phone rang. He swallowed, wiped his mouth with a napkin, and answered.

"Hey Dad, how you doin'?"

"Blaine! Good to hear your voice. I'm doing fine, but I miss everyone. Shelby's parents are doing well watching Dixie and Henry, but I relieve them every day so I can spend time with the kids. They're anxious about Jake and Shelby, so it's good I'm here. They've also grown fond of Joshua's cat, Ernie." Pete wandered into the living room and stared at the tree as he spoke. "I smell pine needles from the Christmas tree, but I have no one to share the season with except Ernie. Nice to have him around for company."

"Sorry about that. Hopefully, we'll be back before Christmas."

"That'd be great."

"Hey Dad, I have Jake here, he'd like to say hi." He held the phone to Jake's ear.

Jake grunted, cleared his throat, and spoke in a coarse whisper. "Hi, Dad."

"Good to hear your voice, son." Pete chewed the inside of his cheek. "I'm looking forward to celebrating a big Christmas with you."

"Me, too, Dad." There was a pause. "Sorry, I'm very tired."

"That's okay, you just get some rest. I love you, and you have multitudes praying for you here. I'll talk to you very soon. Godspeed, son."

Pete hung up the phone and wiped his eyes. He returned to the table and his plate of ham, green beans, and boiled red potatoes. Country music played softly from the small radio atop the fridge. Darkness had taken hold outside.

As he washed dishes in the kitchen sink, an alarm beeped. He checked the console, which noted the alarm was triggered by the motion sensor at the top of the lane. He leaned forward and surveyed the area from the window over the sink. No car lights or any movement.

He dried his hands as a second beep sounded triggered by a sensor midway down the lane. Pete walked out of the kitchen and into the dark adjacent dining room, glanced out the large picture window, and scanned the grounds in front of the house. Nothing was visible, but he heard a faint sound of crunching gravel.

Returning to the kitchen, he turned off the radio and lights, leaving only the occasional hum of the old refrigerator to fill the void. He locked the kitchen door at the rear of the house and retreated to the dining room and secured the two doors at the front of the house.

A strong late fall wind blew hard against the house, and it groaned. He moved low to the ground to the family room at the back of the house, where he retrieved a shotgun from the wall gun rack, and put a handful of shells in the pocket of his hooded sweatshirt. Relocating to a rear window, he scanned the back of the house, recoiling as a figure moved in front of a light over the door of the small smokehouse located twenty feet beyond the screened in porch. The figure disappeared into the darkness on the far side of the house.

Pete loaded three shells into the gun, pumped a shell into the chamber, and crept to the window. He retrieved his cell phone from his back pocket and dialed. The dial tone, although soft, echoed loud enough in the room to cause Pete to put his hand over the phone.

"Effingham Police, Sergeant Riemann."

Pete spoke in a low, urgent voice. "Dale, Pete Grayson. I saw a man behind my house and believe there are probably more with him. I need help."

"On my way, Pete. Hang tight. I'll call for backup."

The screen door to the rear porch creaked open and closed with a soft but audible sound. The knob on the exterior door leading into the kitchen rattled back and forth gently, but the door didn't open. A moment later, planks on the front porch creaked, and the knob to the front door rattled for several seconds before falling silent.

He peered out a window at the rear of the house. A large figure was just outside the screened-in porch, surveying the area, his breathing visible in plumes of mist. Pete crouched and slowly moved back into the dining room. He peered through a corner of a window at the front of the house, where a dark figure stood three feet away, looking in the adjacent window. He jumped back and moved to the enclosed staircase located in the middle of the first floor between the two rooms. There he waited, eyes wide, alternately looking at the door in the front of the house and, on the other side, the family room and kitchen.

"Come on, Dale" he mumbled under his breath.

Noises on the rear porch off the kitchen caught his attention. This time, the noise was louder as the outside door leading into the kitchen was being hit hard.

Pete stood at the bottom of the stairs and looked up. Under his breath, he prayed aloud in a whisper, "Dear Lord, remember me. Oh God, strengthen me just once more, help me protect my home and my family. Be with me."

He took a peek at the front of the house and saw no movement. He turned his attention back to the family room and kitchen just beyond. This time, the kitchen door was hit hard and sprung open.

Pete saw a burly man enter and move slowly into the family room with a pistol in his hand. The man stopped near the staircase landing where Pete stood. Sweat beaded on his forehead, and he began to breathe rapidly.

Moments later, there was commotion at the front of the house as a bright light from outside illuminated the dining and living rooms. The man on the front porch began hitting the door with this shoulder. The old, solid oak held fast.

A loud, clear voice blared over a loudspeaker. "Police! Come forward, hands over your head."

The man from the family room moved toward the front door, which required him to pass through two doors at the foot of the stairs. Hearing the man's footsteps, Pete stepped slowly backward onto the first step of the staircase, his back against a sidewall.

As the burly man started to pass the stairs, the solid wood butt of Pete's shotgun met the side of his head. The man dropped, uttering a very brief, muffled, "Ugghhh" as he crashed to the wood floor. At the same time, the man on the front porch broke a window near the front door and reached in to unlock it.

The voice outside intensified. "I order you to come forward NOW! This is your last warning."

Pete heard a siren in the distance. His eyes were open wide and moving back and forth, scanning the scene at the front of the house; it was challenging to see. He gripped the shotgun tight and stepped further up the stairs, his back against the stairway wall.

As Pete backpedaled, he glanced down toward the bottom of the stairs and caught sight of the burly man's shoes as he crawled away into the family room, quickly moving out of Pete's line of sight. He took another step up the staircase, it creaked loudly, prompting him to squat low. Sweat rolled down from his brow to his nose and began to drip. He wiped his face with his sleeve.

Moments later, three bullets pierced the wall above Pete from the family room. He stepped down quickly onto the landing, stretched his shotgun in front of him, pointed blindly around the wall into the family room, and pulled the trigger, pumped the shotgun, and shot again, one aiming low, the other higher. He repositioned just inside the dining room at the front of the house.

Shots rang out in the front. Pete retreated backward on his knees to a position between the two rooms, reached into his sweatshirt to reload but found no shells. He heard the kitchen door close, and sank low to the family room window looking onto the back yard. Just beyond the rear porch, a silhouette staggered out the screen door and moved slowly toward the smokehouse. He opened the window, leveled his shotgun, pointed it at the figure's legs, and pulled the trigger.

Pete pulled away from the window as multiple shots roared, broke the glass and tore up the door frame. He breathed heavily, his face flushed, and moved to the kitchen looking for shotgun shells on the way, but found none. With no one visible, he stepped onto the screened-in porch. There he had limited places to protect himself and no ammunition. He stayed low and took cover alongside an oversized chest freezer.

The screen above Pete's head was slightly pulled away from the frame. He rose to a squat, pulled it further away, and put the barrel of his gun through the hole as he surveyed the area. The scene was dark, lit only by the glow of the light on the old smokehouse.

Pete heard a new voice on the side of the house, looked out and scanned the scene. He saw a man illuminated by a flashlight, on the ground with his hands out in front of him, gun off to one side.

As Pete stood, a loud sound came from the kitchen. He raised his head as a man with a handgun moved toward him in an unsteady manner, his other arm extended to provide balance. Pete dropped low. The man mumbled, "Grayson" and fired two shots wildly toward the porch, both missing the mark. In the process, the man dropped his gun as he tried to steady himself against the kitchen door frame.

Pete yelled "stop" and began to raise his shotgun. As he did, the man bull-rushed him, closing the distance quickly and pushing him back hard into a wooden porch support, causing the gun to drop. After absorbing two quick punches to the ribs, Pete dropped to his knees, holding his sides and breathing haltingly.

The man looked around the floor frantically in the dark before charging toward the screen door. Pete lifted himself to a squat, and as the man moved forward, he grabbed him around the knees and hit him in the mid-section with his shoulder, driving the assailant into the door frame. The man exhaled loudly as air left his lungs. He reeled backward, hit a wall, and slid to the floor.

The porch was illuminated with a flashlight as a policeman closed in. Pete raised his hands. "I'm Pete Grayson, this is my home!"

Chapter 40

Later in the week, Joshua stepped into Jake's hospital room, with two cups of strong Brazilian coffee. Blaine was groggy but awake and gave a slight nod as he accepted the java. Joshua looked at Jake, asleep, ashen face, an IV in his arm. The men quietly stepped into the hall.

Blaine sipped his coffee. "I think it's supposed to be the last day of the treatment. They said things should be much better by now, but Jake ain't lookin' good. What can we do?"

Joshua rubbed his eyes. "I don't know. The doctors are going to speak today with Dr. Kaymer and specialists from back home. Let's be strong and positive for Jake, Shelby, and everyone else." Blaine kicked at the tile floor and walked off.

Late morning, a nurse entered and put a blood pressure cuff on Jake, who stirred and opened his eyes.

Joshua stepped in close and put a hand on his shoulder. "How do you feel?"

Jake opened his mouth several times and swirled his tongue around in his cheeks. The nurse gave him water. He sipped slowly from a straw, and turned his head to Joshua. "Tired. Hard to keep my eyes open. Where's Shelby?"

"She slept at the hotel and is getting something to eat in the hospital cafe." He saw the confusion in his reddened eyes. "Rest and get your strength back, we'll be here with you. Nothing to worry about."

As Jake's eyes closed, Joshua stepped out of the room into the hallway. He found Blaine leaning up against the wall, finishing a call.

"Glad you're okay, Dad. Wish I'd been there with you. Talk to you soon."

Blaine shook his head as he eyed Joshua, who asked, "What's going on?

"You won't believe what happened. Dad said two guys with guns attacked the farmhouse! He's okay, just in shock. Said the alarms saved him." He looked Joshua in the eye. "Sorry I made fun that you wanted the alarms installed. Good call, cuz."

"I didn't expect that would happen…I think I may have caused it, asking too many questions to too many people." Feeling awful, Joshua walked away, hand on his chest.

Blaine followed, grabbed him by the shirt, and turned him around. "You're the reason Jake has a chance to live.

Don't back down now! I'm with you. Dad's with you. We need you to stay strong and fight."

Joshua bit his lip and ran his hands through his hair. He raised his chin and clenched his jaw. "Let's keep this to ourselves. We don't want Jake or Shelby to worry. Come on, let's sit with Jake."

Dr. Pilla poked his head into the room a short while later and waved for the group to meet him in the hallway. Blaine retrieved Shelby from the café for the update. "We had three specialists on our call today. All had a chance to review the lab results and confirmed the treatment is indeed working. However, the progress is very slow. Maybe too slow."

Shelby raised her voice. "That's good, right?"

Dr. Pilla looked her in the eye and spoke softly. "Yes, that's good as you say. The treatment's active. But it's critically important that the progress of the treatment is faster than the development of the disease. It's sort of a race."

Joshua saw the confusion in Shelby's eyes and asked, "Is there a way to catalyze the treatment effects?"

"No, at least not that we've tried. By this time, patients have usually responded to the treatment. Most of the call was on this subject, sharing ideas including whether or not to continue the treatment beyond one week."

Shelby noted, "Doctor, we're almost at a week now! What can we do?" Blaine put his arm over her shoulder.

"There are two approaches we believe are worth considering. One is to attempt to speed up the DNA replication using various drugs. However, if we do that, we also risk replicating the DNA that hasn't been corrected by the treatment. That means we could make things worse or stall progress. Number two is to slow his metabolism way down by putting him into a medical-induced coma. That may allow the treatment to work faster than the disease and gain momentum."

Joshua felt the growing fear and spoke calmly. "Doctor, can the treatment be adjusted?"

"We've rechecked the medication and it is accurate. We need to follow the proctocol, so no we cannot adjust the medication. I should also say it's still possible the treatment will work without any additional interventions. That said, we're entering uncharted territory."

Blaine leaned gently against Shelby and asked Dr. Pilla, "Was there a final decision on the approach?"

"There wasn't total agreement. Everyone agreed to consider this further and consult with other experts. We have another call later today, and we expect to have a consensus if more progress isn't shown. As you say, we're at the edge of the treatment protocol of one week. Time is becoming critically important."

* * *

As the discussion occurred in Brazil, Pete Grayson brought a chair from the dining room into the farmhouse kitchen and pulled it up to the table. He joined Agent Dan Webber, the locally based FBI agent, the captain of the Effingham County Sheriff's Office, Jesse, and Cole.

Pete was the last to sit and began the conversation. "Agent Webber, what've you found out about the attack? I'm worried about the rest of my family."

Webber set his coffee cup down and opened a manila file. "We ran background checks on the men who attacked you. They were interrogated, and we learned quite a bit. They're from St. Louis, paid to watch you and your family over the last couple months. They turned up at your home looking to, as they said, 'silence' your nephew and anyone who got in their way. Apparently, they didn't know he wasn't here. They weren't clear on who paid them but noted it was a man with a foreign accent, which they couldn't place. They only spoke once with him by phone, and it was a very short conversation. Payments were made online through a St. Louis money transfer office. We're trying to trace the origin of the payments, but so far it's proving difficult."

Pete put his forearms on the table. "Are the men okay?"

"Yes, both remain in the hospital, but they'll recover. Mostly bruises, but one of them had a lot of buckshot in his rear end. Mr. Grayson, can you please walk us through what happened two days ago and why you think it occurred?"

"I'll try. My nephew was concerned about the growing local cancer rate. He felt it might be connected to the GE sweet corn, so we passed word through the community, figuring if it wasn't the corn, it would be better safe than sorry. I can only assume someone wanted to stop us spreading that message. But while I listened to Joshua, I never thought it was true or something like the attack would occur here in Bishop Creek."

Webber took notes and provided more color to the story after Pete concluded his experience. "We previously met with your nephew in Boston. He and his attorney laid out basically the same backstory, with more detail, and he also developed a thesis around the whole. The missing piece, however, has been that there was no clear connection between Golden Helix, Dr. Amaline Currie, and BioMaïs, the company that produces the GE sweet corn seed.

"He suggested that there may be a link between the patents of Dr. Currie's deceased scientist husband and the intellectual property being used by BioMaïs. Yesterday afternoon, your nephew's attorney gave us a well-researched patent trail that seems to provide a link between the two, at least enough to halt seed sales and bring the doctor to the table. She's been resistant to inquiries."

Webber's eyes slowly scanned the men around the table. "I believe your nephew's movements and communications have been monitored. My guess is, they thought he was here at the farm because he's spent time between here and Boston over the last month. Good foresight to add security measures here."

Pete looked up from his coffee. "We made fun of my nephew because he got a new phone and laptop because he thought others were tapping into his communications. I'm glad he stood fast. He had the security installed. God bless him." Pete looked down and shook his head slowly. "I found the whole story hard to believe and told him so. I'm glad he stuck to his instincts; it probably saved my life."

An hour and a half later, Webber closed the file and guzzled the rest of his third cup of coffee. "Although not conclusive at this point, it appears your nephew was spot-on with his hunches. Based on what we've seen between our group, the FDA, the CDC, and other federal departments, Dr. Currie seems to have orchestrated an extremely sophisticated scheme to create a financial windfall for her and investors in Golden Helix. We're unclear as to the involvement of others at this point.

"Given the information we've accumulated so far, we believe we'll be able to obtain an Interpol Red Notice in short order, which is an international request for local authorities to find Dr. Currie and detain her for questioning. We're in contact with the Dutch authorities to execute on the notice once issued, but we need to move quickly. Apprehending a person across borders is very complicated in practice."

After the authorities left, Pete put Jesse and Cole to work, continuing repairs on the farmhouse. He donned a winter jacket and walked up the lane to check the mail, praying over and over under his breath, "Heal, protect, and guide us, Lord."

Chapter 41

Late afternoon the following day, Dr. Currie stood in the lobby of a new eighteen-story tower in the Dutch city of Utrecht, which houses the Medical Evaluation Board Agency. She stood in the middle of a small group comprised of two legal advisors, Anas Hassan, and Dr. Telling. She didn't feel safe but was determined not to convey that fact.

Minutes later, the group was led to a conference table on the thirteenth floor. Arnoud van Whelan, Head of Regulatory Affairs, stood at the head of the conference table.

"Dr. Currie, as I believe you know, we've received calls from the CDC in the U.S. They'd like to speak with you about some urgent genetic medical challenges they're facing and potential applications of DNA Restore to remedy those issues. They've requested we sit with you to see if we can arrange a face-to-face meeting with them in the U.S. They are very concerned and believe you may be uniquely able to help develop a solution."

Currie squared her shoulders and raised her palms. "I've met with the FDA and also consulted with the CDC, as well as the Brazilian health department. We're saving lives with our DNA Restore technology, which they've reviewed and authorized for emergency use, similar to what they did for the COVID-19 situation. Dr. Telling has spoken with them regularly, and I'm not aware of any other needs they have at this time. We have multiple challenges currently to support the BDC situation, let alone take on more. We'll continue to assist in any way possible, but our capacity is extremely tight."

"Yes, but I understand they want to meet with you in person."

Dr. Currie turned to Dr. Telling. "Have you heard this?"

"No, I haven't, and I speak with them weekly."

Van Whelan gave an exasperated sigh. "That's what they've requested. Is that possible?"

"Yes, of course it's possible. I was just in the U.S. recently, assisting them with the potential source of the BDC. But again, I have a business to run." She paused to check the calendar on her phone. "I have little time to travel over the next three weeks, as I have meetings with other countries inquiring about DNA Restore. I can have my assistant contact someone there to arrange a meeting. Do you have a name to contact?"

Van Whelan threw up his hands. "Candidly, Doctor, I'd suggest this be your top priority if you value a relationship with the U.S. agencies. If I were in your shoes, I would fly there today! Here's the name and contact information that was provided to us to schedule a meeting." He pushed a note card across the table to her.

Currie placed her fingers on the card and re-directed it to one of the attorneys. "I'll consult with my assistant and see if I can reschedule other events to meet with them as soon as possible. I trust you'll convey that to your contacts?"

He bobbed his head, then raised his eyebrows. "I have another suggestion. Why don't we call them right now? That might be received as a sign of good faith. It's only eleven o'clock in the morning there."

Currie's eyes darted to Hassan, her attorneys, and Dr. Telling, who all wore no expression or responded by looking for her to take the lead. She broke the silence. "Certainly. I'd be happy to talk and understand exactly what they are looking for from us."

Van Whelan left the room, returned minutes later and dialed the conference phone in the middle of the table. After several beeps, he introduced all parties on the call from Utrecht.

"Hello, everyone, my name is Jeremy O'Neill, I'm with the CDC and in charge of the Office of Genomics and Occupational Diseases. I'm sitting here with two colleagues from the FDA and CDC. Dr. Currie, I'm very sorry I missed you in your last visit here. Unfortunately, I had a family issue and was out of the office for several weeks. I believe Dr. van Whelan has conveyed to you we'd like to sit down with you face-to-face as soon as possible and walk through some serious issues we're dealing with here in the U.S. We're seeing a significant growth in genetic diseases, and you're a leader in genomics. We're very concerned this could spin out of control. Is it possible for you to meet us in Washington in the next day or two?"

Currie sat up very straight. "Van Whelan did mention that, and I'll try to clear my schedule to get to Atlanta as soon as possible. As you said, I was in the U.S. recently to assist the your department on the source of the BDC in your country. Also, we're close to bringing the DNA Restore process online. Dr. Telling has supplied you with all the information you've requested on our DNA Restore therapy, so I'm still unclear why you need to speak with me so urgently and in person."

O'Neill paused, and soft talking could be heard in the background. "To be more specific, we'd like for you to meet some of our genetic experts and see if the DNA Restore platform could be an option for von Willebrand disease. We're seeing unusually high growth with the disease and believe working with you and your platform could be of immediate value and save lives. It would also provide broader opportunities for Golden Helix. We'll, of course, handle all costs." There was long pause. "Doctor?"

"That's flattering, thank you. This is indeed interesting. I was not aware of that issue and of course want to help. Can you send the information you've gathered to review and discuss by video conference until I can change my schedule? I have obligations to the people of Brazil, and other countries are now asking for assistance. I'm being pulled in many directions." She glanced at Hassan out of the corner of her eye and saw him shake his head *no* very slowly.

"Of course, we understand your situation. We'd be in your debt if we could develop a collaboration with you and your company as quickly as possible. Also, we'll bring together leading geneticists here in the U.S. to share ideas.

I'm sorry if I'm pushing you, but it's an urgent matter for us, and perhaps other countries in the future."

The meeting ended with her middle of the road pledge. "I appreciate your need, and I'll do my very best to reschedule some of my obligations to meet with you as soon as possible."

In front of the building, Currie stepped into a black BMW SUV parked at the curb with Hassan. The car pulled out quickly, leaving Dr. Telling and two attorneys watching the car drive away, their ties blowing in the wind. The driver made a few turns before merging onto the A2 north and accelerating toward Amsterdam.

Hassan cocked his head. "It's time. This is a trap."

She replied under her breath, red-faced, with unadulterated anger, "No, no, no, no…" Closing her eyes brought images to mind: Anton Currie in his lab coat, deafening applause to her announcement at the biotech conference, and the email noting FDA emergency approval in the U.S.

She looked longingly into Hassan's eyes. "How can you be sure?"

Hassan brought up a message on his phone and showed her. She noted it was received during the meeting. *"Aviso Rojo de Interpol recién emitido. Muévete rápido!"* Currie reluctantly opened a modest-sized black satchel and inspected the contents. She zipped the bag shut. *"Breng me naar La Maison Amsterdam beauty salon."*

As they moved rapidly north on the A2 motorway, Hassan focused on the vehicles behind and around them. The route was busy and challenging to judge whether they were being followed. As they neared Amsterdam, Hassan provided instructions to the driver. "Do not go to the salon. Take A-10 northeast, Exit S-109 Amsterdam Rijnkanaal." He made eye contact with Currie. "For precaution."

* * *

After the call, Agent Daniel Webber sat with Jeremy O'Neill and Jeanne Jenkins, a direct report to the U.S. Director of Interpol, in a small conference room in The J. Edgar Hoover Building, a low-rise office building located on Pennsylvania Avenue in Washington, D.C.

Webber turned to Jenkins and asked in his deep voice, "We're tracking them, right?"

Jenkins replied, "We have a small team led by our legal attaché in The Hague in a trailing car, along with a backup. He's also confirmed the Netherland Interpol liaison is with them. The Netherlands will not restrain Dr. Currie or any potential interested parties until and unless a Red Notice is approved and put out on the wire. But they've agreed to ride shotgun with us, expecting the approval is imminent, and they'll restrain her at that time."

"Let's get them on the speaker to check in." Webber pointed to the speaker in the middle of the table.

Jenkins dialed, and the group waited half a minute before they heard a voice on the other end. "Hello?" The noise of the car made it challenging to hear.

"Yes, hello, this is Jeanne Jenkins, from the U.S. Interpol office. I'm with FBI Agent Daniel Webber and Jeremy O'Neil of the CDC." She paused as a shrill squeal sounded over the speaker. "We don't have a very good connection, but can you confirm that you are following the car with Dr. Amaline Currie?"

"Yes, we're tailing the car near Amsterdam. They're moving northeast on the A-10. Has the Red Notice been approved? Can we move in?"

As Jenkins spoke on the phone to Interpol for a status on the decision, Webber chimed in, speaking loudly to ensure the message was heard, "Daniel Webber here. Can you pull them over for speeding or bump their car so they stop? The notice is expected imminently."

After he spoke, the line cut out, and the speakerphone transmitted a dial tone. The room in Washington went quiet. Jenkins redialed several times, with no answer on the other end. Minutes later, Jenkins received confirmation that the Red Notice was granted and circulated globally.

The speaker rang. Webber leaned in and opened the line. "Webber here."

The line was clear. "Webber. We followed the car on the A-10 to the S-109. It looks like they knew they were being followed, because they rerouted to a location on the Amsterdam Rijnkanaal, where they transferred to a boat and headed south, which is in the opposite direction. We tried to follow them, but it just wasn't possible. We lost them."

Webber raised his voice, "Can you commandeer a helicopter quickly?"

The legal attache provided a response. "No, I understand that's not possible in a short time period."

Chapter 42

Outside the main entrance of the hospital, Joshua sat alone on a bench under a sparsely leaved cherry tree. People intermittently entered and exited the hospital, largely elderly locals, most wearing smiles and nodding at him when their eyes met.

Walking away from the hospital up the entry walkway, he reflected on his impending call with Pete. A week plus into the treatment, Joshua could see increasing concern on the doctor's faces and in their voices.

At the end of the walk, he dialed. "How are you recovering from the attack, Uncle Pete?"

"Sore, but fine. What's going on with Jake? Shouldn't he be coming home soon?"

"The doctors are getting more concerned that they aren't seeing progress with Jake's treatment. They've been allowed by ANVISA, the Brazilian health authority, to extend the treatment for another week."

Pete's voice cracked. "Can I talk to him?"

"They've had him heavily sedated for the last couple days to slow his metabolism. The doctors believe that might allow the therapy to be more effective."

"Talk to me, Joshua. What's going on here? I'm confused. I thought the therapy had a high success rate and the whole process was one week?" Pete raised his voice. "I'm very concerned."

Joshua closed his eyes and imagined what Pete was going through.

"I don't know what to say. The treatment is working. The problem is that it isn't strong enough at this point to turn the tables on the disease. Several experts, including Dr. Kaymer and the oncologist at Dana-Farber, are involved. They talk and collaborate every day. Jake has an army of experts focused on him looking for an answer."

There was a long silence on the other end before he heard Pete speak in a hopeful voice. "There are a lot of people praying for him. I know he'll come through…please tell him I love him." After a short pause, he added with conviction, "Joshua, tell everyone to remember - faith, not fear!"

Joshua hung up and sat on the grass, head in his hands, and felt a sense of emptiness. A whistle from the hospital entrance caught his attention. He shaded his eyes and looked toward the source.

Blaine waved him over. He rose slowly, tucked his phone in the rear pocket of his shorts, and plodded forward. In the cafeteria, they ate in silence. Joshua felt a sense of déjà vu. The days blurred together. Blaine swallowed a mouth full of fresh fruit; cupuaçu, guava and mango. He finished by loudly licking his lips and fingers.

"They said they hope to have today's labs by ten o'clock. How's Dad?"

Joshua kept his head down. "He's still recovering from the attack at the farm. The FBI was there the other day because they think the attack was linked to my poking around, trying to figure out the source of the cancer. I gave him an update on Jake. He took it hard and was very quiet."

Joshua's phone rang. He stood and walked away from the table. "Hi, Megyn."

"Hi, just calling to check in to see how you're all doing?"

"Trying to stay positive, but it's tough. I'm not used to being in a position where I can't do anything to affect the outcome. I just spoke with my uncle. I'm sure you heard someone attacked the farmhouse."

"Yes. It's a small community. Glad your uncle's okay."

Joshua walked through the reception area and stepped out into the front of the hospital. "Yes, he's a tough guy…" He made his way down the street into the shade under a row of mature trees. "He's struggling though, Megyn. The distance is killing him. The kids miss Jake and Shelby. They've been gone almost two weeks now."

"I'm following things closely on this end. We'll see how the results look today. Dr. Pilla continues to talk with the people at Golden Helix about the case to find another potential option to turn the tide. This is an unusual case for them, especially for someone so young. They've asked ANVISA if another extension is possible. I understand they were very reluctant to approve the current extension, so they'll likely decline the request."

"Megyn, you haven't mentioned Jake's name to anyone, right?"

"Strictly José da Silva…I'm sure you know this, but there's increasing concern the therapy won't work. They've never had an experience like this in Brazil. By this point, most patients have recuperated or a minority of them fade, but while your cousin has regressed by some measures, I wouldn't say he's fading."

"I understand. Thanks for checking in. Nice to hear a friendly voice."

He wandered back to Jake's room. The nurses were busy tending to him: vital signs, IV feeding, washing his body, changing his sheets and clothes. Shelby arrived half an hour later after a good rest at the hotel.

Three doctors entered the room to examine him. After their checkup they stepped into the hall and asked the group to follow. Shelby, Joshua, and Blaine looked at each other with serious eyes. Dr. Pilla provided the update.

"Good morning, we have the results of today's tests. It shows decline in the CA-99 tumor marker, and blood chemistry is within acceptable ranges—"

Blaine mumbled to himself, then elevated his voice. "Doctor, I don't understand!" Joshua put his hand on his cousin's shoulder.

"I'm sorry, Mr. Grayson. I can be too clinical. To be simple, we're still seeing some small positive movements. The sedation may be working, but it may not. We feel we need to bring him out of the sedation to judge better. Also, we've just been notified by ANVISA they will not approve extending the treatment beyond this week. The next twenty-four to forty-eight hours are critical." The doctor group moved down the hallway.

Shelby's shoulders sagged, and her eyes narrowed. "There is some hope?"

Blaine sniffed and shrugged.

Joshua sat on a couch, his hands covering his eyes, and whispered, "Not sure how much more I can take."

Shelby put on a smile, tears running down her cheeks like a sun-shower. She dabbed at her raw red eyes with a tissue. "I'll take this shift. You two have been here all night and yesterday. You go on back to the hotel and get some good sleep, and I'll see you later."

"Come on, cuz," Blaine said.

"Wait, if they're going to bring Jake out of sedation, we should be here for that."

"You boys ain't going to be any good around here. Take a nap and come on back after you get some rest. It'll probably take a couple hours anyway before he's awake. Go on, now." She gave them a no-nonsense look and pointed toward the main entrance.

Joshua and Blaine took a slow walk to the hotel, stopping in the restaurant for a takeout of the Churrasco barbeque lunch special. The elevator again had a handwritten sign taped to the door, *Fora de serviço*, with an "*X*" over the text. The men slowly climbed three flights of stairs, entered their room, dropped their clothes on the floor as they moved forward, crawled into their beds, and put their lunch on their chests. They ate in solitude, eyes forward, the only sounds in the room were chewing, the licking of fingers, and an occasional belch.

Finishing his meal, Joshua wiped his face with a small napkin, balled it all up, and threw it toward the trash can near the door. "I gave your Dad a full update. Should I have done that?"

Hearing no answer, he slowly turned his head to the other bed. Blaine was asleep, barbeque sauce on his face in a random pattern and a quarter of a sandwich in his hand, resting on his chest. Joshua closed his eyes and quickly drifted off.

* * *

The hotel room was quiet and cool as Joshua opened and rubbed his eyes. Blaine's rhythmic breathing was peaceful, almost hypnotic. He turned his head toward the window, where he expected the curtains to be full of light, but instead he saw a soft glow. He sprung from the bed and picked up his phone off the dresser; the clock read four-thirty. He pulled on his pants in a panic and moved to wake up his cousin.

"Blaine, let's get going!"

"Whoa!" Blaine jumped in response to Joshua's face hovering half a foot above him. "Not cool, man!" He sat up and threw his legs over the side of the bed, food dropping to the floor.

"Come on. We slept a long time. It's getting dark."

Cleaning themselves on the run, they rushed back to the hospital, drawing stares. As they speed walked through the lobby, they passed Dr. Pilla, who was in conversation with another doctor. He flagged them down.

"Hello, gentlemen. Your patient is awake. He's recovering from the sedation, but you can speak with him."

The men picked up the pace and made their way to room 218. As they entered, Jake turned his head toward them and struggled to speak.

"Hey."

The men stood bedside and smiled. Blaine asked, "How you doin'?"

"My head hurts somethin' fierce."

Joshua moved to the other side of the bed. "Other than that?"

Jake took a sip of water. "If I didn't have the headache, I'd say I feel okay. They gave me some pain meds, so hopefully they'll kick in soon."

"Did the doctors give you an update on the latest lab results?" asked Joshua.

Jake held his head in his hands. He spoke in a whisper. "Going in the right direction, but still not quick enough."

Blaine stood at the end of the bed, with a slight frown exaggerated by his red barbeque-tinged lips. "Too bad you were out for four months, bro. You missed a lot!"

Jake looked at them wide-eyed and tried to sit up. Blaine, maintaining a blank face, let him stare for a while before he and Joshua began laughing. Shelby laughed and cried at the same time.

Chapter 43

Dr. Amaline Currie's temporary safe-house was a small room in an eight-story apartment building, much of which was crumbling. The window was slightly open, to provide much needed ventilation for the room. The downside was that it let in constant traffic noise and pungent smells from the area: car exhaust, saltwater, and fish being the most prominent. Clotheslines strung across balconies made the place look like an old-time switchboard.

She endured the sounds and smells around the old Sassoon Docks area in Mumbai for the last few days. Currie was in lockdown mode, no travel and no communication except for intermittent, pre-scheduled contact times with Hassan. A local person was paid very well to regularly bring food and water. Hassan was adamant she follow his instructions to the utmost or risk arrest. In this situation, her strong, disciplined nature was her security, protecting her freedom and, considering the wide-scale impact of her human genetic experiment, likely her life.

It was a dramatic juxtaposition for her. No ability to take a shower; only a cloudy, tepid sponge bath from the kitchen sink. She'd entered the apartment a few days prior as a brunette, but now was a dirty blonde.

She spoke aloud to herself to break the silence and maintain her sanity. "This will be temporary...it cannot be happening...we planned too perfectly...I'm so sorry, Anton...we will prevail!"

The walls weren't insulated, effectively wood studs covered with thin wood paneling. Families on each side of her flat spoke incessantly. She rarely found quiet; children crying, men barking orders, and women crying or screaming. The smell of curry was baked into everything. Amaline Currie hadn't slept more than three consecutive hours since arriving. Her phone rang startling her. She checked her watch.

"Hassan...I trust your instincts, but perhaps the discussion with the FDA was legitimate, and it's not too late to go back to them. It could be a rare opportunity to grow Golden Helix much bigger—"

"No! An Interpol notice has been filed, and authorities are looking to question you. You must stay with the plan for your own protection. I promised Anton I would protect you, no matter what."

She raised her voice. "How do you know that?" Her voice began to tremble. "It's terrible here. The smells haunt me, and the noises never stop. I cannot sleep, and I cannot eat any more curry."

"*Sí, Sí, Sí*...I'm working to find out more information. You must be strong, and you must trust me. I wish it were not so, but we live to see another day."

Currie paced back and forth from one wall to the other as she spoke. "When do I leave this place? I cannot breathe here, and nothing is clean."

"We follow the plan. You leave in two days. Do not leave the apartment. We received the second option, funding tranche, and I have moved the money." He laughed. "Stupid Americans."

Currie sat on a chair with a tattered foam cushion. She closed her eyes and paused to concentrate. "Is Grayson taken care of?"

"He has gone underground. The man local to the farmhouse went to eliminate him, but Grayson wasn't there. The uncle farmer was able to protect the home well from the local man and another he hired. They are in jail...but they know nothing about us."

Currie stood and yelled into the phone. "That is not acceptable. Grayson has ruined Anton's science and our dreams. He must suffer a painful death for what he has done. Handle this yourself!"

"*Sí*. I am tracking him down. I will call to check on you tomorrow at oh-eight hundred hours." He hung up.

She sat and sipped on weak Darjeeling tea in a worn, ceramic cup. A moment later, she pulled her head away from the cup and wondered how many lips had touched it. Between sips, she breathed in and exhaled deeply to calm herself. Half a cup in, she began to doze off gently.

Just as her head dropped, her phone rang twice. She jerked awake. The ringing stopped. Seconds later, it rang again three times and stopped. Currie froze, eyes wide.

She stood, threw a scarf around her neck, grabbed her "go bag," left the apartment, and exited down a back staircase. The stairs led to the rear of the building, where a modern rickshaw met her, the front end of a motorcycle attached to a two-wheeled, partially covered passenger seat. The rickshaw immediately took off down one of the many narrow alleys and within a very short time disappeared into a nearby neighborhood of small buildings, corrugated sheet metal, and blue tarpaulin.

Chapter 44

Joshua awoke alone in the hotel room. His first thought was, We're getting close to the timeline of Aunt Sara's passing. DNA Restore has to work quickly.

He slowly rolled out of bed and made his way to the bathroom. As he brushed his teeth, his attention was drawn by the beep of a text message.

Bill Gilchrist's text was short and simple:

[Bill Gilchrist] Check your email.

Joshua pulled up his mail and found a link to a press release on VCJournal.com.

FOR IMMEDIATE RELEASE

Tremont Ventures Invests Further in Golden Helix (Boston, MA)

Tremont Ventures has announced it closed an additional $15 million investment in Golden Helix, bringing its total investment to $25 million. The proceeds are targeted to fund the continuing rollout of the DNA Restore platform in the U.S. and future countries.

Graham Roseboro, the firm's Managing General Partner, commented, "We've developed a very strong relationship with Golden Helix and its world class CEO Dr. Amaline Currie. We believe that the DNA Restore therapeutic platform could indeed be, as Dr. Currie has suggested, a potential cure for many cancers as well as other genetic diseases which will be a future focus of the Company."

Tremont partner Jeffrey Cochran, who led the round for the firm, added, "I'm very pleased that Dr. Currie had the confidence in us to put together this investment on very short notice."

For further details, please contact Tremont via its website.

He texted Gilchrist:

[Joshua] I guess they're blind to the current Interpol situation. How could they let that happen?! I warned them about Cochran.

[Bill Gichrist] Let them ham it up! You should be happy, too. I'll follow up with them ASAP to make sure you get your referral fee, per the agreement, quickly. Merry Christmas!

[Joshua] I should also tell you my uncle was attacked at his farmhouse a few days ago. He's okay. FBI involved. I think the link to this investigation is clear. Just want to make you aware.

* * *

Joshua sat in an oversized chair in the lobby of the Hotel de Esperança with his phone between his chin and shoulder as he peeled a banana. The conference call started with multiple beeps and attendees, representing the FDA, CDC, and Interpol introduced themselves.

"Hello, this is Agent Daniel Webber of the FBI. Thank you all for making time for this call to coordinate our efforts. You've all received a summary of what we believe to be a very sophisticated fraud implemented across multiple countries. I've invited Joshua Grayson to join as well. He has interacted with Dr. Currie several times and may be able to answer questions or otherwise provide valuable information. Mr. Grayson, can you provide us with any thoughts as to where Dr. Currie might be, or anything you believe might have relevance to our search?"

Joshua stood in the lobby looking down as he paced back and forth. "I think it might be useful to also search for a man who seems to be a confidant of hers. Each time I've met with her, he's been close by. I don't recall his name, and I don't think he's the Director of Communications he proposes to be. I sat with him in a meeting with Dr. Currie, and he struck me as her bodyguard.

"Locations to consider include Sweden. She married a man by the name of Anton Currie. He was a professor at the Karolinska Institute in Stockholm, which she attended while completing her fellowship. She must have connections there, and a holding company that owns Golden Helix is also based there. BioMaïs is in Antwerp, a possible location. Lastly, one of the senior people on the Golden Helix staff is Dr. Wilfred Telling. He may have thoughts, and it also might be useful to review her *Time* magazine interview where she described her upbringing."

Webber cleared his throat loudly. "Thank you. Unfortunately, the Dutch regulatory authorities weren't able to convince Dr. Currie to make a trip to the U.S. or anywhere else, and they just missed her after a meeting with the Dutch Medical Evaluations Board. As you all know, the FDA has stopped the sale of BioMaïs seeds in the U.S. Based on our instructions to food retailers and U.S. seed dealers, that information has not been disseminated up the chain to BioMaïs. Fortunately, however, we're not in the growing season, which gives us some cover. That said, it's just a matter of time before word leaks.

"Additionally, we've communicated with the Brazilian authorities and shared our information with them. I believe they've stopped BioMaïs sales as well." Webber paused and reviewed his notes before continuing. "We are confident someone in Dr. Currie's sphere perpetrated an attack on Mr. Grayson's family. We expect that person was triggered by Anas Hassan, the man Mr. Grayson referred to earlier. So, this is quite serious and time-sensitive. Bottom line, we need to move very quickly. Any leads? Thoughts?"

"Jia Kim of Interpol here. We understand Dr. Currie hasn't been seen since leaving the Dutch Medical Evaluations Board meeting where she spoke with the FDA on a conference call. According to Dutch Passport Control, she hasn't left the country. An Interpol notice has been posted. We'll continue to pursue additional information on this case and keep you informed."

* * *

As the FBI-led international conference call concluded, Dr. Wilfred Telling turned into the parking lot of the Lake Winnebago Motel in Fond du Lac, Wisconsin, amid frigid temperatures and falling snow. The doctor rolled his Ford Fiesta to a slow stop in the one unoccupied space left in the lot. Telling's head dropped. He rubbed his eyes and took a deep breath, held it, then exhaled slowly in complete silence. He jerked when his phone rang loudly.

"Dr. Telling? This is Joshua Grayson."

He dropped the phone and looked on the car floor for it. "Hello, Joshua. To what do I owe the honor of your call?"

"I'm sorry for the unexpected call. I'm on the line with someone who'd like to speak with you regarding Dr. Currie. It's quite urgent."

Webber's bass voice immediately followed Joshua's last word. "This is Special Agent Daniel Webber, with the Federal Bureau of Investigation. We're in the process of conducting an investigation and have been attempting to locate Dr. Amaline Currie but haven't been able to do so, and Mr. Grayson suggested we call you."

"Investigation! I'm not aware of any investigation." Joshua heard groaning on the other end of the line, along with muffled curse words, followed by a deep breath. "What can I do for you?"

Webber responded immediately. "Do you know where Currie is?"

"No, I don't. I've been trying to track her down myself for the last several days but haven't heard back from her...which honestly, isn't unusual. What does the FBI want with Dr. Currie? She's not in the U.S. I believe she's in the Netherlands."

"An international Interpol notice to detain her has been posted, and I also need to warn you that if you aren't honest with me, you may be implicated as an accessory to any charges."

Telling raised his voice. "Oh, my! I wasn't aware of that. Why is she to be detained?"

Webber softened his tone. "I'm sorry, Doctor, I can't share that information with you. Do you know anyone who may know her whereabouts?"

"No, I assume, Agent Webber, someone has tried her office and assistant?"

"Yes, of course. The local Dutch authorities have been to her office in Amsterdam, and there's no sign of her. In fact, the offices are virtually vacant."

There was no response. Joshua interrupted the silence. "Dr. Telling? I know this is a shock, but Agent Webber believes they need to act quickly."

"Yes. I'm sorry, I'm just stunned by this news. As I mentioned, it's not unusual I don't speak with Dr. Currie for days, even weeks, but this comes as an overwhelming surprise to me. Afraid I can't help. It seems I'm the last to know."

Chapter 45

As darkness fell on Bishop Creek, Anas Hassan pulled his car into the empty parking lot at St. Aloysius Church, turned off the lights, and found a spot in a far corner. He exited, walked around the cemetery, and made his way to the woods bounding the church grounds. There was just enough light to allow him to find the path he'd scouted earlier in the day.

He walked quietly along the path, eyes wide open, a tactical flashlight providing just enough light to navigate. Hassan adeptly made his way across a broad log over the creek and continued until he breached the far side of the woods. Moving up a slope, and walking to the pond he gained an elevated view of the rear of the farmhouse. Soft smoke billowed from the chimney, barely visible as darkness fell. Scanning slowly with military grade binoculars, he saw lights in front of the old smokehouse, in the kitchen, and the family room at the rear of the house.

Hassan moved down the slope and crouched behind a tree until the darkness settled in deeply. He withdrew a Glock-17 from his military-style shoulder holster, screwed on the suppressor, and moved deftly to the smokehouse, gun drawn. He slowly walked behind the small building to avoid the light, and stayed low to the ground as he made his way to the side of the house under the kitchen window.

The only noise he heard was radio chatter. Advancing to the rear of the home, he scanned the screened-in porch. Seeing no activity, he quietly opened the screen door and walked gingerly to the house door, which was locked. The light over the kitchen table was on, but he saw no one.

He continued around the house, and stepped onto the wraparound porch his back against the wood siding. Hassan peeked in the first widow, no one in the living room; just a reading light on near a chair on the opposite side of the room.

Stepping down the porch stairs he stood against the front of the house behind a tall bush underneath the dining room window a couple feet above him. Holstering the Glock he pulled himself up using the sill and saw a profile of a man through a window shade. The man sat alone at the dining room table, back to the window.

Slowly, silently he lowered himself to the ground, took several backward steps away from the house. Fifteen feet from the window, he could see a clear silhouette of the man.

Anas Hassan took his time, drew his gun. Took aim. Breathed out slowly as he pulled the trigger. While the sound of the gun was suppressed, it was by no means silent, and it was accented by the breaking window. He saw the silhouette drop forward, hit the table, and disappear. He quickly retraced his steps to the woods.

Chapter 46

The uniformed passport control officer at Nanjing Lukou International Airport gave the peroxide blonde hipster lady a slight wave of his hand to come forward. Amaline Currie complied, moving casually forward past the broad yellow line, flowered purple backpack over her shoulder, and handed her passport and Chinese Visa to the man behind the tall counter. The officer glanced at the passport cover–*Bundesrepublik Deutschland Reisepass*–before opening to the photo page. He looked down at the lady in front of him before he swiped it through a PDQ terminal. She adjusted her granny glasses as she waited.

He spoke to her in English. "What is your purpose for coming to our country?"

"Tourist."

The officer stamped the passport routinely, and as he began to hand it to her, the computer beeped, drawing the man's attention to the screen. He pulled the passport back.

Currie looked from side to side out of the corners of her eyes, checking for movement or cameras. She worried about facial recognition technology, not confident the prosthetic devices she wore to change the contour of her cheeks lessened the risk.

She quizzed herself, Did I put them on correctly? Will the adhesive hold?

The officer questioned her in English. "In what city were you born?"

"Berlin."

He asked another question in German. "What is your profession?"

Although shocked at the language change, she kept her emotional reaction in check and responded in German. "*Kunstler*."

After a long pause, the man pointed to the fingerprint scanner in front of the booth. The diagrammatic placard provided visual instructions. She complied by putting her fingers on the scanner. Once complete, she was handed her stamped passport and waved through.

She walked swiftly, becoming part of the crowd moving toward the baggage area. As she distanced herself from Immigration, she dialed her phone. "Hassan?"

The response came quickly and sharply. "No names!"

Currie stepped to a bank of seats away from the crowd and sat down. "I'm now in China. I haven't yet heard further about Grayson."

"I visited the farm. The farmer was able to defend his home well against the two local hires. But I have corrected that and taken the life of Grayson's uncle, the farmer. He is dead, but Joshua Grayson was not there."

Her eyes widened. "Grayson is in Boston?"

Hassan was silent for a short time. "No. He's in Brazil with his cousin, who's getting DNA Restore treatment for his illness."

Currie sat forward on the edge of her seat, eyes bulging, and spoke in a hushed hissing tone, "Whaaaat?!" She stood and paced back and forth, grinding her teeth. "That's not possible! His name was on the blacklist, all trials have queues and only admit local patients."

"The blacklist is only in the U.S. The cousin used a different name. I don't know the details; only the information I've received."

Amaline Currie seethed and started to draw attention. She cupped her hand over the phone. "How do you know he's there? There are several hospitals running trials. Do you know which one? Do you have men in Brazil, or can you take care of him yourself? *He has cost us everything! Our fortune!"*

Hassan spoke calmly and matter of factly. "We have tracked a message from the wife of the cousin of Grayson. He's in São Leopoldo. I will take care of Grayson. His life will end very soon." He shifted the topic, not waiting for a response from Currie. "Many authorities are searching for you."

Currie sat down. "Yes, I am following the plan. Where are you?"

"Not important. Follow your protocols, and next contact is two days at twelve hundred hours GMT."

She hung up and immediately accessed a bank account in the Isle of Man from her phone. Scrolling down to the latest deposit entry, she murmured under her breath as she saw the recent bank transfer, "Thank you, Tremont."

* * *

Hassan walked through the crowd at the Porto Alegre airport, around the luggage carousels, and out to the arrivals area. Putting his hand over his eyes, he scanned the area and walked toward a man waving him over. The car quickly exited the area, following the signs to BR-116 North.

After a silent half-hour drive, the car exited to São Leopoldo and pulled into a vacant parking lot. Hassan broke the silence.

"*Você tem a arma?*"

The man reached under his seat and handed him a towel, which Hassan unfolded to reveal an IMBEL M911 pistol. He de-coupled part of the frame of his carry-on bag and extracted a heavy metal tube. He screwed the silencer on the barrel of the gun and gave the driver brief instructions. The FIAT Palio moved rapidly toward the center of the city.

* * *

Currie took the Terminal Two escalator down to the first floor baggage area. She scanned the area as she walked nonchalantly, earbuds in her ears but with nothing playing. On the far end of the terminal, she identified her contact, a slight man wearing a long black trench coat with a green sweater underneath. He waved as she approached.

They moved at a good pace and exited the terminal into a thirty-degree Fahrenhiet winter evening. Currie felt a cool wind and braced herself, regretting not having a warm winter coat. The smoky, musty smell of exhaust was heavy in the air, as were the loud sounds of jet aircraft taking off.

The Geely two door compact car moved into traffic, and the man serpentined between lanes, causing her to become lightheaded. The airport was twenty miles south of downtown Nanjing, located near the east coast on the Yangtze River, 160 miles west of Shanghai. She new the city history, but all she cared about was an ability to get lost among the population of eight million.

As they approached the city, Currie saw foothills and large mountains to the east. The architecture was mixed between modern buildings and older structures. Traffic slowed as cars moved into the city, which was encircled by a wall as high as forty feet, built in the early 1300s during the Ming Dynasty.

After navigating around the center of the city, the car stopped in an alley in the back of a ten-story tenement on the south side of the Yangtze. The driver caught Currie's attention and extended an index figure, and exited the car.

She watched him move past the rear of the car and into a door in the back of the building.

Currie leaned forward to see out the front window. Under a light over an overflowing garbage bin, she saw dozens of rats scurrying around, several old mattresses, and a few bicycle frames with no wheels. She gagged, pulled her blouse up over her nose, and closed her eyes, willing herself to stay calm.

Chapter 47

Mid-afternoon in São Leopoldo, Joshua paced near Shelby in the long white hallway outside the examination room. She stood quietly, wringing her hands. Joshua moved alongside her as Dr. Pilla approached and waved them into the room. The doctor stood in front of the group, and Shelby leaned on Jake, holding his hand.

"The test results continue to show limited progress," the doctor said. "But not negative."

Shelby dabbed softly at her eyes with a tissue. "How much longer until we can go home?"

"Mrs. Grayson, I'd love to tell you to start making flight arrangements for next weekend, but I can't. Monitoring is important so we can make sure your husband is clearly recovering and stable enough to endure the long flight. He can stay with you at the hotel, which should make it perhaps less stressful for you all.

"Unfortunately, we can't continue the DNA Restore protocols. We've already surpassed the approved levels of treatment with permission from the Brazilian regulator. Now it's up to nature. Assuming Mr. Grayson shows improvement in his DNA tests and is stable, we can discuss flying home, where Dr. Kaymer should be able to handle examinations and take appropriate actions of course. We'll be available to consult with her."

"How long do you think? A day? A week?" She looked down and spoke softly. "I miss my children."

Jake put his arm around her and looked her in the eye. "You can go home now, baby. I'll go back with the guys once I'm cleared." Shelby shook her head as her swollen red eyes welled up. Jake put his palms on her cheeks, pulled her close, and put his forehead against hers. "Let's at least look at the flight options."

Joshua and Blaine made their way to the hospital cafeteria, bought cups of coffee, a few *pão de queijo* rolls, and sat at an empty table in silence. The café was quiet, only a couple on either side of them speaking softly in Portuguese. Blaine left for the hotel after he finished.

Checking messages, Joshua replayed a voicemail from Pete several days prior, noting the authorities still hadn't been able to locate Dr. Currie. The FBI was staying in touch with him, and the local agents checked in regularly. He closed his eyes and ruminated over the news and thought,

How could someone be so evil? For what? Money? Power? Scientific prestige?

Joshua opened his eyes slowly and surveyed the area, looking for Jake and Shelby to emerge. As he glanced across the open space, he did a double take as he thought he recognized the profile of a man talking to the nurse manning the main waiting area. Joshua craned his neck and cautiously stared across the main floor but couldn't place the person in his mind. His instinct caused him to put his head down and cover his face with his hand, as if in thought.

As he looked across the floor, Jake and Shelby emerged from an adjacent hallway, and walked past the man, toward the hospital exit. Immediately the man ended his conversation, turned, and followed the couple. As he walked, he moved his head in a quick sweep of the place, allowing Joshua to get a better view of his face.

Joshua immediately left his roll and coffee on the table and trailed them. His mind shouted, *Danger*! As he exited the building, it clicked…the man from his meeting with Dr. Currie in her Amsterdam office, Hassan! He recalled his exceptionally firm handshake, scars, and dark eyes.

As he moved forward he thought, What's he doing here?! If it was Golden Helix business, why did he immediately start following Jake and Shelby when they passed by? Clearly, no coincidence!

The couple walked very slowly, hand in hand down the street past the multiple funeral homes and then turned right at the end of the street. Hassan trailed them but didn't close on them; instead, he kept at their back with a noticeably consistent buffer.

Joshua crossed the street and trailed Hassan, aware he could turn at any time and recognize him. Given the sparse foot traffic, he held his head down as he walked and looked in store windows when the opportunity presented itself. Once the couple entered the hotel, Joshua saw Hassan close the gap quickly. Joshua followed suit.

Minutes later Joshua arrived and climbed the stairs two at a time. Reaching the third floor, he poked his head into the hallway, looked both ways down the corridor, but saw no one. He knocked on Jake's door with no immediate reply. Moving into his room, he saw Blaine sleeping. He put his ear against the common door between the room and Jake and Shelby's.

"You perv!" Blaine whispered from the bed as he sat up.

Joshua turned to him with a serious expression and knocked on the door. He listened intently as Blaine rose from the bed. He heard Jake and Shelby talking before she opened the door.

"What's up?"

As the group talked, Hassan was working his way down the dank emergency exit staircase, floor by floor, checking access to each. All floors were accessible with no lock, no key required, and lighting was scarce. At the bottom, he opened the door to the rear of the hotel and adroitly disabled the lock.

He returned to the lobby, put 500 Brazilian reais on the counter in front of the elderly front desk clerk, and asked for keys for the Graysons rooms. The clerk slid keys to him, and pocketed the cash. Hassan circled back to the hospital. As he arrived, the FIAT pulled up, and Hassan entered the car and quickly left the area.

* * *

At four o'clock the next morning, the rear emergency door to the Hotel de Esperança opened quietly. Wasting no time, Anas Hassan moved to the staircase and climbed to the third floor, where he silently moved through the door at the end of the corridor. Other than an occasional sound from an ice machine at the far end of the hallway, there was no noise. Hassan turned out the lights in the hallway by shorting out the circuit from the switch near the exit door.

His eyes adjusted to the dark as he moved deliberately down the hall, room keys in one hand, flashlight in the other. Room 333, 331…he stopped as he neared room 323, Jake and Shelby's room, but moved to 321, Blaine and Joshua's room.

Before inserting the key, he pulled the pistol from the belt in the back of his pants and screwed on the silencer. He inserted the key quietly and turned it very slowly, the mechanisms worked quietly, ending with a very soft click. Hassan opened the door, slipped into the dark room, quickly made out the center of the two twin beds, and fired two shots into each.

There was silence. Hassan scanned the room with his flashlight. The beds were slept in, with the bedding clumped in the middle of each—but no one was there. Hassan's face expressed shock and confusion. He immediately moved into the adjacent room, and found the same.

"No!" he whispered. Descending the main staircase, he stopped at the front desk. "*Olá? Olá?*"

A slight middle-aged man emerged from behind a partition. "*Sim?*"

"Where is the man in room three-twenty-three? I have some important medicine for him!"

"*Aeroporto.*"

Hassan gave the man one hundred reais, put an index finger to his lips, flashed his gun, and quickly exited the building, phone to his ear, barking instructions. The FIAT met him in lockstep and accelerated quickly after he hit the passenger seat. They moved rapidly south on BR-116 toward the Porto Alegre Airport.

* * *

At four a.m, the terminal at Caxias do Sul Airport was virtually empty, except for security and a man buffing the floors. The fifty six-mile drive north from São Leopoldo went quickly, given the limited early-hour traffic. Joshua was on his phone as they entered.

"Mr. Grayson, the first flight leaving the airport is at six a.m. There are three open seats on a flight to Rio de Janeiro, connecting in Chicago and on to Indianapolis."

"Okay, hold on." He turned to the group. "Three seats on a flight at six o'clock, followed by a couple of connections, okay?"

Shelby shook her head. "We need four seats."

"I'll fly standby or catch a later flight if needed. I'll be right behind you."

"We'll stay with you. We're safe here, right?"

Joshua shook his head. "As far as I'm concerned, we're not safe until we're home. It's best to get out of here as soon as possible. You two need to get home to the kids. Blaine, you should help Jake."

Blaine spoke over the chatter. "You two go on, I ain't letting Joshua go alone."

Joshua walked away from the group and spoke into the phone. "Can you book two tickets for Shelby and Jacob Grayson on that flight all the way through to Indianapolis?" He looked at the tired couple. Jake was sitting in a seat, head between his legs. "Any chance those could be first-class? Also, two on stand-by, myself and Blaine Grayson."

He scanned the terminal and looked at Blaine, who was doing the same.

"Mr. Grayson, I'm afraid the credit card you have on file has been suspended. Do you have another I can possibly try? Or you can call the issuer." She tried two other credit cards and his debit card. "No, none of those work."

He looked at the array of credit cards in his hand. "I checked out of a hotel just over an hour ago and used the first card. I don't understand." His mind answered him, No coincidence, someone wants to keep us here.

"I'm very sorry, Mr. Grayson, I've tried them all a couple of times."

Thinking through options, he dug through his wallet and found his Tremont Ventures corporate card. "Try this card."

He waited, eyes closed, for several minutes before he heard a response. "Yes, that one worked. You can pick up your tickets at the counter."

Joshua buried his head in his hands and looked up and thought, Thank God! He gave a thumbs up to the group and booked the second back-up flight, departing an hour later and connecting through São Paulo.

Blaine returned from speaking to a security person behind a desk near the main entrance. "If I understood the guy right, security opens in twenty minutes. Let's get our boarding passes and move over to security and be waiting to go through."

The small regional airport began to come alive a short while later. The airline and terminal workers moved slowly and methodically, setting up for the day. The group was queued up for their boarding passes. Blaine had his arm around Jake, giving him support but vocally unhappy with the pace of the set-up.

"Come on, people," he mumbled loudly under his breath.

Chapter 48

As the attendant announced the initial boarding for Jake and Shelby's flight, Joshua kept his eyes fixed on the security line and gate areas. He saw Shelby boarding the flight in his peripheral vision, with a man pushing Jake on board in a wheelchair. He turned his head to see Shelby waving and felt a great sense of relief.

Joshua dialed his phone. After two rings, a deep, groggy voice responded, "Webber."

"Agent Webber, this is Joshua Grayson. Sorry for the early call. This couldn't wait."

"What's going on?"

"I think you know my cousin has been in Brazil, getting the DNA Restore treatment. His wife and brother are also here. We're making our way back home, and I see one of Dr. Currie's people is here, Anas Hassan. He's hunting us."

"Yes we know about him. Often with Currie, he's the enforcer of the organization."

"I saw him yesterday at the hospital in São Leopoldo, where the DNA Restore clinical trials are going on. I believe he's going to be at the Porto Alegre International Airport, waiting for us to catch a flight home. We've re-routed to a smaller airport in Caxias do Sul an hour north of Porto Alegre and are awaiting a flight. If he isn't at the airport, it's possible he may return to the hospital. I'm worried about our safety."

"Smart move. I'm not sure how quickly we can move internationally, but let me put the word out and see if we can intercept him there or when he tries to leave the country. I can reach you at this number?"

"Yes. My cousin Jake and his wife are just boarding a plane. I'm on standby with my other cousin, but we should be gone in the next hour or so if we can't get seats."

The flight boarded with no seats available, leaving Joshua and Blaine to catch the later São Paulo-connecting flight. They stood at the large terminal window and exchanged a buoyant high-five as the plane went airborne.

Blaine turned to his cousin. "Now what? Are we sitting ducks? I don't like this at all."

* * *

While Jake and Shelby Grayson were boarding the Rio de Janeiro flight in the Caxias do Sul airport, Hassan continued searching the Porto Alegre airport, seventy-five miles to the south. He moved to the security line, his eye on the lead group of people, but their faces weren't clear. Three had been cleared through a single passport control checkpoint officer, two men and a woman, the remaining man fit Joshua's height and build. Moving forward, Hassan was stopped by a security guard who asked for his boarding pass and passport. As a result, he was forced to go to the airline ticket counters for a ticket.

A short while later, Hassan arrived back at the security line with a boarding pass for a flight to Brasília on Azul Brazilian Airlines. He passed through cleanly and then to passport control, where he moved through a short line and handed the officer his burgundy Spanish passport and boarding pass. The man looked at the picture and person in front of him. After a pause, he asked him for an additional form of identification and followed with several questions.

With a shrug, the man waved him on. Hassan looked at his watch—thirty minutes until departure. He checked his coat pocket for his weapon of choice, a small expandable black tactical baton, relatively easy to conceal and often mistaken for a battery charger or a wi-fi hotspot antenna. He walked quickly to the gate as the crowd grew more active in expectation of boarding.

No Joshua Grayson or family members to be seen.

The clock in the terminal read six o'clock a.m. Hassan's watch beeped. He dialed his phone. "Have you been identified?"

Amaline Currie sat on a short, worn wooden stool in her small flat in Nanjing. "No. For now, it's quiet. I don't leave the apartment, and the Chinese aren't inquisitive."

"Good." His eyes continued scanning as he spoke. "You need to move soon and change your appearance. Has the contact been in touch with you?"

Currie's eyes dropped to half-open. She caught her head as it began to drop and sat very upright, fighting to stay awake. "Yes." The pace of her speech slowed. "He's preparing the next housing. India was a hideous place. This is no better. Why can't I have better accommodations?"

"We have no time to talk, I must do—"

Currie interrupted in a loud voice. "Don't interrupt me! Have you taken care of Grayson?"

"That is in progress. He will meet his end very soon."

"He has caused this situation. See to it!"

Hassan hung up and systematically surveyed the terminal, looked at his watch, and began to move toward the exit but paused to gauge his next move. After a several minute wait, he left the gate area and moved quickly to the terminal exit. The FIAT was waiting for him. Hassan barked instructions as he hit the passenger seat.

"*Para o hospital São Leopoldo.*"

The driver took off quickly, merging onto BR-116 North. As the car merged onto the roadway, several dark-colored cars could be seen moving south rapidly and exiting BR-116 toward the airport. The car accelerated, and Hassan re-armed himself.

As the FIAT drove north in the direction of São Leopoldo, the car passed a billboard showing a plane and exclaiming in Portuguese and English: "Hugo Cantergiani Airport in Caxias do Sul - Avoid the crowds! Hourly flights to São Paulo."

Hassan spoke over the loud engine. "How long to Caxias do Sul airport?"

"*Un hora.*" The driver held up one finger.

"It's a small airport?"

"*Sim.*"

Hassan stared out the window and rubbed his chin. "Go to the Caxias airport as quickly as possible."

Chapter 49

Joshua sat next to Blaine, watching the clock and activity at the gate. His phone vibrated. Not recognizing the number, he hesitated for a moment before answering.

"Yes?"

"Is this Joshua Grayson?"

"Who's this?"

"My name is Abram Silva. I'm the legal attaché for the FBI in Brazil. I was given your number by Agent Daniel Webber. He's filled me in on your situation, and I've called in the federal police to protect you and your family. We've also send agents to the Porto Alegre airport, but we're in need of your help in identifying the man we believe is named Anas Hassan. Can you provide me with a description or, better yet, a picture of him?"

Joshua considered the question before answering. "I don't have a picture, but I sat down with the man in Amsterdam a few weeks ago, so I'd recognize him if you sent me a picture. He's a little under six feet tall, lean, and in very good physical shape. Semi-dark complexion, thin face, with a few scars and a goatee."

"Webber mentioned you saw him at a hospital in São Leopoldo?"

"He was there yesterday, Oncologia Centenário - Centro de Câncer. He followed my cousin and his wife to our hotel." Joshua put his hand over the phone. "Blaine, did you take any pictures at the hospital yesterday?" Joshua excused himself as Blaine nodded and showed him some hospital pictures. "My cousin took some pictures yesterday at the hospital. There may be something there. However, it's from a distance, and I'm not sure of the quality. I'll look at them, and if I see something, I'll text them to the number you're calling from."

Joshua could hear Silva speaking to others before he responded. "Yes, Mr. Grayson. That may be helpful to us, and we'll also connect with the hospital, as they may have video cameras. Do you know the timeframe?"

"I saw him near the nurse's desk on the main level. It was around four o'clock, late afternoon."

"If you need any assistance, you can reach me at this number. Do you feel like you require security? Where are you now?"

Joshua surveyed the area. "No, my cousin Jake and his wife have left, but there were no open seats for my cousin Blaine and me. We have tickets for a flight scheduled to leave within the hour. I don't believe we're in danger here. We're at the Hugo Cantergiani Airport in Caxias do Sul, thinking Hassan assumes we're flying out of Porto Alegre." Concluding the call, Joshua put the phone in his pocket and stood. He stared down at his quivering limbs. Then very, very slowly, panned the area again thinking, *If we can just get on the plane and get out of here, we should be okay.*

* * *

The gate attendant announced the incoming plane would be arriving half an hour late. Joshua stood in front of the gate among a growing number of passengers. He ran his hands through his hair.

Blaine stared at him. "Hey, you should sit down, cuz."

"We just need to get out of here and make the connection in São Paulo. Should be fine then…man, it's cold in here." Joshua donned his faded Boston College hoodie and hugged himself.

"It ain't cold. You okay?" Blaine put his hand under Joshua's armpit to steady him and helped him sit. "Let's give Dad a call before we leave."

Joshua put the call on speakerphone. After several rings they heard a recording. "Hello, this is Pete Grayson. I'm not available to talk now. Please leave a message, and I'll call you back as soon as I can."

At the beep, Joshua left a message. "Uncle Pete, Jake, and Shelby are on a plane heading home. They have a couple of connections. It'd be good if you, Cole, or Jesse met them in Indianapolis when they land. Shelby's dead tired, and Jake can't walk well or keep food down. He's very weak. I'll send you their flight information. Dr. Kaymer's aware and waiting for him."

Blaine leaned in and added, "Hey, Dad. How are you doin'? I miss you."

They walked to the food kiosk in the middle of the terminal, bought a few Portuguese rolls for breakfast and two large cups of mango juice. They sat at a small, wobbly table and shared small talk.

As they ate, the gate attendant noted the long-awaited plane had landed and would be arriving at the gate soon, but it would need to be cleaned, loaded, and refueled before it could depart. The men relaxed and smiled sheepishly at each other. Blaine stood and moved to the gate as Joshua finished his second *pão de queijo*.

At the same time the announcement was made, the FIAT pulled in front of the small terminal. Hassan barked instructions as he exited, "Wait here. Should be quick."

Inside, he walked the perimeter, systematically scanning the people waiting in lines, using check-in kiosks, checking restrooms, and sitting areas. Beyond security, six gates were arrayed in a semi-circle. In the center of the gate area was a small food cart and eating area.

He moved closer and continued his survey. His eyes grew wide when he saw the tables near the food cart. Quickly, he moved to an empty counter and purchased a plane ticket, then surreptitiously dropped his pistol into a large plant box in tall grass.

Hassan waded through the security checkpoint line. The agent checked his passport electronically. Getting a green light, he was cleared to go through the metal detector. He put a set of keys and his "wi-fi antenna" in a bowl with his cell phone, wallet, and belt, covering the antenna nonchalantly with a handkerchief.

Just beyond the security area, Joshua walked into the restroom. Hassan moved quickly and confidently through the detector, picked up his personal effects from the plastic bowl and walked into the gate area. He followed Joshua into the restroom, pulling an unattended janitorial cart in front of the entrance.

The restroom was empty, and Joshua felt his body relax as he splashed water in his face. He took a deep breath, and raised his face to look in the mirror. Blurred movement behind him in the mirror triggered an instinct to dart to his right avoiding Hassan's vertical baton strike aimed at his head. The baton gave off a high pitched whistle, just missed Joshua's head, breaking a piece of porcelain from the counter.

Joshua moved to retreat but was forced to the far corner of the room, with Hassan advancing. His eyes quickly ran across the area, searching for exits, defensive positions, or weapons he might use to fight the man off, but he saw nothing, not even a trash container. He tried to distract him by throwing his hands in the air and yelling to gain attention.

"What do you want?" He raised his hands to chest level, palms facing Hassan, preparing to defend himself.

Hassan's eyes grew large, wild, and appeared to bulge from their sockets. Joshua's hands curled into fists. Eyes still darting, he inched toward one of the restroom stalls to Hassan's right, but Hassan moved in, swinging madly, hitting Joshua's forearm as he deflected a blow intended for his head, drew blood from Joshua's mouth with a punch, then kicked him in the abdomen with a side kick, bringing Joshua to a squat in the corner. He writhed in pain as he spat out blood.

Hassan hissed, "Before I finish you, I want you to know that I have taken the life of your uncle at the farmhouse. I shot him in the back of his head as he ate dinner. I will take the lives of all your family. I will not rest until they are all dead." Hassan moved in, working the baton in a figure eight motion from side to side.

As he moved closer, Joshua struggled to his feet, feigned left, then quickly shifted right like a running back and moved toward a stall, hands in front of him to push the door open. Hassan moved to his right but recovered quickly enough to counter with a baton strike to Joshua's rib cage, causing him to fall to the tiled floor a short distance from the stall door.

Joshua squirmed in pain, holding the left side of his rib cage, his arms protecting the area from another blow. He tried to yell, but it hurt to breathe, and he could only manage a soft, guttural, "Urgggh."

Hassan moved forward, making a downward strike at Joshua's head, but he hit the floor instead as Joshua rolled away at the last second back toward the corner, where he managed to bring himself to a squat. Joshua leaned back against the tiled wall, then to a wobbly, hunched-over standing position, fists up.

Joshua, was able to deflect another baton strike intended for his head with his right arm and throw a left-handed punch that landed on the side of Hassan's head, but not strong enough to slow him. He gasped for air and leaned forward to catch his breath. Hassan slid behind him and raised the baton over Joshua's head, putting it in position to choke him.

As Hassan raised the baton Joshua was able to get one hand on the baton to hold it away from his throat, but he struggled mightily to fight it off. Hassan pushed him into a wall violently as Joshua fought in vain to kick him, push off the wall, gouge an eye, or spin out of the current position he was in. Hassan put his knee in the small of Joshua's back to gain leverage to crush his throat.

After some thrashing back and forth, Hassan found some leverage using his knee and the wall to constrain Joshua. The baton exerted tremendous pressure, and Joshua was unable to yell. He flailed and tried to use his head to strike Hassan's face, managing only to cause a bloody nose.

As Joshua's resistance ebbed, Hassan hissed in his ear, "Dr. Currie sends her regards."

A wide grin crossed Hassan's face as he leaned back to gain more force on the baton. A moment later, his eyes opened wide as he was hit hard in his right kidney, then his left and right side again in rapid succession, causing him to lose his grip on the baton. He gasped for breath and tried to glance at the source but could not turn his head.

"*BIG MISTAKE, MAN!*" Blaine yelled.

Hassan reached out to steady himself, but Blaine was in control, holding his collar and belt. Blaine pulled up on the belt while pushing down on Hassan's collar and moved rapidly forward, causing the crown of Hassan's head to smash hard into the door of a toilet stall. The door opened, and Blaine propelled him into the stall, where he crashed headfirst into the tiled wall and dropped to the floor between the toilet and metal stall divider.

An elderly man poked his head into the room before quickly turning and running away. Blaine yelled for security as he rushed to help Joshua, who was lying on his side, knees to his chest, bleeding from his mouth and gasping for air. As Blaine attended to him, Hassan crawled out of the stall, made it to his feet, and started to stagger out of the restroom, coughing loudly with blood running down his face.

Blaine turned his head, stood tall, and moved toward him, bellowing, "It ain't your day, man."

As Hassan attempted to move toward the exit, Blaine grabbed the back of his shirt and punched his right arm between the man's legs.

Hassan's feet came up in front of him as his head moved backward and down. A millisecond second later, his whole body, from his face to his feet, met the tile floor with fierce force, driven by the speed of the drop, as well as 230-plus pounds on his back. He lay prone in the middle of the restroom. No movement; only soft moaning sounds as blood arrayed around his head.

Chapter 50

The makeshift interrogation room at the Caxias do Sul airport was cramped. A small group of local police attempted to make sense of the situation, made more challenging by the fact that no one spoke English well enough to understand Joshua and Blaine. Both were handcuffed behind their backs, sitting in chairs side by side in front of a small table and shaking off the unexpected attack.

Joshua was pale, bleeding, and felt severe pain with waves of nausea. He asked, "*Telephono?* FBI?"

They eventually took off one handcuff and allowed Joshua to provide the phone number of Abram Silva, after which they quickly re-cuffed him.

The short, squat man in charge called Silva. Joshua could only hear his responses but didn't understand the conversation. "*Sim eles estão bem.*" Subsequently, "*Aqui está o número de telefone...*" The man hung up and held up an index finger to the prisoners.

A short time later, the phone rang. The leader put the phone on speaker in the middle of the conference table, alongside an audio recorder. "Hello, Mr. Grayson? This is

Agent Silva, and I also have Agent Webber on the line. Are you okay?"

"Hey, this is Blaine Grayson. I'm doing okay, but my cousin here is hurting pretty bad. They tried to bandage him up, but he needs serious medical help."

Silva responded, "We understand, we'll make sure medical attention is on the way."

Blaine added, "Also, can we get these dang handcuffs off? We were just defending ourselves."

Silva spoke to the local authorities in Portuguese, who gave the men a sorry expression and slight bow before removing the cuffs. Silva translated. "He said he's sorry. They weren't sure who was at fault. Let's debrief what went on here."

Joshua moaned. "Do we need an attorney? Are any charges being pressed here? We're in a country we don't know, don't speak the language, and didn't do anything wrong."

Webber broke in. "No, no, no…this is routine to simply get the events on record while they are still fresh and a police report filed. We're going to get you both good medical treatment, and you will be on a later flight today heading home, unless you need to stay for medical reasons. We'll coordinate with the police. You'll be home for Christmas."

As they took Joshua to another area in a wheelchair he caught Blaine's eye, "It's okay."

Blaine described what happened, and a person on the call translated in Portuguese. "We were getting ready to board our flight, and Joshua had to," he looked for the appropriate words, settling on, "go to the toilet. He went off, and I waited near the gate. He was gone for a long time, and the flight was going to board, so I went to look for him. I walked into the restroom and saw the goatee guy trying to choke Joshua with some sort of rod, so I jumped in to help."

One of the locals spoke, and Silva translated. "What exactly did you do?"

"It all happened real quick-like, but basically he was choking Joshua, and his back was to me, so I started hammering his kidneys. He let Joshua go, and I rammed his head into a stall door, then threw him into the stall. I checked on Joshua and saw the guy trying to get away, and I wasn't going to let that happen.

"He was getting away, so I punched him between the legs from behind and flipped him over my hip. He landed on his face and front side of his body, and I landed on his back. Basically, a classic body slam. It was over real quick."

Joshua was brought back to the table and Blaine escorted to a waiting area. Joshua recounted his experience, which synced with Blaine's. "I was fighting for my life and wasn't sure I'd survive until my cousin arrived."

He walked through the conflict, grimacing in pain and with tears in his eyes. "He also told me he…he killed my uncle." Joshua beckoned over the phone, "Please have someone check on him at the farmhouse! I've called and texted him and called but with no response."

Webber replied immediately, "We're on it. We'll get back to you."

The authorities were satisfied, sat the two men at the table, and returned their passports and wallets. Several men shook their hands before departing. Joshua asked Webber and Silva for more current details on his attacker and the whereabouts of Dr. Currie.

Webber's deep voice came over the line. "We don't know much about Anas Hassan yet. The name on the Spanish passport he used to travel to Brazil was Alejandro Machado.

We believe he's Moroccan by birth but grew up largely in Spain. It'll take more time to sort through everything.

"Based on information received from interviews, he has longstanding links to Dr. Currie and her deceased husband. Although he was officially the Director of Communications, he didn't seem to have any duties at Golden Helix. The employees interviewed referred to him as the *waakhond*...guard dog. He'll be in the hospital for quite a while. Last I heard, he still wasn't conscious."

Joshua groaned and spoke softly, "And Currie?"

"We're on her trail but haven't apprehended her yet. But we will. That said, we know she's well funded, as she cleared out everything from the Golden Helix bank accounts. Challenging to track, but we're on that as well."

Webber noted he'd be in touch as soon as they learn about Pete's situation, then wished them safe travels and a Merry Christmas before he signed off.

* * *

Despite the doctor's recommendation for Joshua to spend a night in the hospital, he declined. The men were able to catch a late flight. Joshua walked onto the plane with a temporary cast for a fractured forearm, a tight wrap around his rib cage supporting two fractured ribs, bandages for more minor wounds, and pain medication. After the first leg of the trip, they had a quick connection. They tried to call Pete, but there was no answer.

On the plane Blaine sat next to his cousin, biting the inside of his cheek and rubbing his hands on his pant legs. "Try it again, bro, I'm worried. Dad has to be there."

Joshua wondered if he should tell Blaine about Hassan's boast. He humored him and redialed. No answer. "He's a busy guy. I tried Jake, Jesse and Cole; no answer there either. I left voice mails. They're probably together somewhere." He saw the worry in Blaine's eyes. "I've left messages everywhere, Blaine. We'll get a call back."

Just before takeoff, Joshua received a ping and saw a GIF from Bill Gilchrist. No text, only a laughing Santa and website link. The link brought him to a short industry brief in a venture capital trade journal.

Tremont partners Jeffrey Cochran and Graham Roseboro have some splainin' to do to angry investors as their much-touted investments in Golden Helix–yes, *plural (a total of $25 million in a short time period) disappeared as the company cratered and the CEO is reportedly missing.*

Chapter 51

Joshua peered out the living room window at the front of the farmhouse watching people making their way to the house. Many dabbing their eyes with tissues, others walking slowly, head down.

The lawn surrounding the Grayson farmhouse was covered with an inch of fresh snow, some grass peeking through here and there. Cars filled the long circular driveway, the grassy areas near the equipment barn, and extended up the lane. The temperature hung around the freezing mark but without any wind, perfectly comfortable for the locals.

The house had been updated in the last month. The once-damaged porch was repaired and painted gray, and the house was wearing a new resplendent white tone, which contrasted attractively with the newly painted soft forest green tin roof.

A somber crowd packed the Graysons' large living room. "As you know, there was a shooting here the other night, and we lost someone who was very special." The room was silent except for soft sobs. "I'll miss his humor and his laugh. It was an unfortunate case of mistaken identity. The shooter thought Ted Westendorff was me." Tears rolled down Pete's cheeks, and he paused for several minutes to gain his composure. "Ted stopped in to check on me, as we do here in Bishop Creek. We look after one another. He wanted to see how I was doing without Sara and with Jake being sick." Pete paused and wiped his tears with his red handkerchief. "He was a wonderful man. I'd like to pray, if you all don't mind." Pete cleared his throat and prayed.

After a moment of silence, Pete held a cup of eggnog in his hand. "We also want to thank you all for joining us to welcome Jake home." The words led to smiles and more tears. "This year we didn't have a family Thanksgiving celebration as we normally do, given the circumstances. Even though it's a couple days before Christmas, today you are all part of our Thanksgiving, and part of our family. We give thanks for the blessings we've received. God is truly good.

"We'll be forever grateful to you all for your unrelenting love and support. You each played a part in helping us overcome our challenges, from Sara's going home to Jake's return. God bless each one of you and your families." Pete raised his cup and smiled at Jake, who was sitting with his family.

Jake leaned on Blaine and stood. He held his hand to stop when people moved in to help him. "No, thank you. This is important to me." He scanned the crowd slowly, moving from one person to the next. "If you'd told me a couple months ago I'd get the same cancer that took my Mom, fly to Brazil to get a new treatment, be cured, and be reunited with my brother Joshua..." He wiped his eyes. "I wouldn't have believed any of it. I want to thank you, Joshua, and my family for being there for me. I'll be forever grateful to you all. I will never take the gift of life for granted." He caught Joshua's eye. "Joshua, you're a true hero. Not just for me, but all the other good people who could have died if this evil plot continued." The crowd gave him a rousing applause.

The crowd hovered around Jake, who moved to a recliner in the living room. Shelby and their kids remained close by his side. Joshua introduced Dr. Lange to people he'd come to know by phone or email. The doctor hit it off with Pete, and they spent extensive time at the kitchen table talking and sipping dandelion wine.

Joshua extracted Megyn away from neighbors who were attempting to get free medical advice. "Hazard of the job." She smiled and waved at the neighbors as she walked out of the kitchen and into the family room.

They sat and caught up. Joshua noted Jake's remarkable turnaround. "We were so worried the DNA Restore treatment wouldn't work. It was like Jake was stuck. He started vomiting, and we were incredibly worried."

Megyn grinned. "Not sure we'll ever know what triggered his improvement. Dr. Pilla was shocked to hear how well he's doing. Maybe sleeping for the entire trip back home or coming home and seeing his kids and father jump-started everything…"

Joshua looked up. "I don't think it's a coincidence that he arrived home on the fifty-fourth day after his symptoms started. That was the timeline for my aunt, initial symptoms to her passing."

Megyn's mouth dropped open. "Wow, I didn't realize that!" She leaned toward him and asked, "What's happening with Dr. Currie?"

"I'll show you."

He retrieved his laptop, they put on winter jackets and slipped out of the house through the rear porch. Joshua sat at the picnic table, next to a bonfire Blaine started. Megyn sat close to him as he opened the laptop. He moved closer until their forearms touched and navigated to a bookmarked page.

The screen showed an article entitled, *"From Time to Crime?"* Under the title was a picture of Dr. Currie on the cover of *Time* magazine, taken during her keynote speech at the biotechnology conference. Joshua brought up a news release.

Paris (EuroNews) -- EuroNews has learned that Dr. Amaline Currie, a prominent research scientist who claims to have developed a revolutionary tool to treat and potentially cure cancer, is the subject of a large-scale global manhunt being conducted by authorities in numerous countries. We understand that a Red Notice, the equivalent of an international arrest warrant, has been issued to all Interpol countries. Details behind the warrant are currently unknown.

Dr. Currie is reported to be a notoriously private person; however, it's known that while she was born in the Netherlands, she has lived in multiple other countries, including Germany, Saudi Arabia, India, as well as the UK and Sweden, where she received much of her education. She is fluent in multiple languages and Schengen rules allow her to move around freely within the E.U., which may complicate Interpol's efforts to locate her. Calls to Interpol and Dr. Currie's office were not returned.

Megyn looked up from the screen in silence. Joshua stood and held his hands toward the fire. "One of the FBI agents told me she was tracked to an apartment in Mumbai. But when the India Federal Police raided the place, all they found was a cup of warm tea on a table."

Her eyes grew large. "That's like something out of a movie. It's terrible for the innocent people affected by this mess. What about the guy who attacked the farm? Is that the same man you had a run-in with in Brazil?"

"Yep, same guy. He's in a hospital in Brazil, recovering from meeting my cousin in an airport bathroom. I guess he'll be extradited for trial somewhere."

"Are you scared there are others who may come after you or your family?"

Joshua stood closer to the fire. "Yeah. Unfortunately, we don't know who else may have been involved in the scheme. We may never know. The FBI thinks the odds aren't great, but until Dr. Currie is jailed and the authorities determine if anyone else was involved, we need to stay alert. Currie's being hunted, and they're confident she'll be caught soon. But I'm not so sure."

Megyn stood up from the table, moved next to Joshua, and gave him a nudge. "So, what's next for you? Back to Boston and the world of venture capital?"

He looked out over the snowy fields before meeting her gaze. "I haven't thought much about it. I guess I need to find a job. I've been speaking to people, but for now—" He paused.

"But for now, what?"

He smiled. "I just want to rest and enjoy Christmas with my family for the first time in fifteen years."

Chapter 52

It was a cool, wintery evening in Nanjing, where the temperature hovered around forty-degrees Fahrenheit. A pollution-generated haze hung over the area, created by factory emissions west of the city.

Amaline Currie ran her fingers through her new short honey brown hair as she stared blankly at the city's modern skyline bordering the Yangtze River from a small, narrow apartment balcony. On a small table in front of her sat a modest meal of baozi and green tea.

When she finished eating, she moved back into the apartment. A small room with two chairs and a mattress on the floor. In one corner of the room was a very small cooking space with a one-burner cook-top stove and a sink. Next to the stove was a bathroom with a toilet and shower-head on a sidewall, with one drain in the middle of the floor.

Currie picked up her phone and stared at the screen—no text messages, no emails, no calls. Her thoughts were cloudy, Hassan is two days late…or is it three? Where is he? Shall I call him?

As she considered making a call, a high-pitched scream came from the adjacent apartment, followed by a loud argument in Mandarin. Currie closed her eyes and placed the palms of her hands over her ears to muffle the sound. It was useless and maddening.

She retreated to the balcony, but that didn't provide a respite as sounds of traffic and horns were continuous, and the air quality irritated her lungs. She tried using a scarf as a filter, but it provided minimal relief.

Coughing as she re-entered the apartment, she opened her phone and dialed Hassan. Her hand trembled as she held the phone.

"*Ja?*"

"Why didn't you call me?"

She listened but only heard a man clear his throat and muffled talking. Currie spoke softly. "Are you there?"

"I tried to call you, but you didn't answer."

Currie squinted. "Who is this?"

More muffled voices. "It's Hassan. Do you need anything?"

She rubbed her eyes and looked at her watch. "Who is this?"

"I am close, shall we sit together and talk? I have very important news for you. I had to run from the police in Brazil, so I don't have your local address. Can you give it to me so I can protect you?"

Currie blinked her eyes several times and looked around the apartment. Stained walls. Dripping water from the sink and a lumpy mattress. Tears blurred her sight.

She spoke aloud softly, "I so want it to be true. I am dying here…I am someone! Where do I go? What if they track me here? I've failed, Anton!"

She hung up the phone and rubbed her birthmark as tears rolled down her cheeks. Her body convulsed as her sobs deepened.

* * *

On Christmas morning fourteen hours behind Nanjing, the soft light rose over the fields of Bishop Creek. The light reflected off a thin blanket of snow and gave the Grayson farmhouse a soft, warm glow. A light December breeze rustled the trees around the house, the branches hitting each other, the only sound interrupting the solitude.

Joshua was awake, lying in bed, staring at the ceiling. After stirring and trying to fall back to sleep, he looked at the time on the bedside alarm clock; six-thirty. He rose and glanced out the front window.

He knocked on Pete's door. A few seconds later, the door opened a crack, Pete's eyes were half-opened.

"Merry Christmas, Uncle Pete. I know it's Christmas Day, but how about a run, and after that church? I think my ribs can take it; I'm feeling good."

Pete rubbed his eyes and held up ten fingers, then shut the door.

In the kitchen, they dressed in layers to ward off the winter winds that blew across the empty fields, wool hats pulled down over their ears. They each drew some well water from the bucket near the sink to hydrate themselves and left through the screened porch.

After some light stretching, they jogged slowly up the lane, warming their muscles and getting acclimated to the weather. Instead of turning right, as they'd done since they started running together, Joshua led them in the opposite direction. The wind was light and at their back, nothing stirring yet as they passed St. Aloysius, just the two men running side by side in stride.

After a quick forty-minute run, they slowed their pace as they approached the mailbox, their finish line. They slowed to a walk as they turned toward the house.

"Have you given any more thought to what's next?" Pete asked.

Joshua walked slowly, hands on his hips. "No. I just want to enjoy where I am now, where Jake is, digest everything that's happened, enjoy my first family Christmas in too many years, and see where things lead."

Pete smiled and scanned the scenery. "You surely deserve some time to relax and enjoy yourself. You know, we are…" He paused. "I am very grateful for what you've done for Jake and our family." He continued to look out over the fields. "It's been a true godsend having you here."

Joshua looked down as he walked. "It's been a whirlwind. Thank you for coming alongside me; it means a lot to me. For now, I just want to…heal, that's the best word I can come up with."

"Yeah. Speaking of healing, we need to speed up if we're going to make it to church on time!"

* * *

The church parking area was almost full just before eight o'clock, when the men turned into the lot. They hustled into the church, hair damp, and found seats just before the musicians took their places to start the service.

The pastor's message was focused on the gift Jesus would want for his birthday. Joshua wrote down the quote from the book of Micah displayed on the screen above the pulpit.

He has shown you, O man, what is good. And what does the Lord require of you? To act justly and to love mercy and to walk humbly with your God.

As the service drew to a close, the worship leader asked everyone to stand. The congregation sang a cappella …

"The First Noel, the Angels did say

Was to certain poor shepherds in fields as they lay

In fields where they lay keeping their sheep

On a cold winter's night that was so deep…"

Voices resonated through the building as sunshine began to beam through the old windows. Joshua and Pete sang along as the song concluded...

"Noel, Noel, Noel, Noel

Born is the King of Israel"

The pastor dismissed the attendees with a short blessing. "May God fill you with all joy and peace as you trust in Him, so that you may overflow with hope. Merry Christmas!"

Pete stood and began to leave. After walking halfway down the aisle, he stopped and looked back. Joshua remained in his chair, head down. Pete continued out of the building.

Joshua sat until he was the last person in the church. He raised his head, rubbed his eyes, and took a couple deep breaths as he stood. He put on his coat and walked slowly toward the main doors at the front of the church. Stepping outside, he breathed deeply, taking in the fresh, cool farm air.

He moved slowly down the stairs toward his Pete's car. Two steps into the parking lot, he heard a voice.

"Hey Grayson, need a ride?"

Turning, he met Megyn's eyes. She wore a wide smile and green knit hat, with a red pom-pom.

"Wow…I'm surprised to see you here."

"Why's that? Don't you think I have a soul?"

"Yes, of course." He stopped and smiled. "It's just that it's Christmas Day. I thought you'd be with your family."

"I have to stick around. I'm on call, and your uncle invited me to join your family for the holiday."

Pete caught their attention with a brief honk and stuck his head out the window of his truck. "Hey, you two. Let's go home and have some breakfast. I'm starving!"

Megyn took Joshua's arm, kissed him sweetly on the cheek, and they moved to her car. Joshua stopped before opening the door and looked over the pastoral, fallow fields.

"Beautiful, isn't it?"

"It is. I hope you stay around longer to enjoy it."

He smiled. "I just may do that."

Chapter 53

The farmhouse was filled with gifts, wrapping paper, food, music, laughter, and the smell of pine. Amid the children opening presents, Megyn caught Joshua's eye and indicated for him to follow her into the dining room.

"Joshua, I don't know you that well, but it seems to me what you're missing in your life is a little fun, finding your inner boy. So, I have a Christmas present for you to help you along the way, and as a reminder of who you are." She held out a long rectangular box. "Merry Christmas."

"Really?"

They sat in chairs next to each other as he read the attached card.

Joshua, I've seen the little boy in you and the delight you get from your youth – don't ever lose it. I've also seen the heroic Joshua. You're quite a guy. I hope you stick around so we can spend some time together.

Truly, Megyn.

Joy in his eyes, he peeled off the Christmas wrap, stood, and gripped a wooden baseball bat in his hands. He bent over, kissed her softly, and whispered, "Thank you. Probably the best present I've ever received, just when I needed it."

As the day wound down and everyone departed, Pete caught Joshua before retiring. "There is one last present for you before I head up to bed." He handed him a wrapped gift and put his hand on his shoulder.

"You didn't have to get me a present."

"I didn't…" He gave him a quick smile. "Your Mom and Dad would be very proud of the man you've become. Merry Christmas, Joshua."

Joshua sat in a large armchair by the Christmas tree and a dwindling fire. The envelope taped to the gift was addressed to him at the farm. He opened it, a Christmas card with a traditional nativity scene.

Inside was the handwriting of Aunt Sara:

My Dear Joshua,

A very Merry Christmas to you. I joyfully expect that you've come home to be with Uncle Pete and your cousins, your family. It's been my ardent prayer for as long as I can remember. I'd hoped to be able to spend it with you all, but I'm being called home so, sadly, this will be my last card. I'm quite confident that the Lord orchestrated it this way for a purpose, which will become clearer to you in His time. This gift will bring you real success and happiness in life. It's something that I've cherished for many, many years. It's yours now. May God bless and keep you and do wonderful things through you. I love you, as does your family. Never, ever forget that.

All my Love,

Aunt Sara

He opened the package and found a leather-bound book, with the words "Holy Bible" imprinted on the cover. Scanning through the pages, he saw his aunt's handwritten notes throughout.

Returning to the first page, he read the inscription:

"To our Sara, from your Loving Parents."

Below that:

"To Joshua, from Aunt Sara -

Proverbs 3:5-6: Trust in the Lord with all your heart and lean not on your own understanding, in all your ways acknowledge Him, and He will make your paths straight."

Joshua Grayson bowed his head, closed his eyes, and took in the warmth.

About the Author

Tom Annino was born and raised in Arlington Heights, Illinois, a suburb of Chicago, where he loved playing baseball in the local summer leagues. After college, his job moved his family six times before finally landing in Glen Mills, Pennsylvania, just outside of Philadelphia, where he lives with his wife, near his three children and grandchildren. His focus is now on writing. Still, after many years away from Chicago, he misses Wrigley Field hot dogs and the wind off Lake Michigan at Soldier Field.